STEVEN SHEPHERD

# THE LONG GAME

First published in paperback by
Michael Terence Publishing in 2025
www.mtp.agency

ISBN 9781800949904

Cover image (AI)
Michael Terence Publishing

Michael Terence
Publishing

*For Mum, Dad, Paula, Jess and Joe...*

# One

**18th November, 2021**

It was one of those cold, wet, winter nights in North London that felt like menace could be lurking around any corner. Detective Inspector Michael Dack wasn't sure whether it was his experience working these city streets or if his anxiety was bubbling up again, but he had that feeling that something could erupt at any moment.

Tonight, however, that wasn't his issue. He wasn't cruising around on a mission to stop crime; in fact, he wasn't even on duty.

Michael turned left onto Rookery Drive in Tottenham and pulled his car into an empty residential space. He turned off the ignition and made sure his doors were locked before he surveyed the surroundings.

The typical assortment of London litter was strewn across the pavement and into the road in front of him. Broken glass shards and empty laughing gas canisters scattered the floor outside the Polish mini market. Every shop was protected by rusty, iron shutters, pulled down to detract would-be burglars.

Michael wound down his window a fraction and lit up a cigarette to try to settle his racing heart. The smell of the street oozed into the car as errant raindrops splashed onto his face. He took two deep drags and attempted to collect his thoughts, but movement ahead caught his attention. He flicked the cigarette into a puddle outside and closed his window.

Through the rain-dashed windscreen, he could just about make her out, the bottom half of her white dress peeking from under a tiny black leather jacket. He watched as she walked towards his car, tottering slightly, like she'd had a few drinks. As she got to within ten metres of him, he knew for sure that it was her. This was the girl he'd been waiting for.

He had known of her for a little while now. They'd met once, albeit briefly, but there was something about the girl that captured his attention, her alluring green eyes, her broad Romanian-accented voice interspersed with dashes of cockney from her time in London.

Since that first meeting, he'd painstakingly researched her and now felt closer to her than some members of his own family.

He felt a rush of adrenaline course through him as she came within touching distance of his car. Her dress was soaked through and clung to her damp skin. Her mop of jet-black curly hair was wet and bedraggled, stuck to the side of her face.

She passed by, barely a metre from where he was sitting, oblivious to the fact she was being watched. Michael began to have second thoughts. He had an unblemished police record stretching back over forty years; he'd never committed a minor crime before, let alone one this serious. He thought of his ex-wife, Paula, and his daughter, Josie, and then he thought of his new partner, Samantha, and his two stepdaughters. How would they feel if this ever came out?

His nerves buckled, and his hand reached to start the ignition. He had an urge to drive off and leave this squalid situation behind, but then he looked in his rear-view mirror as she walked away, and that feeling washed over him again. There was no choice in the matter. He needed to do this now.

Michael got out of the car quietly, leaving the door slightly ajar to avoid making any noise. He looked around to make sure no-one was watching and began to follow her, slowly at first, then speeding up as she approached the junction ahead. He couldn't allow her to walk down another street; he had to do it here and now.

The rain helped to drown out the sound of Michael's footsteps as he got within touching distance of her. He glimpsed left and saw his reflection in the window of a dry-cleaning shop. An old man with myriad demons inhabiting his soul stared back. He hated what he saw, and anger grew within him.

As the girl made to turn left, he reached into his pocket and pulled out the syringe, easily flipping the lid off to expose the needle. He grabbed her from behind with his left arm, wrapped it around her shoulder and clasped his hand firmly over her mouth. In one expert movement, he tilted her head to the side, stabbed the needle into her neck, and unloaded the anaesthetic.

She tried to cry out, the sound meek and muffled. She struggled for what seemed like fifteen seconds or so, but she was small and weak in his arms. He felt her drift into unconsciousness and then dragged her back to his car.

He pulled open the back door and threw her in, making sure nothing spilled from her jacket as he did, aware that any evidence left could scupper his whole plan. Glancing around the streets one more time, he climbed into the driver's seat, and sped off into the stark, London night.

# Two

A multitude of flashbulbs popped off, momentarily blinding Metropolitan Police Commissioner Morgan as she stepped into today's press briefing at Scotland Yard.

She silently berated herself for once again forgetting to cover her eyes as she made this familiar, short journey. After three years in the job, she ought to have become accustomed to it by now.

Commissioner Morgan had attracted a fair bit of criticism from the media throughout her period in charge of the Metropolitan Police, but that was nothing her broad shoulders couldn't take. To Suzanne Morgan, the press were an unwelcome sideshow from her main goal of jailing as many criminals as possible.

She was aware that much of the criticism was down to her appearance. She was probably the most un-stereotypical police commissioner in the Met's history: an overweight and unattractive lesbian, hailing from the north of England. She knew she didn't provide the most aesthetically pleasing photo opportunities, but, in her own words, she 'couldn't give two fucks about that.'

Suzanne was brought up in Sunderland in the early '70s, a single child to a single parent, her mother having died when she was barely a toddler. Her father was a coal miner, and he had done his best to instil some femininity into her upbringing but had failed miserably. Still, what he couldn't provide in some areas, he more than made up for in love and laughter. He taught her to never back down from anyone and to always chase her dreams, no matter how many toes she had to tread on in the process.

Whilst Suzanne was no press darling, most of her colleagues held her in the highest regard. They saw her as brave, loyal, and personable, and they rewarded her with their trust and dedication.

Today's press conference was probably the most high-profile one she had ever been involved in. There were more journalists there than she'd ever witnessed before. She felt a rare pang of nerves as she took to the stage, tapped her microphone, and cleared her throat loudly, causing some of those in attendance to grimace.

"Ladies and gentlemen, thank you for your attendance today. As you are no doubt aware, five days ago, the body of a young girl was discovered on Hackney Marshes. Today, I can officially name the girl as Natasha Shaw. Her family have already been notified and are currently being looked after during this horrendous time for them. There's evidence that Natasha had been sexually assaulted before being strangled. She was just fourteen years old.

"As you know, this is just the latest incident in our capital involving attacks against under-age girls – or, as I prefer to call them, children. I am here today to let you know that going forwards, we will be doubling down on our efforts to bring the perpetrators to justice.

"As of today we are introducing a new taskforce dedicated to solving these crimes. This taskforce will be given unparalleled powers to investigate the darkest areas of society, and to eradicate this vile abuse against our young girls. To head up this expert team, I would like to introduce one of our finest police officers. He's someone I've known, worked with, and respected for many years, Detective Chief Inspector Michael Dack."

# Three

"Commissioner Morgan, do you feel that your office has taken its eye off the ball in regard to these crimes? My second question is for Detective Chief Inspector Michael Dack. What do you feel you can bring to this case?"

Suzanne Morgan quickly replied.

"The answer to your first question is no. I don't feel we've taken our eyes off the ball, and I can assure you that every member of my team shares the same determination, to help drive such heinous acts from London streets.

"The introduction of this taskforce entirely supports our seriousness in combatting these crimes, and I can think of no better person than Michael to lead the team. I'll now hand over to him to answer the second part of your question."

Michael leant forwards to speak into the microphone as Suzanne looked on. He was in good shape for his age, strong as he always had been. At six-foot one and fourteen stone, he carried a masculine air of authority. He still looked reasonably spritely, especially considering the numerous years he'd spent abusing his body with alcohol and tobacco. But there was something in his eyes. He looked haunted.

Michael paused for a few seconds before leading into his response.

"Thank you for your question. I think firstly, it's important to point out that, as of yet, we haven't been able to connect any of these cases to each other.

"I've been a serving policeman now for over forty years and have been involved in similar investigations around the country. In fact, I first met Commissioner Morgan around twenty years ago, when we worked together to solve a case involving the abduction and trafficking of young girls in Newcastle."

As soon as Michael said the word 'trafficking,' he regretted it. This was why he hated doing press conferences; he could never stick to the script. Hands shot up throughout the press before one of them, an older man seated towards the front of the auditorium, shouted out,

"So, do you think these cases bear the hallmarks of a trafficking ring then, Detective Chief Inspector?"

This caused a female journalist to shout out, "There have long been rumours of a VIP paedophile ring operating in London. Does your experience tell you that this could be a possibility?"

Michael waited for the bedlam to die down slightly before motioning with his hand for silence. "I apologise for that slip of the tongue. I did not mean that the cases show there is a professional operation to blame, I was referring to the nature of the cases, the disappearance of young girls."

"So, do you think that this could all be the actions of a lone person?" shouted another journalist from the back of the room.

"I'm not here to speculate, I'm here to investigate and dedicate."

Michael smiled to himself at his little soundbite before he looked up and realised that no-one else was impressed.

"I promise that my team will leave no stone unturned in this investigation. We will work every hour possible to ensure that the perpetrators of these hideous crimes are brought to justice."

"You mention your team. How many are on it, and can you name them?" shouted the same female journalist as before.

Michael hadn't been briefed on the answer to this question. He glanced at Suzanne for reassurance, but she was staring vaguely into space. He took this as a sign that she was happy for him to tell the truth.

"We will have a four-person team, including myself, and I can't currently name them as they're not yet in place."

The press erupted in a loud gasp before more shouts started to ring out. He looked at Suzanne again and she glowered back at him.

"Only a four-person team! How do you expect to crack these cases with that?" shouted one journalist.

"Chief Detective, if your team is not yet in place, are you telling us that basically all the Met have currently done is put you in charge of an investigation?" shouted another.

Suzanne Morgan stepped forwards again to the microphone. "We are in the very latter stages of confirming the personnel for the taskforce. Each individual has been specially chosen for their own skillset and experience. Please remember, we aren't looking to create a large, bulky team here. I want a small, flexible, and skilled unit, capable of moving quickly on any new evidence."

As she stepped back, she gave Michael another look, as if to say, 'That's how you do it'.

Michael felt like walking off the stage. He looked around for a friendly journalist and pointed towards a chubby-looking, young male with glasses. As soon as the man spoke, Michael instantly regretted it.

"Iona Radociou, a fifteen-year-old Romanian immigrant who disappeared on her way home from school in March 2021. Lisa Cattermole, a twelve-year-old girl snatched from her Shoreditch bedroom in June 2021. Simina Albescu, aged fourteen, a schoolgirl on holiday in London from Romania in November 2021 who never returned home to her family."

Michael tried to interrupt, but the young journalist ploughed on, revelling in his moment in the spotlight.

"Claudia Jenkinson, a fifteen-year-old traveller girl who ran off from her site in Debden one evening in April 2022 and never returned. Joanne Buckley, fourteen, and Lucinda Wallace, thirteen, two vulnerable girls staying at a YMCA in Stratford. They disappeared one evening in August 2022.

"Cristina Petrescu, thirteen years old, a Romanian immigrant who disappeared from a funfair in London Fields in June 2023, never to be seen again. Lena Nowak, a Polish immigrant aged twelve, taken from a Christmas market in London Bridge two days before Christmas Eve 2023. And now, Natasha Shaw.

"These crimes are all located within an eight-mile radius of each other. Every girl is aged between twelve to fifteen. Are the Metropolitan Police seriously trying to tell us that they can't prove these crimes are linked, and are they seriously trying to tell us that they have no leads on the perpetrators?"

Michael looked over again at Suzanne and realised it was going to be him who had to respond, no matter that he had only been in the job for less than twenty-four hours. He sighed audibly.

"I can assure you that no-one at the Metropolitan Police is happy with this situation, and no-one has rested on their laurels. My team will be looking at every single one of these cases with fresh eyes and a clear mind."

"Can you confirm the rumours that Natasha was found wearing a bracelet that seemed to contain a barcode? And can you also confirm that this was similar to a bracelet the very first victim, Iona, was found wearing?"

This question rang out from the same female journalist as before. Both Michael and Suzanne were taken aback. Whilst the fact that Iona was wearing such a bracelet had been well known, it was supposed to be confidential that Natasha had been found wearing one that bore extreme similarities.

Suzanne stepped forwards to the microphone. "I'm sure you are aware that some facts have to stay confidential in order to protect our enquiries. As such, I will neither confirm nor deny that rumour. Now, we would like to wrap up this conference and press on with our work on the case, so just one more question."

Scattered hands shot up throughout the media, but one voice again rang through loudest, her middle-class, home counties accent rising above the cacophony of the other attendees.

"Final question then to Detective Chief Inspector Michael Dack. How do you feel your own personal history, regarding your still-missing daughter from thirteen years ago, will affect your judgement in this case? Do you feel her memory will drive you on or in fact be a hindrance?"

Suzanne looked at Michael to see if he was willing to respond, but no words came out of his mouth. She stood up to the microphone again.

"We won't be answering personal questions. That will wrap up the press conference for today, thank you for your time, and we will update you going forwards with anything we deem relevant."

# Four

"Well, that was a complete shit show, wasn't it, DCI Dack? Shall I book you in for some intensive media training before we start this investigation?" Commissioner Suzanne Morgan stormed down the Scotland Yard corridor with Michael trailing in her wake.

"I couldn't agree more, ma'am. I'll tell you what might have come in handy, a little pre-event briefing, perhaps? I'm a bit too old to be out there on stage winging it."

"Oh, don't be such a worrier. You didn't say too much wrong, apart from the bit about the similarity in cases. Or the part about the team not being in place yet. Or the part about how many officers were in the team."

"I don't know if you noticed, ma'am, but I looked at you for a bit of guidance on that point, and you were too busy staring into space! Did you have something more important on your mind?"

"You noticed, did you? Very observant. Yes, as a matter of fact, I completely drifted off. I suddenly remembered that I was going out for dinner tonight, and I was wondering if there was any way I'd be able to get away with a starter, main course, and dessert whilst sticking to my Weight Watcher plan. There I am, working out how many points a tiramisu contains, and the next thing I know, you've provided the country's media with classified police information!"

They both stopped in their tracks and stared at each other for a few seconds before simultaneously bursting out laughing.

"Seriously though, ma'am, how did that journo know about my past?"

"You have heard of a thing called Google, haven't you? It's hardly confidential information. One thing I am sure of though, now that it's out in the open, they'll all be looking into the matter. Are you sure you can handle that?"

"I'm sure, ma'am. I've learned to live with that part of my life for a long time now."

"I'm glad to hear it. Now, let's crack on, we'd better put this team together quickly!"

Ten minutes later, the pair were sitting in Suzanne's office, each with a cup of coffee and a file containing twenty possible candidates to join the taskforce.

"So, did you have a chance to look through this last night? All these candidates have expressed an interest in working this case, and I feel they could all add something to your team. I've got three favourites in mind, but I'd like to hear your thoughts."

"I'm happy to go with any two of these candidates you recommend. You know I trust you implicitly, ma'am."

"Stop buttering me up and tell me what you want."

"I think I need the third person to be someone I can rely on and someone with a bit more experience."

"Here we go. Let me guess what's coming next." Suzanne sat back in her chair and took a sip of her coffee.

"What do you mean?"

"Cut the bullshit, Michael. I can see your brain ticking over. You want your old mate, Robert Archer on the team, don't you? Well, don't bother, because I knew you would, and I've already sounded him out. He's not interested."

"Why not? What did he say?"

"He said he's too old to be running around East London on a revenge crusade with you. Trust me, Michael, his fire has gone out. You'll get no joy out of him."

"A revenge crusade? He really said that?"

"I'm afraid so."

"Give me a chance to speak to him. I know he'll do wonders if I can get him up and running again."

"He also said that the last time he saw you, it didn't end too well. He didn't divulge further but said you'd know what he meant."

"Oh, that was nothing, he's a stubborn old goat. Let me go and see him. If he's not in by the end of next week, then I'll choose someone else."

"For god's sake, I knew you'd do this. Okay, I can't have this discussion going on all day. If Rob still says no, then I choose the third member. Deal?'

"Deal."

"Okay, good. You've got Nisha Sharma and Matt Gardiner."

"Fine. Tell me about them."

"Nisha is nosey, pushy, a complete pain in the arse and probably the most aspirational copper I've ever met. She wants my job, and she thinks she'll get it within five years.

"If you put her on this case, she will do absolutely everything to crack it and then use it to get herself a promotion. Don't get me wrong, she'll try to take all the credit for it as well, but I couldn't give a toss about that. She's a bloody good copper, and she'll work every hour possible."

"She sounds like a barrel of laughs. What about Matt?"

"He absolutely loves himself. But he's tough, and I think this investigation could lead you into some scary places. He won't be intimidated easily. He's six-foot three and full of muscle. He does cage fighting or some bollocks like that. Either way, I think you need a physical presence."

"Are you saying I don't possess that anymore?"

"That's exactly what I'm saying. Not at your age. Anyway, are you happy?"

"I will be if I get Rob."

"Well, don't rely on that, you've got till Wednesday to convince him. Speak to my PA, Lizzie Oakley. She'll take you down to your new office. You'll find everything already set up for you down there. If you need anything else, you come directly to me, okay? Now, get out."

"Blunt as always, ma'am. Thanks for your time."

"Don't be a smart-arse, Michael. There's only room for one in this building, and you're looking at her."

"Thanks, ma'am." Michael turned and started to walk towards the door.

"Oh, Michael, one more thing. I can't help thinking that if you do your job well in this case, you're going to find out information that could have some huge repercussions for law and order in this country. Just make sure you're mentally prepared for that."

# Five

As her eyes flickered open, she experienced once again those familiar few seconds of hope, these precious few moments that had grown to be the best part of her day – until realisation set in.

The darkened room was no nightmare. The stained, single mattress was no mirage. The bucket in the corner was no illusion. This was her reality, and it had been ever since that fateful night.

She did not know how long she had spent imprisoned in this room. Without any windows, the days and the nights had rolled into one. She couldn't work out if it was weeks, months, or maybe even years since she had been taken against her will. She did know that she wouldn't be able to survive much longer.

She sat up on the mattress and glanced at the bracelet fastened around her wrist. The tag around her ankle read, Emilia. It was the name that had been foisted upon her by those two men whom she hated with all her heart. The two men who had taken her, drugged her, and locked her up in this hellhole.

She had never wished harm upon anyone before in her life, but if she was given the opportunity, she swore she would happily kill these men with her own two hands. How could anyone take another human against their will? How could people be so callous, so devoid of emotion, to be able to rip someone from their family without a care in the world?'

How she longed to see her father again. What she would do to be back in his arms and feel his comforting embrace, that familiar smell she had known since she was a child. If he knew where she was, he would come looking for her with fury and vengeance. If he knew the things that these men had done to her, he would tear them limb from limb.

She started to sob – a regular occurrence for her these days. It was quietly at first but gradually grew louder as her eyes surveyed her torso and limbs, covered in bruises, aching and pale, unrecognisable from the young, healthy body it had been prior to her kidnapping.

Her crying began a chain reaction. She heard one other girl start to sob, and then another. The cries came from nearby rooms that she presumed were like hers. She did not know how many other girls there were; she had never dared to ask.

Occasionally, one of the girls would attempt to communicate with another, some in English, some in languages she did not understand. Through the thin walls, they shouted out, longing for companionship, but the punishment for being caught was severe. If the men heard any of them, then they would be subjected to beatings, torture, or sometimes even worse. It was enough to deter most girls from trying again.

As her tears ran dry, she lapsed into her regular daydream. It was one in which her two captors were put in handcuffs and bundled into the back of a police van after policemen dressed in black with machine guns invaded the building.

She pictured her day in court, confronting the captors. Emboldened and powerful, she would tell them to their faces just how low they were, before she would watch them sentenced. She imagined waving at them with a smile on her face before she would go off to rehabilitate and make the most out of her life.

She knew she was strong enough to get over this ordeal, if she was just given the opportunity. If she was given a second chance she was convinced that she could cope and prosper. She just wasn't convinced that she'd ever get the opportunity.

She was jolted out of her dream as she heard that dreaded, familiar sound – a large door lock clanging open at what she presumed was the end of the corridor. She had never seen outside of her room so could only guess at what lay out there, but she imagined a long, gloomy hallway with rooms on each side, imprisoning other girls like herself.

She heard a collective gasp go up throughout the prisoners. They knew what this typically meant. Each of them would pray that it was not their room door that was opened.

As the footsteps drew closer, she heard the two men speaking in a foreign tongue. Then came the sound of a third male, one whose voice she did not recognise.

The footsteps grew louder and so did the voices. She put her ear to the door, and it sounded as if the men were bartering. Her heart sank. It was another customer, depraved and desperate, looking for a cheap thrill in this squalid hell.

She jumped back onto the bed and lay face down, head in hands, repeating her prayers over and over, 'Please don't let it be me. Please, God, don't let it be me.' Silence fell outside for a few seconds, and her pulse quickened. She knew the decision was near.

The lock of her door began to turn, and a small tear formed in the corner of her eye.

# Six

It was late evening when Michael finally walked in the front door of his four-storey townhouse on Conewood Street, Islington. He loved the location, but despite living there for nearly four years, it had never felt like home.

He hadn't contributed anything financially towards the property. His partner, Samantha, had previously been married to a futures trader called David, who'd suffered a fatal heart attack six years ago. The money he'd left in his will enabled Samantha to pay off the mortgage on the house whilst also comfortably providing for her two teenage daughters, Rebecca and Georgia.

The shadow of David still hung over the house. The girls had never warmed to Michael. They would cringe when he sat down on a seat next to them, his breath usually smelling of alcohol or cigarettes.

As Michael walked through the front door, he was relieved to see only Georgia sitting in the front room; she was the quieter of the two. He greeted her with an overly cheery, 'Good evening, Georgia,' from which he received a mumbled reply of, 'Hi, Michael,' and a semi-smile.

"Evening, darling. You're late! Dinner's nearly ready. Did you have something important on today?"

Michael grinned as he heard Samantha's voice call out from the kitchen and wandered down to see her.

"Go on, then. Just how bad was it?" Michael said as he hugged her from behind. The smell radiating from the oven was like nectar to his nose. Samantha had promised him his favourite dish tonight – a Moroccan lamb tagine.

"Don't be silly, you were great," she replied, briefly turning to kiss him on the lips, "Now, what are you drinking? Whisky? Wine?"

"Both, please. And a vodka chaser."

"Darling, it really wasn't bad at all. Just maybe don't go on social media for a few days."

"I think I can manage to avoid that."

"I'm sure you can. Can you shout the girls, please? Dinner's ready."

Georgia walked in and sat quietly to Michael's right before Rebecca entered shortly afterwards and crashed down on the chair to Michael's left without saying hello. Rebecca caught him staring at her.

"Yes, Michael? What are you looking at, you creep?" she said in her sharp North London accent.

"Just wondering if you were going to say hello, that's all."

"Errr, wouldn't have thought so. I'm a bloody laughingstock at school after your performance on TV today."

"Becky, that's enough!" called out Sam, but Rebecca wasn't finished.

"Bit ironic, isn't it? You've been hired to search for missing young girls. It's like your perfect job, isn't it? I'll bet you'll be well good at it."

Georgia stifled a laugh as the words came out of Rebecca's mouth. They had a running joke about him being a dirty old man, especially after they'd heard the rumours about his missing daughter.

"Becky! Stop that right now. We are going to have a peaceful evening tonight, and I won't have you ruin it," said Samantha as she poured herself a large wine.

"It's okay, Sam," said Michael. "I'm sorry I embarrassed you both on TV. If it helps, I hated it as much as you. Press has never been my thing."

"Young girls are though, right?" Rebecca snapped back, prompting another stifled laugh from Georgia.

"Oi! One more comment like that, and you're up to your room, do you hear me?"

Michael smiled resignedly and took another gulp of wine; it was going to be a long weekend.

# Seven

It was 6.53 on Monday morning as Nisha Sharma stepped out of Westminster Station. A surge of excitement ran through her body. Today was the start of a new chapter in her life.

She'd received the call just three days ago from Detective Chief Inspector Michael Dack, informing her that she'd been chosen as part of a new taskforce. It was the sort of position she'd been longing for ever since she'd progressed through the training course at Hendon with flying colours.

She cast her mind back to those days and smiled as she thought of how jealous some of her colleagues would be if they could see her now. She had never been the most popular person. Her dedication to the job and propensity for sticking her nose into other's business often rubbed people up the wrong way, not that she cared about the opinions of others.

She took a deep breath of the warm London air and started out on the short walk to Scotland Yard. She had been told to meet at 8am for an introduction to her new team, but she wanted to be in at least forty-five minutes early.

Her thoughts turned to her new boss. She'd re-watched Friday's press conference a couple of times over the weekend, and she wasn't impressed with what she had seen. To her, DCI Michael Dack had looked underprepared and indecisive in front of the full glare of the media.

She was, however, prepared to give him the benefit of the doubt. She'd heard good things from Commissioner Morgan about his previous work, and she appreciated that not everyone was comfortable dealing with the media. Perhaps his strengths lay in other areas, and her skills could complement them.

She looked across the river at the Houses of Parliament, and her eyes narrowed. Like everyone else, she had heard the rumours that circulated on social media about the involvement of a VIP trafficking ring. Whilst Nisha typically paid little attention to conspiracy theories, she had to admit that it certainly seemed plausible in this case. She had never heard of an investigation with so many victims that had failed to turn up even a single suspect.

She had, so far, only been privy to a limited amount of information and was excited about being filled in on the rest. She strode through the gates, took a deep breath, and walked through the entrance of Scotland Yard.

At the same time, approximately fourteen miles away in Dagenham, Matthew Gardiner's second reserve alarm went off. The noise took a while to work its way into his deep slumber, but when it did, he jolted up. Today was his first day in a new role for the Metropolitan Police, and he was already late.

He had been celebrating all weekend with his flatmate, Liam. They'd only intended for one big night out, but Friday rolled into Saturday, and then Saturday rolled into Sunday as they moved from pub to pub before ending up back at their flat with two girls.

As his eyes adjusted to the light, he felt the pain surging through his head and cursed himself for self-inflicting this state.

He reached over and groggily grabbed the phone from his bedside table, pressing the screen at least three times before the alarm stopped. He squinted at the display: 7.05am. "Shit!"

Eleven minutes later, he was running down the stairs half-dressed. He found his shoes and threw on his jacket before he sprinted out of the front door. He looked slightly bedraggled, but at least he was passable for a human being.

He made it to Dagenham East Station with a minute to spare and started to collect his thoughts. It dawned on Matt that he hadn't looked into the case at all over the weekend. He had blurred recollections of someone in the pub telling him that his new boss had crashed and burned at a press conference. He then remembered the tray of jägerbombs that Liam had ordered just before closing time. He had downed three of those, no wonder he'd had trouble sleeping.

Sweat poured down his forehead as he realised that he'd be meeting his new team in fifteen minutes time. He cursed himself again.

The doors slid open at Westminster Station, and he darted through them and up the escalators, pausing only at the exit to check his phone's Google Maps for the directions to Scotland Yard. Six per cent battery! "Get your head on this, Matt, would you?!" he grumbled to himself.

He ran as fast as he could, arriving at the entrance at 7.56am, sweaty and unkempt, but at least not late. He swore to himself that today was the start of a new him. Today was the day that he'd finally start to grow up and take responsibility. The same promise he made most Mondays.

# Eight

Philip Strevens opened a bottle of Vodka and poured himself a large glass, before he shuffled to the study at the rear of his one-bedroom house in Croydon.

He switched on the light bulb which dangled bare from the ceiling. Laptops, desktops, screens, and servers were scattered around, all in various states of working order. He pushed any equipment that related to his professional life to one side, he wouldn't be needing those tonight.

He felt a rush come over him as he anticipated the next few hours of computer time. He looked forward to these days like most other people would look forward to a night out with friends. In here he felt safe, his physical frailties were insignificant. For Philip Strevens, a good time was one spent behind the anonymity of a computer screen.

He sat down on his dark, leather desk chair and clicked a mouse which stirred a large desktop into action. Next to the keyboard, a green, glass ashtray overflowed with cigarette butts. He pulled out a packet of Mayfair Blue's and lit one up, sucking greedily on it as he tapped on his keyboard. The smoke exhumed from between his yellow cragged tooth, and floated across the room, before it settled on the stained, brown wallpaper.

The walls were sparse, except for one display case which contained a series of Scout badges obtained during his many years in the organisation. They reminded him fondly of his time spent as an Akela. He cherished those days, even though he still held a grudge about the way he was forced out of the role.

He perched the cigarette on the side of the ashtray, as his screen flashed open. The first page that came up displayed a Tor browser, and an option appeared asking him to either connect or configure, he chose to connect. A green tick informed him that the connection had been successful. He smiled, safe in the knowledge that his actions would now be completely untraceable. 'God bless the internet'.

He clicked onto the Snapchat app and logged in with the username Jordan645. A profile photo appeared at the top of the screen. It was that of a good- looking boy, probably aged around 16 or 17, posing on a beach with his top off. He checked into the inbox and was disappointed to see that no-one had responded to yesterday's raft of messages.

He brought up his sent items to ensure they had all been delivered. There were 24 of them just from yesterday, all the same. A photo of a boy, lifting up his t-shirt to show his tanned washboard stomach, with the words written underneath, '"Fancy seeing further?"' He inspected the range of recipients, all happy smiling young girls, and cursed under his breath, 'Why are you ignoring me?'

He closed Snapchat and signed into Facebook under the username AlexW2005. A similar profile image appeared at the top, but of a different boy. Next to it were his personal details: Date of birth (23/4/2005), location (London/LA) and hobbies (music, football, cinema).

Further down the page were several photographs of the same boy engaged in various activities with friends or family. Comments or jokes were posted underneath, each one by other profiles created by Strevens. He congratulated himself yet again on how intricate his system was. He took a final puff of his cigarette before he cast it into the ashtray.

A message alert appeared at the bottom of the page. It was Jessica.

'Hey Alex, back online I see? :) Xox'

Strevens rubbed his hands together and began to reply but then paused. 'Give it ten minutes, keep her keen,'

He opened another tab and typed in a different web address. This one took him to a page that was completely black except for a couple of letters written in dark grey on the bottom right of the screen. They would have been indistinguishable to the naked eye had you not known they were there. He clicked on them and was asked to enter a username and password. His username was tHe iNSAtiable1...! And his password was over 20 digits long.

A grin spread across his face as the site opened. Sprawled across the screen were a series of images and videos of children, all in various states of undress.

This was Strevens's utopia, an online playground where he could watch his innermost desires being played out, whilst being able to communicate confidentially with like- minded people.

As he tried to decide which video he would watch first, a message sprung up at the bottom of the screen from a username SAtan'sCHILD666

'Are you selling or buying?'

# Nine

The office was dingy and old fashioned, located deep in the bowels of Scotland Yard. It was an environment in which Michael felt at ease. He didn't need the latest technology to carry out his work, he just needed his own keen eye and intuition.

It normally helped if there was a raft of evidence. The four meagre cardboard boxes that sat on the desk in front of him were surprisingly sparse for an investigation of this size.

There were some scraps to feed on though. He'd spent all weekend combing through the pages and knew where he would start the investigation. He was looking forward to letting his new team members do the same. He would judge if they possessed a similar mindset to him, or indeed, if they noticed something that he may have missed. He smiled. As if he'd ever miss something.

Michael looked up to the far end of the office and the smile drained from his cragged features. Staring back at him from the wall were nine young girls, caught in random poses, some happy, some oblivious, some solemn, but all now brought unwittingly together under one morbid umbrella.

Michael fought back the grief by reminding himself that only two were confirmed dead. He locked on to the gaze of one of the girls, a familiar, haunted face reminding him of a moment in his past that he'd rather forget.

He was startled out of his trance by the office door opening and turned around to see Lizzie Oakley, PA to Suzanne Morgan, walk in, followed by two people.

The female strode in like she owned the office. She was of Asian descent, approximately five-feet two inches and, whilst a little plump, was pretty with large, dark brown eyes and perfect bright white teeth. She was dressed professionally in smart dark blue suit over a white shirt. She clearly knew how to make a first impression.

The same could not be said of the male. He was tall and athletic looking, but his skin was blotchy, and his spiky brown hair looked dishevelled instead of stylish. His eyes were semi-closed, as if the lighting in the office was too bright for him. He was almost certainly hungover. Michael made a mental note to pull him up on that later.

He extended his hand out to greet them. "Good morning. You must be DS Sharma, and you must be DS Gardiner. Welcome to the team. I'm DCI Michael Dack."

"Good morning, guv," the pair chimed back in unison.

"Right, I've had a look through your files. You both came highly recommended from Commissioner Morgan. Congratulations on that. I know from first-hand experience how hard it is to get praise from her."

Both sergeants laughed awkwardly at Michael's attempt at humour.

"I must say, though, that the cases you've worked on previously pale in comparison to this investigation. You've both shown that you have potential, but now you need to step up and fulfil it. We cannot let this investigation fall flat. If we do, it will probably be the end of my police career, and it will derail yours before you've even got started. If we're successful, though, it's the fast track for you two, and I can sail off into the sunset, cigar in hand, reputation enhanced. Are you following me?"

"Yes, guv."

"I take it you've acquainted yourself with the case as much as possible before we begin?"

"Yes, guv."

Michael noticed that Nisha replied to this question a lot more confidently than Matt did.

"Okay, so what do you think?"

"What do you mean, guv?" asked Nisha.

"First impressions, straight off the bat. From the limited info you have, what's your gut feeling? DS Gardiner, you go first."

"Erm, well, I think it's too early to draw any conclusions. Are the cases linked? If so, how many of them? I need to see more evidence before I state my impression." Matt knew straight away his answer was inadequate and was furious at his booze-addled brain for failing to think of a better response.

"Okay, so we have a serious case of fence sitting over here. Interesting. I was told you were the cocky one. Maybe a weekend on the sauce is making you a little anxious, eh?"

Nisha smiled. She had also noticed the smell of alcohol on her new teammate.

"Okay, DS Sharma, your turn."

"I'm of the belief that they're all linked, guv. You can rule out a serial killer, there's obviously more than one person involved. For me it's either an Eastern European trafficking gang or..." She paused.

"Or what, DS Sharma? Speak your mind, this is a safe place here."

"Or there is a highly influential and powerful trafficking network in operation."

"Very interesting, you've gone for the nuclear option. Are you easily affected by social media or things you read in the gutter press, DS Sharma?"

"Not at all, guv, but—"

"There's nothing more to say. Thank you both for your observations, they've helped me paint a picture of the characters I'll be working with."

Nisha and Matt looked on in concern. He surely hadn't drawn a conclusion on them from this opening exchange, had he?

"Right, those are your opinions from the facts you know. Here in these boxes are the facts you don't know. Take your time and go through all this evidence today. I'll be looking forward to getting back later and seeing if your opinions have changed."

Nisha's eyes seemed to light up at the thought of rafting through the evidence, whilst Matt's stared blankly.

"Okay, guv. Should we know where you're going?" asked Nisha.

"No, you shouldn't, but I'll tell you anyway. I'm off to sign up our fourth team member. Enjoy your day."

# Ten

Across the city, Detective Inspector Robert Archer was at his desk in Wood Green Police Station. As he observed the buzz in the office created by his colleagues enthused by their work, he got that familiar, sinking feeling.

It wasn't that he hated his job, it was more a feeling of demotivation. He no longer possessed that passion for bringing criminals to justice. He was tired, and at sixty-one years old, he felt like his time was coming to an end.

The police force had been his whole life, and he didn't regret that for a second. Growing up as a young black man in Tottenham in the 1970s and '80s, he'd bucked the trend amongst his friends and community and started work with the establishment that so many of them viewed as the enemy. He was considered a pariah amongst many peers, but that didn't concern him. He had always been strong of will and possessed a razor-sharp wit that enabled him to swat aside any insults that came his way.

He boasted an impressive CV, having worked on some of the most notorious cases in North London. But now his limbs were tiring, and his mind, whilst keen as ever, just didn't have the fight anymore. Increasingly, he felt like a man out of time with the modern age and the 'new' police force. He hankered for the older, simpler times.

Robert drank the last of his coffee and immediately felt the urge for another. He heaved himself out of his chair and walked towards the communal kitchen. He was just about to switch on the kettle when he heard a familiar voice from behind.

"Congratulations, Granddad."

Robert slowly turned to see his old friend, Michael Dack, standing in front of him, holding a bottle of Johnnie Walker Blue Label.

"Michael Dack, as I live and breathe. Thanks for the present, I'll drink it all to myself later. And by the way, the answer's still no."

They stared at each other with straight faces for a good five seconds before they broke and embraced in a hearty bear hug.

"So, how have you been, old mate? You certainly haven't been eating salads since the last time I saw you," said Michael with a grin on his face.

"Pots and kettles, mate! Look at those trousers, you could hold a rave in them."

"Ha, well, when you get to our age, who cares? So, how's the family? I can't believe you're going to be a granddad. Is Patti doing well?"

"She's doing fine, thanks. They all are. And you shouldn't be so shocked, it's not unusual for people in their sixties to be grandparents! Most are doing it earlier you know."

"Yeah, you're right, I forget how old we are sometimes. When the hell did that happen?"

"God only knows. So, how about you? Has Sam finally pressured you into having more kids?"

"Don't be ridiculous, we'd need to have sex for that to happen! Plus, I've got enough problems with her two girls without bringing another issue into our lives."

"Is that drama still going on? I would have sworn they'd have warmed to you by now."

"It's got even worse if anything. And my performance at the press conference on Friday didn't give me any more points in the cool stakes."

"Performance at the press conference? Don't know what you're on about, mate." Robert frowned and shook his head.

"Haha! Don't give me that, you've probably been watching it on repeat."

"What do you mean?" Robert put on his best cockney accent. "Er er er, I do apologise for that slip of the tongue."

"All right, stop it now! I've had enough grief from Morgan over it. She told me she'd already been in touch with you. She knows us well."

"Yes, she does, and I'm sure she told you that I will not be swayed. Not for you, and not for anyone."

"She did tell me that, and I told her I'd get you to change your mind."

"You shouldn't go round making promises you can't keep."

"Tell you what, let's go and grab a bite to eat, my treat. If you don't change your mind after that, then I promise I'll leave it."

"I'd never say no to a free breakfast. Let's go to Kenily's. Give me a minute, I'll leave this bottle on my desk."

"Bring it with you, mate, I fancy a taste."

"It's nine AM!"

"Yeah, I'm starting late today."

Twenty-five minutes later, the two friends were sitting opposite each other with a full English breakfast in front of them, a mug of coffee, and a pair of empty plastic cups into which Michael had just poured two large shots of whisky.

Robert took a sip and smiled in satisfaction. "Ah yeah, that's the good stuff. So, tell me, why have you taken this job, mate? Why do you need this hassle at your age?"

"I have my reasons, Rob," Michael replied through a mouthful of hot sausage and egg.

"Well, I just hope your reasons are the right ones."

"And what's that supposed to mean?"

"You know exactly what that means. I hope you don't believe this case has anything to do with Josie. Because if you do, that's madness."

Michael placed his fork down on the plate and leant back. "Is that what you seriously think of me?"

"Don't bullshit me. There are similarities, even all these years apart. It's so rare, kids just disappearing into thin air, no clues, no witnesses, no suspects. It happened with Josie, and it's happened with these girls. You're telling me that this has played no part at all in your decision?"

"I'm a policeman, Rob. There are girls out there who are missing or dead and so far, no-one has been able to make any inroads. That's what made my decision, the thought that I can make a difference. That's what drives me on, and that's what used to drive you on as well. When did that change?"

"That changed when I turned sixty and realised that I was too old to be running around playing 'Dirty Harry' in London. This city is more dangerous than it ever has been. Do you know what I see come through our police station every day? The cases I hear about, the scum I see on the streets, and what they're willing to do to earn a bit of coin nowadays? London is like the Wild West now. The job's changed, and I'm too old to change with it."

"But surely you must care that people like this are brought to justice?

"Of course I care, but my family are my priority now. My house is paid off, my pension's coming up. I'm ready to retire and help Patti look after my grandchild."

Michael paused. "It's a girl, isn't it?"

"Don't go there, Mike."

"Would you be happy bringing her up with people like this still on the loose?"

"I said don't go there!"

"Oh, come on. I need you, Rob. No-one works as well as us two together. Forty years of success in bringing down criminals. We've still got it in us. And yeah, you're right, we would have to deal with some scum on the streets. But this investigation doesn't end there. It ends as far away from there as you can imagine."

"What do you mean?"

"This isn't some Eastern European trafficking gang calling the shots, and it's not a band of gutter thugs in charge. This goes to the top, trust me."

Rob paused. "How far to the top?"

Michael extended his arm as high as possible above his head to make the point. "Right to the top."

"Oh, come on. Now you're peddling some conspiracy theory to me. You want me to start chasing round shadowy Westminster figures? You don't surely believe that."

"I do believe it, mate. It's not just a conspiracy theory, I've read the evidence, and I've spoken to my contacts. If my suspicions are right, this doesn't just stop at Westminster."

Michael watched Rob and knew he had touched a nerve. Rob hated the establishment and loathed privilege and entitlement.

Rob looked back at Michael and could tell that he was convinced in his words. He could see that old determination in his friend's eyes. He remembered that Michael's instincts were rarely wrong. He felt motivation rise through his body, and suddenly, after too long a time, he started to feel his old self again.

# Eleven

"DS Sharma, DS Gardiner, let me introduce you to the fourth member of our team, Detective Inspector Robert Archer."

Nisha was taken aback by how loud Michael was as he burst through the door of the taskforce office. He seemed more boisterous than before. She quickly concluded that this was down to two things. Firstly, the man standing next to him was an old friend, and secondly, they'd both had a drink. She watched as he put arm around Rob and saw her second suspicion confirmed.

"Not only is Detective Inspector Archer a bloody good friend of mine, he is also one of the best policemen you will ever meet. We've solved hundreds of cases together, me and this man here, and do you know what? We're gonna solve this one as well. Of course, with your help. So, listen to this man, follow him, learn from him, and love him, just like I do."

As Michael planted a kiss on Rob's cheek, the effects of early drinking were so obvious that even Matt, in his hungover stupor, could tell his boss had been at the booze.

Nisha stood up and offered her hand. "Pleasure to meet you, DI Archer. I'm DS Sharma."

"It's pleasure to meet you too. I've heard a lot about you."

Nisha's eyes widened. "Have you really? Who from? Commissioner Morgan?

Rob gave Michael a wink. "No, not really, I thought it was just a nice thing to say."

Matt stifled a laugh at Nisha's crestfallen face before standing up himself. "DS Gardiner, guv. It's good to have you onboard."

"I'm not your guv, son, Michael is. And I have heard about you. I was told that you turned up drunk for your first day of work. Is that true?"

"I had a bit to drink celebrating my new role over the weekend. It won't happen again, guv. Sorry, I mean DI Archer." Matt felt aggrieved at having to apologise for his drinking to a pair of men who were clearly under the influence themselves but thought it prudent to swallow his pride on this occasion.

"Apology accepted. And by the way, it's not just 'good' to have me onboard, it's fucking great. You two have hit the jackpot being placed on a team with us old boys. You're about to get an education in police work that a lifetime at Hendon couldn't buy."

Michael chuckled as he watched Rob launch into his traditional 'initiation' routine with the younger colleagues. It was something he had witnessed many times over the years but had feared he may never see again.

"Right, that's the introductions over. You've both been looking through the evidence. Tell me and Rob what you think."

"I'll go first, guv," said Nisha. "The most significant piece of evidence we have is the bracelet. Out of all these crimes, we have just two bodies, Iona Radociou and Natasha Shaw. No significant DNA was found on either body, no foreign fibres, but both had a white plastic bracelet on their left wrist. A bracelet with what looks like a QR code on it."

Nisha laid the photographs of both bracelets out on the table, "Investigations into the QR code have led nowhere. We've tried multiple devices to scan them, but nothing works."

"DS Gardiner, what does that lead you to believe?" Michael butted in.

"That if these codes do mean something, they're only scannable with encrypted devices," said Matt.

"Encrypted devices, the bane of a copper's life! It's a good place to start, DS Gardiner, so why don't you get onto it? Speak to any informants on our books who have a history with encrypted phones."

"Okay, guv, I'm on it," Matt replied, a forced keenness in his voice.

"Good lad. Okay, so what else do we have, DS Sharma?"

"In two of the crimes, a pair of men were spotted at the scene. In the case of Lisa Cattermole, two separate witnesses saw two men running down the street carrying what looked like a young girl. Lena Nowak was taken from the Christmas market in London Bridge by two men, and three witnesses corroborated that."

"And what did SOCO tell us about the crime scene of Natasha Shaw?" asked Rob.

"It looked like two sets of male footprints around the body," said Matt.

"Have we got the analysis back on the footprints yet?" asked Michael.

Matt leaned back in his chair, "Indiscernible brand, both sets look like heavy duty work style boots, approximately size eleven or twelve."

"So, they're two big men," said Michael, standing on his tiptoes and holding his arms out to accentuate the point. "Undoubtedly, they got disturbed and ran off. There's no way they'd have left the body lying in the open like that, with the bracelet on, if someone hadn't spooked them. The question is, who? We've still had no-one come to us saying they witnessed anything that night, correct?"

"No-one, guv. Perhaps it was just a dog walker or some random drunk out late at night."

"Maybe, but these guys don't seem like the type to get spooked easily. If it is the same men, then they've firstly taken a girl from her bedroom and secondly taken a girl in full public view from a busy Christmas fair."

"The only difference is those girls were alive. Natasha was dead," said Nisha.

"So, tell me your hypothesis, then, DS Sharma."

"She went missing ten days before her body showed up. I'd say she was kidnapped first and then died during an escape attempt. This leads me to believe she was either being held in the vicinity of Hackney Marshes or she was in the process of being transported at the time."

"We need to speak to the family again. I'll arrange for us to meet her mum and brother," said Michael. "DS Gardiner, you crack on with the encrypted phones. DS Sharma, I want you to get in touch with the previous witnesses. Make sure you go to their homes, go over the old stories, and match them up against what they told us at the time. Check and see if there's anything suspicious there."

"Okay, guv."

"DI Archer, cast your eyes over those boxes and get acquainted with the case. Let's talk when I'm back, and I'll get your views on where we should be looking."

# Twelve

Michael stepped into the car park at Scotland Yard and was engulfed by the heat. "There's no better place in the world than London when it's sunny," he smiled to himself.

He checked his watch and saw he had approximately eight minutes before he had to be upstairs in Commissioner Morgan's office.

He fished into the pocket of his jeans, pulled out his phone, and tapped in the number. Simultaneously, he pulled out his box of cigarettes, lit one up, and took his first drag. He quickly secured a meeting with Natasha Shaw's mother for the next morning, then threw his cigarette onto the floor, ignoring the ashtrays stuck to the wall. He walked inside and took the lift to Suzanne's office on the fourth floor.

"How have you been, ma'am?"

"Do you mean besides the increase in violent crime, online fraud, immigration crime, burglary and muggings? Yep, apart from all that, I've been great. So, how are your team are getting on? Have you made any headway with Rob yet?"

"Well, funnily enough, ma'am, he's downstairs with us now."

"You're kidding me?"

"Nope, told you I'd crack him."

"Well, I didn't see that coming. I was sure he was ready to rot away in North London for the rest of his years. He shouldn't already be here though. There's paperwork we must do to get him transferred. Oh, shit, is that why the governor of Wood Green nick keeps ringing me?"

"Sorry, ma'am, when I convinced him, he just couldn't wait to get started."

Morgan shook her head. "For god's sake. Okay, I'll take care of it. Now, are you ready to meet the biggest wanker you've ever met?"

"That's surely no way to talk about your boss."

"Spare me the sensitivity. Anyway, it wasn't him who hired me, he inherited me, and I know that he wishes that wasn't the case. He's an old sexist who would much rather have a man in charge of the Met. Watch how he acts and tell me I'm not right."

"You were Peter Marshall's appointment, right?"

"Yep, good old Lord Peter Marshall. I'm not saying he was perfect as home secretary; he had his faults as we all do, but at least he respected your thoughts. I'll never forget the warning he gave me, do not trust David Parkinson. He's only out for himself and cares about nothing else."

"It sounds like the guy was born to be a politician. What's he even doing coming here anyway? Shouldn't we be meeting him over at parliament?"

"It's a good photo opportunity for him, isn't it? You know how these slippery bastards work. They like to show the press they're on top of things when nothing could be further from the truth. And trust me, Michael, this bastard is this slipperiest of the lot."

"You've got a good working relationship with him then?" Michael smirked.

"He's a condescending prick. I'm getting worked up just thinking about him. I should have had a fag. Have we got time?"

"It doesn't look like it, I think your man's arrived."

Suzanne's heart sank as she saw the Rt Hon David Parkinson, the incumbent home secretary of the UK, striding across the floor towards her office, his long-suffering assistant, Ania, scuttling behind him.

Suzanne gave Michael a look, straightened her face, and stepped out of the office to hold open the door. "How are you, sir? Welcome to HQ. Would you like any refreshments at all? Tea or coffee?'

"Oh, don't be so silly, Sue, do you think I'm going to subject myself to a PG Tips with long-life milk?"

Michael watched as the home secretary briefly shook Commissioner Morgan's hand and pushed past her into her office. His voice was exactly as Michael had imagined it would be, posh, rasping, and nasally.

David Parkinson was the sort of man who exuded privilege. Aged fifty-two, he was in decent shape at nearly six feet tall, with only a small hint of a belly starting to appear. His grey hair was slicked back and, judging from his deep tan, he had either recently been on holiday or owned an expensive sunbed. His tailored, dark grey suit was combined with deep brown leather shoes, a white shirt, and a royal blue checked tie, held in place with a silver tie clip.

"And you must be Michael?" He was also clearly no respecter of titles, or maybe just not those titles he considered beneath him.

Michael reached out and shook his outstretched hand with a forced smile that Suzanne would have been proud of. "Pleasure to meet you, sir. I'm DCI Michael Dack."

"And as you doubtless know, I'm the home secretary, the Right Honourable David Parkinson, and this is my assistant, Ania. Let's all take a seat, shall we?"

The group moved towards the back of Suzanne's office, where four black leather armchairs were located around a small brown coffee table.

"So, you're the chap who's going to solve these blessed missing girl cases? Lord knows they've been a noose around my neck for as long as I've been in power. Sue hasn't been able to make any headway, so it's good to get a fresh pair of eyes on the case."

It spoke volumes to Michael that the home secretary described his job as 'being in power.'

"Yes, sir, we'll get these cases solved for you. Trust me, I know how hard Commissioner Morgan has been working on them."

"Working hard without any results. It's the worst sort of work in my mind. No offence of course, Sue, I know you have a lot on your plate, darling."

Michael saw Suzanne's face start to redden and decided to step in before she snapped back. "Well, I'll be honest, sir, it's extremely rare that an investigation like this has such little evidence. It's almost impossible in fact. These people are either the most professional criminals I've ever seen, or…" Michael stopped. Out of the corner of his eye, he could see Suzanne staring at him.

"Or what?" asked Parkinson, leaning forwards to look Michael squarely in the eye.

"Or they've just been extremely lucky so far. Either way, we'll get to the bottom of this, don't worry."

"I appreciate your confidence, Michael, I really do. I hope you understand, though, that I've received similar promises, from policemen like yourself, many times regarding this matter, and it's still rumbling on. I'd like to be kept fully abreast of the investigation on a regular basis. I'm not one for micromanaging typically, but in this instance, I feel like I have no choice.'

"I'm very happy to keep you as fully updated as possible, sir. Of course, always taking case confidentiality into account."

Parkinson grimaced. "I don't think you understand, Michael. I'm the home secretary, case confidentiality doesn't apply to me. I want to be kept *fully* updated. Do you understand?"

Michael felt his adrenaline rise. Through years of training and police work, he had learned to deal with all sorts of bullies, liars, criminals, and charlatans. He held the stare of the home secretary for approximately ten seconds, letting an uncomfortable silence hang in the air, before he replied in a considered voice.

"As I said, I will endeavour to keep you as fully informed as possible. There will, however, be occasions I have information, and I will not share it with anyone if I feel doing so could damage the investigation. I wouldn't share it with Commissioner Morgan, my team, my partner, and I'm afraid, sir, I wouldn't share it with you. I want to be as honest as possible from the start in our relationship. I'm sure you wouldn't have it any other way."

The two men continued to stare at each other. Suzanne and Ania both shifted uncomfortably in their seats, awaiting Parkinson's response. He wasn't used to being challenged in this way.

Eventually, Suzanne felt the need to interject. "What DCI Dack is trying to say, sir, is that, in any investigation, there is always information that is vital to keep confidential until such time the investigating officer deems it necessary."

"Do you think I'm a fucking idiot, Morgan?" Parkinson replied, throwing his hands up in the air. "I know exactly what this man is trying to say. I'm just exceptionally surprised he's saying it, and I'm even more surprised you're allowing it. You seem to forget who's in charge here. And perhaps if your colleagues did keep you fully abreast of all information, we wouldn't be in this predicament now."

As he finished his words, he leant back slightly in his chair and softened his glare. "Okay, Michael. I appreciate your determination to crack this case. Ania, please write down that Michael will be taking full responsibility for the results of this investigation. Make a note that he doesn't wish to share the burden with peers or colleagues who may be able to assist him. I will ensure in all my dealings with the media that these facts are made aware."

"If you're trying to intimidate me, sir, I should let you know that I care not one bit about the media or my public image."

"Yes, that much was obvious from your appearance at the press conference," Parkinson snorted.

"Exactly. My stepdaughters told me that I've been pilloried on social media, and honestly, I couldn't give a toss. I've taken this job to get justice for these girls, and I'll go to any lengths to get it. Coming out of this looking like a plonker on Twitter or Facebook is the last thing on my mind. Do you understand what I'm saying? And Ania, you can note that down as well."

A small grin began to form on Parkinson's face, an expression of either admiration or contempt. Eventually, he held out his hand for Michael to shake.

"Okay, Michael, well I'm glad we're both clear on where we stand. I wish you the best of luck with your investigation, and I hope you bring these bastards down. Now, if you wouldn't mind running along, Sue and I have some other business to attend to."

"Very well, sir. I hope you have a nice evening. Goodbye, ma'am. Nice to meet you, Ania." Michael shook Parkinson's hand and nodded towards the two women before he exited the office, receiving a wide-eyed look from Suzanne as he did.

# Thirteen

It was just after 9am when Michael pulled up outside Robert's house in Southgate. He considered beeping the horn, but he hadn't seen Robert's family in over two years now. His sense of manners got the better of him.

He was greeted at the door by Robert's ten-year-old daughter, Latisha, who was beaming from ear to ear.

"Uncle Michael's here," she shouted out and was soon joined by her younger brother, Henry, who ran up and hugged Michael tightly around his right leg.

"Hello, Michael," came a voice from the living room. He looked up to see Judy, Robert's wife, walking towards him with a grin on her face. She had put on weight since he last time he saw her, but she still looked healthy. Her eyes had a few more lines around them, but they twinkled like they always had, shining out from her smooth, dark skin.

"Judy, it's good to see you. You're looking well, my darling." Michael put Latisha down and enveloped Judy in a long hug, Henry still clinging to his leg.

"Don't you try to flatter me. What have you got my husband into this time? He was nice and comfortable, heading towards his retirement, until you showed up again!"

"His waistline is certainly looking comfortable, Judy, I'll give you that. It must be something to do with your lovely home cooking!"

Judy burst into one of her long, rhythmic laughs that warmed the heart of anyone who heard it, "Well, you must come round one night for dinner. How about you bring that partner of yours?"

"That sounds fantastic. We'll get something in the diary. Is Patti around? I'd love to see how big her bump is."

"She's at the hospital having her scan. Can you believe it? Only five more months and I'll be a grandmother!"

"You'll be the youngest-looking grandmother I've ever seen. Make sure you pass my love onto her. Now, where's that husband of yours? We've got to be in Debden in fifty minutes."

"I'm here, I'm here." Robert came out of the kitchen holding a slice of toast.

"You want any toast with that butter, mate?" Michael said, noticing the melting dairy dripping over Rob's hand.

"It's too early for your wisecracks, I get enough backchat from my family."

As the pair headed out, Judy called after them. "Michael, I mean it, please take care of him. He's going to be a grandfather soon."

"You know us, Judy, we're always all right."

They arrived at Stacey's address just after 10am, a two-bedroom council house located in the middle of Debden's largest estate. The smell of marijuana hung in the musty morning air as they walked up the uneven path, flanked either side by overgrown grass littered with rubbish and the occasional pile of dog faeces.

Before they'd knocked, Stacey opened the door. She was dressed in an old pink dressing gown that looked like it had seen better days, bright pink pyjama bottoms, and a scruffy white t-shirt. Her hair was greasy and scraped into a bun. Her pale, make-up free face housed reddened eyes.

"Good morning. I'm DCI Dack, and this is DI Archer. Are you Stacey Shaw?"

"That's me. Please, come in. Sorry about the state of me, I ain't slept a wink. Would you like a cup of tea?"

"I'd love one thanks, two sugars, please," replied Rob as they made their way inside. He was surprised by how clean and tidy it was.

They sat themselves down on a tatty, brown sofa whilst Stacey boiled the kettle. She returned with a tray containing three cups of tea and a packet of custard creams, which Rob instantly delved into.

"So, how can I help you, officers?'"

"There's no need to be so formal, Stacey. You can call me Michael, and you can call him Robert. Before we begin, will Nick be joining us?"

Stacey let out a sigh. "Well, he said he would be, but who knows? He stayed out again last night. He's been a bit all over the place since the murder. He's started hanging round with some new friends. I'm not sure if I agree with them, to be honest."

"Were he and Natasha close then?" asked Robert.

"They were. He always looked out for her."

"I know you've already been formally interviewed about Natasha, so we're not here to dig up old ground. We just want to have an informal chat, introduce ourselves properly, and see if there's anything else that you may have remembered in the last week or so that may help, no matter how small."

"Oh, so you're not here to provide an update then. I was hopeful you may have made some progress. Wishful thinking, eh?"

Robert detected the tone of frustration in her voice. "I'm sure it seems like the police are moving slowly. All I can say to you is that things are heading in the right direction, and you have a really strong team working on this case now."

"What about all these other girls? I'm sure that if any of them were posh, these cases would have been treated more seriously. It looks to me like they've been pushed to the back of the queue."

"I can assure you that's not the case. We are on the job, and we will solve this for you. We just need a little patience and, if possible, a little help. Is there anything useful at all you can tell us?"

Stacey held her hand to her chin and stared straight ahead. "I'm sorry, but I just can't think of anything."

As she finished her sentence, there was a noise at the front door. A stocky figure dressed in a blue tracksuit and black dirty trainers walked in with a scowl on his face.

"Nick!" Stacey got up and threw her arms around her son, although the warmth was not reciprocated. He brushed past her and walked into the living room, followed by three other men.

Two of the men looked around Nick's age, late teens to early twenties, but one of them was clearly older. He was six-foot tall and lean, with an angry-looking face adorned with pock marks. His hair was shaved aggressively at the sides and spiked with gel at the top. He wore a black leather jacket and dark-coloured jeans accompanied by a pair of green biker boots. He ignored Stacey and stared directly at the two policemen.

"Hello, Nick, glad you could make it. I'm DCI Dack," said Michael.

"Why are you bothering my mother again? She's told you all she knows. You should be out there catching these nonces instead of in here drinking our tea."

"Nick, don't speak to them like that, they're trying to help," said Stacey.

"It's okay, Stacey," said Robert. "We'll be out there catching them soon, son, don't worry about that. We just came to see if there was any further information you or your mother could give us."

"Well, as it happens, there is. While the police have been twiddling their thumbs, we've been out there doing some investigating of our own. My mates here, they've been a lot more useful than you lot have."

"What have you been up to?" said Michael.

The older man stepped forward and spoke in a confident yet monotone manner. He seemed devoid of emotion whilst at the same time exuding a quiet rage. "I'll take it from here, Nick. DCI Dack, my name is Mason Greenwell, and I'm the founder of the group Street Shield."

Michael rolled his eyes.

"We heard about this case and reached out to Nick through Facebook. Street Shield help catch sex offenders all over the country. We've been responsible for banging up eighteen of them, and our network is growing. We've recently started investigating some unsolved cases, and we've found disturbing links between them."

"Are you qualified to investigate crimes, son?" said Michael.

"We are convinced that there is a VIP sex trafficking ring operating in the higher echelons of society. Westminster, Scotland Yard, well-known businessmen and celebrities, you name it. We've been gathering evidence that we'd be willing to share with you one day, once we know that you are of the right calibre."

"What do you mean, 'of the right calibre'?" asked Robert.

"Forgive me for being cautious, DI...?"

"Archer." Rob was surprised that Mason knew he was a Detective Inspector.

"Forgive me for being cautious, DI Archer. In my numerous dealings with the police over the years, I have learnt that many of them are not to be trusted. Once I am sure that you are trustworthy, then I'd be willing to talk. Until then, we'll continue to operate in our way and let you operate in yours."

"Listen, son," said Michael, "I know what type of group you are. I've seen your sort online before with your honeypot tricks. You dangle a pretend minor in front of a suspected sex offender and then accost them at the meeting place. I have no doubt that your heart is in the right place, and I'm not saying I disagree with you giving these bastards a dig or two, but you're not the police, and I can't justify endorsing you in any way."

"Oh, I understand, DCI Dack, and I knew you'd trot out that old line, they all do. What you need to realise is that we are the ones who are prepared to get our hands dirty. We can go to places the police can't, and we also receive information from people who are scared to talk to the police. There are many out there who operate on the wrong side of the law but hate nonces just the same as us. They don't want to talk to the Old Bill but they're happy to pass information to us. Do you understand that?"

Michael and Robert remained silent, but inside they appreciated there was a bit of sense to what Mason had said.

"Now, if I'm honest, DCI Dack, I do think I'm going to be able to trust you because I know that you've been there, haven't you?"

"What do you mean?"

"You've been affected by a nonce personally, haven't you? Same as I have, same as how most of our group has."

Michael froze. Mason had obviously done his research.

Mason continued. "Because of your history, I know you feel the pain in the same way that we do, and I know you want justice as much as we do. As such, I think I'm going to be able to trust you, but just not fully yet. However, as a sign of faith, and in hope of a working relationship, we're going to throw you a little bone. Please show them, Nick."

Mason stepped back and ushered Nick forwards. He took out his phone and brought up a photo. It was of a young blonde girl dressed in tracksuit bottoms, converse trainers, and a white vest top.

"This is Harriet Kennedy," said Nick. "You need to find her. We've been trying but haven't got the resources to track her down. She lives around Bow somewhere. She's a little wrong 'un apparently, only sixteen years old, but heavily into boozing and drugs, and she likes socialising with older men.

"From what we've been told, Tash started hanging out with her a couple of months ago. They met at a rave and grew closer after that. It sounds like she's a bad influence. This is her number. She won't pick up the phone to me. You better find her before I do," said Nick.

"Son, you better not do anything stupid if you do find her," Michael tried to warn Nick, but he could see his words had no effect. He watched as Nick walked up to his teary-eyed mother and planted a kiss on her forehead.

"Don't worry about me, mum, I'm gonna get this all sorted." Nick headed out the front door without looking at Michael or Rob. The rest of the group followed him, but before he exited, Mason turned again to address the room.

"Good luck with your investigation. We'll be watching your progress, and if we find out anything further, and if we can trust you, we'll be in touch."

# Fourteen

It had been a week since the initial meeting of the taskforce, and Michael had grown frustrated with how little progress had been made, especially from himself and Rob.

They had yet to track down Harriet Kennedy. Her phone had been switched off, and all attempts to trace the device had been futile.

Nisha and Matt had been working on their own objectives for a few days now, and Michael was eager to get an update from them. He had arranged a team briefing for 8am that morning and had woken early in anticipation. He tiptoed out of bed and showered and changed as quietly as possible, trying not to disturb Samantha as she slept.

Michael felt guilty as he closed the door. He was aware that he'd been spending less time with Samantha as the investigation had begun to dominate more of his life. He also knew that this situation was likely to get worse before it got better.

Michael entered the office at 7.23am and was not surprised to see Nisha already sitting at her desk. It pleased him that he had a colleague just as determined to crack this case as he was.

"Good morning, DS Sharma. How have you been?"

"Morning, guv. I've been working on the previous witnesses to the two men from the other cases, but I must be honest, I haven't made much progress."

Michael chuckled, "I was asking on a personal level, we've got plenty of time to discuss work."

"Oh, okay. Yes, I've been fine, I've just been working on the case."

"Good to hear. I've been fine as well, thanks for asking."

Nisha missed the sarcasm in his voice and carried on staring at her screen.

Michael rolled his eyes. "Do you want a coffee?"

"I'm fine, thanks."

"I'll take one. White with no sugar, please." Matt had appeared at the door, and he was looking pleased with himself.

"I'm sure it's meant to be the other way round. You lot should be making drinks for me. What are you so chipper about anyway, DS Gardiner?"

"I think I've made inroads on the phone encryption side of things."

"Okay, well at least someone's making progress. You've earned your coffee."

Rob appeared at 8.07am, sweating profusely and clutching a large Costa cup.

"Glad you could finally make it," said Michael.

"Sorry I'm late, the trains were a nightmare today."

"Still had time to grab yourself a coffee though, I see."

"I couldn't risk having to drink one of your cups, Michael, we all know what they taste like, don't we, Matt?" Rob motioned towards Matt and the mug in front of him, which was still full. There was a brief silence before all four of them started laughing.

"I must admit, your coffees aren't the best, guv," said Nisha.

"Bloody hell, this is the thanks I get for trying to look after my team? Well, I won't bother next time. Anyway, enough of this, let's all take a seat. DS Gardiner, you seem the most positive today, so you go first. Cheer me up, please."

Matt stood up straight, holding his A4 ring-bound notepad out in front of him.

"Okay, I've managed to get in touch with an informant of mine who knows quite a bit about encrypted phones. He helped us massively in that huge bust back in 2020 when the French police managed to crack the encryption."

"With the Dutch firm, right?" asked Michael.

"Correct. He was well connected with that firm, and he told me they had all sorts of different software for reading QR codes. I'm talking about hundreds of applications. It was the next big thing they were working on, online payments through the dark web for drug deals. They were going to use crypto to pay, and it would just be a simple scan of the QR code and then an easy online transfer. This Dutch firm were in the process of setting themselves up as a payment intermediary, with the potential to create their own crypto currency in the future if it worked. It would have netted them billions they reckon. If, of course, they hadn't been compromised."

"All very interesting, DS Gardiner, but tell me how this can help our case."

"My contact is going to try to set up a meeting for me with one of Dutch mob, called Joost."

"And you reckon he's prepared to talk?"

"No guarantee yet, but apparently, the whole group are still running scared since the bust, not just from the Old Bill but from the crooks they sold these phones to as well. They've got some of biggest hitters in Europe after their blood. If he can assist in any way, and we can help him, then there could be a potential deal."

"And how do you think he could actually help us?" asked Rob. "Forgive me, my tech knowledge has diminished in my older years."

"You barely knew how to switch on a computer when you first started in the job," said Michael, causing Rob to throw a biro at him.

"My contact reckons Joost was the tech wizard for the group. He's probably still got access to software that can read QR codes. If we can get hold of him, he may be able to help us scan these two bracelets," said Matt.

"Nice work, DS Gardiner, let's make sure we speak to him. This is your number one priority to work on."

"I'm on it, guv."

"Okay, good. Well, I already know how you've got on, Rob, and precisely how much progress you've made... Sod all!"

"About the same as you, I reckon."

"Correct, so let's see if our other young protege can show us up. What have you got for us, DS Sharma?"

"Honestly, not much I'm afraid. I've managed to speak to both witnesses from the Lisa Cattermole case. They were drunk that evening, so the descriptions they provided were not exactly crystal clear. They went for a night out in Shoreditch and were walking down the same side of street approximately fifty metres apart. They noticed two large men dressed in dark clothes running in the opposite direction, one of them holding what seemed to be a girl under his arm."

"Exactly what they'd told us before then. How about Lena Nowak?"

"This is a little bit more interesting. Out of the three witnesses that night, I have only been able to track one of them, two are still unaccounted for."

"Unaccounted for how?"

"The first was a homeless man known only as Ed. He gave police a witness statement that night, but after that, they never saw him again. He couldn't be tracked down, and no-one has heard from him since."

"Yes of course, very helpful."

"Exactly. The second was a tourist visiting from China. His name was Huang Tzao, and he was initially very helpful. He gave perhaps the most detailed description of the two men. He said he was prepared to help as much as he could. He'd attend an identity parade if necessary or do one online from China if required. He was quite confident he could pick the men out."

"Okay."

"But then he flew back to China and wasn't heard from again. The contact details he provided went cold and all attempts to trace him through the Shanghai police also fell flat. It was like he completely disappeared."

"And have you tried to get in touch with Shanghai yourself?"

"I haven't, sir. I was going to ask you about the protocol for that."

"I haven't got a clue, DS Sharma. Get working on it and come back to me if you hit any obstructions. Now, what about the actual witness you did track down?"

"Caroline Flaherty. She's a pretty unremarkable witness who provided very basic information and no change from the original witness statement."

"Do you think she had anything to hide?"

"I don't think so. She seemed a little nervous maybe, but that's it."

"Okay, let's keep an eye on her anyway. Anything else?"

"Nothing. Sorry. I wanted more, but I just can't believe how little evidence there is."

"You keep saying this, but maybe rather than wonder why there's so little evidence you need to investigate why."

"Sorry, guv, what do you mean?"

"In my experience, there's only two reasons for such a lack of evidence. Either the police involved in the investigation didn't do their job well enough or… they did 'their' job very well."

Nisha frowned, "I'm still not following."

"Have you investigated who conducted the original interviews with the witnesses? Have you looked into the coppers involved in each case?"

"I haven't. Are you suggesting what I think you are? And if so, isn't that a job for anti-corruption?"

"I'm not suggesting anything. But you need to investigate where the case leads you. In this case, the lack of evidence is leading you to find out the reason for the lack of evidence. Do you understand?"

"Fair enough, I'll get onto it."

"Very good, now let's talk about next—"

Michael was interrupted by the office phone ringing.

"Is that DCI Dack?"

"Yes, it is. How can I help?"

"We have a young girl in reception. She said you've been trying to get hold of her. Her name is Harriet Kennedy."

Michael's eyes lit up. "Make sure she doesn't leave. I'm coming now." Michael put down the phone and gave the room a smile.

"Rob, come with me please. Harriet Kennedy has just shown up. Now, she's a young girl and may well be scared, so let's be nice. On second thoughts Rob, you stay here. Nisha, come with me."

"Oh, charming that is. You think I can't be nice?" Rob chortled.

"Don't be sensitive, mate," Michael shouted as he and Nisha exited the office and made their way upstairs. They reached reception and saw a young, blonde girl standing by the desk, wearing a bright yellow tracksuit.

"Harriet, my name is DCI Michael Dack, and this is DS Nisha Sharma. Thank you for coming down to meet us." Michael offered the young girl his hand, and she gently shook it back.

"Didn't really have much choice, did I? You'd left me about a hundred voicemails," she replied in an abrasive manner tinged with street attitude.

"Why was your phone switched off? We've been trying it for nearly a week."

"Cos I'm scared, ain't I?! I got people after me, fucking weirdos who think I had something to do with Tash going missing. All these paedo catchers and that, they won't leave me alone. I had to go and buy a new phone. I only turned this one on the other day to check my messages."

"If someone is threatening you, then that's not okay, and we can help with that," said Nisha.

"Nah, I ain't no grass. I just want this all over with. The last thing I need is Old Bill chasing me down, so let's get this done, yeah? What do you wanna know?"

"Why don't we go somewhere with a bit more privacy? Do you want a drink or anything?" asked Nisha as sympathetically as she could.

"Nah, I'm fine."

"Okay, follow us."

The three of them made their way to a lift. There was an uncomfortable silence as it descended two floors. As the doors opened, Nisha was surprised to see Michael turn left instead of right.

"The interview rooms are this way, guv," she motioned.

"It's okay, we'll use one of the rooms down here, there's no need to make this too formal."

Nisha frowned. Surely Harriet was a key person of interest, and the interview should be conducted in an official interview room, with recording equipment. She decided not to question the wisdom of her superior officer in front of Harriet.

Michael held the door open to a basic room which sometimes served as a makeshift waiting area. Inside were two worn sofas, a couple of armchairs, and a coffee table with some outdated magazines laid out on it. Nisha gave Michael a quizzical look as she entered but was ignored.

"Thanks for coming in, Harriet, this should only take ten minutes. Now, firstly, how long were you friends with Natasha?" said Michael.

"I met her just under a year ago at 93 Feet East."

"What's that?"

"It's a rave down in Brick Lane."

"Bit young for raves, aren't you?" Nisha butted in, causing Michael to give her a stern look.

"Don't be silly, there are loads of youngsters who go to raves nowadays. You should try it; you may have a bit of fun," Harriet gave Nisha a smug smile.

"It's not my thing really, drugs and kids. So, Tash must have been fourteen at that time?" said Nisha.

"We're not here to judge underage drinking, DS Sharma, let's stick to the task, shall we?" Michael interrupted. "Okay, Harriet, so you made friends at that rave, and it went from there. Would you describe your relationship as close?"

"Yeah, I'd say so. We kept bumping into each other at different parties and then started hanging out more. She used to come down to Bow and visit me cos she hated where she lived in Debden. She said it bored the life out of her."

"You don't seem that upset considering someone close to you was murdered a few weeks ago," said Nisha.

"What, cos I'm not sitting here bawling my eyes out? People deal with grief in different ways you know, Mrs Sharma. I'm absolutely gutted, and I'm scared."

"It's DS Sharma, not Mrs Sharma."

"DS Sharma, why don't you go make us some drinks?" said Michael, trying to alleviate the tension, "I'm in need of a coffee. Harriet, do you want anything?"

"Just a water, please."

Nisha cursed to herself as she made her way to the kitchen. She'd gone in harder than Michael wanted. Whilst waiting for the kettle to boil, she promised that she'd change attitude when she returned to the room.

On her way back, as she got to within ten metres of the door, it flew open, and Harriet stormed out, ignoring Nisha as she passed. She was visibly upset, with reddened eyes, as if she'd been crying. Michael came out a few seconds after her.

"What's happened, guv?"

"Interview's over. I've got what I needed. Let's get back to our office and I'll fill you in then. I'll just walk Harriet out."

Nisha stood in the corridor for a minute after they left, thoughts racing through her head. What on earth happened? Should she have left them two alone in a room? She made her way back to the office, still in a slight state of shock.

"How did it go?" Rob asked.

"Hmm, it was all a bit—"

"—Tense, I'd say." Michael had arrived back. "I've got an apology to make, Rob. I should have taken you instead. DS Sharma is useless at playing good cop. Either that or she hates women. Which is it, DS Sharma?"

"Women? She was a sixteen-year-old girl."

"She was a vital person of interest who we needed to manage carefully to extract information from. Your hard-bitch act was the exact opposite of what was required. Make sure you read the room next time."

"Did you get anything useful?" said Matt.

"Yes, I did," said Michael. "I hope you're feeling hungry; I'm taking you all out to the pub for lunch."

# Fifteen

A repetitive, agonising ache pulsed throughout her head, bleeding into her sleep, feeding her nightmares. On the rare occasions she had a normal dream, the ache was still there, looming on the outskirts like an evil voyeur, acting as a reminder that when she woke, she would do so into darkness.

As her eyes twitched open, the stench of the toilet bucket, still uncleared after two days, hit her senses first before the sight of those dank, depressing walls followed. She had almost grown to accept the smell as a friend. The bucket only got cleared when she had a male visitor eager to abuse her. The worse the smell of the bucket, the longer she had been free of a pervert's company.

She'd been imprisoned here for so long now that it wasn't just the depravity of the situation that infuriated her. She had, in her bored and frightened mind, started to consider the economics of the situation, and it made no sense.

She would typically experience a visitor every one or two days. It was rare she had two in one day. In her warped state, it angered her that she was being held like this for such scant reward. It could be justified if she was getting multiple customers a day, making her captors a decent profit. For five or six times a week, they were probably earning just a few hundred pounds. Was her life not worth more than this?

She sat upright at the sound of the corridor door opening. She heard the two men walk in, laughing and joking loudly, oblivious to the feelings of the women they had imprisoned.

The collective gasp of the girls was quieter this time. Undoubtedly some had not yet woken; it seemed early for a visit. She listened for a third voice, but none came. She breathed a small sigh of relief. It must be a food drop.

Every few days, the men would deliver a bag of shopping for the girls. It usually contained items that did not need to be refrigerated: crisps, bread, fruit, water. The basics, but enough to survive on.

She heard doors to some of the other rooms being unlocked and then closed. She was hungry and comforted herself with the thought that food would be with her shortly. She obediently sat on her bed and faced the wall opposite the door, knowing that her captors would order her to do so anyway. They always took great care to avoid the girls seeing their faces.

A minute or so later, the lock in her door started to turn, followed by a voice which called out aggressively.

"Turn round. Face wall, now!"

"I am, come in," she replied, trying to sound as inoffensive as possible. The door opened, and footsteps entered.

"Stand Up! Face wall!"

She did as she was told. A large pair of hands grabbed her shoulders and then begun to tie a blindfold around her eyes.

"Shower time for you," a voice said, close to her face. She smelt the man's breath – a putrid combination of cigarettes, alcohol, and rotting food. It took all her effort not to gag.

The hands on her shoulders spun her around and frogmarched her on the short walk to the bathroom. She prepared herself for the ritual humiliation that was about to unfold. She had become hardened to it. She knew it was just another step in process of dehumanising her.

She started to undress as soon as they stopped walking. When she was naked, she was handed some soap, and a shower head with lukewarm water trickling through it. Before she began to wash, she suddenly received a heavy slap to her backside. The force of it made her stumble forwards. Both men started laughing uncontrollably.

It brought up memories of a similar incident, an occasion in school a year or so ago, when a boy had crept up behind her and groped her. She recalled spinning around and confronting him, pushing him backwards, screaming at him in front of his mates. All her friends immediately had her back and came storming up to support her, shouting at the boy, belittling him publicly. She remembered his tears as he was forced to apologise for what he had done. She remembered feeling so proud that, together with her friends, she had stood up for her rights and her body.

In here, naked, vulnerable, and alone, she had no friends to support her. She had no method of revenge. She had no power. All she could do was accept the abuse.

Underneath her blindfold, tears started to pour from her eyes again.

# Sixteen

"You seem like you have something to say to me, DS Sharma. Are you going to get it off your chest?"

Nisha knew this moment was coming as soon as Michael had asked her to ride with him, "I have quite a bit to say if I'm honest, guv."

"You'd better get started then because we're going to be at this pub in fifteen minutes."

"First of all, I didn't appreciate the way you just ripped into me in front of the rest of the team back there. I felt that could have been handled privately."

"If you think that's a 'ripping into,' DS Sharma, then you are in for a rude awakening. I was told by Commissioner Morgan that you were a tough nut. Was she wrong on that?"

"No, guv."

"Good, because I haven't got time to deal with shrinking violets in this investigation. There may come a day when giving someone a dressing down is not permitted by the police, but when that day comes, I will either be retired or dead. Until then, I will continue to speak bluntly. Do I make myself clear?"

Nisha nodded.

"Glad that's sorted. What else do you want to say?"

"Why did you decide to do the interview in that room?"

"Because I read the situation. She was a girl who thought she was street smart and had come into the police station as bold as brass. I wanted to maintain that attitude so that we'd be able to keep her talking. I thought she may get scared if we put her into a formal environment, switched on the tape recording, and took her out of her comfort zone."

"But what if she gave evidence that was vital to the investigation, and we didn't have it recorded? What you did went against all basic police training."

"That was my instinct and that was my call. I've been in this job for over forty years, and I like to think that I know what I'm doing. Your police training will only take you a certain distance in this career. After that, you must start learning to trust your instincts."

"Okay, but…"

"I brought you in to act as a confidant for her, someone younger and female who she could relate to more than some old fart like me. You went completely in the opposite direction. I asked you to leave as you were brushing her up the wrong way. She was clamming up instead of opening up."

"I'm sorry, guv, but I didn't like her. She was hiding something."

"Yes, she was, and it was our job to get it out of her."

"And what was it you got out of her? What did she say about this pub?"

"It's a place that she'd started visiting with Natasha. This pub let them drink in there even though they were underage. They befriended a few men in there, and she heard recently that Natasha had started visiting the pub on her own."

"And do you think she was telling the truth?"

"I think most of it's the truth. If my suspicions are confirmed, then she's not the criminal here, she's just a naive young girl who's been manipulated."

"And how did you get this information out of her?"

"What do you mean?"

"When I came back with the drinks, she seemed visibly upset. She wasn't like that when I left her. How did you make her spill the beans?"

"I let her know a few facts about the cases we'd been investigating and the sort of men who were involved. I gave her a bit more information about how dangerous it could be if she didn't have the police in her corner."

Michael swung the car left down a side street in Islington and broke sharply, "Here we are. Hop out and I'll go and park up."

Nisha stared despondently at the decrepit building in front of her. It was hardly worthy of being called a pub. Paint was stripping from the exterior walls, and two of the windows had cracks sprawled across them like elaborate glass spider webs. Above the entrance, a decaying sign read, 'The Shallow Pond.' It was hard to tell from the outside whether this place was still open for business.

"Not up to the standards of your usual establishment, DS Sharma?"

She turned to see Rob and Matt walking up the street towards her.

"You couldn't be more wrong, DI Archer. I can eat a pack of pork scratchings and down a pint of crap lager with the best of them."

"Good to hear, girl. Let's go in. I'm buying."

The door creaked loudly as Matt pushed it open, causing the occupants of the pub to stare over in unison. There were only eight customers and one member of staff inside. All were male and over the age of fifty. It seemed from their reaction that they weren't used to many outsiders in here.

The carpet was old and worn, a chequered red, black, and orange design that looked like it hadn't been replaced in decades. The walls were adorned with a cream, pimpled wallpaper that bore an uncanny resemblance to rice pudding – if that rice pudding had been left out in the sun for three years. The smell of stale beer and cigarettes hung in the air, even though it had been many a year since smoking was permitted in pubs.

"There are some real charmers in here, aren't there?" said Nisha as they sat down at an empty table in the corner.

Rob laughed. It was certainly an odd clientele. Each patron looked either depressed or angry, sporting faces damaged by decades of alcohol and nicotine. Beyond them at the bar stood a portly, balding man in a green jumper, who hadn't stopped staring at them since they'd walked in.

"Right, what are we having? Let's go and say hello to the beauty behind the bar," Rob said, far too loudly for Nisha's liking.

"Pint of lager for me, please, DI Archer," said Matt.

"Let's forget the formal shit today, shall we? It's Rob from now on. What about you, Nisha, do you drink?"

"I'll drink you under the table, you cheeky bastard. I'll have a double G and T, please."

All eyes in the pub focused on Rob as he walked up to the bar. It reminded of him of times many years ago when he would be the only black face in places such as this.

"What can I get you, officer?" said the barman, confirming Rob's fears that they had already been outed.

"Very observant of you, mate," Rob replied. "Used to spotting coppers, are you? That normally means one of two things."

"What's that then?"

"A, you're a copper yourself, or B, you have a substantial interest in avoiding coppers. Now, judging from the fact that you're about to pour my drink, I think we can rule out A."

Rob saw the colour drain from the man's face as he sensed his act of bravado had backfired.

"Now that the pleasantries are over, I'll have a pint of lager, a large Gin and Tonic, and two large whiskeys please. And what is your name?"

"You can call me Bill."

"Old Bill, eh? That's ironic. Are you the guv'nor round here or just the barman?'

"I'm the guv'nor, mate. I run the place," Bill replied aggressively, slamming down the drinks.

"You should be very proud," Rob turned to walk back to the table only to find his way barred by a large, menacing-looking man. He looked out of place in this pub, standing at least six-foot three and almost the same distance wide. His huge biceps bulged out from underneath a tight, grey t-shirt with visible sweat patches underneath both armpits. His head was completely shaved, and across his left cheek was a thick scar that ran from lip to ear.

"Is this man bothering you, Bill?" he said in an Eastern European accent.

"The 'officer' is fine, Marius, he's just in here for a drink."

Rob refused to take his eyes from the man. They continued to stare at each other, nose to nose, as the rest of the pub watched in anticipation. The tension was broken by the sound of the entrance door opening.

"Making friends already, Rob? That's what I like to see," said Michael. He strode over to the pair and put his hand on Marius's shoulder. "I do apologise for my friend. He can get a bit excited when he's let out."

Marius turned his stare on Michael for a few seconds and then moved to the side, allowing Rob to pass.

"You always did take us to the nicest places, Michael," said Rob as he sat down.

"Yeah, I've got to agree, guv, for our first team bonding outing, you could have picked somewhere a little friendlier," said Matt.

"Don't be so soft. This is a proper London pub experience. Now, did anyone pick up the menu? I'm starving."

"I'm not sure they do food in here, which is probably for the best," said Nisha.

"What a shame. Looks like it's an assorted selection of nuts and crisps for us."

"Yummy. So, anyway, what's our plan here?" asked Matt.

"It's an easy gig for you. I just want to have a drink and get to know you both a bit more. At the same time, let's keep an eye on who comes in and out and see if anyone acts shady. Although they'd have to be stupid to do something like that since we basically came in with flashing blue lights on our head."

"So, why are we here if we're not going to question them?" asked Nisha.

"What are we going to question them on, DS Sharma? Underage drinking? I just want them to know that there are police sniffing round. I don't want them knowing why, but I'd like to unnerve them a little. Let's have a few drinks. After a while, you lot can move on, and I'll stay here and get to know the place a bit better."

"Sorry to ask again, but what's the point in that? They already know you're Old Bill. Wouldn't you have been better off—" Michael cut Nisha off.

"You have no trust in me whatsoever, do you, DS Sharma?" Michael laughed.

"She's just like me when I first met you. Don't get offended. You do take a while to warm to," said Rob.

"I'm sorry, I don't mean to question. I'm just not used to unorthodox methods," said Nisha.

"I know, and I'm not trying to dig you out, but you need to know that some investigations can't be solved through going by the book. You said yourself that you believe all these cases are linked, yes?"

"I do."

"And I agree with you. So, how long has this all been going on for? At least three years from what we know, probably longer. Everything's been done by the book so far, and guess what? We've got nowhere."

Nisha and Matt both nodded. Michael took a large gulp of whisky and continued.

"There's a reason I was brought in on this case. Commissioner Morgan has worked with me for years and knows my methods better than anyone. Do you understand?"

They spent the next hour laughing and joking together, mainly about Michael's and Rob's 'war stories' from working past cases. The tales got louder and louder, and the laughs attracted more glares from all corners of the pub. Marius and Bill stood at the bar the whole time and hadn't taken their eyes off the group. It wasn't lost on Nisha and Matt that in the time they had finished two drinks, their older colleagues had downed four double whiskies each.

After Rob finished off his fourth, he stood up and clapped his hands together. "Right, come on you two, we're off."

"Are we going back to the office?"

"What, when we're just starting to get on so well? Don't be silly. We're off to another pub, just maybe one that you don't need a tetanus injection to enter. See you later, Mike, have a good night." Rob held his hand out, and they both exchanged an awkward handshake-cum-high five.

"Have a good time you lot. See you bright and early in the office tomorrow. Do not be late, DS Gardiner. I've got my eye on you." And with that, Michael walked unsteadily to the bar to order another drink.

# Seventeen

There were only eighteen journalists and two photographers in attendance, all of whom felt privileged to be given the golden ticket of access to a Richard Banks press conference.

True, it was hardly a press conference in the usual sense of the word. It wasn't like they'd be able to ask questions or probe him on pressing matters. They were more than aware that this was a PR event for Richard Banks, but they were just grateful for the opportunity. After all, this man was a notorious recluse. He hadn't spoken to the press in over six years, quite unusual for someone whose personal wealth the latest *Sunday Times* Rich List had estimated at £2.7bn.

Richard Banks was a controversial and polarising character in British society. Some saw his rags to riches story and no-holds-barred approach to business as inspirational and deigned upon him a demi-god status. Others who had access to solid sources, or had experienced working with him first hand, had witnessed his contempt for colleague's feelings, his rudeness to staff, or the underhand methods he would use to manipulate people.

Rumours had consistently surrounded his personal life, but allegations never made it to court. It seemed obvious to his detractors that complainants were bought off with large sums of money and non-disclosure agreements. Whilst these rumours had circulated on social media, they never seemed to make the mainstream media – much to the consternation of those who would have loved to have seen him knocked off his perch.

The press knew why they were there today, packed into a room which was to be used as the common area for a new women's refuge in the Docklands. It was the latest move in the positive image campaign conducted by Richard Banks PR team, desperate to reinvent their man in the eyes of the British public.

The Richard Banks Foundation had contributed many millions of pounds towards good causes, both in the UK and overseas. This refuge was the most recent of a line of buildings they had opened in conjunction with a government who were desperate to combat the ever-growing problem of homelessness.

A collective hush spread throughout the room as the man himself breezed in through the back doors. He looked fit and tanned at fifty-nine years old, his dark hair combed into a side parting. He was dressed in a navy blazer teamed with an unbuttoned white shirt, dark denim jeans, and brown cowboy boots. He was flanked by two huge security men, dressed casually in white shirts and dark jeans, both sporting the obligatory sunglasses.

Richard Banks possessed that intangible presence which seemed to make everyone else in the room shrink. Many a tale had been told of how VIPs and royalty would fawn over him at private events, in awe at his charisma and knowledge. Those closer to him were aware that this was his public face, the personality he displayed when others were watching. As he took to the microphone, silence fell upon the room.

"I've been fortunate enough in my life to have accumulated a substantial amount of wealth. I've always believed in trying to give back as much of that as possible through the Richard Banks Foundation. Our charity now operates in over sixteen countries worldwide, with the main beneficiaries being the youth of today.

"Whether we are helping young people displaced from their families or communities affected by wars and atrocities. Whether we are providing opportunities in education or employment for young people who don't have the resources to achieve these goals themselves, or whether we are providing accommodation, food, and water to young people who live in poverty, the Richard Banks Foundation prides itself on its holistic integration. We get involved at ground level and provide full, hands-on assistance wherever possible.

"Today marks the latest chapter in the Richard Banks Foundation's commitment to a better life for young people in our capital city of London. It gives me immense pleasure to announce the opening of this refuge for young women, many of whom have experienced extreme hardship in their lives and just want an opportunity to do better." Banks paused to look around the room.

"We converted this building from a disused, rundown factory in the Docklands to a high-quality, multi-faceted accommodation and education facility. We have 152 bedrooms here, which will house young women from all areas of society. We have single mothers who have been abused by their partners and need a safe haven in which to bring up their children. We have economic refugees who have been separated from their families and need a roof over their heads. And we have women who were homeless, without a family of any kind, and who would not survive living on the streets.

"We would like to thank the government for assistance in the development of buildings such as these, and I am delighted that the housing secretary, Ian Stebbing, is here today to help us open our fourth London refuge of this nature, and seventh in the UK. Believe me, this will not be the last. So, it gives me great pleasure to hand over to Mr Stebbing so he can tell you more about our collaboration and officially open our Docklands refuge."

Banks stepped back and allowed Stebbing to come to the microphone. The housing secretary was a nerdy-looking figure, with grubby spectacles and a thinning hairline. He was dressed in an ill-fitting brown suit with black shoes that seemed like they hadn't been polished in years. Richard Banks looked him up and down from behind and rolled his eyes. He could never understand people, especially those in positions of power, who didn't take pride in their appearance.

As Stebbing waffled on in the way that politicians tend to do, Banks felt his phone begin to vibrate in his top pocket. He let it go to voicemail, but then felt it ring for a second and third time. Most calls for him went straight to the phone managed by his PA, Caroline Nolan, but this was his personal number, and it was rare that someone tried to call him on it.

Banks discreetly pulled open his blazer and gently lifted the phone out of the inside pocket. He was annoyed to see the name on the screen: Bill Lowthy. 'Why the hell is he calling me?'

Banks stood silently seething through the next five minutes of Ian Stebbing's speech before watching him clumsily cut a piece of cheap ribbon. He forced a smile and a wave to the press in attendance, then walked off to an empty room, making sure that no-one followed him.

"What the hell are you calling me for?" he spat down the phone as Bill answered.

"I'm sorry, sir, but we've got a bit of a problem down here. I thought you should know."

"Down where?"

"At the Shallow Pond, sir."

"Why on earth would I care about a problem down there?"

"We've had some Police in today."

Banks paused. "What did they say?"

"There were four of them who came in initially, and it didn't seem like there was much purpose at first. But now three of them have left, and their boss has ended up staying. He's been here for about five hours. He's completely wankered and making a right tit of himself."

"Surely you and Marius can handle a drunken man in your pub, can't you?"

"The issue is, sir, we found out his name, and Marius googled him. It's DCI Michael Dack."

"Should that name mean anything to me?"

"He's heading up the new Scotland Yard taskforce, the one that's looking into Natasha Shaw and all the girls." Silence fell at the other end of the phone. Bill waited for a few seconds before checking. "Sir, are you still there?"

"I'm still here. What's he been asking?" said Banks.

"He asked who owns the pub, who owns the building, is there accommodation upstairs, things like that. I'm not sure how to respond."

"Give him as little information as possible. Ensure he drinks a load more, treat him well, and then get him a cab when he can't walk. Now, get rid of this phone you're talking on, and we'll be in touch soon about a meet."

"Okay, sir."

Banks stormed out of the room and down the corridor. He spotted his PA talking to one of the journalists and called out at her, clicking his fingers in the air as he did so. "Caroline, here now." She dutifully walked over to him, attracting wandering eyes from some men in the room. She was dressed powerfully in a tight black pencil skirt and white blouse. She was an attractive woman, but her face was sharp and harsh, mainly due to the amount of plastic surgery she'd had done.

"Caroline, get the car out front, we're leaving. Pull Stebbing away from the press before he bores them to tears and get him over here. I must speak to him. Oh, and I need you to dispose of this phone," said Banks.

"No problem, sir." Caroline took the phone and sidled up to Ian Stebbing, whispered discreetly in his ear and pointed towards Banks. Within a few seconds, Stebbing was standing next to him.

"How can I help you, Richard?"

"We have a situation. Get hold of David Parkinson and let him know that it's imperative we arrange a meeting this week."

# Eighteen

Nisha was struggling to stand at the bar. She looked down at her watch and was shocked to see it was 10.42pm. "Bloody hell, how's it that time already?" she spluttered out to no-one.

After paying for the round, she made her way back to the table where Matt and Rob were sitting, their arms around each other, both talking intensely about their shared love: Tottenham Hotspur Football Club. Nisha immediately vowed to go straight home after this drink.

They had managed to end up, via a few other bars, in the Fox on the Green pub on Upper Street in Islington. Rob felt a little out of place as it was full of a younger, hipper crowd, but Matt and Nisha were right at home.

As she sat down shakily, a question entered her head, and before she could stop to consider whether this was an appropriate time to ask, it had already left her mouth.

"Rob!" she slurred, whilst clumsily pulling at his arm. "I've got a question for you."

"Okay, go ahead, Nisha."

"You've been close to Michael for years now. What do you know about his missing daughter?"

Matt rocked back in his chair and puffed out his cheeks, unsure where to look. Rob was unmoved and stared back at Nisha with a blank look on his face, contemplating his response.

"Well, first of all, DS Sharma, thank you for ruining the mood."

"I am sorry, I'm just, you know… We're working with him on a missing girl case, and he's obviously suffered through the same situation. I wondered how it may affect him."

"Well, that's a valid concern I suppose. Look, I don't really like to talk about it to be honest. None of us know the full details of what happened that day because he's never really spoken about it. He obviously took it very badly, as you can imagine."

"Yeah, it must have been awful," said Matt.

"Neither of you have kids, do you? Well until you do, it's impossible to imagine how painful something like this would be."

"So, what do you know?" said Nisha.

"Josie was just nine years old, and she was such a lovely little girl. She was so bright as well…" Rob paused and took a breath as the emotions rushed back to him. "They were due to go on holiday to Marbella, but around a month before, Paula, that's Mike's wife, found out she was pregnant with their second child. They were going to cancel the holiday, but then Paula insisted that Michael and Josie went without her. She said it would do them good to get away. So, off they went. It was on the second day that it happened. I'll never forget him ringing me in tears, screaming down the phone. I could hardly make out a word he was saying.

"They were on the beach. Josie was playing in the sand, and Michael walked to the beach bar to get a beer and an ice cream." Rob took another long gulp, and his eyes started to water. "He looked away for a second, and when he turned around, she'd gone."

"Was he drunk?" asked Nisha, but Rob instantly shot her a look that told her not to go down that path.

"Bloody hell, that's awful," said Matt. "He must hate himself."

"How many witnesses were there?" said Nisha. "Surely someone must have seen something?"

"It killed him, absolutely ruined his life. It's a miracle he's still here standing today because back then, I would have bet big money on him topping himself within a year. And that was just the start of the nightmare."

"What do you mean?"

"Well, in answer to your earlier question, there were no witnesses at all. As such, the Guardia Civil arrested Mike and he was their number one suspect for a while. They grilled him for a few days, and they wouldn't let him speak to Paula. We had to pull some strings to get him out of there."

"Why did they think he was involved?" said Nisha, eager for more details, but Rob ignored her.

"He came home and hit the bottle hard. Paula blamed him, and he blamed himself. They were arguing every day, it was a toxic environment. Their marriage deteriorated. He left the force for a while and kept flying out to Europe after receiving tip offs from coppers overseas. He was chasing leads, hunting down suspected paedophiles, getting into trouble. He completely lost his mind."

"And Josie has never been found?" asked Matt.

"Never. She'd be twenty-two now."

"Is he still with his wife?"

"No. They soldiered on for a few years, trying to bring up Jacqui as best they could, but the marriage was broken. They ended up divorcing when Jacqui was three, and it was the best move, to be honest."

"Wow," said Matt, taking a slow sip of his beer. "That's an horrendous story."

"Yep, and on that note, I'm off to the toilet," said Rob, standing up and pushing past their chairs to make his way downstairs. He looked on the verge of tears.

Matt turned to Nisha. "What did you ask that for? We've had a good day together. Couldn't it have waited?"

"I'm sorry, I just needed to know. There's something I'm not too sure about with Michael, something I can't put my finger on."

"What do you mean?"

"I don't know. I don't want to start making accusations, but when we were with Harriet Kennedy the other day, he acted very strangely. I was a bit creeped out, to be honest. And then what about earlier? He wants to stay in that dirty old pub all on his own. Now I find out he was a suspect in his daughter's disappearance."

"What are you trying to say, Nisha?"

"Ignore me, I've had too much to drink. Apologise to Rob for me. I'm going home." Nisha ran out of the bar before Matt had the chance to protest. She turned left and walked towards the cab rank.

If she had turned right, she would have seen Michael staggering along Upper Street in the general direction of his house. He had finally left the Shallow Pond after refusing their attempts to get him a cab. Despite being paralytic, he still had enough wit about him to know that he shouldn't give out his home address.

As he reached the taxi rank, he found that no driver was willing to take him, so he decided to walk home, thankful it was a warm evening. A thought entered his head, and he decided to ring his ex-wife, Paula. The call rang through to her voicemail.

"Paula?" Listen to me. I'm so sorry, I am so, so sorry for what happened with Josie. You know that don't you? But don't you worry. I am on to them, darling. I'm going to get those bastards who took our daughter. You mark my words. I'm going to find out what happened to Josie. You just watch me bring them to justice."

# Nineteen

"Mum! Michael was stumbling around the landing naked last night when I got in. It was vile."

The words rang through Michael's aching head as he rose out of his inebriated slumber.

"All right, I'll have a word with him, Bex. He was out last night with work, so I think he had a bit to drink," called out Samantha's exasperated reply.

"A bit to drink? The house smells like a brewery. We shouldn't have to put up with this, mum."

"I said I'll have a word with him."

"A word isn't enough, mum!" Michael heard Rebecca shout, then the sound of the front door slamming.

"Jesus, it's not even eight AM and I've already caused a row," he thought to himself. As he lay in bed rubbing his forehead, his mobile phone started to ring. He rolled over and saw it was Matt calling.

"Have you checked your messages, guv? We've got a problem."

"Give me a minute, Matty."

"Matty now, is it? What happened to DS Gardiner? You must be still drunk."

"Don't be smart, and yeah, I'm not feeling the best if I'm honest. Now, what is this you've sent me?" Michael was squinting at his phone.

"It's a link to Facebook video. Just click on it."

"Facebook? What on earth makes you think I've got a Facebook account, DS Gardiner?"

"Okay, hold there a minute, let me send you the video file."

"Can't you just tell me what's on it?"

"Michael, we need a word." Samantha appeared at the bedroom door with a face like thunder.

"I know, I heard. I'm sorry, darling, I was absolutely smashed."

"Aren't you a bit too old to be getting in states like that? You're meant to be setting a good example to these girls."

"It was for work reasons, and anyway, I wasn't naked, I had my pants on."

"They're teenage girls, Mike, they don't want to see you in your pants!"

"Guv?" came the voice from the other end of the mobile in Michael's hand, "you still there?" Michael and Samantha exchanged an embarrassed look before she turned and walked away.

"DS Gardiner. I don't suppose there's a chance you didn't hear all that, is there?"

"I heard nothing, guv," Matt replied unconvincingly.

"That was my partner, and she was talking about my stepdaughters. I walked in completely pissed last night. Anyway, where's this video?"

"Go on our WhatsApp group, guv. I've posted it there. You know how to use WhatsApp, don't you?"

"Cheeky this morning, aren't you?"

Michael pressed play on the video. Unfolding in front of him was a scene on what looked like a London street. There was a man, probably in his fifties, surrounded by four younger men and a girl. They were shouting at him aggressively whilst videoing him.

Michael struggled to hear any words at first due to the poor sound quality, but it soon improved. There were taunts and accusations coming from each of the younger men. "Dirty bastard, you thought she was fourteen, didn't you?" "You travelled across London to try to meet a schoolgirl, you nonce." "This is all being recorded and will be handed over to the police. Have you got anything to say?"

It soon dawned on Michael what was happening. His focus intensified as he recognised two of the younger men on the video. The one doing most of the shouting was the man he'd met at Stacey's house, Mason Greenwell. The other man was Nick Shaw. Michael sat upright, instantly forgetting his hangover.

The older man, greasy and bedraggled looking, kept apologising and begging to be left alone. He looked petrified, but Michael felt no pity for him. The man tried to walk off and barged through Nick to do so, but this only caused tensions to escalate. Nick squared up to him, and then, out of nowhere, launched a right hook to the temple, sending the older man crashing to the floor.

"Oh, for fuck's sake," Michael said out loud as he watched the footage.

Bedlam erupted. Nick crouched down to deliver another punch before Mason grabbed him from behind. The camera focus wobbled as the person holding the phone tried to get involved in the melee, and suddenly, the video came to an abrupt halt.

"When did that happen, DS Gardiner?" Michael asked.

"That was posted on the Street Shield Facebook account last night, with the title 'predator gets decked.' It got taken down after twenty minutes, probably when they realised it could be used to prosecute Nick."

"Do we know what's happened to the victim?"

"Apparently, he was left unconscious on the floor as the group ran off. He got taken into hospital last night with a fractured jaw and concussion. His name is Philip Strevens, a fifty-four-year-old with no prior convictions. He's informed the attending officers that he wants to press charges."

"The cheek of these lot. He's travelled across London to do a bit of kiddie-fiddling and then wants to press charges when he gets a dig for his trouble."

"I couldn't agree more, guv, but he's saying he was set up and had no intention of underage sex."

"Okay, let's hijack his interview. Obtain his details, and we'll get in touch. And can you get DI Archer and DS Sharma into the office, we need to go over this together?"

"They're already here, guv. You're the only one who's not."

"Blimey, you lot are keen. Did you have an early one last night?"

"Nope, we can obviously just handle it better. See you soon."

On the journey to the office, Michael watched the video back four times. He received a message on the way from Matt to say it had now reached some Twitter sites and was gaining traction. There was the typical plethora of comments underneath: 'wish I had a chance to deck that nonce.' 'I hope they stuck the boot in too when that dirty old man was on the floor.' 'If he'd been trying to meet my daughter, he wouldn't be alive right now.'

"Morning, guv," chimed Nisha and Matt in unison as he walked into the office.

"Fuck me, you look like death warmed up," said Rob.

"How was the rest of your day? Did you make friends?" asked Nisha.

"I certainly made myself known, put it that way. Right, we need to find out who owns that pub."

"I'm way ahead of you. That building is owned by a company called Lantern Property Limited. They own a few similar establishments around the city. Lantern Property are owned by an offshore company registered in the Cayman Islands called Equisea. They're a multinational organisation with properties all over the world, mainly here in the UK, or around Eastern Europe," said Nisha.

"That's interesting," Michael replied.

"Not as interesting as this. The main shareholder in Equisea is Richard Banks."

"What? *The* Richard Banks?" said Matt.

"Yep, billionaire philanthropist and massive dickhead, Richard Banks," Nisha replied.

"You're not a fan then, DS Sharma? Funnily enough, I saw something about him in the news this morning. I think he was opening some sort of refuge yesterday," said Rob.

"That's right, all part of his plan to convince the public that he's not a huge arsehole."

"Well, arsehole or not, he probably owns hundreds of buildings around the world in which he has no clue what goes on inside. We should start looking for links in his organisation though. Let's dig into Bill who runs the gaff, and see what we can find out about Marius," said Michael.

"And let's also start looking into the refuges. He's got a few of them operated by his charity, according to this article," said Rob, who had found the piece in the *Daily Mail* that morning.

"I'll get onto it. I didn't have you down as a *Mail* reader, DI Archer. I'm very disappointed," said Nisha.

"I'll read anything that helps me catch criminals."

"DS Gardiner, how are you getting on with locating your Dutch guy?" said Michael.

"It's moving a bit slowly, as you can imagine."

"Okay, let's try to get that nailed. It could be a vital cog in this investigation." As he finished his sentence, Michael's phone began to ring. It was an unknown number.

"Hello, this is DCI Dack."

"Hello DCI Dack, this is Mason Greenwell."

"Thought you'd save us the trouble of coming to look for you, did you?"

"What happened to Philip Strevens was regrettable, and I need you to know that Street Shield has never condoned violence against a perpetrator. This is the first time anything like that has ever happened, and I take full responsibility. Nick is still probably too emotional from his loss to be out on the street with us."

There was something about Mason's blunt approach that Michael admired.

"An 'alleged' perpetrator, Mason, don't forget that. This is exactly why I told you not to go taking the law into your own hands. Any chance of banging him up now has gone, and Nick is more than likely going to get into trouble. I'll do all I can to make it go away though. The last thing that family needs is another court case."

"So, Philip Strevens is looking to press charges, is he?"

"He is indeed. Hopefully it doesn't get that far."

"Well, let's not be too hasty, DCI Dack. You may want to speak to that man yet."

"What do you mean?"

"Philip Strevens isn't just one of the chatroom predators we tease out with generic messaging techniques. He was targeted a bit more succinctly than that."

"I'm still not following, you're going to have to be clearer."

"Philip Strevens's name was handed to us by one of our sources. We believe he's linked to the VIP network that I spoke to you about. I think you're going to want to interview him. He could prove to be very useful."

"Oh, yeah? And these sources you keep mentioning. Rock solid, are they?"

"Some of them are, some of them aren't. As a previous victim, I like to think I know my way through the bullshit now."

"Look, son, if you're getting evidence that's vital to my case then the best way of helping us both is by sharing it."

"I've told you before, DCI Dack, not until I can trust you. There's a huge leak in the Metropolitan Police. Some of these people who approach me are terrified for their lives. They've been a victim at the hands of the police before, and I've had to swear to them that this info stays with me. They just want to see these abusers humiliated in public. That's a form of revenge that they can handle."

"Son, this is not—."

"Don't patronise me again, DCI Dack. I'm a serious man, and you should speak to me as such. Do you not understand? If these victims came to you and provided their testimony, there's two ways it can turn out. A, they're hunted by the members of this group, or B, the case gets dragged up in court, they must relive all their horrors again, and their integrity is called into question by one of the most expensive defence barristers in the land. Can you see why it may be more appealing for these victims to come to me instead?"

Michael paused to take in what Mason had just said, "Okay, so what are you suggesting?"

"Speak to Strevens, treat him as a victim, show him sympathy and get him to open up. I've talked with Nick, and if he must be arrested, then so be it. With the extenuating circumstances, he'll get an ABH and a suspended sentence at worst. By the time his case comes to court, hopefully you've used Strevens to crack this group."

"You better not be having me on here, Mason."

"Just do your job, and I'll do mine." The phone went dead. Michael turned to see if his colleagues had heard the conversation, but all seemed focussed on their computer screens.

"DS Gardiner, what's the deal with this Philip Strevens? Is he still wanting to press charges or has he come to his senses yet?" Michael shouted out.

"He's still keen on pressing ahead. I spoke to him twenty minutes ago. He's coming in for an interview tomorrow afternoon."

# Twenty

Nisha walked through the door of her Wembley flat just before 11pm. She was used to working long hours on cases, but this one was proving to be more arduous than any before.

She collapsed into her armchair and was joined by her tabby cat, Fred. Nisha felt a pang of guilt that she was seeing less of him since she started on the taskforce, then realised how sad that sounded. Most police officers lamented the missed time with their family. She lamented it with her cat.

She couldn't stop thinking about the investigation; her brain wouldn't let her. She had found out today that the two investigating officers on the Lena Nowak and Lisa Cattermole cases were DCI Brian Stock and DS Alison McKenzie.

Brian Stock had since progressed to the heady heights of Detective Chief Superintendent, and as one of the highest-ranking policemen in the capital, Nisha was nervous at the thought of contacting him regarding a past investigation. It embarrassed her that she hadn't yet drummed up the courage. She had always thought of herself as a fearless investigator, but there was something about looking into colleagues that didn't sit right.

Alison McKenzie had since left the police force and moved to Liverpool to start a new life with her family. Nisha was more comfortable investigating someone who was no longer with the police, and had managed to track down a contact number through one of her old colleagues. So far, she had only been able to reach Alison's voicemail.

Her thoughts drifted to Michael and the doubts she still harboured about him. She had tried to push them to the back of her mind, but a comment this afternoon from Matt had stirred those doubts up again.

"Your imagination would have run wild if you'd have heard my call with DCI Dack," Matt had said.

"Oh, yeah, why's that then?"

"Well, you know what you were saying last night?"

"I told you to forget all that. I was drunk."

"Yeah, I know. But I was on the phone to Michael. His missus came in and started having a go at him for walking round naked in front of his two stepdaughters."

"You're kidding! How old are they?"

"God knows, 'young teenagers' is all I heard. I knew you'd like that," Matt had said and then walked off, leaving his revelation hanging in Nisha's head.

Now she was at home, she had time to properly digest the conversation. She grabbed her laptop, opened Google, and typed 'Josie Dack missing girl'.

There were hundreds of pages dedicated to the incident. The mainstream media were generally sympathetic towards Michael, despite the odd piece that casted doubts on his suitability as a father for leaving a young girl alone whilst he went off to get a beer.

The comments section provided a different flavour of opinions. Whilst she usually detested the vitriol poured out on such platforms, she couldn't resist trawling through them.

'This man should be investigated IMO! No way does a nine-year-old girl get taken from a public beach with no witness.'

'He's either to blame for negligence or the actual crime itself. I'm sorry but his story just doesn't add up.'

'Lock this clown up, supposed to be a policeman and he loses his own child. He's either completely incompetent or had a hand in her disappearance.'

"Idk why but I just don't trust this man. Spanish police have it right, investigate him.'

Nisha scrolled through, letting the comments seep in. She downed the rest of her wine and went to pour another before she was interrupted by her phone ringing. She answered the withheld number to hear a female voice on the other end.

"Hello, is that DS Sharma?"

"It is, yes. Who's this please?"

"This is Alison McKenzie. I understand you're trying to get hold of me."

"Oh, thank you so much for calling back, Alison. I wanted to speak to you ab—"

"—I know what you want to speak to me about, but you're wasting your time. I've got absolutely nothing to say about those cases. I put my concerns on record at the time, and they were ignored."

"Your concerns? What do you mean, Alison? I didn't know you had any concerns."

"Like I said, I've got nothing further to say, so please leave me alone."

"But, don't you want to help us try to bring these—"

"—Please listen to me, DS Sharma. I'm hanging up now. I have nothing further to say about those cases, and I have nothing further to say about Brian Stock."

# Twenty-one

"Thank you for coming down today, Mr Strevens. That's some nasty bruising you have there. How are you feeling?" It was rare that Michael began an interview so placidly.

"Do let us know if you start feeling unwell throughout our chat and we'll do anything we can to help," added Rob.

They were both sat opposite Philip Strevens and his solicitor in one of Scotland Yard's interview rooms. Michael had instructed the taskforce to ensure a gentle approach was taken for this interview, although he hadn't told them why. Until he was sure of Mason Greenwell's credibility as an informant, Michael had decided that he wouldn't let his team know who his source was.

"Thank you, officers, that's very kind of you, and thanks for the tea and biscuits as well," replied the spindly-looking man sat in front of them.

Rob fought hard to hide his disgust as biscuit crumbs scuttled out from between Strevens's jagged, nicotine-stained teeth. Aged fifty-four, and around five-feet eight inches tall, this balding, frail man probably only weighed about nine stone and certainly didn't present a frightening image.

"Isn't it a bit strange that we have a DCI and DI interviewing the victim of a minor GBH charge?" said Strevens's solicitor, who had previously been more interested in the contents of her mobile phone than her client's situation.

"Normally, yes. but the group who attacked Mr Strevens have been on our radar for a while now. Vigilantes like this are the scourge of the police department, and these lot seem to be particularly militant. The fact they've done this to an innocent man sickens me." Michael spoke through gritted teeth.

"Well, I'm glad you're taking it seriously," said Strevens. "I've suffered some serious damage here, and I will be looking for compensation."

"As is your right as a law-abiding citizen, Mr Strevens. Now, please, in your own words, can you talk us through the events of the other night?" said Rob.

"You've seen the video, surely all the evidence you need is on there? I got surrounded by a pack of unruly youths and then, when I went to walk away, I was the victim of an unprovoked assault."

"It was an appalling assault, and you certainly did not deserve that. We just require some information on the build-up to the event because if we can prove that they lured you to that location with the intention of assaulting you, then we could really throw the book at them. Why were you there on that street in Romford? You live in Croydon, don't you?"

"Yes, Croydon born and bred, but I am a bit of a man about town. I'm often out visiting friends or acquaintances in other parts of London."

Both Michael and Rob struggled to keep a straight face at the thought of the person in front of them describing himself as a 'man about town.'

"And is this what you were doing in Romford? Visiting a friend?" said Michael.

"I was due to visit a female, actually."

"How did you know this female?"

"I met her on a social media site. We started chatting and struck up a friendship over the course of a few weeks. We then arranged to meet. Her name on the site was Cassidy, and she seemed lovely. Of course, it turned out to be a ruse. There was no Cassidy, just a bunch of yobs waiting to jump me.

"You've seen the video, so don't try to play me for a fool. They thought I was sexual predator, but I've been through all my chat history with her, and not once did she mention she was underage."

"And I presume you've got the full records of the chats?" said Rob.

"I have, although I didn't bring them in today. She was the one leading me on, saying provocative things and teasing me the whole way through. I just thought she was a little promiscuous, you know."

"And do you often arrange to meet up with strangers over the internet?"

"Quite a bit. It's a brave new world out there, you know. Everyone's at it."

"I'll take your word for it. And just so we're clear going forward, how old did you think Cassidy was?"

"You don't have to answer that, Mr Strevens," said the solicitor.

"That's okay, I've got nothing to hide. I thought she may be a teenager. She looked young, but I placed her around eighteen or nineteen. I definitely didn't think she was under sixteen. That is not my thing at all."

"And you didn't find it surprising that someone of her age was flirting with someone of your age?"

"Not at all, Detective. It happens a lot. You find a lot of girls online who are interested in sleeping with an older man, especially the more vulnerable ones. You know, those with daddy issues."

The solicitor winced.

Michael leant forward and looked Strevens in the eyes, lowering the volume of his voice as he spoke. "I do know what you mean. We see so many girls like this in our line of work. So, here's what we're going to do next. We have already identified the young man who assaulted you, and we're going to put an arrest warrant out for him today. I'll be in touch as soon as we bring him in."

"Is that it? Is that all the information you need from me?"

"Like you said, it's all on camera, so we can work from the footage for now. Once we have him nicked, we'll be in touch."

"Okay, that sounds good to me. Thank you for your time. This was very efficient, I must say."

"Not at all. Thank you for your time. Are you off to work now?" asked Rob.

"I am. No rest for the wicked."

"And what is your line of work?"

"I'm an IT engineer."

"You must know a lot about computers then. You could help me on that. I haven't got the foggiest."

"Of course. Feel free to get in touch if you ever have any questions. Here's my business card."

Philip handed Rob a tatty business card bearing the name PSIT in the form of a crude blue logo. He then limply shook both of their hands before he left the room with his solicitor.

A few seconds after he left, Nisha burst through the door. She'd been monitoring the interview through a video link.

"What was the point of all that? We didn't ask him anything about any of our cases."

"We decided against it, DS Sharma. We went with a different tactic instead."

"And when was this change of tactic communicated? Why wasn't I informed of it?"

"You weren't informed because you don't have to be. We chose to build a rapport with him instead. The man's clearly a few sandwiches short of a picnic basket. If we can get him on his own, I reckon we can pull some valuable information out of him."

"That's if he is connected to our investigation. You still haven't told us why you think he may be."

"It's just a line of enquiry I'm following. We'll give him a call in a few days, let him know the progress on arresting Nick, and try to get him in an informal setting when his solicitor isn't there," said Michael.

"She was hardly QC of the year, was she? She barely managed to stay awake," said Robert.

"Typical duty solicitor, just here to collect her fee. Anyway, I'm going up to speak to Commissioner Morgan and see if we can get some surveillance put on him."

"Why, guv? We've got no indication that he's involved with our investigation at all. Are we just presuming that all sex offenders are intrinsically linked to each other now?" said Nisha.

"Intelligence that I have been given through an informant. You should try to find some informants of your own, DS Sharma. They can be pretty useful," Michael called back as he walked out of the door.

On the way to Commissioner Morgan's office, Michael gave Mason a call.

"Good afternoon, DCI Dack. How can I help?"

"I've just had Strevens in. Are you serious about this guy being involved?"

"My sources say so."

"I'm placing a lot of trust in you here, Mason."

"That's because you have nothing else to go on, DCI Dack."

"You're not wrong there. Do you have records of the conversation Strevens had with your catfish girl? He's saying she never admitted to being fourteen."

"I have the records. She clearly pointed it out, but he didn't respond to it in the messages. He'll probably try to claim he didn't notice that part of the conversation, that's what they normally do. Do you need me to send you the chat?"

"Not yet, hold onto it for a bit but make sure you don't lose it. I may ask you to bring Nick in for questioning, and if so, I'll probably have to charge him. Now, trust me on this, I'll get it thrown out and will use your records of the chat to do so, but if you're serious about this guy being involved, then we're going to need to play along with him for the time being."

"That's fine with us, DCI Dack. It looks like we're starting to build a reciprocal trust process."

"I'll be in touch," said Michael, hanging up the phone just as he reached Morgan's office.

"So DCI Dack? Have you cracked this case yet or what?" said Morgan as he entered her office.

"Nearly there, ma'am, just a couple of minor points to process and then the arrests will flood in."

"Hmm. I detect sarcasm in that voice. I'm guessing you're here to ask for my help?"

"I may need to get some surveillance on a person of interest. That won't be a problem, will it?"

"Not if you can prove how interesting they are.'

"The level of interest is not exactly obvious at this moment in time, but I have some information to suggest he may be very useful."

"Doesn't exactly sound solid, but you know I'm here to support. Tell me, is this person all we have currently, or are there any other lines of enquiry?"

"There are a few things we're working on, ma'am. If any of them pan out into anything more significant, you'll be the first to know."

"I would very much hope so. Now, what's all this I hear about a pub? Very convenient that your investigation leads you to a drinking establishment."

Michael stood open mouthed. Suzanne let him stew for a few seconds before putting him out of his misery.

"Don't worry, you haven't got a leak in your department. Well, not a purposeful one anyway. Lizzie overhead DS Sharma and DS Gardiner talking. You may want to tell them to keep it down when they're in common areas."

"For god's sake. Yes, a pub has arisen as a place of interest. Have a guess who owns the holding company."

"Go on, tell me, I've got no time for guessing games."

"None other than Richard Banks."

Suzanne stopped writing and stared up at Michael, "What are you doing tomorrow night?"

"No plans, ma'am. Why?"

"Keep it free. We're going on a trip."

# Twenty-two

"We've got a call for you from Scotland Yard, sir. Did you want me to put it through?" asked the nervous-sounding desk sergeant at Liverpool Street Police Station.

"That depends on who's calling, doesn't it, lad?" boomed the reply in a thick Yorkshire accent.

"It's a DS Nisha Sharma, sir."

"A DS! Do you think I've got time to talk to a bloody 'DS'?"

"She said to tell you it's quite urgent, sir."

"Did you not hear me? Unless she's ringing to tell me that I'm being knighted in the next honours list, then I'm not interested."

"Yes, sir. Sorry, sir."

Detective Chief Superintendent Brian Stock slammed down the phone, seething that someone so lowly was trying to get in touch with him.

Stock was an old-fashioned copper who ruled by fear. He believed in strict discipline and a deferential conformity to rank. He had worked his way up from the crime desk at Barnsley Police Station to one of the highest positions in the country, and he never missed an opportunity to remind anyone just how important he was.

He'd be in an even higher position if it wasn't for that modern-day enemy to the straight, white male hierarchy: political correctness. Stock believed he should be the Metropolitan Police Commissioner, and he only wasn't because Suzanne Morgan was a homosexual female. 'Political box-ticking at its finest' was how he described her appointment to anyone who would listen.

He was confident that his time would come. Commissioner Morgan was bound to screw up sooner or later, and when she did, he would be the natural choice to take over. He now had the two necessary components to ensure such a promotion: impressive results and influential friends in high power.

He stood up to check on his subordinates and bore an intimidating presence. At five-foot eleven and nearly twenty stone, his imposing bulk was matched by a steely. dark stare which sat aggressively within his boulder-like head. He was always clean shaven and had sported the same haircut for all his 56 years: short back and sides.

As he strolled through the office, he took pleasure in watching how the eyes of his team would switch straight to their computer, terrified of being engaged by him. They abhorred the way he would stand over their desk, demanding instant answers to questions. He was known as the last dictator of the constabulary, and he took that as a huge compliment.

A phone started ringing from his inside blazer pocket. It had been a while since this device had received a call and he marched back to his office to answer it in private.

"Hello, DCS Brian Stock speaking."

"Hello, Brian, long time no speak," came the well-spoken voice from the other end of the phone.

"Who's this?"

"Forgotten me already, have you? And after all we've been through. It's Trevor Wood here from the British Embassy in Shanghai."

"Trevor. It has been a long time. Is all well over in China?"

"Not really, old bean. Are we talking privately here?"

"We are."

"I had a call from my contact at the Shanghai Police Department earlier. Apparently, there's a detective sergeant from the Metropolitan Police sniffing around, trying to locate our old friend Huang Tzao."

Stock fell silent for a few seconds before responding, "And just how much sniffing around has he been doing?"

"It's a 'she'. And by the sound of it, she's put in quite a few calls. It doesn't seem like she's going to let it lie. Is she someone you could speak to?"

"That depends, Trevor. What's her name?"

"DS Nisha Sharma."

"Okay, well that is interesting."

"Why's that?'

"Because I had a call from her myself this morning."

"Hmm. Why do you think this is all getting brought up again? I thought we'd quashed it."

"I'll have to look into it, but off the top of my head, I'd imagine it's something to do with the new taskforce they've just announced. I'd bet your bottom dollar that this DS Sharma is a part of that."

"Are we going to have a problem here, Brian? The last thing I need is another political incident."

"It's nothing I can't handle, Trevor. Leave it to me."

"I very much hope so. Do keep me updated."

Stock hung up, grabbed his office phone and rang through to the desk sergeant.

"Lad, it's DCS Stock here. Get me DS Nisha Sharma back on the phone."

# Twenty-three

Michael yawned as he stepped outside of Scotland Yard late in the afternoon sun. The last thing he wanted was to join Commissioner Morgan on her mystery excursion. He was, however, intrigued as to what could be so important that she felt the need to show him rather than tell him.

"Put that thing out, you dirty bastard. You're in your sixties, it's time to quit," Morgan's voice called out from behind him through the open passenger window of her silver X-type Jaguar.

"Typical. I'd just lit it up, ma'am. The one time you're not late."

"Oh, bring it in here then. And light me one up while you're at it, I've had a stressful day."

Michael got into the passenger seat and sparked up a cigarette for her.

"Been a while since I've seen you smoke, ma'am, something stressing you out?"

"Are you joking, Michael? I'd like to see you walk a mile in my shoes. It's constant pressure from the moment I wake up to till the moment my head hits the pillow. I tell you now, you made the right decision not trying to climb the ladder. If I had my time again, I'd do exactly what you done."

"It wasn't exactly all my decision, was it? But yeah, I must admit, I don't envy you. So where are you taking me tonight? We're not going out on a date, are we?"

"You'd be so lucky. Strap yourself in, it's a long ride. We're off to Surrey."

"Surrey? We won't be home for hours. What's down there?"

"Someone who I think may be able to shine a little light on this investigation for you."

"Could we not just call them?"

"No, we bloody well can't. I can't guarantee that his phone isn't being listened to. If you've got something more important planned, then let me know. You were the one who said you had nothing on."

Michael's mind drifted guiltily to Samantha, who would have to spend another night without him. She hadn't said anything to him yet, but he knew that she was annoyed with the constant absence, "No, you're all right. Surrey it is," he replied.

The following ninety minutes passed quickly as the pair took the time to catch up with each other. It seemed that growing old, combined with the pressures of the job, had led them further apart in their friendship than they'd realised. Michael was unaware that Suzanne was now single, having split up with her girlfriend eight months prior. Suzanne didn't know that Michael's ex-wife, Paula, had a child with her new man.

It made them appreciate how little interest they'd taken in each other's personal lives over the past few years. They promised not to let it slip again.

By the time they pulled into their destination – a leafy road in Cobham that boasted huge multi-million-pound houses on either side – Michael was grateful for the long journey and the opportunity it provided to reconnect with his friend.

"Blimey, Suzanne, this road is like something out of a High Grant movie. You're not going to tell me you've bought somewhere down here, have you?'

"People on our side of the law can't afford places like this, Mikey boy, you know that."

Morgan swung the car into a huge driveway barred by metal gates. She pressed the buzzer on the system and was greeted by a posh voice at the other end of the intercom. "Is that you, Suzy?"

"It is indeed, sir?"

"Hahah! Buzzing you in now, old girl. Make your way to the front door."

"Are you going to tell me who this is yet?" said Michael as he watched the gates in front of him jolt, then slowly start winding open.

"I'm about to introduce you to my old boss, Michael."

They parked up and made their way to the entrance of the country-style manor. Before they reached it, the door was opened, and a tall elderly-looking man emerged, holding his arms outstretched to Suzanne with an exuberant beam across his face.

The gentleman looked healthy for his age, tanned with short grey hair and oversized ears. He was dressed in a yellow jumper, grey chinos, and brown loafers – the sort of outfit that only the upper class could get away with. As he enveloped Suzanne in a bear hug, Michael couldn't help but notice the Patek Phillipe watch on his wrist. About eighty grands worth, he reckoned.

"Michael, this is Lord Peter Marshall, former home secretary and the man who went out on a limb and hired me."

"Yes, and just over a year later, I was sacked, although I'm sure there was no correlation." A wry smile spread across Peter's face.

"Stop it, you old bugger, I got better results than anyone else you hired."

"Only you could get away with calling a lord that, Suzy! Anyway, it's a pleasure to meet you, Michael, and please let me clarify that she is right. She was the best police commissioner I ever hired." He leant in and whispered into Michal's ear. "And my favourite, although don't tell her that."

"It's a pleasure to meet you, too, sir. And don't worry, your secret is safe with me."

"Good, good. Well, please do come in. I've arranged for drinks in the annexe."

Michael's mouth was wide open as they walked through the house. It was huge but somehow felt homely. Grand beams of oak sprung up throughout the hallway and corridors. Michael peered inside one of the rooms and saw a bookcase that contained more publications than most libraries. As they turned right and walked down a long corridor, he was thrilled to see old black and white photos adorning the walls. Moments of a different era captured, displaying the lord in various conversations with many notable names from world politics, show business, and sport.

"So, this is where they send lords to see out their final days, is it?" Michael asked, hoping he hadn't misjudged his host's sense of humour.

"Ha! I wish our government looked after us like this. No, I'm ashamed to say that this is all from family money. The House of Lords pension is barely enough to warm the swimming pool."

The annexe turned out to be a room larger than an average London flat. It had sliding glass patio doors at the far end which opened onto a spectacular lawn resembling Kew Gardens. Michael wondered just how much family money there was in the Marshall clan.

"Please, take a seat," said Peter, beckoning them towards four beige, leather armchairs positioned around a vintage coffee table. "What can I get you to drink? Are you a whisky man, Michael?"

"You could say that. One of those would be lovely, please."

"Just a bottle of lager for me. I'm only having the one, as I'm driving," said Suzanne. "I'll tell you what, every time I've been to this house, I find a new room. Is there one for every day of the month?"

Peter chortled as he brought the drinks over and took a seat. "Not quite, but there's more than enough. Since my Patricia passed away, though, it does seem rather empty. I should be downsizing really, but I just can't bring myself to move away from the place. I've lived here for so long."

"Do you live alone, sir?" asked Michael, taking a sip of the whisky. His tastebuds immediately confirmed what he predicted: this was a very expensive drink he'd been handed.

"Just me and the two girls," Peter replied, pointing to the garden, where two overweight Labradors were passed out on the grass. "How do you like the whisky? It's a rare double malt from Scotland that I was given as a gift a few years back."

"It's delicious, sir. Just the sort of gift I like."

Peter smiled back at him briefly before the expression on his face turned serious.

"So, how are you getting on with the investigation?"

Michael glanced at Suzanne, unsure of how much information he should divulge, but was met with a reassuring nod.

"It's a bit of a slow burner currently. We've made some headway in certain areas, but not the progress I would have liked overall."

"And you've met my successor, I understand. What did you think of him?"

"I must be honest, I think he's complete arsehole. He's not a friend of yours, is he?"

"Not at all, and your judgement is very sound, although probably not quite damning enough. Suzanne told me yesterday that one of your lines of enquiry led you to a building owned by Richard Banks, who, by the way, is another huge arsehole. Is this correct?"

"That's correct. I'm gathering from the tone of your voice that you think this is quite relevant."

Peter and Suzanne both looked at each other in silent conferral. It was the commissioner who eventually broke the silence.

"Being a pair of arseholes isn't all these two men have in common, Michael. We think it's time to fill you in on a few parts of this case that Lord Peter and I have previously discussed. Do you want to start, sir?"

"Yes, of course, Suzy. So, despite appearing to be clueless, David Parkinson is probably the most dangerous man in Westminster. During my time as home secretary, when he was coming through the ranks, we initially got on well, and he factored a sort of mentor-protege relationship. He used to confide in me some pretty personal stories and, as such, over time, I began to trust him and confide in him similarly.

"It turned out to be a complete ruse. He was playing me from day one, always with his eyes on taking my job. The stories he confided in me were completely made up. Hours and hours of them. Do you have any idea how twisted someone has to be to maintain such lies over so many years? Believe me, I've worked in Westminster my whole life. I've seen the worst of them. Nobody compares to David Parkinson and the lengths he went to for power."

"I'm shocked, sir, and a little disappointed in my powers of deduction. I had him pegged as being a useless arsehole. Annoying, but harmless," said Michael.

"Yes, that's the problem. Most people do underestimate him. He plays the game very well, and he moved through the ranks of government quicker than anyone could foresee. It was startling in fact, and before long, it became very apparent that he was being backed by some big money as well. Anyone who questioned him internally was swiftly seen off. He became a figure of fear throughout Westminster.

"Eventually, he came for my job, and I saw exactly how he had earned such rapid promotion. It started off with the typical petty stuff, a bit of public mudslinging, some private denigration to the

PM about my advanced years. This was nothing I couldn't handle, but things soon took a sinister turn.

"When he was making his power play, I found out some information about him and a young girl. Now, she wasn't underage in the legal sense, but she'd barely turned sixteen. The whole thing was pretty unedifying. I decided to confront him privately about the allegations, and to my eternal regret, I didn't go straight to the PM or the police. Of course, he denied them, and there was a furious row late one night at Parliament, which ending in me telling him I'd be going to the PM the next day and would be expecting his resignation.

"The next morning, I woke up and made my way in to work, only to be greeted by the sight of Parkinson standing outside my office with two of his cronies. He advised me that overnight, there had been a security scan conducted on all MP's computers and that mine had turned up some disturbing stuff. They sat me down in front of the screen and brought up a whole raft of images, complete filth involving children, bestiality, you name it. It was disgraceful, and before you ask, of course it had nothing to do with me, they had somehow hacked in and planted it there."

"Why didn't you go to the police?"

"Parkinson had played me. He said if I offered my resignation that day and went quietly, this would never come out. I would get to keep my reputation intact and retire gracefully. I was well past retirement age anyway."

"I'm still upset you didn't come straight to me, sir. You know I'd have had your back," said Morgan.

"I know, Suzy, but I didn't want to put that on you. The way I saw it, the more people who knew about it, the more chance it had of coming out. You know what it's like nowadays with all this social media stuff. It's a public court. Fake news can completely ruin someone's reputation. And, in my case, there was actual evidence, however false it was.

"I've seen what happened to my friend, the former head of the Armed Forces. He went to his grave with a dark cloud hanging over him, despite a lifetime of stellar public service. My Patricia was very ill at the time. I didn't want her seeing out her final hours concerned about me. Besides, what did I actually have against him? It was my word against his, and my accusation was about a girl who, despite being young, was legal at the time. I couldn't win. I choose to retire and keep my good name."

"I don't blame you. That's a terrible position to be in. But what does this have to do with our investigation?" said Michael.

"After Patricia passed away, I started to yearn for revenge. I went to Suzanne and told her everything. Luckily, she believed me. She looked into the hacking episode for me."

"And believe me, I did it as discreetly as possible, Michael," said Suzanne, "but not discreetly enough. Within a few days, I had a visit from David Parkinson, who was now my boss. He ordered me to stop all investigations into Peter, or I would be immediately fired and subject to criminal charges."

"How did he find out?" said Michael.

"Obviously a leak in the police force," replied Suzanne.

"He has a lot of contacts, Michael, people in every sort of position throughout the system," said Peter.

"I played the innocent, silly woman. I apologised profusely and said I'd heard rumours about Peter and wanted to see if there was anything further to investigate. Parkinson bought it. He is a chauvinist, after all. He's kept a very close eye on me since though. But before I got shut down, I did find something of interest."

"Go on."

"I managed to trace the source of the hack."

"How did you do that? You can barely turn on an iPad."

"You cheeky sod. It was with the help of a trusted and skilled colleague. Anyway, the source of the hack came from within an organisation with links to Richard Banks."

Michael's eyes widened. Peter gave him a few seconds to digest the information before he continued.

"It was clear that Banks and Parkinson had grown close. Banks had been prioritised as a preferential partner in a few government housing schemes, but that sort of thing goes on all the time. When we found out that there was a strong possibility that he assisted Parkinson in this, Suzanne and I realised just how far his slimy tentacles spread within our system."

"Okay, so Parkinson's corrupt, and his billionaire mate helps him. But what does that have to do with our investigation? Do you truly believe they're involved in the kidnapping, exploitation, and murder of underage girls? It's a big accusation to throw around without much proof," said Michael.

"Well, that's your job, isn't it? To find the proof? Look, I can tell you now that the rumours of a so-called VIP paedophile ring in government haven't just swirled around the press for all these years, they've been circulating in Westminster as well. Hushed discussions in dusty corridors. That moron who went to the police last time, backed by the labour minister, was a clear fantasist, and those cases should have never got out of the interview room. The problem is, they became public knowledge, and now everyone involved has such egg on their face that the whole concept of the VIP ring seems preposterous. Well, it's not. I'm convinced there is one, and I believe it goes right to the top."

"To the PM?"

"No, not him. He's a fool, but an honest fool at least. It goes beyond the PM and beyond the government. I'm talking about the Palace."

"You truly believe that? Even if you are right, how are we ever going to be able to get close enough to prove it?"

"Well, this is why we decided to go down this route, Michael. This is where you and the taskforce came in," said Suzanne.

"No-one said it would be easy, Michael. You must tread carefully. Taking down a home secretary is almost akin to taking down the prime minister himself. There will be dark and powerful forces at work, and you won't know who to trust. But believe me, Parkinson's involved in all this. Him and Banks will be driving it with their power-hungry egos, but the reach of the group will spread wide. There will be other politicians involved, and they've got at least one copper on the inside for sure. I don't know who, but it's someone high up, more than likely someone who's been over-promoted since Parkinson became home secretary."

"Bloody hell. I knew there was a chance this investigation would lead us to a high-profile group, but this is like a script from Hollywood."

"I told you when you joined that it could take us anywhere," said Suzanne. "I wouldn't have brought you here tonight if I didn't think there was any substance to it, but when you told me that pub had a connection to Banks, I couldn't leave it any longer. You're playing with the big boys here, Michael, so play well."

"Just to be clear with you both, this conversation never happened," said Peter. "I can't be getting involved in this. As a former home secretary, they'll be watching me. If I stumble across anything important, I'll try to discreetly let you know, but you can't be coming to me for more assistance. I wish you the very best of luck, but you're on your own in this one. Now, let me get you another drink, Michael, and you can let what I've told you sink in."

"Make it a double, please, sir."

# Twenty-four

It was bank holiday Monday in August, and the meeting place was a private room located above a run-down pub in Tower Hamlets – one of the most deprived areas of London. It was exactly the sort of location where no-one would expect to find a billionaire, the home secretary, and the housing secretary, seated around a large table with six other men.

The two security guards did not look out of place in this establishment. Both were dressed similarly in dark, denim jeans, heavy construction boots, and black leather jackets.

Bernard was the larger of the two, standing at around six-foot five inches and weighing in at just under nineteen stone of solid muscle. The jacket he sported was an XXL, but it struggled to contain his huge frame. His face was unshaven and full of scars. His piercing, green eyes darted around the room, keeping a hawk-like watch on the attendees.

Murat was shorter but wider. His bulldog-like features were the epitome of raw aggression. He ran his fingers through his long, dark, greasy hair, scowling at anyone who looked in his direction.

The pair were friends, having known each other since they were five years old. They attended the same school in the Albanian capital city, Tirana. As they grew up together, through childhood to adulthood, they ruthlessly established a reputation as two of the hardest men in a city full of hard men.

It was their foray into people trafficking from Eastern to Western Europe that eventually led them to the UK. They decided to make the move a permanent one when they both turned thirty and realised the extent of the money that was on offer in London.

Anyone who was in their company felt uneasy. A sense of violence hung over them like a dark cloud struggling to contain the thunderstorm within. The only person who didn't seem intimidated by them was Richard Banks, due mainly to the vast sums he paid them to carry out his many forms of dirty work. He liked having them around in meetings such as this, where high-profile people could feel their presence.

As Banks sat at the head of the table and surveyed the nervous chit chat amongst the attendees, he knew that his two enforcers were having the desired effect.

"Right, gentleman," Banks began, "I think it's time we get this meeting underway, as I can't stay in this shithole for too long."

"Yes, amen to that," said David Parkinson, the only one of the men who uttered a reply.

"I've called this meeting, as it appears that our little network is starting to get a bit sloppy in their actions, and this is un-fucking-acceptable!" The raise in volume as he delivered the last words made everyone in the room jump.

"We were ticking along quite nicely until the Natasha Shaw incident." Richard's glare turned towards Bernard and Murat, both of whom looked down at the floor. "Since then, this fucking taskforce has been announced, and within a few days, they turn up and start sniffing around one of my bloody pubs!

"The first thing I need to know is how the Shallow Pond got linked to Natasha Shaw. Bill, have you got something to tell me? Don't you dare lie to me."

Bill Lowthy looked up sheepishly from the other end of the table. A simple landlord, he was not used to being in such exalted company. He decided that this was no time to try to feign ignorance.

"Look, boss, she used to visit, and we'd let her and her friend drink in there. She seemed to fit the profile we look for, right age, right background. So, we found out a few details about her, and Marius passed them onto Bernard and Murat." Bill looked over at Marius, who nodded his head solemnly.

"You never told us she drunk down the pub, you dickhead!" Bernard shouted, pointing his finger at Bill, whose face instantly drained of colour.

"If we didn't pass on that bit of information, then I'm very sorry."

"No, fuck that," Marius shouted. "We shouldn't have to say sorry. It was you two who had her and let her get away. It was you two who killed her and then left her body there to be found with the bracelet. How is this our fault?" The room fell silent as everyone looked at the Romanian in shock.

Despite his own size and appearance, Marius was no match for the two Albanians, who would regularly mock him. He had never stood up to them before, and even though his words were true, he instantly regretted them when he saw the look on the their face's. They weren't used to being questioned by anyone, especially in public. Eventually, it was Murat who broke the silence.

"If you have a problem with how we operate, you Romanian pig, then why don't you come outside, and we will sort it out man to man?"

Marius stood up, not wishing to lose face, but inside, he was praying that someone would stop the confrontation from happening. He had seen the two Albanians in action and knew that he stood no chance if the argument turned physical. His prayers were answered by the interjection of Richard Banks.

"Enough of this. You're all to blame. Firstly, Marius is right, it was an absolute shitshow how you two let that girl out of your grasp and then didn't clear up the mess."

"Boss, I have told you, she escaped out of the car when we were transporting her, and then when we caught up, we were disturbed by a dog walker. We had no choice but to leave."

"Yes, and I suppose she just strangled herself, did she? I know what happened. You were both drunk again, and your temper got the better of you after she escaped out of the van you forgot to lock. Even if you couldn't take the body, you take the bloody bracelet! That's what caused this mess. The same thing happened with Iona. How have we let this happen again? Richard banged his fist down on the table, his face reddening.

The two Albanians looked back at him solemnly. They knew he was right. They'd messed up, and it was mainly due to the fact they'd drunk a bottle of vodka before attempting to move Natasha from one location to another.

"Secondly," Banks continued, "your actions are unforgivable, Bill. How many bloody times have I told you? You are not to conduct this business in any of my premises. There cannot be any links to me whatsoever."

"I'm sorry, boss, but I'm sure they won't link the pub back to you. When that inspector turned up, we treated him like you asked. I don't think we'll be hearing from them again."

"Really, Bill? Then please tell me something. Why have we had members of that taskforce pulling up files on Equisea on a police computer?"

"Are you sure, boss? How do you know that?"

"Because I bloody well told him," Came a voice with a gruff Yorkshire accent from a dark corner of the room. Everyone except Richard looked around, startled; they didn't know there was anyone else in attendance. As the person stepped forwards into the light to reveal themselves, most of the room was still unsure who it was – except for David Parkinson.

"Brian, good to see you chap. That was a bit dramatic of you, wasn't it?"

"You know me, sir, there's only so long I can stand listening to bullshit before I have to step in."

"Gentlemen, I felt it was time to introduce you to our man on the inside of the constabulary and the man who is going to clear up this mess you've caused. This is DCS Brian Stock. Bill, be a good boy and let him sit down, would you?" said Banks.

Bill meekly stood and offered his chair to the policeman, an embarrassed look on his face.

"Good evening, gents. As Richard mentioned, I'm going to do my best to quash this investigation, but I need you to help me as much as possible. Bill, Marius, you mentioned Natasha's friend. I'm guessing this is how the taskforce found the pub. What's her name?"

"Harriet Kennedy," replied Marius.

"Does that ring any bells, Brian?" asked Banks.

"No. I've checked through the list of everyone they've officially interviewed in this investigation. Her name's not on it. That doesn't mean they haven't spoken to her though. DCI Michael Dack isn't exactly renowned in the force for doing things by the book."

"Ah, yes, the head of this taskforce. So, what do we know about him?"

"He's a decent copper but a bit of a loose cannon. Should have probably got further in his career, but he had a family incident a few years ago that nearly sent him to the nuthouse. His nine-year-old daughter was taken from a Spanish beach while he was propping up the bar. She's not been seen since. His wife ending up leaving him, and he became a raging alcoholic."

"His daughter wasn't one of ours, was she?" asked David Parkinson, prompting the whole room to start chuckling.

"That would be some sort of coincidence, wouldn't it?" replied Banks. "Anyway, this tells me two things. Firstly, he's probably more motivated than most to try to crack this investigation. Secondly, I'm guessing this man has some serious demons. Let's start looking into him and see if there's anything we can use to manipulate him. Toby, can you get onto that?"

A small, bespectacled man in his mid-twenties looked up from across the table and nodded his head in a jerky manner, sporting a creepy grin that unnerved most in the room. He had yet to speak throughout the meeting and had spent most of it staring intently at his laptop.

"Do you not want me to investigate him, Richard? I'm sure I can dig up some dirt by speaking to some of his former colleagues," said Brian.

"I'd rather you concentrate on monitoring the taskforce. Find out where they're going and who they're speaking to. If you start asking colleagues about him, it may arise some suspicions. Let Toby investigate Dack. From my experience, someone's online history is usually far more revealing than their public persona."

"No problem at all. Is there anything else you need from me?" said Toby.

"Just a guarantee on that QR code. You promise me they'll never be able to scan it?"

"They've got more chance of winning the National Lottery three times in a row. It's the most secure encryption ever developed."

"Okay, good. Now, David, what can you do to alleviate the pressure on us? I mean, after all, this taskforce was born under your watch."

"Some things are out of my control. I do report back to a parliament, you know. If I'm seen to be complacent in my job, I can be swiftly replaced. I can assure you, though, that I will be working from the inside to undermine this whole investigation and use its failure to replace that fat, dyke commissioner I got lumbered with."

"And then we can get Brian in that position?"

"That's the plan, Richard."

"Good. Final point from me, then, can someone please get that moron Philip Strevens to drop his case on the kid who gave him a slap? He's a liability and another example of our network getting sloppy. The last thing we need is that simpleton speaking to the police after he's been caught travelling across London for a cheap thrill."

"I'll sort it out, boss. It's the least I can do," offered Bill.

"I'll leave that task with you. Don't let me down again. Now, can you please all pay attention to this? Every person here is in this room because I trust you, or at least I *did* trust you, to do your job. I cannot be getting involved in the minutiae of this operation. I'm funding it, I've provided locations, and I've put people in place. I should now be able to leave you to get on with it. If anything like this incident happens again, I'm going to have to seriously reconsider the personnel in this team. Do I make myself clear?"

The table nodded in unison with a few grunts of acceptance.

"We need to be cautious, but operations must also continue. We have our biggest ever event coming up in a few months. Our special guest is now confirmed to attend, so we need more stock for it. We'll be making some moves within the next few weeks."

# Twenty-five

"Talk to me, DS Sharma, tell me you've got some good news for me." Michael appeared in an ebullient mood as he walked through the office door.

"It has been an interesting morning, guv. I finally had a call back from DCS Brian Stock. He's agreed to meet with me sometime next week."

"Tell me about Brian Stock. What's his profile?" asked Michael, recalling the conversation he'd had with Lord Peter Marshall a fortnight ago.

"Profile? What do you mean?"

"Have you looked into his background? How long's he been in the force? Has he had a rapid rise through the ranks? What got him into the position of DCS? He must have had some serious career success to be promoted to that lofty height. Are there skeletons in his closet? Are there any investigations he's worked on that have grey areas?"

Nisha grimaced. Snooping around a detective chief superintendent's CV sounded like career suicide to her.

"Well, he sounds Northern on the phone to me, so I'm guessing he didn't start off in the Met." As soon as the words had left her mouth, she regretted them. Michael walked over to Nisha's desk and stood in front of her.

"DS Sharma, you're in this team because I heard from good authority that you are fearless, perceptive, inquisitive, and aren't afraid of a bit of hard work. Now, one of those points is certainly correct, but to be honest, the fact that you spend more hours in this room than anyone else isn't the biggest selling point for me. I sense some trepidation from you about looking into a colleague. Am I right?"

If she was investigating any other policeman, it should be him, Nisha thought to herself, but repressed the urge to say it out loud, "yes, I am a little, guv."

"You need to get that out of your system now and start doing work befitting of a DS, or I will find someone else who can. Telling me that a man sounds Northern on the phone and therefore probably didn't start in the Met is not the level of work I expect. Do I make myself clear?"

"Yes, guv, I'm sorry, I'll get right onto it."

"Okay, good. Have you heard from Alison McKenzie yet?"

"I haven't. She won't answer her phone," Nisha lied.

"You may very well have to go up to Liverpool and speak to her then. Ignoring the police is not acceptable, and as a former officer, she should know better. You mentioned it had been an interesting morning. What else happened?"

"We had a call at six AM from Philip Strevens. He asked if you could call him back."

"Pass me the phone, please."

Michael dug out the card he was given by Strevens and punched in the number; it was answered almost instantly.

"Is that DCI Dack?"

"It is. How can I help you, Mr Strevens?"

"I've changed my mind. I no longer wish to press charges against that kid who slapped me. Can you ensure they're dropped, please?"

"Erm, yes of course. What made you change your mind?"

"I was angry at the time, but I'm over that now. There was no damage done. I don't want to waste police time when I'm sure there are more pressing matters to deal with."

"Assault is quite a serious charge, Mr Strevens. It's not one we'd usually take lightly. Are you sure of your decision?"

"I am."

"Okay, no problem, I'll get it done for you."

"Thank you very much."

"Just one more thing, Mr Strevens. My personal laptop has been playing up. Is there any way you'd be able to have a look at it for me?"

"I'm sorry, DCI Dack, I'm completely booked up. I don't think I'll be able to help." The phone went dead.

"All okay, guv?" asked Nisha.

"Have we arranged that surveillance detail for Strevens yet?"

"There's been a delay in getting it signed off. I'll chase it up."

"What sort of delay? I requested this through the commissioner and got approval."

"I don't know, guv. I've just been told it's still pending."

"That's not good enough. Find out why. He's hiding something from us, and I want him followed."

Nisha wrote down a reminder on her notepad. As she did so, the office door flew open, and Matt charged through.

"Guess who I've just been on the phone with," Matt shouted.

"I'm in no mood for guessing games, DS Gardiner. Just tell me, please," said Michael.

"I've finally spoken to Joost. I think there's a willingness from him to work with us, if we can offer the right assurances."

Michael jolted back in his chair. This was positive news indeed. He had recently read up in further detail on the Dutchman's background and was more convinced than ever that he could prove pivotal in this case.

Joost was part of a Dutch network of nine hackers who, nearly seven years ago, had designed the technology they thought would make them all multi-millionaires. They called themselves the 'Balling Brothers,' adapted from the Dutch word for outlaw – balling. Whilst their creation did indeed make them rich, it subsequently grew into a living nightmare.

Operating exclusively on the dark web, the Balling Brothers had created an encrypted phone technology that they marketed as the most secure network in the world. Through purchasing one of their handsets for the price of 2,500 euros, the client would receive six months' worth of calls and messages that were impossible to trace. Users were promised complete privacy on any communication conducted on the handset.

The Balling Brothers initially had good intentions with their product. They had designed the phones as a reaction to the phone hacking scandal, conducted by various media outlets, that had targeted the private messages of many celebrities. The Balling Brothers sold their encrypted phones as the perfect solution for cash-rich, private individuals who needed their online activities to be secure. The plan worked for a while, and many customers signed up, paying 5,000 euros for 12 months' usage.

The operation soon took a sinister turn. The Balling Brothers realised that the money coming in from celebrity customers was not enough to keep their enterprise running. Word of their venture had, however, got out to crime syndicates around the Netherlands, mainly large-scale drug dealers who recognised the technology as the ultimate platform on which to conduct their illicit transactions.

A meeting was held by the Balling Brothers, and the group voted narrowly in favour, by five votes to four, of making their product available for criminal use. They updated the devices to make them more attractive for criminals by introducing a 'kill button.' This option completely wiped all communication from their phone if the user ever thought they were in danger of having it confiscated by the authorities.

It didn't take long before criminals across Europe used the phones to conduct a whole raft of illegal activity – drug dealing, people smuggling, large scale theft, even contract murder. The criminals felt so secure conducting their activities on these devices that they used them brazenly, without fear of consequences.

The enterprise carried on for over four years, until one day, the French online crime agency managed to crack the whole system and open a proverbial treasure mine for Europe's police forces. The history of every communication conducted by anyone who owned the phone was laid bare for the law to see. It was like shooting fish in a barrel.

The investigation yielded some of the biggest results ever seen in Europe. Huge drugs busts were carried out daily, contract killers were rounded up, and trafficking gangs were smashed. In a three-week period during the Covid-19 crisis, some of the most powerful criminals were taken off Europe's streets and locked up for life. Those who weren't immediately arrested, but knew they had used one of the devices, went on the run to places like Morocco, Northern Cyprus, or Dubai, and they weren't the only ones who had to flee.

The Balling Brothers had sold these devices on the guarantee that they provided the ultimate in online security. When this turned out to be false, it didn't take them long to realise that they had now made enemies out of some of the most dangerous people in the world. The network immediately disbanded. They took as much money as each of them could and they went on the run, going their separate ways with the intention of making new lives for themselves. Unfortunately, it didn't quite turn out that way.

Of the nine original members, six turned up dead in suspicious circumstances over the next eighteen months. There had been a huge ransom placed on their heads by the criminal gangs, and it was one that any small-time crook was only too keen to cash in. There were still three members of the Balling Brothers who had not been located, but they were now set for a life perpetually on the move, anonymous and hunted for the rest of their days. Joost was one of them.

"How have you got him to talk? I didn't think any of them lot would ever show their faces again," asked Michael.

"He's terrified, he's tired, and he's got nowhere else to go. If we can get him a fresh start in the UK with a new identity, I'm sure he'll come in. He wouldn't tell me where he is now, but he can be in the UK in the next few weeks if there's a deal on the table."

"And you're convinced he can help us with this code?"

"One hundred per cent, guv. This guy knows everything. He designed the whole technology. If anyone can help us, he can."

"Okay, get it arranged, and I'll speak to the commissioner."

# Twenty-six

Summer was starting to give way to autumn, and the nights were drawing in.

Claudia Wells and her best friend, Ruby Bell, had just finished playing a year ten netball match for their school in Hackney and were in good spirits after a resounding win.

They walked out of the school gates, still in full netball kit, where one of their parents would usually be waiting to take them home.

Tonight was different. The girls had lied to their parents and told them they were visiting the other's house for dinner after the game. They skipped out of the gates excitedly, turning left to head down towards the high street.

They had arranged to meet two boys from their class, Harry and Freddy, who had asked them to go to the café for dinner. They were excited at what would be their first ever date. Claudia had taken a shine to Harry, and Ruby liked Freddy. They didn't know the boys felt the same way and were delighted when they were asked out on a double date.

They were both well-behaved girls, and lying to their family didn't come easily, but they were now at an age where boys were becoming of interest, and a rebellious streak was starting to creep in.

It was nearly dark as they walked together, linking arms. They talked about the game and laughed about how nervous they were at the thought of dinner with the boys. They wondered if the boys would pay or if they would be expected to contribute. Claudia already knew what she was going to order: burger and fries with a large chocolate milkshake. Ruby asked if it would look greedy if she had an ice cream sundae for dessert.

The chill wind began to bite into their bare legs, and they wished they'd brought something else to wear. Claudia zipped up the front of her black coat, and Ruby pulled the hood of her orange puffer jacket over her head.

In their youthful excitement, they did not see the dark blue transit van slow down as it drove past them. They didn't notice it drive on to the next junction before it made a sinister U-turn.

The girls turned into an estate, which offered a shortcut to the café. They were already running late and knew the boys would be waiting for them. Ten seconds later, the transit van turned into the same estate and crawled along the road, following them with its headlights now turned off.

As the girls reached the end of the estate, they made to cut through the alleyway, which led in the direction of the high street, when a man's voice shouted behind them in a strange accent.

"Hey, girls, where you off to tonight?"

They spun around and saw the transit had pulled up to the pavement, around ten metres from where they were standing. A large, scary-looking man leaned out of the driver's side window, and there was another man in the passenger seat.

"Keep walking, Ruby, ignore them," whispered Claudia, tugging at her friend's arm. They turned and headed towards the alley.

"Hey! I'm talking to you. Don't ignore me." The shout was more aggressive this time, and it sent fear through both girls. This part of the estate was isolated; there was no-one else in the immediate vicinity who would be able to help the girls if the situation turned nasty. They kept walking and prayed that the men would leave them alone.

As they got to the entrance of the alleyway, they heard a noise that filled them with terror: the sound of two van doors opening and then slamming shut. Ruby let out a shriek and broke away from Claudia. She sprinted down the alleyway in a blind panic. Claudia froze, her legs pinned to the ground, devoid of energy. She knew that she should run with her friend, but for some reason, her body wasn't letting her.

As the two men converged on Claudia, she screamed at the top of her lungs, but it did not deter them. It was only when they got to within a few metres of her that she found the energy to run, but by then, it was too late. The men bundled her to the ground. She felt a large hand that smelt of cigarette smoke clamp around her mouth and an arm envelope her waist. She went limp, knowing that fighting was pointless. She was like a rabbit in the jaws of a wolf.

As Ruby reached the end of the alleyway, she turned to check on her friend, expecting to see Claudia right behind her. She was shocked to see her on the ground with one man on top of her and the other getting to his knees. She screamed Claudia's name and contemplated returning for her but knew there was nothing she could do to help. The scream alerted the attention of the man on his knees, who rose to his feet and started to run towards her.

Ruby turned and ran. She was one of the fastest in her year. She knew that the man would probably catch up with her after a while, but she just needed to make it somewhere public, somewhere there were people around whom she could alert to the danger.

She saw traffic lights about a hundred metres ahead, that was where the high street began. If she could make it there, she would be okay. She heard the man's heavy footsteps converging on her, and she screamed again. Every second she ran, she thought she would feel him grab her from behind. But she kept running, and as she turned, she saw the gap between them wasn't closing; she was pulling away from him.

She reached the traffic lights and turned left onto the high street. There were plenty of people milling around; she was safe. She screamed once more and pointed back down towards from where she had run. The man had now turned and was jogging back towards the alleyway. An elderly couple approached Ruby and asked her what had happened. The woman took her into her arms, and Ruby erupted into tears.

\*\*\*

DS Matt Gardiner burst into the taskforce office, disrupting the calm atmosphere that had been prevalent just a few seconds before. "There's been a schoolgirl snatched off the street in Hackney."

"Fuck me, when?" said Rob, jumping out of his seat and grabbing his coat.

"The call just came in. It happened about five minutes ago. Where's Michael?"

"He went home about an hour ago, he wasn't feeling too good. Get the car, and we'll call him on the way."

# Twenty-seven

She was jolted out of her trance by the sound of the door at the end of the corridor clanging open. She then heard the screams and pleading of an English girl.

"No, please! Don't do this this! Please!"

They had captured more prey.

She knew she should feel disgusted. She wished she felt sympathy for the girl, but she had been locked up in here for so long that her mind had become distorted through the isolation and longevity of negativity. It was now a small source of joy when another girl was forced into their shared prison.

She consoled herself with the fact that she wasn't alone in her suffering, that other parents out there would be just as worried as hers. She hated herself for this most skewed form of schadenfreude, and she wished that her pure heart would reappear and enable her to feel human again, but that heart was a distant memory.

She heard the breath get slapped out of the new girl's face as one of the two beasts decided the screaming had gone on long enough. There were a few seconds of silence before the inevitable crying started.

She heard the door to the room next to her creak open; it must have been empty this whole time. She listened as the girl was thrown inside, a sound like she'd crashed into the wall at the far end, and then another bout of hysterical crying. She wished the ordeal was over for the new girl and that they would lock her in and leave her to cry alone, but she knew they didn't operate that way. A pang of sympathy crept into her. She grabbed onto it gratefully; it proved she was still human.

She heard the men walk into the room and the door slam behind them. The girl started to whimper and began pleading to be left alone. There was another loud smack and the sound of the girl hitting the floor.

She put her hands over her ears, so she didn't have to listen to the filth that was about to occur; she had heard it too many times before. She had listened as girls were brought in, terrified and alone, believing that they were at their lowest ebb – until those two animals proved there was an even lower place to be taken to.

She clamped her hands tighter, and dug her head into the mattress. It couldn't drown out the noises coming from next door.

She tried to zone out and push the screams, to the back of her head. She willed positive thoughts, forcing them into her brain to push out the depravity occurring just a couple of metres away. There were no positive thoughts strong enough. Any happy memories she held had long retreated to a part of her mind that was locked away, as if to protect them from the enduring nightmare.

The only emotion powerful enough to combat the sordidness, was hate. She concentrated on how much she loathed these two animals. She focussed on her fantasies of revenge, on the intense levels of pain she would inflict on her captors should she ever get the chance. These thoughts consumed her, coursing through her veins. The noises from next door now acted as a distant crowd, cheering her on as she carried out imaginary violence on the two monsters.

And then the noises abated. She removed her hands from her ears; the only sound now was gentle sobbing. Her new neighbour had been broken, and the monsters were revelling in their ungodly act.

Sympathy overwhelmed her again. She wished she could cradle the girl in her arms and attempt to comfort her. She wished she could tell her that everything would be all right, that they would soon escape, and that she would not have to go through that experience again. She also knew that if she did so, it would be a lie. She said a silent prayer for the girl instead.

The men walked past her room laughing. As she listened to them talking in their foreign language, she was sure that she made out two words in English:

"His Majesty."

# Twenty-eight

Michael took a deep breath as made his way towards Suzanne Morgan's office. He was in for a dressing down, and it was one that he deserved. As he reached the entrance, he saw that the commissioner and home secretary were already waiting for him.

"Nice of you to join us," said David Parkinson as Michael pushed the door open.

"Sorry I'm late, sir. I had some issues getting in."

"Issues getting in? It's ten-fifteen AM. What time do you usually start? No wonder this case is going nowhere fast," said Parkinson.

Michael bit his lip.

"Take a seat, Michael. We have a few issues we need to discuss," said Suzanne. "As you know, we had a schoolgirl called Claudia Wells snatched from the streets of Hackney yesterday. You were completely unavailable to reach. Can I ask where you were all evening and why you were out of contact?"

Before Michael could answer, Parkinson butted in, "We lost a valuable opportunity to nail a perpetrator at the point of crime, and now we have another missing girl. I'm about to go in front of the press and offer up a ham-fisted excuse. It's completely unacceptable that the lead detective on the case was out of action. I hope you have a good explanation."

"I left here at four PM yesterday to follow a line of enquiry that required me to be incognito. Without divulging too much information, I was in a location where I could not be recognised as a copper, and as such, I left my phones at home," said Michael.

"That's very convenient, hiding behind case confidentiality again. I'm guessing you're not going to be able to divulge the location you were in?" Parkinson asked, his face contorting in contempt. Michael looked him in the eye and then turned back towards Morgan.

"On top of that, ma'am, I have a team in place for a reason. All of them, especially Rob, are more than capable of leading a rapid incident response in my absence, just like they did yesterday. There was nothing more I could have added to that response had I been there."

"If there's nothing you would have added, Inspector, then why the hell have we got you in charge?" David sneered.

"It's Detective Chief Inspector, sir, and the reason I am in charge is—"

"—I don't care about your rank, and we all know you're in charge because of your friendship with the commissioner. So far, I don't see any other rationalism apart from that. Your taskforce hasn't proved to me in the slightest that it's capable of cracking this case. It's been nearly two months now and not one arrest has been made. I am severely underwhelmed."

Michael opened his mouth to argue his case but decided against it. The quicker he accepted his admonishment, the quicker he would escape this man's presence.

"So, what have we got from yesterday?" Parkinson continued. "Any useful CCTV? Any witnesses who saw the blue transit van? I suppose a lead on that would be asking too much?"

"My team got the plate back from a CCTV image and ran a check on it this morning. It's a fake. It was also too dark for the images of the men in the van to show anything meaningful. We managed to track the van as it made its way in the general direction of Central London, but then lost it as it entered a blackout area."

Michael was sure he could see a faint satisfaction appear on the home secretary's face.

"And can I ask if there has been any other progress made in this case? Anything I can give the press to prove we may have even the slightest idea what we're doing?"

"Well, we did have a line of enquiry, sir, but you blocked the request for surveillance on Phillip Strevens," Michael replied.

"Ah, I see, so it's my fault, is it? And remind me, what relevance did this Phillip Strevens have to the case?"

Michael paused to contemplate his reply, and Parkinson jumped on it.

"Ah yes, that's right. He may or may not have thought he was speaking to an underage girl online. A girl who turned out to be fake anyway. Do you think every man in the UK who expresses an interest in young girls has something to do with this case?"

"Sir, I interviewed him, and there was definitely something worth looking into."

"I read the transcript, Inspector, and there was nothing linking him to our investigation. I can't sign off surveillance on any old weirdo who gets horny and goes online. God, I do hope this isn't the extent of your investigation, or I'm even more worried than when I walked in here!"

Parkinson waited for a response, but none came. He stood up and cast a disappointed look at them both.

"I think I've heard enough. I'll do what I can with the press, but I must warn you that we're on thin ice. Publicly, I'll defend you, but privately, I want this meeting recorded as my first notice of discontent with the taskforce. If substantial improvements aren't made, I'll have no hesitation in making changes."

Parkinson marched out. Michael waited for a few seconds before he turned to Suzanne.

"You didn't fancy sticking up for me a little there did you, ma'am? How can you let him talk to me like that when you know what Lord Marshall told us the other day?"

"Be careful how you question me, Michael. As much as I respect Peter Marshall, what he told us the other day amounted to no more than his opinion. He gave his advice, but it's down to us to establish facts. And for the record, I don't disagree with everything Parkinson just said. I cannot defend the fact that you were unavailable on what could have been a vital day."

"I was following—"

"—Don't give me that shit. I can tell when you're lying. I don't want to know what you were up to, as it could put me in a precarious position, but you better not have been face-down in some boozer."

Michael looked up guiltily.

"And why the hell did you mention Strevens again? I told you he'd already vetoed that line of enquiry!"

"Because there's something there, ma'am. You put me on this case because you trust my instinct, but you won't back me on it."

"I need more than instinct to go to a home secretary with. Just because I trust you, it doesn't mean he will. You know full well he doesn't even trust me!"

"Well, I'm just going to have to follow Strevens myself then, aren't I?"

"If you think that's the best use of your team's time, then that's up to you."

Michael paused. "I need you to get a deal on the table for a witness as well, ma'am. I didn't want to say in front of Parkinson, but this could be a huge part of the case."

"Remind me again, who he is?"

"I'm not giving names out, but he's to do with the encryption side of the investigation. We think we can get him to help us on the bracelet if we can offer a deal."

"Have we actually made contact yet?"

"Only via a third party so far, but it should be happening in the next week or so."

"I can't request anything until he's been spoken to directly. Once he has, then come back to me, and we'll go from there. The case needs to be compelling though."

"Okay, I'll let DS Gardiner know. Now, is there anything else, ma'am, or can I get back to work?"

"Go on, get out of my sight."

As Michael was about to close the door, Suzanne called after him.

"Michael, you know what you have to do, don't you?"

He looked back at her solemnly and gave a small nod. He knew she was right; he just didn't want to admit it.

\*\*\*

In the car park, David Parkinson had just got into his silver Bentley. He took a few deep breaths to compose himself before making the phone call. He knew he had to be firm but couldn't risk losing his temper, no matter how angry he was. The call was answered straight away by Richard Banks.

'Hi, David, how are we looking?"

"Honestly, Richard, I think you've got away with that by the skin of your teeth. You're very lucky that the man in charge of the taskforce is a useless old drunk. This sort of thing cannot go on. Get those two apes under control, and make sure that fucking van is destroyed."

"I've spoken to them already. It wasn't them."

"What do you mean? Was this not the work of The Club? If that's the case, then I'll go back up and read the riot act to that inspector."

"No, don't do that, David. We do have the girl, but it wasn't Bernie and Murat who took her."

"Who was it then?"

"It was Marius."

"Marius! What the bloody hell? He's a glorified pub bouncer, what's he doing getting involved?"

"Don't worry, he will be dealt with. Are you sure we've got away with it?"

"It looks like it, but I can't go on clearing up messes like this. You really need to get your team under control, Richard."

The phone went silent for too long, David regretted his tone.

"David, I understand you're angry. Believe me, I am too. In the future though, before you decide to talk to me like that, please remember who works for whom."

# Twenty-nine

It was a quiet night at the Shallow Pond pub; only three customers were inside, each nursing a sorrowful pint at separate tables. At the bar, Bill and Marius were talking in hushed tones.

"What did you do that for? We were already on dodgy ground with Banks," said Bill.

"I'm sorry. I saw an opportunity, and I took it. I thought he would be happy. He told us we needed more stock," said Marius.

"We were also told to be cautious, and then you go and do that. You've never been told that procurement was part of your role in The Club."

"Like I said, two girls appeared in front of me, and it seemed too easy."

"Yes, and you only managed to get one of them. Now there's another girl out there who can identify you."

"No chance. It was too dark. Don't worry about that."

"Don't worry?! You don't understand how serious this is. I think you've been drinking too much lately. And who were you with? The press are saying there were two men."

"It doesn't matter who I was with."

"Of course it matters, you prick. We can't have outsiders getting involved in group activities."

Marius stood up to his full height and pushed his forehead into Bill's. "Do not speak to me like that." Both men clenched their fists, neither backing down. They were interrupted by the door opening.

"Everything okay, gentleman?" Michael walked in, with Rob behind him.

"All fine here, thanks, Inspector, just a little argument about football. How are you both? I didn't expect to see you here again so soon," said Bill.

"Football, eh? Who's your team?" asked Rob.

"I'm West Ham, and Marius pretends to support Millwall just to wind me up. Are you having a drink?"

"We'll have two double whiskies please, Bill," said Michael, heaving his black leather carry bag onto the bar. The zip on it was open, and the contents were clearly visible.

Marius had a glance inside the bag before he informed Michael, "Hey, your bag is open. You don't want that all spilling out in here."

"That would be just my luck. Thank you, kind sir," Michael said, zipping it up.

Bill poured the drinks, acting as casually as possible. Inside, he was panicking. What were they doing in there again? Have they got a lead on that girl? He brought the drinks back to the bar, where Michael and Rob were now both perched on stools. "These two are on the house. Is there anything we can help you with, or are you just here for a drink?"

"Just here for a quick drink, Bill. You can stand down," Michael said.

"Well, while we're here, I guess we may as well ask," Rob added. "You haven't seen this girl around, have you?" He pulled out a photo of Claudia Wells from his jacket pocket.

After a few seconds of pursing his lips, Bill broke the silence. "I think I have. Hasn't she been on TV a bit? Ah yes, that's right. She's the girl who went missing from Hackney, didn't she? Why do you think she'd be in Islington?"

"I don't know, it was just on the off chance. You two seem like you're 'men of the world'," said Rob. Whilst he wasn't certain, he was suspicious about their reaction. From looking at Michael's face, he knew his colleague had picked up on it too.

The policemen sat at the bar for another half an hour, enjoying chit chat occasionally interspersed with questions. It was still unclear to Bill whether there was some sort of investigation going on or if they were simply there for a drink.

Eventually, Rob downed his third whisky and stood up. "Right, I'd better be off, or I'll be in trouble with the wife. Are you coming, Mike? We can share a cab."

"No, I think I might have a few more. I've only got two angry stepdaughters waiting for me at home."

Bill's face dropped.

"Well, don't be too late, we've got an early start tomorrow," said Rob before turning to Marius and Bill. "Thank you for your hospitality, it's been a pleasure. Before I go, I couldn't have a photo with you, could I?"

"Erm, what? I'm not sure," Bill protested, but before he knew it, Rob had given Michael his phone and put both his arms around their necks with a smile on his face. Michael snapped the shot and gave the phone back to him.

"Thank you, gentlemen. I've recently made a point of taking more of these. I've realised my memory is failing me, and I hardly have any photos to fall back on! Have a good evening."

The next two hours followed a similar path to Michael's first visit to the pub. He downed drink after drink and told stories about his past. It reached 10pm, and he showed no sign of going home.

Bill walked upstairs to the flat he lived in and brought out his burner phone. After the last meeting, he'd been told never to call Richard directly again but to go through his PA. She answered after two rings.

"Caroline Nolan here."

"It's Bill at the Shallow Pond. Can you talk?"

"Yes, go ahead."

"Michael Dack's in here again. He's been asking questions about Claudia Wells."

"Okay, and have you handled it?"

"I think we've played it as well as possible so far. His colleague, who was in here earlier, took a photo of me and Marius though."

There was a long silence on the other end of the phone before Caroline responded. "Bill, in your honest opinion, do you think Marius has been pinpointed as a suspect?"

"I don't know."

"Okay, I'll let Richard know."

"Caroline, there's one more thing that Richard may find of interest. Michael's absolutely hammered, and he's carrying his laptop around with him in a bag."

"Yes?"

"Well, I don't know how Toby's getting on with his research, but I was thinking that it may be useful for him to have access to his laptop. You never know what it may have on there. It could give us an insight into their investigation."

There was another silence before her reply. "That's not a bad idea. Don't you try to do anything, it will look too suspect. I'll sort something out."

As Bill walked back downstairs, he winced as he heard Michael regaling one of the blurry-eyed regulars with more stories of days gone by. Did this guy ever shut up?

"Billy boy! Come and have a drink with us," Michael shouted from the corner table.

Bill couldn't think of anything worse than spending time in the company of a pissed-up policeman, but if he was able to get Michael as drunk as possible, it may make the job of relieving his laptop a little easier. "Coming right over, mate, and I'm bringing shots with me."

An hour later and after imbibing half a bottle of tequila to himself, Michael was struggling to walk to the exit.

Bill put a steadying arm around him. "Come on, mate, time to go. I'll get you a cab."

"But I need a slash," Michael slurred whilst trying to pull at his jean zip as if he was about to start urinating in the pub.

"You can do that outside. The toilets are closed in here now."

Michael shuffled forwards with one eye closed and the other squinting and made his way to the main road. He walked past a commercial waste container and remembered how desperate he was to relieve himself. He staggered over and stood beside it, facing the wall.

As he struggled again with the zip, he didn't notice the youths who appeared about ten metres behind him. They had been following him ever since he'd left the pub. All three were dressed in black, their hoods pulled over their heads.

Michael finally managed to undo his jeans and pull down his pants. He didn't hear the footsteps approach him rapidly from behind. He barely felt the blow to the back of his head that was administered with a heavy, blunt object. He was unconscious before he hit the floor. As he lay prone and vulnerable, the three youths rifled through his pockets and took his wallet and phone, before they picked up his bag and fled.

# Thirty

Matt pulled up the collar on his grey, herringbone Zara jacket to try to shield himself from the bitter October morning. His hands curled around the cup of takeaway coffee he'd bought from the café on the corner of Silver Street in Edmonton, North London. He took another glance at his watch.

After nearly a month of phone calls with their mutual acquaintance, and many broken promises, he had finally managed to arrange a meeting with the elusive Joost. He now had one shot at convincing this paranoid criminal to flip sides and help the police. He was desperate to go back to Michael with positive news.

Matt's thoughts drifted to his boss. He was starting to have doubts as to whether Michael was cut out to handle a case of this size. He was arriving for work later and later each morning, normally with the smell of alcohol lingering on him. He was also acting erratically, especially since he was mugged outside the Shallow Pond pub a week ago. It appeared that Michael was starting to crack under the psychological burden of the case.

Last week, Matt had brought up his concerns with Nisha. They discussed whether to raise Michael's behaviour with Rob but had decided that this probably wouldn't help. DI Archer was a loyal friend, and as far as Matt and Nisha could see, was oblivious to his friend's ongoing problems.

The pressure on the taskforce had intensified dramatically over the last few weeks. The brazen kidnapping of Claudia Wells had worked the media, public, and government into a frenzy. With no progress made so far on finding her, there were rumours of Michael being sacked and the whole taskforce being disbanded. Matt felt a heavy burden. This meeting with Joost was crucial.

The morning rush out of Silver Street tube station began to die down as the time reached 9.30am. Joost was now an hour late and Matt was starting to lose hope. He had presumed the Dutchman had asked for an 8.30am meet time, so they could be blend in amongst the public. As the streets became more deserted, Matt grew convinced that the window of opportunity had been missed.

It was then that he noticed a man sitting on a bench at a bus stop around fifteen metres away. He was dressed in a black bomber jacket and blue jeans and was wearing a beanie hat, which made it difficult to identify him. Matt kept his eye on him but made no move to approach yet. He remembered what Joost had told him: "If I want to speak to you, I will make myself known."

Matt watched him for the next couple of minutes, praying he would receive a sign. Suddenly, without even turning to look at Matt, the man held his arm in the air and made a beckoning sign with his hand. Matt felt adrenaline pump through his veins. He took a deep breath, walked as casually as possible to the bus stop, and sat on the same bench just a couple of metres away.

"Good morning, Mr Gardiner," the man said in a clear Dutch accent. Matt's heart skipped a beat.

"Thanks for agreeing to meet with me."

"Can I ask why we're meeting in public?"

"Because a police station isn't always the most confidential place."

Joost frowned, "That's not very reassuring."

"I agree, but it's a huge case we're working on, and we can't risk any internal leaks."

"Do you believe you have a rat then, Mr Gardiner?"

"You can call me Matt, and yes, we believe so."

"That doesn't sound like an enticing prospect for me. I'm a wanted man all over the world. Someone inside the police who could blow my cover could be fatal for me."

"I'm fully aware of that, and that's why, if you agree to help us, it would be under the strictest confidentiality. There will only be five people in the whole force who know. I can guarantee your safety."

"I see, but please tell me this. What if one of those five people turned out to be the rat?"

"I can assure you they're not." Matt felt his voice waver. He was making promises that he wasn't confident he could keep.

"You don't seem too sure, Matthew. You have some doubts about your police friends, maybe?"

Matt paused to consider his response. "I'm certain that none of my team are corrupt. The only other person who'd know about you is the commissioner. If she's dodgy, then God help us all. And let's be honest, mate, what other hope have you got? It's either this, or you stay on the run for the rest of your life."

Joost fell silent and stared pensively at the pavement. Matt knew he'd struck a chord.

Eventually, the Dutchman spoke. "You are correct in your assertions. I have grown sick of constantly looking over my shoulder, of roaming from city to city in the hope of finding peace. There is none for me living this way. I need a new solution. What terms can you offer me?"

"Complete immunity from any previous crime committed and a new life for you anywhere in the UK."

"I'd need to see a signed agreement before I start."

"Of course." Sensing victory, Matt delved into his pocket for his phone and pulled up a photo of the bracelet found on Natasha Shaw. He showed it to Joost. "Do you think you can help us?"

Joost took the phone and zoomed in on the photo, studiously examining the bracelet before handing the device back. "It looks complicated, but I can do it. I'll have it cracked within six weeks. Where will I be working from?"

"We can't bring you into Scotland Yard – you're a wanted man, and there's only a few of us aware you'll be assisting. We'll get you in accommodation close by. You'll be working and living from there for the duration. It will be basic, but you'll have all the equipment you require."

"And who will be setting the equipment up? That will be another person who knows of my identity. Can they be trusted?"

"It will be someone from our IT department, but they won't know your identity. They'll be informed the setup is for an undercover police officer. I'll pop in every now and then to check on you and bring you groceries, but essentially, you'll be working from there alone. We recommend you don't leave the flat at all."

"That's no problem. I'm used to staying hidden."

"Good. Have you got somewhere to stay for the next few days whilst we get everything set up?"

"I have."

"Let me know how to contact you. I'll get the agreement drawn up and the location ready for you."

Joost stood up and passed Matt a scrap of paper with a number scribbled on it. "I hope I can trust you, DS Gardiner." He turned and scurried back to Silver Street tube station.

Matt watched him disappear inside the entrance, then leant back and allowed a contented smile to spread across his face. He'd made the breakthrough that could finally help to crack this case.

# Thirty-one

Nisha was pleasantly surprised as she walked up to the entrance of the Punchbowl pub. She had anticipated a much grottier establishment, due to its location just off Kilburn High Road, but the well-maintained exterior and modern interior were much to her liking.

She found it strange that this place had been suggested as the meeting point, but after weeks of chasing DCS Brian Stock, she had no other option but to go along with his recommendation. She'd tried to arrange a suitable time during work hours but was informed that he was too busy to do an interview at the station. He was, however, able to give her an hour at his favourite pub.

The pub was surprisingly busy for a Tuesday night in early November, but she noticed there was a football match showing on the TV which seemed to be the main attraction for most of the customers. She scoured the faces for Brian Stock.

Her eyes settled on a man in the corner whose gargantuan frame dwarfed the two-seater table at which he was sat. He was tucking greedily into a large dinner of pie, chips, peas, and gravy. In front of him were three pint glasses, two of which were empty. Something about him made Nisha feel uneasy.

"DCS Stock?" she asked as she reached the table, holding out her hand.

"Oh, hello. You must be Nisha?" he answered in a broad Yorkshire accent, he wiped his fingers with a napkin before shaking her hand. "Call me Brian, we're out of work hours now. Go on, take a seat there, love. What are you drinking?"

Nisha's skin bristled at being called 'love' – it was one of her pet hates, but something she'd grown used to when speaking to men of his generation. "Condescension is an overwhelming tool in the patriarchy's arsenal," she always said to her friends.

"I'll have a mineral water, please. Now, once again, thank you for—"

DCS Stock scowled. "A mineral water? What the hell's that? You're drinking with me now, love. Have a proper drink. Don't worry, it's on me. I know a Detective Sergeant's salary doesn't really cater for much."

"A mineral water will be fine, sir. I've got an early start tomorrow, and I could do without the alcohol fog."

DCS Stock shrugged his shoulders. "Suit yourself, love. And like I said, call me Brian." He turned towards the bar and shouted over at a young barman, who was busy pouring a glass of wine for another customer. "Eddie, bring me over another pint of ale and a mineral water for the lass. There's a good lad."

The barman nodded with a smile on his face that Nisha could tell was forced.

"As I was saying, thanks for agreeing to meet with me today, Brian."

"No problem. It didn't sound like you were going to stop chasing me if I didn't. So, remind me, what's all this about? Something to do with them missing girls from a few years ago?"

"That's correct. I've just got a few questions to ask and see if there's anything further you may remember that could help us." Nisha delved into her bag and pulled out a small recording device, which she placed on the table in front of them.

DCS Stock grimaced. "There's no need for a tape recorder is there, love? I told you, I'm happy to answer your questions, but we don't need to make this too formal. Let's put that away, shall we?"

"Sir, I'm sure you're aware, it's just standard procedure. It means I don't have to spend time writing notes or remembering details later."

"It's standard procedure in a formal interview, DS Sharma," Stock replied sternly. "Now, if you wanted one of those, you should have arranged a suitable time to come to my office."

Nisha felt like screaming at him. She'd been trying for weeks to arrange a formal interview only for her requests to fall on deaf ears. She took a deep breath. She couldn't risk Stock terminating the interview before it started.

"Of course, sir. I'll put it away."

"How many more times? Call me Brian! Jesus Christ, what are they teaching you lot at Hendon nowadays? Certainly not listening skills."

"Sorry, Brian. Let's crack on, I don't want to take up too much of your time. So, as I understand, it was yourself and DS Alison McKenzie who interviewed the witnesses to the two kidnappings involving Lisa Cattermole and Lena Nowak. Is that correct?"

"That sounds about right," Stock replied without looking up, as he carried on shovelling chips into his mouth.

"Well, we've tried to follow up with those who were interviewed, and we've hit a few brick walls."

"I'm not surprised, love. These crimes were a couple of years ago now. No-one likes to be reminded of things like this from their past, do they?"

"Do you recall interviewing Huang Tzao?" Nisha looked for a reaction in Stock's face as she asked the question, but there was not even a flicker.

"I do, as it happens. He was a nice guy. A tourist from Asia, if I remember rightly. Japan or China or somewhere."

"He was from China. Shanghai to be precise. I noticed on the witness statements that he was the one who provided the most detail and had the clearest description of the two men. He flew back to China but promised he would be able to help should we require him to. He seemed certain that he could pick the men out from an identity parade."

"I don't recall exact details, but I do remember him being quite helpful."

"Did you ever speak to him again after he flew back to China? Did you or Alison follow up with him?"

"From what I remember, Alison tried to follow up with him a few months later, but he couldn't be reached. I think his phone was switched off, and that was the last we heard of him."

"Were you suspicious about that at all?"

"Not really. China's a big place. I'm sure people go missing there all the time. Anyway, we had no real use for him, it wasn't like we'd managed to find a suspect to identify."

"Do you find it suspicious that out of the three witnesses to that crime, two of them are currently unaccounted for?"

"Why? Who's the other one?"

"A man who gave his name as Ed."

"The homeless chap? Are you seriously asking me if I'm surprised that we can't locate a homeless chap from a few years ago? Fuck me, love, I hope your questions are going to improve, or this has been a right waste of my time."

Nisha ignored the attempt to demean her, "And how did you find Caroline Flaherty when you interviewed her? I spoke to her a month or so ago, and she seemed a bit nervous talking to the police. Would you remember any reason for that?"

"Nothing springs to mind. Some people are just scared of authority, aren't they?"

"Have you spoken to Alison McKenzie recently?"

"Recently? No. She left the force a year or so ago, didn't she? I heard she moved up North somewhere. Lucky girl. She got away from this shithole. Have you spoken with her?"

Nisha paused. "I have spoken with her." She thought she saw Stock's eye twitch as she replied.

"Oh aye, and what did she say?"

"I'm not currently permitted to divulge that information, sir." Stock's expression changed. It was only for a second or two, but a look that read half angry and half anxious appeared. She felt like she'd found a chink in his armour and decided to let her words stew in his brain for a while – a tactic she often found worked when interviewing suspects.

"Would you mind if we had a quick break? I'm dying for a wee," she asked.

"You crack on, love, but remember I'm on a schedule here, and it's getting shorter by the second."

"I won't be too long."

As she walked to the toilets, Stock took a deep breath and let some of his pent-up aggression come to the fore. How fucking dare she question him like this? The jumped-up little madam. As soon as he was made commissioner, he'd make sure she was out on her arse.

He noticed that she'd left her bag on the seat and an idea formed. He looked around the pub to check that no-one was watching then reached under the table to pull the bag over to him. He unzipped it and probed inside. It didn't take long before he found what he was searching for; Nisha's notebook.

He pulled it out and opened the book, confident she was the type of officer who liked to keep notes of ongoing cases. He was not disappointed. He scrolled through ten pages of scribbled notes all about the current investigation, but her handwriting was messy and difficult to read. He pulled out his phone, turned on the camera, and took photographs of each page. He then placed the notebook back in the bag, zipped it up, and pushed it back over to her side of the table. "Fucking amateurs," he scoffed to himself.

As Nisha returned, she noticed that Stock's plate had been cleared and another pint sat in front of him, which he was already halfway through.

"Where's the mineral water?" she asked as she sat down.

"I cancelled it. I didn't think we had much further to go in this chat, so I thought, why waste the money?" Stock was in no mood for niceties now he had what he wanted.

Nisha was relieved. She had no wish to spend any longer with this man than she needed to. She would ask her remaining questions as quickly as possible and escape his presence.

After twenty more minutes of blunt, belittling responses from Stock, Nisha had finally had enough. She said goodbye and made her way outside. "What a complete arsehole," she exclaimed out loud, happy that the ordeal was over but unsure as to what she had achieved apart from upsetting a very senior officer.

She thought about how Stock had bristled when told about Alison McKenzie. There was definitely something there. She decided she would have to go up to Liverpool and speak to Alison in person.

She pulled her phone from her handbag and saw she had two missed calls from Matt. She rang him straight back.

"Hello, mate, how's it going? Did you ring me?"

"I did, yeah. Are you able to talk for a minute?"

"Of course. What's up?"

"I'm starting to have real concerns about Michael."

"Jesus Christ, finally. I've been saying this since day one. What's made you see the light?"

"This has to stay between you and me."

"Of course."

"Well, we left the office earlier, and he was the only one there. I got home, and I'd forgotten my house keys. I had to come all the way back in to get them. Anyway, I walk into our office, and the lights are off, so I thought it was empty at first. When I get inside, I notice him in the corner, passed out on his chair, snoring, with an empty bottle of whisky in front of him."

"He's a massive pisshead, Matt. We've discussed this. He's not cut out to run this case."

"I know that, Nisha, but it gets worse. I walked around to his desk to wake him up and…" Matt paused as if unable to speak the next words.

"Yeah, go on," Nisha encouraged.

"He had the photos up of the two dead girls on his screen."

"Are you sure? Just those two girls?"

"Yep, just the two murdered ones. It was weird. It's like he'd been sat there drinking and staring at them."

"What did you do?"

"I couldn't do anything. I just got my keys, ran out, and called you."

"I knew there was something odd about him. We have to do something about this."

"Yeah, but what? It's hardly a standard situation, is it? What's the protocol in matters like this?"

Nisha paused. "I don't know the answer, but I know the first step we should take. I need to speak to Harriet Kennedy again and find out what really went on in that interview."

# Thirty-two

Michael turned off the ignition, rolled his seat back, and lit up a cigarette. He guessed this was the thirtieth one he'd smoked today.

The rain lashed against the car. It was a brutal November's evening in London. He decided against unwinding his window to let the smoke out. What damage could passive smoke do to his lungs that he had not already inflicted on himself?

Michael's mind was in turmoil. He couldn't remember the last time he'd had a decent night's sleep. He was feeling pressure from every direction: pressure from above to crack this case, pressure from his team to be the leader they needed, and pressure from his partner to spend more time with her.

He needed an escape. Alcohol had provided him with a withdrawal from reality over recent weeks, but he was craving more.

He began to drift off, and a few minutes' peace set in, but then his eyes sprang open, and his brain clicked back into focus. He looked over at the front door of the house on this suburban road in Croydon. A chill ran over him.

He had been stalking his prey for a few days now. He'd been coming here straight from the office every night, keeping a close watch on them, studying their every move. His only company had been a bottle of whisky and BBC Radio Two.

As he sat there, waiting for movement from his target, his mind cast back unintentionally to a similar night in similar circumstances a few years ago. An unwanted memory that he had tried to push from his conscience. He took a large gulp of whisky and tried to concentrate on anything else.

He settled on another issue, but it was not one that brought comfort to him. The stolen laptop had been causing him consternation for a few weeks now. He was concerned that its contents would soon come to back to haunt him.

The door to the house opened, his heart raced. The chase was about to begin. 'Come on, then, where are you going to go tonight?'

A figure appeared in the doorway, frail and dainty. It walked down the path to the pavement, taking care to look around, almost as if it knew it was being watched. It turned left and scuttled away.

Michael had a quick decision to make. Follow his target on foot or by vehicle. Despite the rain, he swiftly deduced that foot was the most efficient method and least likely to attract attention. He stepped out of the car, the raindrops smashed aggressively into his face. He started to walk down the street in the same direction as his target but on the opposite side of the road.

\*\*\*

At that very moment, just a few miles away, Richard Banks strolled through the door of his Knightsbridge penthouse. He had just completed a day full of back-to-back meetings and was ready for a warm bath and an early night. As he went to hang up his jacket, he heard his wife, Janet, call out from the living room.

"Good evening, darling. Did you have a good day at work?"

Banks bristled. He found it astounding how such an innocuous question could antagonise him. This is how their marriage had been for many a year now – loveless and barren. He was sure they had been in love once; he couldn't remember the feeling, but he remembered that he used to tell Janet he loved her.

Those feelings had died decades ago. There was now just acceptance from her side and hate from his. He abhorred everything about her. He detested how her skin had become stretched, pale, and blotchy as she grew older. He hated how her backside wobbled, and her breasts drooped when she took off her clothes, even though he was very rarely in the room when she did that nowadays.

He loathed how she had begged to stay with him, even after he confessed to affair after affair, sometimes with friends of hers. His blood boiled as he recalled her pleading with him not to walk out, how she told him that he could sleep with whoever he wanted, that she didn't care if they never had sex with each other, and how they could even sleep in separate rooms if that was his preference. She cried as she told him she could not go through the public ignominy of divorce, which would be seen as sacrilegious in the critical eyes of her demanding parents.

He detested her for not being able to give him the children he craved, and he knew that her guilt was a large part of why she was so desperate to maintain the facade of a happy marriage. More than anything, though, he hated the fact that, without her, he would have never got to the position he now found himself in.

Janet came from an extremely wealthy family, whilst Richard Banks came from a council house. It was her money which provided him with the opportunity to open his first business – a property development company which failed spectacularly. It was her money that bailed him out of bankruptcy and enabled him to start again, rebuilding his company more methodically, learning from past mistakes.

The public were unaware that he had been bankrolled by his wife. They preferred to buy into the story that he'd built himself up from poverty. He was terrified at the thought that the truth would emerge one day, and his aura would be shattered. That was half the reason he had agreed to stay with her all these years. The other half was that he enjoyed the cover that being a supposedly happily married man provided for his more nefarious activities.

"Hello, Janet. Yes, it's not been bad, thank you," he replied emotionlessly.

"David's in here, darling. He popped over to see you."

Banks frowned. He wasn't used to having guests pop over unannounced. "Which David?"

"Parkinson, of course. Which other David do you know, darling?"

Banks bristled again at her continued use of the word 'darling'. He knew she was saying it to maintain an image in front of a guest, but it still riled him. He walked through to the living room and saw the home secretary sitting on the sofa, holding a cup of tea.

"Good evening, Richard. Sorry for turning up like this. I've got something I need to discuss with you quite urgently. Is there anywhere we can speak?"

"Oh, don't mind me," Janet chimed dutifully. "I'll go upstairs and run myself a bath. It was lovely to see you again, David."

Banks took Janet's place on the sofa. The pair waited until they heard her go upstairs.

"We've got a problem, Richard." The tone in Parkinson's voice was serious enough to grab Banks's attention.

"Another one? I thought I was paying you to sort out the problems."

"Yes, well, this one is pressing, and it's going to need us to make a joint decision."

"Go on."

"Brian Stock has been in touch. Yesterday, he managed to get hold of one of the taskforce member's notes on the case, a DS Nisha Sharma. They make for concerning reading."

Parkinson pulled out his laptop and brought up the images that Brian Stock had sent him. He handed the device to Banks. "I didn't want to send these to you, hence the reason for my visit."

Banks took the laptop from him and started to scroll through the images. Though the notes were scribbled, messy, and written in broken English, they could be deciphered with a little work. Most of them were irrelevant to Banks, but there was one page that stood out.

The headline read, 'The Shallow Pond - Natasha Shaw.' Underneath were various notes about Harriet Kennedy and what she had told the police about the pub and its relationship to Natasha. "That fucking pub!" Banks exclaimed out loud, causing Parkinson to nod in agreement.

His anxiety rose as he read on and saw a line that read, 'Marius/Ruby Bell - photo identification.' Banks started to feel lightheaded. He read on, and at the bottom of the page he saw the line, 'Lantern Property Ltd - Equisea - Richard Banks.'

He'd already heard through Brian Stock that the taskforce had investigated the files on Equisea, but to see his name written in black and white, on the same page as notes about a young girl's kidnapping, rocked him. The shock caused him to lash out at Parkinson. "Why's your name not on here?"

"There's more. Go to the final page," Parkinson calmly responded, as if he'd anticipated Banks's exact reaction.

Banks scrolled to the bottom of the roll of images. The final page contained just two lines of notes:

'Philip Strevens - Mason Greenwell'

'Harriet Kennedy - MD - investigate'

After a few seconds of pondering, he turned back to Parkinson. "Who the fuck is Mason Greenwell, and who the fuck is MD?"

"I have no idea who Mason Greenwell is. I'm getting it looked into. I can only presume that MD relates to Michael Dack."

"Why would she need to investigate him and Harriet Kennedy? That doesn't make sense."

"I don't know, and to be honest, that's the least of our worries. If Ruby Bell has identified Marius, then it could open a huge can of worms."

"I know that, David, I'm not stupid. But what can we really tell from these notes? It doesn't specifically say that she has identified him."

"I guess not, but do you really want to sit around and wait to see? I think that moment has passed. It's time to act."

"What do you have in mind?"

"As chance would have it, the two Albanians are meeting with Marius and Strevens at this very minute to start sorting out the Christmas party."

Banks stared back at Parkinson. A dark realisation spread over him at what the home secretary was suggesting.

# Thirty-three

Rob walked through the door and dropped his bag on the floor with an overexaggerated sigh. He was relieved to be back home after another long, gruelling day in the office.

He heard the footsteps of his two children run down the stairs to greet him, a huge smile spread across his face. It felt good to be amongst family. He hadn't been spending as much time with them lately as he would have liked.

"Hi, Daddy," Latisha and Henry shouted in unison as they reached the bottom of the stairs. They gave their beloved father a cuddle and then ran into the living room to watch twenty minutes of TV before dinner.

Robert was so proud of them. Everyone agreed that they were two of the most adorable children you could ever wish to meet. Both were popular at school with teachers and pupils alike. Robert put most of the recognition at the feet of his wife, Judy, his childhood sweetheart.

Judy was the rock upon whom Rob could always rely. She was the sounding board for any advice he required, and she was, in his eyes, the best mother to ever walk the face of the earth. He had never stopped loving her since the first time they'd met, and he felt privileged that she felt the same way about him.

His chosen career could have negatively affected any relationship, but Judy had only ever been supportive. She had never once expressed misgivings in his work, never given him a hard time for working long hours and had never once asked him to leave the police force.

As he walked into the kitchen to greet her, Judy turned to look at her husband. The impact this case was having on him was clear to see. His feet dragged along the floor as if lifting them was too much effort. The bright, energetic, fun-loving husband she had enjoyed at home over the last few years had been replaced in just a few months by a tired and withdrawn replica.

"How's your day been, sweetheart?" she asked as Robert hauled himself onto the armchair, head in hands.

"Same as every day. Bloody awful. How about you, my love?"

"Mine's been very relaxing. I took the children to school, met Patti for lunch, and then went and had a coffee with Suzi. I took the dog for a walk, watched the TV for a bit, picked the children up, and then came back here to prepare dinner."

"That sounds like bliss," Robert replied jealously.

"I wish you were with me to do all those things together." She glanced over to see his response, but he turned away to stroke their Cockapoo, Bert.

"It won't be long. Just a couple more years, and I'll be right by your side."

Judy raised her eyebrows but chose not to push the point. "So, how is the case going?"

"It's going nowhere fast, darling. It's like there's an invisible brick wall preventing us from making any progress. It's infuriating."

"Do you regret taking it on now?" Judy held her breath, hoping the question wouldn't anger him.

Robert shrugged his shoulders, a reply that spoke volumes to both.

"And tell me, how is Michael coping?" Judy said.

Robert paused, caught between wanting to open up to his wife but not wishing to worry her. He decided that complete honesty was the best route. "Keep it between you and me, but I'm worried about him. He's very rarely at the office. He leaves most of the groundwork to us. He's acting erratically, and I'm pretty sure he may be drinking heavily again. And..." Robert paused again.

"And what?"

"I had a phone call from Stacey Shaw this morning. She's the mother of one of the victims. Apparently, Michael's been ringing her a lot, at all times of day and night. He's left a few messages on her phone, and she played some to me. He's clearly drunk or on some sort of substance."

"What is he saying on them, Robert?"

"He's repeating himself over and over. Saying things like, 'Don't you worry, Stacey, I will find these bastards for you. I'm on them now, I know what I have to do,' etcetera, etcetera. He's not saying anything inappropriate, but it's weird and unprofessional.

"She wanted to make an official complaint, and I had to talk her out of it. I told her that I'd speak to him. It's a shambles, if I'm honest. The other two members of the team clearly don't trust him now. They're carrying on regardless, as it's a big opportunity for them, but he's not providing any leadership."

Judy nodded, as if the revelation didn't surprise her.

Robert picked up on her reaction, "Have you heard something, Judy?"

"This also has to stay between you and me. I've been sworn to secrecy."

Robert nodded.

"Paula rang me earlier. She's very concerned."

Robert frowned. "Paula? How does she know about any of this?'

"Michael has been calling her, too, relentlessly. Similar to how you just described, but the messages are even weirder. He keeps saying he's going to find her. He keeps saying he's close and he'll bring her back."

"Who? Bring who back?"

"Josie."

Robert's eyes widened. If Michael truly believed that this case was going to lead him to his missing daughter, then his mental state was even worse than Robert had thought. Judy knelt beside him and put a large, comforting arm around his shoulders.

"I'm worried about you, Robert. You shouldn't be running around at your age in investigations such as this. I know you done it out of loyalty to Michael. I know you two were great friends, but it sounds like he's losing the plot. I'm scared. I don't think you should be involved anymore."

Robert turned and looked deep into her pleading eyes. He knew she was speaking sense. "I should never have taken this case on."

Judy nodded.

"Okay. Well, I don't even know where he is right now. He's probably passed out in a pub somewhere. We've got a meeting first thing in the morning. I'm going to speak to him then and quit the taskforce."

# Thirty-four

Michael watched from behind a tree as his target stopped walking directly next to a narrow, gravel pathway. They looked left to right, scouring the vicinity to see if anyone was watching them, and then darted down it.

"Where are you off to now, Strevens?" Michael whispered under his breath. He jogged to the pathway and peered down it but could only see darkness. He decided to follow, moving as slowly as possible to avoid making a sound.

As he reached the end, he was surprised to see that it opened out into a courtyard area. He tiptoed forwards and saw a small building ahead of him. He moved closer, and realised it was an old scout hut. From its decrepit exterior, it didn't appear to have been used recently. He remembered that Strevens was once an Akela.

Michael crept forwards, gently using his hands to feel his way along the wet wooden slabs of the hut. The surface beneath his fingers changed from wood to wire mesh, causing him to stop in his tracks. He let his eyes refocus. He was standing at a window, covered with wire protection. The curtains inside the hut were drawn, preventing him peering through. He continued onwards, taking even more care with his movements.

Michael froze. The sound of footsteps came from the pathway he had just walked down. There was more than one person, and they weren't bothered about keeping quiet. As they came closer, he heard the voices of two men conversing in what seemed to be an Eastern European accent. Michael looked around for somewhere to hide.

He squinted into the darkness towards the end of the hut and saw a wheelie bin. He scrambled over and knelt behind it, making himself as small as possible.

The men reached the end of the path and strode into the courtyard. Michael heard them walking towards him, and his heart started to pound. He peered around the corner of the bin and realised it was right next to the hut entrance. Michael had hidden in the worst possible place.

The men were now barely one metre from him, separated only by the bin. They stopped outside the entrance door. Michael held his breath as the two men continued talking for what was probably twenty seconds, but to Michael, it felt like a lifetime.

Two cigarettes hit the floor just a few inches from him, and the men walked inside. He peeked over the top of the bin and noticed that the entrance door had not closed properly behind them. There was a gap large enough for Michael to squeeze through without making a sound. What awaited him on the other side was another question entirely.

After a few seconds of contemplation, he knew there was no other option. He crept to the door, breathed in, and slid his frame sideways through the opening.

He found himself in a darkened entrance foyer which smelt of damp. Ahead of him was a pair of white double doors with two small windows through which a light was coming. Michael tiptoed up to them. There were muffled voices coming from the other side, one of which he was sure was Philip Strevens.

Michael pulled his phone out and started to record on his voice memo app, holding it as close as possible to the hinges. He then raised his head up to the window to see what was happening inside.

Four men were sitting on plastic chairs inside a dusty-looking hall. They were engaged in what appeared to be animated discussion. One of them was Strevens. He was the only person not talking and seemed intimidated by the other men, all of whom dwarfed him in size.

The two men whose faces were also visible to Michael were huge, brutish individuals, both wearing leather jackets and mean scowls. Michael glanced at the entrance door to check it was still open, conscious that if he was spotted, he should choose flight over fight.

The fourth man had his back to Michael. It appeared from the conversation that he was arguing with the other two in a foreign language perforated with broken English. Michael couldn't make out the words. He pressed his phone slightly harder into the hinge of the door, hopeful that technology would enable him to transcribe the conversation later.

A phone started ringing from within the hall. One of the two men pulled it out of the inside pocket of their leather jacket and answered. He spoke into it for a few seconds before he stood and walked to the far end of the hall.

The unknown person sat with his back to Michael, stretched out his arms, and turned his head to the side, enabling Michael to get a look at his face. He recognised him instantly. It was Marius.

The man on the phone was now pacing. He had a serious look on his face, as if the caller was bearing bad news. He turned and walked back, directly towards the door from where Michael was watching.

Once more, Michael held his breath as the huge bulk of the man's head passed by the window, enabling Michael to see his scar-filled face in all its aggressive glory.

Michael pondered his next move. Maybe it was time to get out of there; he didn't want to be caught in that place alone. He breathed a sigh of relief as the scar-faced man walked back to the group, hanging up the phone as he went. It wasn't long before Michael's relief turned to horror.

With his right hand, the man pulled out a huge knife from the back of his trousers. In one foul motion, he grabbed Marius from behind with his left arm and pulled his head back so that his throat was exposed. In a clinical swipe, he slit Marius's throat before he had any chance to react. Blood immediately poured from the gaping wound and cascaded onto the ground. Marius grabbed his throat with both hands to try to stem the tide, but it was too late.

Philip Strevens rocked back in his chair, open mouthed. He tried to scream, but no words came out. The man holding the knife pointed it at Strevens and started to walk towards him, a maniacal grin spread over his face.

Michael looked on helplessly. He couldn't overpower these two men, but he needed to do something. He lifted his phone to call for backup but as he did so, the device caught on a screw protruding from the door. It fell from his hand and smashed onto the floor. He looked through the window and prayed again that he hadn't been heard. This time, his prayers went unanswered.

Strevens and the two men turned in Michael's direction. As Marius slumped to the floor, the man who had not carried out the killing stood and sprinted towards the door. Fear shot through Michael; he made a dart for the exit, leaving his phone where it lay.

He barely made it outside before the huge brute burst through both sets of doors and leapt on him. Michael felt gravel embed into his skin as his face crashed into the floor. As he staggered to his knees, his assailant followed up with a huge kick that landed flush on the back of his head.

When Michael came round about ten minutes later, he was inside the hall, sitting on one of the plastic chairs. There was a gag in his mouth, and his hands were tied behind his back. Sat next to him was Philip Strevens, and on the floor was the lifeless body of Marius, lying in a puddle of his own blood.

As Michael's brain refocused, he saw that the man who had attacked him was sitting opposite him, holding the large knife. The other man was on the phone again.

'No, Strevens is still alive. The fucking copper turned up. What do you want me to do, kill the bastard in front of him?"

Michael strained his ears to see if he recognised the voice on the other end of the phone; it wasn't familiar. He could tell, however, that the man was English, and he was furious.

"Has the policeman got a phone on him?"

"Yes," replied the thug. "He dropped it outside, but we found it."

"Okay, that means you need to get him moved. When he doesn't turn up to work, the Old Bill will triangulate for his last position and will swarm that place. This is a fucking problem, Bernard. You need to make sure you clean that hall of all the blood. There cannot be any trace."

Bernard, Michael thought to himself. At last, he had a name, although a fat lot of good it would do him in this position.

"This is not our fault, boss," Bernard barked down the phone angrily. "You told us to kill them here. How should we know there was a pig here?"

"You should have checked, like a professional would. Anyway, you need to move him and Strevens to where we discussed, and you need to clean up and get rid of the body. Don't fuck that up. I need to think tonight how we can clean this mess up. I'll call you tomorrow."

\*\*\*

In Knightsbridge, Richard Banks hung up the phone and felt like the world was caving in on him. "Can these morons do nothing right?" he shouted at David Parkinson, who was sitting next to him with an ashen look on his face.

"This is bad, Richard. Killing a couple of criminals is one thing, but a fucking policeman? That's a whole new level."

"Thanks for your insight, David, very helpful. Need I remind you that this was your idea?!"

The pair sat in near silence for over half an hour, contemplating their next move. Every so often, one of them put forward a suggestion, which the other one shot down instantly. It was then that Banks's phone started to ring again.

"What now?" he shouted without checking who was ringing him.

"Hello, sir. I hear you're in a bit of a pickle," came a calm voice from the other end of the line.

"Toby? How did you hear about it? I hope you're ringing with some sort of solution, otherwise, now's not the time."

"I had a call from Bernard, he told me all about it. I thought I'd better put your mind at rest."

"What do you mean? Speak to me," Richard's heart began to settle. Toby was his most trusted accomplice, a highly skilled operator who he could always relay on.

*Toby Trent was, at the age of 27, already a legend in the underworld hacking community. His deeds had long been whispered about on dark online forums. He was widely regarded as the ultimate internet outlaw, due to his infiltrations into some of the most secure systems on the planet. His real identity was a secret, for he was hunted by crime agencies and criminals alike – a fact he wore as a badge of honour.*

*It was Toby who, years before, had been instrumental in the creation of The Club. He'd created a forum on the dark web where like-minded men could share illegal footage, discuss their darkest desires, and boast about their debauched lifestyle. Banks had instructed him to reach out to fellow members and float the possibility of a secret in person meeting. After much negotiation, the meeting took place one night, with five men who were eager to expand their appetites. Of those five men, three were still members of what they termed 'The Club': Richard Banks, Toby Trent, and Phillip Strevens.*

"Well, I was going to save the good news for our meeting tomorrow, but it seems like you need it quicker than that. Anyway, there's no need to worry. We've got him, sir."

"Got him how?"

"Boss, I've hacked into his deepest darkest secrets, and we've got him like you'll never believe."

"This is no time for riddles, Toby. I need info."

"Let's just say that DCI Michael Dack shares the same taste in women that we do."

# Thirty-five

"Let me guess, he's not turning up again." Matt leant back in his chair and yawned.

"Seriously, how many times are we going to let this slide?" said Nisha. "Have you even heard from him, DI Archer?"

"I've tried to ring him three times this morning, but each call's gone to answerphone," said Rob.

Nisha threw her hands up in the air. Matt shook his head and tutted.

Rob wanted to admonish them for being petulant, but he knew they were right; Michael was becoming a liability to the case. He walked to the front of the room and cleared his throat. "Right, there's obviously a large elephant in the room that needs addressing."

"It's a huge elephant, and the problem is that it's very rarely in the room," Nisha retorted, earning her a scowl from Rob.

"There's clearly something the matter with DCI Dack at the moment, and I promise you I'll get to the bottom of it. I share your anger, and when I speak to him, I'll make it clear that this behaviour can't continue."

Matt was the first to respond. "With all due respect, I think the time for talking to him has passed. His heart clearly isn't in this anymore. I think you should speak to the commissioner and put yourself forwards as Michael's replacement."

Rob saw Nisha nod in agreement, and his heart sunk. He'd arrived this morning with the intention of quitting the taskforce. How could he ditch these two when they needed him the most?

"The best thing for this case would be for Michael to sort himself out and get back on top of it. I know you two don't think so, but he was making some headway behind the scenes. I think there's a lot more going on with this case than even we know," said Rob.

The room fell silent, Nisha and Matt turned to each other. Rob could tell they weren't happy with his explanation, but there seemed to be something else, "If there's anything further you two want to add?"

"Well, there is something." Matt was immediately cut off by Nisha. She'd already told him that she didn't want their concerns raised until they'd had the chance to speak to Harriet Kennedy.

"It's not for now, Matt," she said.

"DS Sharma, if there's anything important going on, I'd like to know."

"It's fine, honestly. I do think you need to speak to the commissioner about Michael's performance though. The longer we let this drift on, the worse it could be."

Rob nodded. "Your point is noted, and I'll give it consideration. Now, let's crack on. DS Gardiner, can you give us an update on where you are with things?"

"We now have Joost set up with all the gear he needs. He's in a little flat not too far from here. I've been popping in from time to time, and he's doing fine. He's confident he'll have the code cracked within a few weeks."

"And what do we think the code will show when we can scan it?"

"We can't tell for sure at this point. It should provide information on what exactly is being scanned and hopefully take us through to the next step that someone would experience when they scanned it. Joost is also confident that as soon as he cracks this, he'll be able to tell exactly who produced the code. Apparently, there are only a few people in the world capable of writing encryptions this sophisticated."

"Okay, good, thanks for the update. How about you, DS Sharma?"

"Well, following on from my meeting with DCS Brian Stock the other day, I've doubled down on my attempts to try to contact Huang Tzao. The authorities over in China are not helpful at all, but I've gone down a different route with the help of my old friend from university who used to live over there. She's helped me access some social media accounts, and I managed to track Huang down. The problem is that all accounts linked to him seem to be inactive. I've reached out to a few of his contacts and left my phone number with them. I'm waiting to hear back."

"What did you make of DCS Stock?"

"He's a complete arsehole. There's something not right about him. Hence the reason I've decided to go up to Liverpool and speak to Alison McKenzie face to face."

"I think that's the right move, DS Sharma. Anything else from your side?"

"That's it from me, sir. How are you getting on?"

"I've decided I'm going to bring Marius Barbaneagra in for questioning in the Claudia Wells investigation."

Nisha frowned. "I thought he was in the Shallow Pond all night and had an alibi? And you said Ruby couldn't be sure it was him from the photo you showed her."

"Bill Lowthy has a solid alibi, Marius doesn't. His phone shows he didn't leave the pub, but that means nothing. He could have quite easily left it there on purpose. And yes, you're correct, Ruby wasn't sure with her identification, but she didn't rule him out either. I think it's worth bringing him in for questioning, even if just to ruffle his feathers a little. What more have we got to go on? It's hardly like we're drowning in evidence here."

Both Nisha and Matt shrugged. They thought the link between the Shallow Pond and the investigation was spurious to say the least, but other lines of enquiry were running thin.

The meeting drew to a close. Rob waited until his colleagues had left before he pulled out his phone and dialled Samantha's number.

"Oh, hello, Rob, I wonder what you could be ringing about."

"Do I ever call about anything else? How is he, Sam?"

"How the hell should I know? You see him more than me nowadays. He didn't come home at all last night. If he does come home, it's normally well past midnight, usually pissed out of his head. I'm sick of it, Rob. I'm close to the end of my tether."

Rob had never heard Sam this angry before. "I haven't heard from him in two days, Sam. His phone's been off, and he didn't turn up for meeting he'd arranged this morning. Have you spoken to him at all in that time?"

"I haven't heard a word from him and to be honest, I'm past caring. We're living separate lives at the moment, and I'm starting to think I'm happier that way. If you're sending out a search party for him, I'd probably start with every gutter outside every pub in North London."

# Thirty-six

As Michael gravitated back into consciousness, the first thing he noticed was a searing pain in the side of his head. He winced and tried to raise his right hand to rub it, but found it was tied to his left hand behind the back of the chair he was sitting on.

The confusion lasted for a few seconds before his memory drifted. He recalled the events in the Scout hut and quickly realised the perilousness of his position.

The room he was currently sitting in was modern looking and clean, although it was sparse, with just a few chairs and a table in the far corner. Michael did not know how long he had been unconscious for, but Bernard and his friend had obviously taken the decision to move him. He noticed that there was no sign of Phillip Strevens or Marius.

The sound of a door swinging open came from behind him. He tried to call out, but the gag in his mouth, stuffed so far in that he could feel it scratch against his tonsils, prevented him from doing so. He heard footsteps approach, and was then sent reeling from a slap delivered to the back of his head.

"DCI Michael Dack," a voice he recognised as Bernard's said, "you have been a naughty boy, haven't you?"

Bernard and his partner appeared from either side of Michael. They grabbed the table and chairs and sat down on them in front of him.

"I'm going to do you a favour and remove that gag from your mouth. Before I do, you should know that there is no-one close enough to hear you and there is no-one who will be able to save you. If you try to scream, we will just inflict more pain. Nod if you understand."

Michael nodded, and Bernard leant forwards and pulled the gag from his mouth.

"Are you surprised you are not dead?"

Michael hesitated. "I'm not sure. You have no reason to kill me."

The other man scoffed. "We never need a reason to kill anyone."

Bernard smirked. "Please forgive Murat's bluntness, and don't worry, we are not planning to kill you. What I am trying to say, though, is… can you think of any reason we why wouldn't? You saw us kill Marius. What good would it do us to keep you alive?"

Michael shrugged.

"Perhaps you need a clue," Murat said, before he beckoned to the back of the room.

Michael heard another set of footsteps approach. A runty-looking man with glasses, dressed in a dirty, baggy t-shirt and oversized jeans appeared from the side of him and placed a laptop on the table. He flipped open the screen and stared at Michael directly in the eyes with a smirk.

"DCI Dack, my name is Toby, and I'm the person who's just ruined your life."

Michael looked at the device in front him and almost vomited. It was his laptop – the one that had been stolen from him outside the Shallow Pond.

Toby's skeletal-like finger reached out and opened a media player. He chose a file and pressed play.

The film was eight minutes and forty seconds long. It opened with a young girl tied to a chair in a darkened room. She was incoherent and erratic, clearly under the influence of some sort of substance. The videographer, out of shot, approached the girl and circled her in a slow and deliberate motion, being sure to capture every inch of her vulnerability. He then returned the camera to its original position, perched on a stand in front of her.

After a moments silence, the videographer began to ask the girl a series of questions: "How old are you, darling? What's your name? Where are you from? Do you like older men?" Bernard, Murat, and Toby all started to snigger.

"Sounds like someone we know," said Toby. Michael winced.

As the video reached four minutes, the questions stopped, and the man stood and walked towards the girl, appearing in shot for the first time. He strode slowly behind her and leant down, grabbing her around the face before kissing her suggestively on the cheek. The identity of the man was clear to see; it was DCI Michael Dack.

"Turn it off, I've seen enough!" Michael shouted out. He knew what happened next. Disgust surged through Michael as the memories of that night three years ago came rushing back.

"Poacher turned gamekeeper," Toby sneered.

"It's not how it seems," Michael said weakly. "She wanted me, she came to me, we were in love. It wasn't about sex. I'm nothing like you lot."

Toby stepped forwards and closed the screen.

"That girl is Simina Albescu. She went missing on the eighteenth of November 2021, and her body has never been found. I need to warn you now that if you do not co-operate with us, or if you try to bullshit us in any way, this video will be on every mainstream media channel by nine o'clock tonight. We will leave you hanging from the ceiling of some crack den in East London in what will appear to be a suicide. Your reputation will be in tatters, your child will grow up knowing what kind of man their father is. Do you understand?"

A tear tumbled from Michael's eye and rolled down his cheek. He nodded his meek compliance back at Toby.

"First of all, where did you take her from?"

Michael stared at the ground in shame. "I took her from a street in Tottenham."

"What's the name of the road? And what time was it? Can you remember anything more specifically about the location of the abduction?"

"Rookery Drive. I can't remember what time exactly, but it was late, past two o'clock in the morning. Everything was shut. All I know is that there was a dry-cleaning shop and a Polish mini market. I don't know if they're still there now."

Toby walked to the back of the room and exited through the door, leaving Michael alone with Bernard and Murat.

"And where is she now?" asked Murat.

"I threw her body out at sea, down in Southend. I took a boat out one morning, weighed her down, and chucked her overboard about three miles from the coast."

Bernard nodded his approval. "Very professional, Michael. Such a shame you had to be silly boy and keep a porno for your pleasure, eh?"

"How did you find out about the Scout hut?" asked Murat.

"I've been following Strevens the last couple of nights. He led me there."

"Why were you following Strevens? What do you know about him?"

"Ever since he came to the police station to press charges, I had my suspicions about him. He said a few things in the interview that didn't seem right."

"Fucking Strevens," Bernard said to Murat. "He should have been put down a long time ago."

The door opened again. Michael turned his head and saw Toby with two other men. "How many more of you lot are here?" he shouted, before he stopped in shock as the men came into view. David Parkinson and Richard Banks.

"Well, well, well, I didn't know you had it in you, Michael. My opinion of you has changed dramatically, I must say," said Parkinson.

Michael was stunned into silence. Lord Peter Marshall had been right.

"He's telling the truth," Toby placed a different laptop down on the table, pressing play on another video. This time, it was CCTV footage, and Michael quickly recognised the scene: Rookery Drive in Tottenham. The date and time at the top of the screen read 18.11.2021, 02:43.

The room watched the scenes unfold as he approached Simina Albescu from behind. Michael couldn't help but be impressed at just how quickly Toby had managed to hack into a CCTV system and locate footage from a few years ago. No wonder this group had operated so efficiently for so long.

As the video finished, David Parkinson turned to Michael. "So, DCI Dack, we have a problem, and we're going to need your help to get us out of it. Your taskforce, however incompetent they are, have somehow been stumbling slowly towards the truth. You have two choices. We need you to work in conjunction with us and help to divert their attention away. If you don't, both videos will get leaked, and your life is over. Are you ready to start answering some questions?"

Michael nodded again.

"Good. Let's begin. Who the hell is Mason Greenwell, and what's he got to do with us?"

Michael frowned. "Mason? He's just a kid. He's got nothing to do with anything."

Parkinson rolled his eyes and glanced at Murat who launched a punch to the side of Michael's head.

"That's not how we play this game, Michael," Parkinson continued. "The only thing you can do is tell us the whole truth. "You must comprehend this."

"I'm sorry. Mason is a friend of Natasha Shaw's brother. He's been helping him get over the death."

"And he's also recruited him to Street Shield by the look of it," Toby said from behind the laptop he had been typing into.

Michael realised he was going to have to offer complete transparency, "Yes, and as I was about to say, he's a part of Street Shield, a paedophile entrapment gang. They were the ones who filmed themselves attacking Strevens. They're just a bunch of street vigilantes."

"Good, we're getting somewhere. Now, tell us, who is this witness you have holed up somewhere?"

"Witness?" The question stumped Michael; he wasn't aware of any witness they had.

"Yes, we know you have one. We've been reliably informed through police sources. You need to tell us who they are and where they've been placed."

It dawned on Michael that they were referring to Joost. He wasn't quite a witness, but he was helping them with their enquiry. How did they know about him?

Sensing his apprehension, Richard Banks stepped forwards and grabbed him around his cheeks aggressively.

"I've got a question, Michael. When was it that you turned?"

"Sorry?"

"When did you turn? When did you become one of us? Was it after you lost your daughter Josie? Did the thought of her being kidnapped by some dirty old man drive you on? Did you want to make others feel the suffering that you did?"

Michael's face twisted. "How dare you speak about her like that! Don't you ever mention her name again! Who the fuck—" He was interrupted by Banks slapping him around the face.

"Listen to me, Michael. We haven't got the time for these games you're playing. We need to know everything about your investigation. We're going to ask you as many questions as we need answering. If you can convince us that we can trust you and if you can prove to us that you're going to be useful going forwards, then we may just allow you to live.

"If not, then we won't be content with simply ruining your life. We've done our research. We know all about your daughter Jacqui and your little stepdaughters, Georgia and Rebecca. They'd fit in quite nicely on our roster. You've already lost your ex-wife one child. You don't want to lose her another, do you?"

# Thirty-seven

Rob slowly pulled his car into the street in Croydon. It was past 9pm, and frost was puncturing the fresh, wintery night. Some of the houses had already started to put up Christmas lights in their gardens.

He was nervous as to what he may find down here. After discovering that Michael's phone was last active in Croydon, it hadn't taken him long to connect the dots. His friend had come down here for Philip Strevens.

What concerned Rob more was the reason for Michael's visit. Was he there to simply tail Strevens? Did he intend to confront him, or were his intentions even darker than that? The way Michael had been acting lately, it would have been no surprise if the combination of elements boiling up inside him had caused him to erupt.

It was of even greater concern that all attempts Rob had made to ring Strevens over the last two days had also fallen flat. He'd driven down here on his own, without any police backup – in case he needed to help his friend out of a predicament.

Rob parked up and looked over at Streven's house. There were no lights on. He checked his phone again to look at Michael's last known location and was confused to see it was over a quarter of a mile away. Maybe he'd turned it off before he'd paid a visit to the house. That thought didn't comfort Rob at all.

He walked up the path and hammered on the front door for a few minutes, but there was no answer; not even a stir from inside. He briefly considered breaking down the front door but was unsure he'd be able to do so without drawing attention. Rob got back into his car and drove to Michael's last location, hopeful it would provide more answers.

He pulled in adjacent to the location spot. There was no building but there was an eerie-looking path leading to a place unknown. As he turned off the ignition, the heckles on the back of his neck rose. Something didn't feel right.

He pulled out his police baton and held it firmly as he walked down the gravelly path, which soon opened out into a courtyard. He crept forwards at a snail's pace now, shining his torch around the area before it came to rest upon the corner of a spooky looking hut.

Rob scanned the torch along the windows of the seemingly empty building before he continued to walk forwards. As he got to the final window, he froze. There was the shadow of a person inside.

Rob paused. Thirty years ago, he would have gone charging in with no concern for his welfare. Now, fully mature and with responsibilities, he no longer possessed that mindset. His hand reached for his police radio, and he came close to calling in backup, but out of loyalty to his friend, he decided against it. What if that was Mike in there? What if he had Strevens tied up in there, or worse? Rob's took a deep breath and tried to calm himself. It was more than likely just a squatter. "Stop being so stupid, Archer," he whispered.

He took his hand off the radio and reaffirmed his grip on the baton. He walked up to the entrance door, and shouted through the gap, "Whoever is in there should make themselves known. I am a police officer, and there is backup on the way." There was no reply.

"I know there is someone in there. Make yourself known now and come out with your hands up. If you are a squatter, I promise you that you're not in trouble."

Again, there was no answer. If it was Mike, he would surely have recognised Rob's voice.

"I'm going to enter the building now," he shouted. "If you are in there, you should make yourself known to me or risk further action." Rob waited for a few seconds and then edged forwards through the door, shining his torch around the small entrance hall. He saw double doors ahead of him that led to the main hall. He pushed them open and stepped inside.

Rob shone the torch around the hall like a prison spotlight searching for escaped felons. There was nothing except some discarded sports equipment. He shone the torch on every single area he could find. The light created a dancing display of shadows as it ricocheted off walls and windows. There was still no sign of life. Maybe the figure inside had been a trick of the light.

Rob's torch then skirted over a scene that caught his attention. In the middle of the floor, were four chairs positioned to face each other.

He stepped forwards to inspect them, still scouring the room for any sign of movement. He bent down and put his hand on each one to check for warmth, but the surface was freezing cold. There certainly hadn't been anyone sitting on them in the last few minutes.

Out of nowhere, he was startled out of his skin. From the far end of the room came the sound of footsteps sprinting. Rob spun, expecting to be attacked, but his torch caught the back of a figure running across the hall and through the exit.

"Stop!" Rob shouted and started to run after the person, but he was too old and too slow. By the time he reached the courtyard, the stranger had already disappeared down the path. By the time Rob reached the street, there was no-one to be seen. "Fuck it!" he shouted, exasperated at his failure to catch the person but relieved that he was out of the hut and any potential danger.

He stood on the street for a minute or so, gathering his thoughts. There was only one logical solution left. He got back into his car and dialled Suzanne Morgan's number.

"DI Archer, to what do I owe this rare pleasure?"

"Hi, ma'am, sorry for ringing your mobile, but I thought it shouldn't wait."

"Oh dear, that sounds ominous. Go on."

"I'm afraid to say that we've got a bit of a problem with Michael."

There was a pause from Suzanne's side of the phone before she replied. "Right, and what seems to be the problem?"

"I don't know where he is. He's been missing for a few days now. I can't get through to him on his mobile. I'm starting to get worried."

The pause from Suzanne was longer this time. Rob closed his eyes and braced himself for the verbal backlash, but it did not come. Her reply was almost jovial.

"That is a huge surprise that you can't find him."

"I know, I've been looking everywhere I can think of."

"Well, you can't have been looking hard enough. Are you sure you're still up to being a detective?"

"Pardon?"

"I'm sitting with Michael now. He's right opposite me. I'll put it on speaker phone for you."

"What?" Rob stuttered out.

"Hello, Rob, no need to panic, mate, I'm here at the station," Michael's voice bellowed out, clearer and chirpier than he'd sounded in ages.

Rob's surprise gave way to anger at the casual way Michael introduced himself, "We've been worried sick about you. Where have you been?"

"You couldn't have been that worried, mate. You didn't tell Suzanne or any other Old Bill to come looking for me. Anyway, I'm fine. Get yourself home and be ready for a briefing at nine AM tomorrow. We've got a case to crack."

# Thirty-eight

She felt like she hadn't slept in days. There were the irregular lurches from consciousness into semi-consciousness, but these lasted barely a few seconds. They were just long enough for her mind to slip into some alternative world, a place that was better than where she currently lay. She couldn't remember the last time she'd had meaningful sleep. The memory of those blissful few seconds when she used to wake was now just a distant recollection.

She had accepted that this was her life. There was no pretence now that she would ever escape this confinement. There were no remaining fantasies about revenge. There was no hope. She had banished it from her brain. It was the hope that hurt the most.

The door at the end of the corridor clanged open. She stared expressionlessly at the wall in void acceptance.

She did not baulk at the footsteps. She did not care if it was her door that opened. She gave not a second's thought to the monsters on the other side of the walls. She was empty inside.

The screams started from next door, but where that noise would once pierce through her soul, it was now an irrelevant whisper in the cold, dark wind that crashed against her skull. If she'd had her wits about her, she would have noticed that the screams were different this time. They were more anguished, even more terrified.

"Noooo, please, don't do it! Don't do it! I'll do anything you want, please, don't kill me.'

The words finally registered with her. What did she mean, don't kill her? That was not what they did.

She cocked her head to listen closer. The next sound she heard was one she would never forget: a plunging noise followed by a scream, and then a sound like gurgling. Her eyes sprung open. Did they kill her?'

The sound of something dropping to the floor was followed by more thrusts and strikes and kicks. The girl could not be heard anymore, but a noise rang up from the other rooms: a murmur which morphed into a whimper and then developed into full blood-curdling screams as the other girls realised what had just taken place.

She stayed quiet; she wasn't scared, she wasn't sad. The overwhelming emotion was jealousy. She was jealous that her neighbour had managed to escape from this hellhole. Why her? she pleaded inside. Why couldn't they take my life?

She heard the men exit the room, dragging the body with them.

"Shut the fuck up, or you'll be next," one of them shouted.

That was the invite she needed. She started to scream as loudly as she could, the only girl still doing it, but the men continued walking down the hall, ignoring the threat they had just made.

Fury grew within her. She could not go on any longer. She lowered her head and charged at the wall in front of her, hoping she would be able to damage herself fatally.

Pain shredded down her spine at the first effort as she bounced back from the collision. Weak and delirious, she felt the blood begin to trickle down her head. Maybe this could work; maybe she could bleed to death. She stepped back, lowered her head, and charged at the wall again.

# Thirty-nine

"Good morning, DS Sharma. Have you missed me?"

Nisha wasn't sure what surprised her more – the cheeriness in Michael's voice or that he was in the office before her. "Good morning, guv. It's nice to see you here," she said politely but firmly.

"Nice to see me *at this time*, you mean?"

"Nice to see you at all. I was beginning to wonder if you'd taken yourself off the investigation."

"I know I have some explaining to do. Let's wait for the other two to arrive, and I'll talk you through what I've been working on."

"Well, it better be good, guv. I'm going to grab a coffee before we start. Do you want one?"

"Black, no sugar, please. Make it strong."

The greeting from Rob and Matt as they arrived was equally frosty. When everyone was sitting down, Michael stood to address the room.

"The first thing I'd like to do is apologise. I've obviously been uncontactable for a few days, and my behaviour has been erratic the last few weeks. I'm sorry for this. It's unprofessional and disrespectful to you all. I won't try to make excuses for it, but all I will say is that I had my reasons."

His three colleagues had the same muted response: a slow nod of the head combined with pursed lips. None of them had expected an apology like this, especially Rob, who knew from experience just how hard Michael found it to say sorry.

"I'm sure you'll be pleased to hear that I return with a renewed vigour for this case. I am more confident than ever that we are on the verge of cracking this thing."

Rob wasn't convinced. Michael's performance seemed fake. Michael was a born pessimist. He felt he had to say something, "Are you sure that's not just because you've been sober for a few days?" It's all well and good being optimistic until you're at the bottom of a bottle again."

"I appreciate your concern, but I promise you that there is a reason for my absence, and believe it or not, it has brought us closer to solving this investigation."

"I'm not having it, mate. Do you expect me to believe that you've been on some undercover operation or something? It's not acceptable, Mike. This team needs consistency and leadership."

Nisha and Matt exchanged awkward looks; they had never heard the two friends argue before.

"I understand your anger, Rob. I'm not going to pretend I've been working efficiently these last few weeks. I've been in a dark place, and you're right, most of it was at the bottom of a bottle. I'm out the other side now though."

"Share the progress with us, then," Rob shouted back.

"I'm sorry, I can't do that yet."

The answer earned an exasperated sigh from Rob who flung his arms up in the air.

"I just need you to trust me," Michael continued. "I know I've done nothing in this case yet to earn that, especially from you two, DS Gardiner, DS Sharma. I've asked too much of you already without giving enough back, but please, bear with me. The end is in sight."

Silence fell upon the room. Nisha and Matt wanted to trust Michael, but they'd been burnt by their experience of working with him. They looked at Rob for guidance on how to react.

Rob glared at Michael, aware that the onus was on him to make the first move. Eventually, he turned to both detective sergeants. "Would you mind giving me and DCI Dack the room? We've got some things we need to iron out."

Nisha and Matt didn't need asking twice. As the door closed behind them, Rob pulled his chair closer to Michael.

"How long have I known you, Mike?"

"You know the answer to that."

"Humour me."

"Over forty years now."

"And how many times have you tried to lie to me over those years?"

"Are we calling them lies? That insinuates a deviance. I prefer to call—"

"—Just answer the fucking question."

"I don't know exactly. I'd have to say multiple."

"Too many to count. And how many times have you got away with lying to me?"

"Never. You always know when I'm lying."

"Exactly. So, why do you think you can lie to me now?"

Michael stared into Rob's unflinching eyes. "Rob, I'm not lying to you, I just can't tell you the whole truth. I will be able to soon, and I swear to you on my daughter's life that these last few days have seen me make serious progress on unmasking the identity of these criminals."

Michael congratulated himself on the clever wording of his answer, none of which was false. He watched as Rob analysed his facial expressions and tone, in the way that only detectives could do.

"Why didn't you check in with us, Mike? We were worried."

"I can't tell you why yet."

"Samantha was worried, even Paula was worried."

"Oh, shit, you didn't call Paula, did you?"

"I didn't know what else to do. I thought you were in a ditch somewhere." Rob paused. He wanted to tell Michael that he'd followed his path to Croydon, but something told him not to. "I came in here today with the intention of quitting. It's been on my mind for a few days now, but I haven't been able to speak to you."

"You can't quit now, Rob. We're so close, I promise."

"The family want me to, and I want to. I'm over it all. I'm too old, and I don't care anymore."

"Now you're lying to me. Not about the age thing, you're right on that. But I know you still care. You always have done. It's what makes you a great policeman, mate." Michael leant forwards and put both of his arms onto Rob's shoulders, "I can see in your eyes that you want to nail these bastards. I promise you from the bottom of my heart, we will do this, and it will be soon."

Rob shook his head, "Why do I fall for this shit every time?"

"Because you know I'm right, and you'd never forgive yourself if you walked away now and left this case unsolved."

Rob pretended to consider it, but he already knew what his response would be, and so did Michael.

"I just need you to help me convince the other two to see this through. They have to be onboard with us," said Michael.

"They've never been offboard. It's a real shame that you can't see that." With that, Rob stood and walked towards the kitchen, already fretting about how he would break the news to Judy.

Michael sat back and smiled. He decided he'd treat himself to a cigarette.

He got outside and walked to the far corner of the car park, away from any prying ears. He pulled out a new mobile phone, looked around to check the vicinity, and then dialled a number.

"How did it go?" the voice on the other end barked.

"I got away with it, David, they don't suspect a thing."

"Very good. From our side, the first part of the plan has gone ahead as discussed. The next part is down to you. You know what needs to be done."

Michael's heart sunk as he remembered what the first part of the plan was, but he was too deep to have second thoughts. This was now about survival.

"Yes, sir, I know what needs to be done."

"Don't mess this up, DCI Dack. It's your only chance of keeping your life as it is."

Who said he wanted to keep his life as it was? Michael thought as he hung up the phone.

# Forty

It was the third ring that finally registered in Nisha's head and nudged her out of the deep sleep she was currently enjoying. It took a further two rings before her brain stuttered into gear. Someone was calling her. What time was it?

She fumbled clumsily for the device on the bedside table, nearly knocking over her glass of water in the process. She squinted through the dark at the illuminated screen. The time was 3.53am. The number ringing began with an overseas dialling code: 0086.

Nisha frowned. She briefly considered not answering, angry that the one good night's sleep she'd had in a while had been disturbed. Curiosity, though, as so ever with Nisha, got the better of her.

"Hello?"

"Hello, I am looking to speak to Detective Sergeant Nisha Sharma, please." The softly spoken female voice had a succinct accent that Nisha placed as East Asian in origin.

"You're speaking to her. How can I help?"

"You left a message on my Weibo account about Huang."

Nisha sprang upright. It had been nearly six weeks since she'd sent messages to several of Huang's contacts on Weibo, a Chinese social media site, but she hadn't received one response – until now.

"Thank you for getting in touch. Can I ask your name, please? Are you a friend of Huang? Do you know where he is?"

There was a pause at the end of the line. "Is anyone else listening to this call?"

The question confused Nisha. "No, this is my mobile phone. I'm currently at home."

"But are your calls recorded or listened to? I need to know I'm speaking in complete confidence."

"Yes, I can assure you the call is in complete confidence. Don't worry, I don't need your name, I just need to find Huang. Can you help me?"

"They do not need my name to track me, they just need my voice. I need you to promise me that I'm not being recorded."

Nisha's confusion grew. What did she mean by 'they'?

"I promise, it's just you and me speaking, no recording. What is your concern? Is Huang okay?"

"Huang is dead, Detective Sergeant. He was killed around two years ago."

"Killed? What happened? And if he's dead, why is his Weibo account still active like he's alive?"

"Because that's how they want it to seem."

"Who are 'they'?"

"Surely you must know. This all started after he came to your country, after all."

"Look, I'm a little bit lost here. Let me get a pen so I can take this down."

"I don't have time to answer questions, Detective Sergeant, I just wanted to let you know that he is no longer around."

"Wait, please just give me a few seconds. Can you tell me how he died?"

"Officially, it was a heart attack, but that's just how they operate. We all know he was poisoned."

"Poisoned? But why? What was he involved in? And who you mean by 'they'?"

"After Huang returned from holiday in England, he told his friends that he had witnessed a serious crime. A few days afterwards, he was contacted by Chinese authorities. He never told us exactly what was said, but his whole personality changed after that. He became paranoid. He was convinced he was being followed. Just two weeks later, he was killed."

"What makes you so convinced that he was…" Nisha trailed off as she heard a click at the end of the phone. "Hello? Hello?" The line was dead. Nisha tried to dial the number back, but it would not connect.

She turned on her bedside lamp, thoughts racing through her head. Could the caller be trusted? Surely Huang's death was nothing to do with the case? There was no actual proof that he was poisoned or even dead.

The conversation had unsettled her. There was something about the caller's voice, calm and measured, but demonstrably scared, which gave Nisha some faith in it. She weighed up her options. There was zero chance of her getting back to sleep now.

She had no way of following the lead up, that much was obvious. Tracing the phone number would have to involve the co-operation of the Chinese police and was therefore virtually impossible.

Nisha rose slowly out of bed and trudged to the bathroom, still undecided on what the best move should be. She stepped into the shower, deciding she may as well go into the office and get some work done.

After two minutes of hot water cascading onto her, she had a better idea. She cut her shower short and hurriedly wrapped herself in towel before opening the National Rail website on her laptop. The first train leaving from London Euston to Liverpool Lime Street was at 5:13am, just over an hour's time. "Perfect," she said out loud before booking a seat. "It's time to meet Alison McKenzie."

Two hours later, Nisha was staring out of the train window at the English countryside flashing by. The early morning sun was just starting to rise, illuminating the rolling fields with bold cracks of light, creating a masterpiece of sullen beauty from the dark desolation that had been in place just minutes before.

Nisha had never been to Liverpool before; she'd barely been farther north than Birmingham. She wondered what sort of city would greet her when she disembarked.

The train pulled into the platform; Liverpool Lime Street Station was bustling. Nisha was the first passenger out of the carriage door, and the freezing air hit her instantly, catching her by surprise. She knew it was colder up north, but this felt like a temperature she'd never experienced before.

That unmistakable pre-Christmas vibrancy hung in the air. Even though the big day was still over four weeks away, a buzz and vigour perpetuated through people, a tangible excitement at the season of festivity that lay ahead. It warmed her inside. Christmas was her favourite time of year. She let out a smile then realised it was the first time she'd smiled in weeks. It evaporated almost as soon as it arrived.

The taxi rank was directly next to her platform. She was surprised to see the majority of them were black hackney carriages, just like she was used to back home. She'd previously thought that was solely a London trademark.

"142 Sefton Park Road, please," she said to the driver as she climbed inside the cab.

"No worries, love, I'll get you there in just a jiffy," came the jovial reply from the elderly Scouse driver. "How was your journey? You come from London, have you?"

"Yes, not bad, thank you," Nisha stammered out. The friendly tone of the man's voice threw her. She was used to her drivers being moody and untalkative.

After a twenty-minute journey in which she barely managed to get a few words in, but was given the history of music concerts that had taken place in Sefton Park, the driver finally parked up.

"Here we go, love, number 142 is just there. That'll be twelve quid please."

The door at 142 opened to reveal a small, nervous-looking woman still dressed in her pyjamas.

"Alison McKenzie?" said Nisha.

"Erm, yes. Who's asking?"

"DS Nisha Sharma. We spoke briefly on the phone. Is it all right if I come in?" Nisha noticed Alison's face drop.

"Oh, it's a bit of bad time, to be honest. I told you all I could on the phone."

"Please, Alison. I've travelled all the way up from London this morning to see you. I promise I won't be too long. I just need a bit of professional courtesy from a fellow copper."

"Professional courtesy? Is that what you lot have been giving me since I left the force? I just want you all to leave me alone."

Nisha stepped forwards. "What do you mean 'leave you alone'? Who's been bothering you, Alison? I want to get to the bottom of this."

Alison sighed. She craned her neck and looked each way down the road before she turned back to Nisha. "Go on then, I guess you'd better come in."

# Forty-one

Matt walked into the taskforce office and was surprised to see Michael and Rob chatting excitedly in the corner with Commissioner Morgan.

"What's going on?" Matt shouted across the office.

"I've just had a call from an informant with some strong intel," said Michael. "Don't bother taking your coat off, we're heading out. Where's DS Sharma?"

"I got a text from her this morning. She's gone up to Liverpool to speak to Alison McKenzie."

"Typical. She's going to miss a big day."

"Why, what's happened?"

"We're going down to Croydon. We've got a lead on a missing girl."

"Bloody hell. How strong is the tip off?"

"Strong enough," Suzanne Morgan butted in. "Now, stop your chinwagging and get down there. Uniform are already on their way and will position themselves outside the house until you arrive."

The journey to Croydon was quiet, a complete contrast to how a police car would usually be on the way to a bust. As Matt weaved through the dense, early morning London traffic, he couldn't help but notice that Rob had barely spoken a word. His face in the rear-view mirror looked anxious. Matt hadn't seen him like this before. He felt the need to break the awkward silence, "So, what's the info you received, guv?"

"One of our suspects has been spotted walking into his house with a young girl. Funny thing is, he lives alone and has no young female relatives," said Michael.

"Suspects? We barely had any suspects," Matt said.

"You may not have done, but I did. Take this left, this is the road."

As they parked up, Rob glanced at the house, and a feeling of dread spread over him. He'd knocked at that same door just two

174

weeks ago but hadn't investigated any further. If Michael's informant was right, and Strevens was holed up inside with a girl, then Rob could have missed an opportunity to save her. He pushed the thought to the back of his mind and prayed the information was wrong.

Two police cars pulled into the road and parked up. A woman exited one of them and approached the taskforce with three uniformed policemen following behind her.

"DCI Dack? I'm DS Loughter." She held her hand out for Michael to shake.

"Pleasure to meet you. Have you been monitoring the house?"

"Yes, for the last thirty minutes or so. No sign of movement whatsoever."

"Okay, thank you. Set up a perimeter, and block the entrance to the road. Have you got an enforcer with you for the door?"

"We have. DS Garrett, can you grab the ram, please?" she shouted over at her colleague.

"You come with us, son. The rest of you be prepared in case anyone tries to run," said Michael.

They approached the front door, and Michael hammered on it. After waiting a few seconds and hearing no movement inside, he hammered again. "Phillip Strevens, are you inside?"

Again, there was no answer. Michael looked over at DS Garrett. "You're up, son."

The young man stepped forwards and swung the enforcer at the door, aiming directly at the lock. It took only two swings before the door came flying off its hinges, and all four men sprinted inside.

"DI Archer, you and DS Gardiner sweep down here. I'll go with DS Garrett upstairs," Michael shouted out. The house was small, and there were only three rooms for them to investigate on the first floor: a bathroom, bedroom, and an office space. They began to check the bedroom but were stopped by Matt's voice shouting from downstairs.

"Guv, get down here, now!"

Michael flew down the stairs, almost tripping over as he did. They ran towards the back of the house and saw Rob walk out of a small room. Michael tried to speak to him, but Rob brushed past, unresponsive, an ashen look on his face.

Michael took a deep breath and walked in. It was dirty, and sparse, containing just a bed and a bedside table. Matt was standing over the bed with his back to Michael. He held his police radio in his hand, as if he was about to make a call but hadn't yet found the will to do it. Michael soon saw why.

The bed was not empty. There were two bodies lying in it, two heads resting on a stained pillow. Both had their eyes open. Neither of them were breathing. One of the bodies was Phillip Strevens; the other was Claudia Wells.

# Forty-two

Nisha walked into the taskforce office at 4pm to be greeted by darkness. The team must still be down in Croydon, she thought.

She contemplated driving to Strevens's house but deduced that this would be a decision based on the fear of missing out rather than one made for practical reasons. SOCO would be all over the crime scene by now. There was nothing she could contribute that they wouldn't be able to.

She walked to the kitchen to make herself a coffee. At the far end of the corridor a group of colleagues were gathered, staring at the wall-mounted TV.

"Breakthrough at last. You must be happy, Nisha?" said one of the group.

Nisha nodded back and smiled. She looked up at the screen to see that David Parkinson had just taken his place to address the media.

"Thank you for coming here at such short notice. I am pleased to confirm that we have today made a major breakthrough in the investigation into—"

"He wastes no time, does he?" Nisha shook her head.

"I am, however, afraid to say that in making this breakthrough, there has been another victim. We found the body of Claudia Wells, the young girl who was recently abducted from the streets of Hackney.

"We also found a body of a man. We will reveal his identity in the near future. Through combing his house, and seizing his computer equipment, we have found firm evidence that he was responsible for the spate of crimes against young girls in London, dating back over the last three years. Although it appears that he acted alone in the majority of his crimes, we are also actively seeking another person of interest, who may have been his accomplice in the kidnapping of Claudia..."

As Parkinson droned on, Nisha's face screwed up. 'He's talking like the whole investigation has been solved. There are still missing girls out there.'

"I would like to thank both Commissioner Suzanne Morgan and DCI Michael Dack, who I will welcome to the stage in a moment. Their tireless work together…"

Nisha couldn't listen any longer. She stormed back to the taskforce office, shoved open the door and let out a scream. Unable to work, she sat silently stewing for over an hour before Rob entered and walked straight to his desk without acknowledging her. Matt followed shortly behind.

"So, job done then, yeah? We may as well pack up and go home. Phillip Strevens, criminal mastermind. Who would have thought it?" Nisha said, turning back to her computer.

"Why do you say it like that? We've had a good result. You should be happy," said Matt.

"Oh, come on, mate. You don't seriously think he was the kingpin in all this, do you? Doesn't anything here seem a bit suspicious to you?" Nisha noticed Rob's ears prick up.

"Not really, no. It sounds to me like you're just annoyed you weren't there when we made the bust," said Matt.

"So, there's three years of investigation yielding no clues at all, then suddenly, Michael gets an anonymous call out of nowhere, and lo and behold, it leads straight to the perpetrator. Oh, and he just happens to conveniently be with one of the victims at that time. And, by the way, I wouldn't really call it a bust."

"What would you call it, then?"

"Well, they were both dead, weren't they? It's not like you had to do anything. How did they die?"

"Strevens assaulted her, stabbed her multiple times, and then poisoned himself. We found an empty vial next to the bed."

"So, he just suddenly decided to kill himself, did he? Why on earth would he do that?"

"His note said that he couldn't take it anymore. He felt the police were closing in on him, and he couldn't risk being caught. He took Claudia as his last victim."

"Ah, yes, the note. Let me guess, he confessed to all the other crimes in it as well, I suppose?"

"Don't condescend me, Nisha."

"I don't feel like I have a choice. You can't see the woods for the trees. Go on then, what did the note say?"

"Yes, he confessed to nearly all the other crimes. The only one he didn't was Simina Albescu."

"Of course he did. And the note was in his handwriting, was it?"

"It was typed out, but he'd signed it, and yes, we checked that the signature matched."

"Ever heard of a forged signature before?"

"Can you turn down the sarcasm a few notches and actually tell me what you're trying to say?"

Nisha ignored him. "So, in this note, what did he say happened to all the other girls?"

"He admitted to killing them."

"Perfect, but let me guess, he didn't say where he'd buried them."

Matt paused.

"Of course he didn't," Nisha shouted.

"I don't know why you're getting angry at me, Nisha."

"For fuck's sake, can't you see? Something stinks here!"

"Shut up!" a voice bellowed out from the corner. In the heat of their slanging match, they'd forgotten that Rob was in the room. "You're bickering like two schoolchildren."

"Well, I'm sorry, but let's have your opinion here. Doesn't it smell a bit funny to you?" said Nisha. "And why are you so cut up about it? You know something's wrong, don't you?"

Rob ignored the question. He wasn't ready to admit that he'd been banging on Strevens's door recently, "What did you find out in Liverpool, DS Sharma?"

"I met with Alison McKenzie."

"And?"

Nisha paused. "This stays between these four walls, okay?"

Both men nodded.

"She is adamant that there is corruption running through Whitehall and the Metropolitan Police."

Matt shook his head, but Rob remained unmoved.

"When she was working on this case originally, she felt like every attempt to investigate was blocked. Witnesses disappeared or refused to talk. Evidence would go missing. She kept getting put onto other minor cases rather than being allowed to concentrate on this. She raised her concerns to Brian Stock, but he admonished her. He told her to back down, or he would ruin her career. She was terrified of him. She said he was a bully."

"Okay, so a DCC was overbearing. So what?" said Matt.

"She tried to go above his head and express her concerns to another senior officer, but that only made it worse. That was when it started."

"What started?" asked Rob.

"A campaign of harassment. She started getting people knocking on her house at all hours of the night. Faeces posted through her letterbox and left in her locker at work. She was sure she was being followed by strange men. Eventually, she couldn't take it anymore. She quit and moved up to Liverpool. And additionally..." Nisha trailed off.

"Additionally what, DS Sharma?" Rob snapped.

"She was convinced there was someone influential involved in helping to block the investigation. Either someone in the Met or somewhere even higher."

"Not Brian Stock?"

"She thought it went above him."

"Did she get any proof of this?"

"No, but she was convinced of it."

Matt scoffed. "So, you won't believe the evidence of a dead body and a written confession, but you'll believe the words of a bitter ex-policewoman who was probably too weak to do the job?"

Nisha spun to face him. "That's how you see policewomen, is it? Weak and bitter?"

"You know I didn't mean it like that."

Nisha turned back to face Rob. "I know you don't want to hear this, but..."

"Don't say it, DS Sharma."

"You know how strangely he's been acting though. I get he's your friend, but come on, an informant message out of nowhere that leads us right to a dead body?"

Rob stayed silent.

"Did he ever tell you why he brought Strevens in for questioning in the first place?"

Rob remained silent.

"I can see that you're suspicious, DI Archer."

"You're mistaken, DS Sharma. But we need to remain vigilant. Matt, check on Joost. We need him to come through with something. Now, listen, both of you. What we just discussed must remain amongst us, do you understand?"

# Forty-three

Michael afforded himself a smile as he walked into the car park and lit up a celebratory cigarette. His performance at this press conference had been a lot more polished than his first one. Even Rebecca and Georgia may not be embarrassed by him.

"I need a word, Mike."

The voice came out of nowhere and made Michael jump. He turned around to see Rob who had a serious look on his face. "Of course, mate. What's up?"

"Not here." Rob motioned over to the corner of the car park.

"I need to know who your informant is, Mike."

"What do you mean, mate? You know I can't tell you that."

"Don't give me that bullshit. We've broken a thousand rules in our lifetime. What's your problem with telling me this?"

"It's not about the rules, mate. I promised the guy I wouldn't tell anyone. He doesn't trust the police at all."

"Oh, but he trusts you, though, yeah?"

"What is that supposed to mean?"

"Just tell me who it is."

"We've just had the biggest breakthrough of our career, and you're out here questioning me like this?"

Michael tried to walk past him, but Rob pushed him back. The frustration that had been simmering inside him the last few weeks finally boiled over. He flew forwards and grabbed Michael around the collar, throwing him against the wall.

"Enough of this. Tell me now who the informant is, or I am done. With you and this case."

Michael held his arms out by his side. "What is wrong with you?"

"You're hiding something from me, and you've been doing it for a while. You begged me to sign up on this case, and now you're treating me like a mug. I'm going to give you one more chance. Why did you first suspect Philip Strevens of being involved in all this?"

"For god's sake, Rob. It was Mason Greenwell."

Rob frowned, and his grip on Michael loosened. "Mason Greenwell? The bloke from Street Shield?"

"Yes. I haven't told anyone because it's a bit embarrassing getting information from some vigilante. No one would give him any credibility, but he's been absolutely spot on. That was why Street Shield beat up Strevens. Greenwell found out that Strevens was a key player in this paedophile ring."

Rob paused. "Who told you there was a girl spotted at Strevens's house?"

"Greenwell. One of his group was staking it out. Why are you so cut up about it anyway, Rob? Why are you acting like this?"

"Because I was at his fucking door. I was knocking on it. There was no answer. If I'd have banged it down, I may have been able to save her."

Michael frowned. "When were you there?"

"When you went missing. I followed your phone signal down to Croydon to try to find you. I went to his house because I thought you might have done something stupid. Then I went to that Scout hut."

Michael's pulse quickened. "What Scout hut?"

"Your phone signal led me down an alley to some abandoned hut. That's why I've been so messed up today. I'm feeling guilty. I'm sick to death of this job. I want off it."

Michael sensed the weakness in his friend. He gently pushed his arms away and then enveloped him in a bearhug. Rob buried his face into Michael's shoulder and started to sob.

"You have nothing to feel guilty about, Rob. It's not your fault. She probably wasn't even there that night. You've been fantastic on this case. And guess what? We've caught the bad guy again. That's why I wanted you with me. Because we get results."

"This is the last one, Mike. I swear, I'm done now," Rob sobbed.

"Of course, mate, that's fine. We'll put this to bed very soon, now we've got Strevens. We'll soon catch his accomplice, and the case will be closed. You can retire a hero and settle down to help raise your grandchild. When's she due again?"

"Fifth January, just five weeks now." Rob pulled his face from Michael's shoulder and started to wipe away his tears.

"Five weeks. That's amazing, mate. Your whole life is mapped out now. You can leave policework behind you. Now, look, why don't we go have a few quiet beers to celebrate?"

Rob wiped his nose and nodded. "Can we go to the Cock and Dragon in Cockfosters? It'll be easy for me to get home from there. I don't fancy a late one."

"Of course we can. Are you ready to go now?"

"Let me just go back inside and get my things."

Michael waited until Rob was out of sight before he took his phone out and dialled David Parkinson's number.

"Well, I think that went rather well, old chap." Parkinson's voice made Michael feel sick whenever he heard it.

"It did, but we have a little issue. I've just found out that DI Archer has been to the scout hut. Are we sure it was properly cleaned after the incident? I'm worried he'll decide to go back."

"I was promised it was cleaned thoroughly, but we can arrange for them to go down again if you like?"

Michael paused. "Hold off on that for a minute. I've just had another idea."

Rob made sure that the tears were no longer visible before he walked back into the office. Only Nisha was in there.

"Where's DS Gardiner? Rob asked.

"He's gone to check on Joost, like you asked him to."

"Okay, well, you can tell him when you speak to him that your thoughts on Strevens are completely wrong. I've just spoken with DCI Dack and found out who his informant was. It's all legit."

"What? But how do you know it's legit?"

"Just trust me on this, DS Sharma. I've met the informant before and know how he gets his info. Now, please drop your suspicions and be happy that this case is nearly over. I know I am."

# Forty-four

Just over a mile away from Scotland Yard, Matt arrived at Joost's front door. The safehouse was a one-bedroom flat in a rundown housing estate with one of the highest crime rates in London. Matt chuckled at the irony of a safehouse located in one of the most dangerous places in the capital.

"Hey, buddy," Joost answered the door in jovial fashion, greeting Matt with a friendly high five. He'd been locked down in this flat for nearly two months now, and Matt was the only human interaction he'd had during this time.

"I bring supplies," Matt announced proudly, walking through the door with two carrier bags, one full of food and the other of alcohol. "I hope you fancy a drink."

"I'm Dutch, of course I do. Beer to start?"

"Beer to start," said Matt, cracking open two cans of Stella Artois and handing one to Joost. He took a seat on an armchair in the corner of the room and let out a sigh.

"Long day?" said Joost.

"You could say that."

"Well, you'll be pleased to know that I am getting very close to cracking this code, my friend. I think I'll have it done in a week or so."

"I take it you haven't watched the TV today?"

"Are you taking the piss? How am I meant to watch this thing you left me with?" Joost pointed to an ancient-looking television in the corner.

"Good point. Well, we've actually made a major breakthrough today. In fact, we think we've found the main guy." Matt noticed a worried look spread across Joost's face. "Oh, don't worry, it won't affect your deal with us. We'll still need your evidence to put the case together. Not that the accused will have much say in it. We found him dead, cuddled up with one of his victims."

Joost frowned. "You think there's just one guy?"

"Well, he maybe had an accomplice. We're still looking into that."

They tucked into the alcohol for the next few hours, going through beer and wine in excessive fashion. It got to 10pm and Matt decided to order a Chinese takeaway and some more wine.

"Matt, tell me about the guy you caught today," Joost slurred.

"You know I can't do that. It's confidential."

"Ah, come on, who am I going to tell? You're the only person I ever speak to. I may be able to give an opinion."

Matt thought about it for a few seconds and concluded that Joost was right.

For the next twenty minutes, Matt unburdened everything about the case. He veered from Phillip Strevens and Nisha's concern about him, to Alison McKenzie and her belief of an influential VIP running things. By the time the takeaway arrived, Joost had received the full debrief.

As they started to eat, Joost broke his silence, "You do know that your friend Nisha is right, don't you?"

"What do you mean?"

"There is no way that someone like Phillip Strevens and a friend could be running this operation."

"Why do you say that?"

"The level of technological expertise alone is mind boggling. The finances behind this operation would have to be huge."

"He works in IT."

Joost started laughing. "My friend, I don't think you understand. The encryption on this bracelet is something that probably only five or ten people in the whole world would be able to produce, and their expertise will not come cheap. I guarantee you that anyone with that ability or knowledge is not living in a one-bed flat in Croydon fixing computers for a living."

Matt dropped his fork and stared at Joost.

Joost stopped talking, stared back at Matt directly in the eye, and then stuffed a whole pork ball into his mouth, which caused them both to drunkenly burst out laughing.

They were interrupted when Matt received a message. He squinted at the screen. Michael had sent a photo to the taskforce WhatsApp group chat: him and Rob in a pub together, smiling and chinking a glass of whisky. The quote underneath the photo read 'Remember - Taskforce Christmas Party - This Friday. Attendance is compulsory.'

# Forty-five

Bill Lowthy was about to ring the bell for last orders. He'd been dreaming of this moment for the last few hours. It had been a long Thursday night and surprisingly busy by Shallow Pond standards. Bill put the increase in custom down to today being the first day of December, a date which would typically bring more drinkers out of the closet as the anticipation of Christmas started to swirl in the air.

The nights had been harder for him ever since Marius had disappeared. Despite the fact they spent half of the time at each other's throats, Bill enjoyed his company a lot more than any of the regulars', most of whom were either half dead or half paralytic. He also felt a lot more uneasy without the giant Romanian by his side.

He didn't dare question Bernard and Murat as to what had happened to Marius, but it didn't take a genius to work it out. Marius hadn't been seen or heard from in nearly a month, and that told Bill all he needed to know. He was well aware how ruthless the two Albanians could be.

He cursed Marius for being so stupid. Why did he have to grab Claudia Wells that night? He'd warned him so many times about getting ideas above his station, but Marius hadn't listened. He didn't believe that Richard Banks would have the balls to finish him. He was wrong.

And then, there was Strevens. He'd been offered up as the group's sacrificial lamb. A wiry decoy that enabled them to go on carrying out their activities. Bill shook his head, thinking about the callousness The Club had demonstrated. He wished he'd never got involved with Richard Banks. The negatives were now far outweighing the positives.

Bill could only hope that he would be spared the same fate. He'd tried to convince himself that his services were worthwhile. There was no need for The Club to get rid of him as well, was there? He was living each night on tenterhooks.

He took a slug of brandy and started on his customary walk round the pub, asking the stragglers to drink up and wishing them a safe journey home. In truth, he couldn't give a toss if any of them were run over by the nearest bus.

As the last punter staggered out of the door, sending a blast of freezing London air into the pub, Bill swept up some empty glasses and took them back to the bar. From behind, he heard the door open again.

"Pub's closed, mate," he shouted out without turning to see who it was.

"It fucking well will be," came a voice he didn't recognise.

Bill spun around. The scene in front of him made his blood turn cold: four men dressed in black, all wearing balaclavas. Two were carrying baseball bats, and two were holding hammers.

Bill stood in shock. Had The Club come for him? He reassessed and saw that the people in front of him were too small to be Bernard or Murat. The two Albanians were also too bloodthirsty to let anyone else do their dirty work. "Now, now, lads. There's not much in the till, but whatever there is, you can have. I'm no hero. There's no need to harm me."

One of the men sent a baseball bat smashing down on the nearest table, scattering glass across the pub.

"We don't want your dirty money. We're here to close this pervert's paradise down."

Bill's stomach dropped. He held his hands out by his side and edged around the back of the bar. "I don't want any trouble. I'm just the landlord here."

"Yeah, course you are, mate. You just pour the drinks and leave the abusing to Phillip Strevens yeah?" Two of the group sprinted towards Bill, and the other two started to demolish the pub. Bill bent down and tried to grab the iron bar that Marius kept under the till, but he was too slow. The men were on him in a flash and dragged him from behind the bar and back into the pub.

Bill felt blow after blow across his body. One cracked into his skull and opened a gaping wound above his eye. The next hammered into his kneecap, then his shin, and then his elbow.

The final devastating blow sent his head spinning. Blood poured into his eyes, his body fell limp, and his tongue lolled out of the side of his mouth as he lapsed into darkness.

# Forty-six

Nisha opened her eyes and simultaneously sighed in despair. Today was a day she'd been dreading for a while: the taskforce Christmas party.

In truth, it was more of an all-day pub crawl than a party, but it was the last thing she needed right now. Nisha was in no doubt that Michael would use the recent developments in the case as a cause for celebration – something that made her feel sick.

Two dead bodies, one of whom was an innocent child, was no reason for joviality. The convenient circumstances surrounding the discovery were playing on her mind. Just because her team was willing to bury their heads in the sand, it didn't mean Nisha had to.

She dragged herself out of bed and wailed as she saw what was hanging up on her wardrobe, ready to be worn. Michael had insisted the whole taskforce were kitted out in Christmas jumpers for their big day.

Ninety minutes later, she walked into Dishoom restaurant in Shoreditch, to be greeted by a loud cheer from a table in the far corner. She looked over to see Michael, Rob, and Matt, all dressed in the most garish Christmas jumpers one could imagine. They already had three empty pint glasses in front of them. She put on her best false smile and walked over.

"Stop being a party pooper and get your jumper out, DS Sharma," Michael shouted.

Nisha shook her head, closed her eyes, and then undid her jacket to reveal the sartorial monstrosity lurking underneath. The three men cheered and made space for her at the table.

"We've got four bacon naan rolls on the way for breakfast. Have you tried them before? Bloody lovely," said Rob.

Nisha rolled her eyes. To her, the bacon naan rolls, that were a staple of Dishoom's famous menu, were just another example of the Westernisation of Indian cuisine. A crude hybrid of a dish, designed with the simple intention of luring British customers into an Indian restaurant for breakfast – something that was previously unthinkable.

"Right, this is the plan for the day. After breakfast, we've got crazy golf booked at Swingers underneath the Gherkin tower. Should be good. A bit of lunch booked at an Italian restaurant around the corner, and then we're off into Shoreditch for a bar crawl," said Michael.

"Sounds good, guv. Quick question though. Have you and Rob been out in Shoreditch lately?" said Matt.

"Can't say I have, but I've heard it's lively."

"Yeah, you can say that again," Matt replied, giving Nisha a raised eyebrow, which made her giggle. They imagined how two men in Christmas jumpers, both approaching pension age, would go down in young and trendy Shoreditch.

The bacon naan rolls arrived, accompanied by another round of drinks. Nisha decided to start the day off with a gin and tonic. She reasoned that she'd have to get as drunk as possible, as early as possible, to be able to enjoy today.

"So, have we made any inroads into the identity of Strevens's accomplice? Nisha asked as the first taste of Gordon's hit her lips.

Michael slammed his beer down. "DS Sharma, I have one rule for today, no-one is allowed to talk business. This whole day is all about fun. Now, I know that'll be hard for a workaholic like you, but do you think you can manage it?"

Nisha paused and then nodded back.

"Good girl," Michael replied and held his beer in the air. "Cheers everyone, and Happy Christmas."

Eight hours later, they stumbled into a cocktail bar on Shoreditch high street, creatively named called The Shoreditch. The day had gone pretty much to plan, and even Nisha had to admit that it hadn't been as bad as she'd feared.

They huddled around a poser table in the corner of the bar, with Nisha and Michael grabbing the only two high stools available.

"This isn't fair," Rob pleaded. "You're thirty years younger than me, Nisha. I need a seat."

"Yes, but I'm a lady. Where's your sense of chivalry?"

"Oh yeah, course, that's right, you women are all for equality until you can use your gender to get something."

"Well, I suppose it's about time. Men have been using gender to their advantage for hundreds of years now."

"Good point well made, DS Sharma," Michael slurred. "I'm going out for a fag. Anyone fancy joining me?"

"I'm good, guv, I'll keep your seat warm while you're gone," Matt replied, jumping on the stool before Rob had a chance to act.

"Oi, you cheeky bastard, get off, that's mine," Rob shouted and tried to playfully wrestle his younger colleague off the stool.

Michael laughed as he walked outside. It had been a good day so far. He pulled out a cigarette and started to scour his pocket for a lighter.

"Need a light, DCI Dack?" came a voice from his side.

"Mason? What the hell are you doing here?"

Mason held out a flame from a Zippo, which Michael cupped his hands around and clumsily lit his cigarette.

"Are you enjoying your night, DCI Dack? Celebrating the progress in the case, are we?"

Michael thought he detected a hint of animosity in Mason's voice and paused before his reply, "We're not celebrating anything about the case, we're just out for our Christmas drinks. How about you?"

"I'm not surprised you're not celebrating. You've made a bit of a pig's ear of it so far, haven't you?"

"What do you mean?"

"I told you about Strevens months ago, and you done nothing about it. You left him free and able to offend again and now look what he's done. Claudia's blood is on your hands, DCI Dack, make no mistake about it."

"Son, I can see why it looks like that, but trust me, it's not. We can't just lock people up for no good reason."

"I'm disappointed in you, DCI Dack. I was hoping you'd be different, but you've proved me wrong. You're just a slave to legislation and procedure."

"Mind your tone, son." Michael pushed his face closer to Mason's and stared him in the eye.

"Oh, please, don't try to intimidate me. I know now that you're all mouth and no action. Luckily, Street Shield are the complete opposite. We've made the decision that we're going to be a lot more active. In fact, it's already started."

"What are you talking about?"

"That shithole pub that Strevens and his cronies were using as some sort of headquarters. Let's just say, it won't be opening again anytime soon. I'm guessing the landlord was part of his group too. He had nonce written all over his face."

"You'd better not have done anything. I've told you to keep out of this and leave it to the police."

"Keep out?! The only reason you had Strevens is because of us! Without him, I can't see that you've made any progress on this case at all."

Michael hesitated. If Rob or any of the group came out and saw Mason here, it could cause huge problems.

"Okay, fine, you've made your point. We need to work closer together going forwards."

"The time for that has passed, DCI Dack. My faith in the police is now completely gone." Mason walked away into the throng of festive revellers, just before Matt walked outside on his mobile phone.

"What, really? You're kidding me?" said Matt.

His excited tone pricked Michael's attention. "What's going on?" Michael asked, only to be shushed by Matt. Nisha and Rob then tumbled out of the bar door.

"It's too busy in there, it's doing me in" Rob shouted.

"Shuusssh!" Matt hushed even more loudly, "Okay, that's great news. Can you let me know what you've found out?" said Matt.

Michael leant in and heard a Dutch accent reply, "There's too much to discuss over the phone. You must come over." Michael's heart started to pound; Matt was speaking with Joost.

"Can you tell me one thing? Is it to do with Strevens?" said Matt.

"Strevens? He's just a tiny cog in this game. What I've found out is going to blow your mind," said Joost.

"Right, I'll come straight over." Matt hung up the phone and then turned to the taskforce. "That was Joost. He's cracked the code. He reckons he's found out everything."

"Great news. Get over there, son. I'm ready for bed anyway," Rob shouted and gave Matt a huge slap on the back.

"Anyone else fancy coming?" Matt looked at Michael.

"Erm, no, I'm good. This is your part of the case. You deserve the glory. I think I'm ready for bed too."

Nisha frowned. Michael's response was very understated considering what he'd just been told. "I'll come with you, Matt," she said.

Rob turned to Michael. "Fancy a nightcap somewhere empty and quiet?"

"Not tonight. I've got to get back to Sam."

"Suit yourself then. I'm heading off. Have a good weekend." Rob gave Michael a hug and walked across the road to the cab rank. He didn't care how long it would take; there was no way he was getting on a tube home with the Christmas crowd.

Michael waited until Rob was out of sight before he pulled his phone out of his pocket and punched in a number.

"David, it's Michael. We've got a big problem."

# Forty-seven

"Is this where we've put him?" said Nisha as the estate appeared in front of them, "Doesn't look very safe to me."

"That's exactly what I said," laughed Matt.

They climbed the three flights of concrete steps that led to Joost's floor, and both stopped, panting for breath at the top. "I'd rather not be doing this after an all-day session," Nisha huffed out.

Matt raised his eyebrows in agreement. "Come on, it's just along here."

As they approached the flat, Matt suddenly grabbed Nisha. The front door was open, and the lock looked like it had been busted. Nisha's instinctively reached for her police cosh before she remembered that they weren't in uniform tonight.

Matt held his finger to his lips and gently pushed the door open. The flat was pitch dark, complicit with an eerie silence that raised their hackles. They edged forwards, unsure as to what may be awaiting them.

They reached the living room and stopped, listening for any sort of noise. Matt reached his arm out towards the wall and fumbled for the light switch. The sight that greeted them as the dull bulb flickered on was one they'd never forget.

Joost was lying on the floor, face up, with a gaping hole across his neck. Blood was seeping out of it and towards each corner of the room, covering the floor in a sticky red carpet.

The flat had been destroyed. The computer equipment was smashed into hundreds of pieces, which were strewn across the room. Matt knelt next to Joost's body, unable to utter a word.

There was a noise from outside, heavy footsteps sprinting along the external walkway. Nisha turned and saw two silhouettes run past the window. "Matt, they're still here!" she screamed.

Matt jumped up and ran out of the door, with Nisha following close behind. They looked to the far end of the walkway, around fifty metres away, and saw two men bounding down the staircase.

Matt got to the stairs first and looked over the side, but there was no sign of the men. Nisha caught him up, panting heavily. They continued down the stairs, jumping two or three steps at a time.

As they reached the second floor, they both peered over the side, but again, there was no sign of the men.

"I'm not sure they've gone down to the ground floor," Nisha said. "We would have seen them running across the path, wouldn't we?"

Matt paused. She was right. There was only one way out of the estate: a path that led to the main entrance. The men were either hiding somewhere on the ground floor or had tried to stay on one of the other floors to trick them.

"Okay, you have a look on this floor, I'll go down to the ground floor. These are the only stairs in this building, so we should have them cornered. Shout if you find them. Do not try to engage them," said Matt.

Nisha nodded and ran around the walkway. Matt reached the ground floor and walked out into the car park and turned to stare back at the building. His eyes scoured the first and second floor walkways, but he could only see Nisha.

He turned and looked for potential hiding places on the ground floor. While the estate was sparse, there were some overgrown bushes next to the wall. He started to walk towards them, constantly checking back towards the stairs in case the men made a run for it.

A bloodcurdling scream punctuated the night sky. It sounded like it had come from the far side of the building. Matt sprinted over towards its direction.

As he turned the corner, another scream came, this one even more terrifying. Matt looked up to the second floor, and in what seemed like slow motion, he saw Nisha's body somersaulting over the side as if she had been tossed like a caber. He could only watch in horror as she fell over ten metres and landed on the cold, concrete floor with a sickening thud.

# Forty-eight

"Sorry, DS Gardiner, you're going to have to repeat yourself. What do you mean, everything has gone?"

"Everything, guv. Whatever evidence Joost uncovered has been taken. All the equipment has been smashed to bits." Matt stared at the floor in the Chelsea and Westminster hospital waiting room, still unable to comprehend the events of the previous night.

Michael puffed out his cheeks. "And how's DS Sharma doing?"

"Not too good. She's got a broken leg, fractured ribs, and a busted elbow. But she'll survive, thank God. Considering the height she was thrown from, she's had a massive result. I can't believe she didn't break her neck."

"And tell me again, DS Gardiner, why didn't you call for backup when you realised the flat had been broken into?"

Matt bristled. It was 6.30am, and he hadn't had a wink of sleep. The last thing he needed was the Spanish Inquisition.

"I've already told you, it all happened so quickly. One second, we found the body, the next, the suspects were sprinting past us." Matt took his gaze from the floor and directed it firmly at Michael.

"And you let DS Sharma go off on her own, drunk, to try to accost two grown men?"

"We spread out to try to stop their escape. I told her to scream if she found them," Matt raised his voice.

"Well, you're lucky you don't have the death of an officer on your conscience. Whether you have the death of a witness, we're still to find out."

"What do you mean by that?" Matt stood to his feet.

"How did they know the location of the safehouse? You must have been followed there on a previous visit. It's the only explanation."

"I was never followed. I was always cautious. Maybe if you'd decided to come with us last night rather than go for another drink, this could have been avoided."

"Oh, so it's my fault now, is it? I've heard it all now."

Rob noticed other people in the waiting room staring over and decided it was time to interject. "All right, calm down. We're all emotional. The main thing is that Nisha will be all right. She's the one we should be thinking of now."

"Yeah, and the fact that we've lost a huge opportunity to close this case once and for all," Michael spat out.

"I think the one thing we do know is that this case is far from solved. There's a couple of murderers running around now with access to privileged police information," said Rob.

Michael shrugged. "Well, we don't definitely know that these two are related to our case, do we? Joost was one of the most wanted men in Europe. Plenty of crooks out there needed him dead."

"Oh, come off it," Matt shouted, "they took all the evidence. Of course this was to do with our case."

"Maybe they didn't know what was on the computer. They could have thought he was helping the police with other investigations. Let's not jump to conclusions. I still think we've broken the back of this case with Strevens. We just need to find his accomplice now."

"That's bullshit. This thing is much bigger than Philip Strevens. Joost told me on the phone that Strevens was insignificant."

"He could have been saying that to justify his side of the deal. We can't rely on the words of a desperate criminal, DS Gardiner."

"I can't listen to this anymore. You're burying your head in the sand. I'm going back to see Nisha." Matt turned and stormed off.

Michael looked over at Rob. "Thanks for sticking up for me there. A voice of reason could have helped."

Rob didn't reply. He stared at Michael, looking him up and down.

"Okay, fine, you're taking his side, are you? Sod this. I'm going back to the office," said Michael.

Rob remained in his chair for the next twenty minutes, thoughts racing through his head. Eventually, he stood and made his way to the toilets. He found a spare cubicle and sat down on the floor, his back propped against the door.

He held his head in his hands and started to sob, quietly at first, but it grew louder. Soon, he was crying hysterically as the reality of the situation overwhelmed him.

Nisha was right. Michael, his best friend of forty years, was lying.

# Forty-nine

"Are they for me?" Nisha pointed at the sorry-looking bunch of flowers in Rob's hand. "Are they supposed to make me feel better? I think I'd prefer chocolates next time."

"Bloody hell. You're in a state like that, and you're still as demanding as ever," Rob replied.

Nisha laughed but then winced almost immediately. "Ouch, please, no more jokes. Every bit of me hurts when I move."

"How are you feeling?" said Rob, taking a seat on an empty chair next to her bed.

"Surprisingly, not too bad. At least my face isn't damaged, and that's my main selling point. Think it'll be a while before I try flying again though."

Rob smiled. He had to admire her spirit.

"Michael not with you?" asked Nisha.

"He was, but he had to leave. I need to speak to you both anyway. Without him around. I'm beginning to share your concerns about DCI Dack. I think you could be right, Nisha."

Nisha's and Matt's eyes widened. This was the first time they'd ever heard Rob express misgivings about Michael.

"I need you both to play along for the time being. Don't let onto him that anything is up. I'm going to be looking into a few things discreetly from my side. If I find any concrete proof, I'll report back to you straight away."

"What exactly do you suspect him of? And what's made you change your mind?' said Nisha.

"I don't know exactly what or how far he's involved, but I do know that he was lying to me and DS Gardiner this morning. I've been friends with him long enough to know when he's covering something up."

"What you were you talking about this morning?" asked Nisha.

"How these men got the address for the safehouse."

"You think he may have had something to do with it?" said Matt.

Rob gave Matt a look.

"But if that's true, then he's an accomplice to murder. And what's more, he's responsible for getting me nearly killed!"

"Keep it down, DS Sharma. These accusations are very serious, and that's why I need to be sure before we start making them. I'm going to try to find the proof, and I've got a good idea where to start."

The next hour passed in a flash as multiple scenarios raced through Rob's mind. He weaved through the traffic and considered the implications if his suspicions about Michael were correct. One thing was certain: he needed evidence. He indicated left and turned into a now familiar road.

Rob pulled into an empty parking space and looked over at the alley that led down to the Scout hut. He reached into his glove compartment, pulled out his police cosh and radio, and exited the car.

The entrance to the hut was still open. Rob puffed out his chest and walked inside. In daylight, the place looked even more decrepit. Paint was peeling from the walls, window frames were rusting, and equipment was scattered across the floor.

Rob walked to the far corner of the hall and then started to pace slowly in a straight line to the opposite end. When he got there, he turned, took a step to the right, and repeated the exercise, combing the floor for any signs of evidence, no matter how small. There was none to be found.

Rob walked to a pile of discarded sports equipment. Gym mats, ropes, a solitary medicine ball, old bibs, and gym clothes. He reached into the pile and started tearing through it. There was something of use in this hall, he knew it.

As Rob picked up the last gym mat, he heard something fall to the floor. Next to his foot was a large chunky gold bracelet. Rob knelt and picked it up, his brow furrowed. He was sure he'd seen this before.

The bracelet was uniquely designed, twisted gold interspersed with dashes of silver and black. Rob wracked his brains for a few minutes before it hit him. He took out his phone and checked through his photographs. On one of the most recent images: Rob,

Marius, and Bill together in the Shallow Pond. The bracelet was clearly visible on Marius's right wrist.

# Fifty

Michael passed the taxi driver a twenty-pound note, told him to keep the change, and stepped out into the misty evening gloom.

He zipped up his jacket and observed the surroundings: a deprived council estate in Brixton that looked like it hadn't seen a street cleaner in years. Pigeons picked greedily at discarded crisp packets and overflowing bins. Empty bottles of alcohol were strewn across an overgrown patch of grass that was meant to resemble a playing area for children.

Michael took a swig from the bottle of whisky he'd been nursing since 3pm. He tried to piece together his memories of the previous day. He recalled a huge row with Samantha after she'd confronted him about his drinking again. He remembered storming out and had vague recollections of a late-night bar. After that, it was blank.

He felt guilty about Sam; he'd been drinking too much lately, but it was the only thing helping him cope. He downed the rest of the whisky and sent the bottle hurtling into the play area, where it landed with an anti-climactic thud on the grass.

Michael walked down the alleyway in front of him. As he reached the end, he saw his destination: a small community hall that had been closed today for a 'private event.'

He walked up to the door and knocked eight times as instructed. It swung open, and he was greeted by Bernard and Murat, wearing identical smiles.

"Please, come in, Mr Officer." Bernard bowed and held his arm out in an exaggerated fashion, causing both men to laugh.

"Humour in Albania must be pretty basic," said Michael as he walked through an entrance hall and into an old-fashioned room with a bar at the far end. There was a table in the middle, around which sat five men and one woman.

"DCI Dack, what a pleasure to have you here," Richard Banks grinned and motioned towards an empty seat.

"I have to admit, I was expecting some plusher surroundings bearing in mind the guestlist," Michael replied, collapsing into the chair.

"We like to rotate our meeting points around different venues such as these," said David Parkinson. "The rougher the better in our eyes. It helps to keep things discreet for The Club."

"I'm guessing they're all venues owned by yourself, Richard? So, is that what you call yourself, is it? The Club?"

"All these questions, Michael. You're beginning to sound like a policeman," Banks chortled, earning loyal laughter from each of his guests. "Don't worry, all will become clear. You're part of us now."

"I feel very privileged," Michael replied with a false grin.

Banks stood up. "So, let me do some introductions. We have here the Rt Hon. Ian Stebbing, current housing secretary. My PA, Caroline Nolan, and, despite you being colleagues, I don't believe you know DCS Brian Stock."

"By reputation only," Michael replied and nodded at each of them. Stebbing was the only person who reciprocated. Caroline was too busy looking at her iPhone, and Stock responded with a scowl.

"And, of course, you already know Toby. He was the one whose work enabled you to become a member of The Club," Banks chuckled as Toby gave Michael a sarcastic wave.

"I'm a member now, am I?" said Michael. "I don't recall filling out any forms."

"Yes, we like to think of you as a member now. With the information we have on you, I don't think you'll be looking to leave us anytime soon. I have to say, your work has been especially useful so far. We're very impressed, aren't we, David?" said Banks.

"Certainly. Your help with the Phillip Strevens and Claudia Wells situation was much welcome. And the information you provided the other day regarding the code cracker was invaluable. Bernie and Murat got there just in time, didn't you?"

"The Dutchman squealed like a pig when we cut his throat," Bernard laughed from his position at the entrance door and gave Murat a high-five.

Michael felt sick at the man he'd become. The Joost situation affected him the most. Whilst he'd helped with the Strevens and

Claudia Wells cover up, The Club had already decided to kill them both. He told himself that there was nothing he could have done about that. Joost was different. Michael's actions had led directly to that man's death. He pushed the pain to the basement of his brain. It was either Joost's life or his, he told himself.

"You didn't have to throw my officer over the balcony though," Michael said, looking over at the two Albanians. "That sort of thing is sloppy and could be costly. One dead copper and the whole Met would be diverted after us." He used the word 'us' through gritted teeth.

"Fuck that bitch. We needed a diversion to get out of there," Murat shouted back at him.

"All right, shut it," Banks ordered. "Michael's right, it was sloppy."

"I have some more information that you may find valuable," Michael said, leaning back in his chair. "I know who smashed up your pub."

"Pray tell," Banks purred, leaning forwards to rest his chin on his hands.

"It was Mason Greenwell and his little crew."

"The Street Shield guy?" said Parkinson.

"That's the one. Now, where can I get a whisky round here?"

"This bloody kid," Banks spat. "I've had enough of him. Bernard, arrange to take care of Mason Greenwell, please. And can you also bring Michael a large whisky?"

Bernard stomped to the bar, grabbed a bottle of whisky and a glass, and slammed them down on the table in front of Michael. Michael poured himself a large measure and downed it in one.

"So, the next part of our plan is in motion, Michael," said Parkinson. "Your friend found the clue in the Scout hut."

Michael's eyes raised. "How do you know?"

"We had him followed. He came out of the hut holding the bracelet in a clear plastic bag. We tailed him to the Shallow Pond. He obviously didn't know it was closed. By our reckoning, he'll probably visit Bill in hospital either today or tomorrow."

Michael's heart sank. Rob was suspicious of him. "I knew he'd go there. I knew he'd find it," Michael muttered in response.

"Yes, your instincts were proved right again. Anyway, Bill's been briefed about what to say and how to act. If he pulls this off, we should be home and dry."

"We're going to need more than just Strevens and Marius as scapegoats. My colleagues are convinced there's a VIP involved," said Michael.

"Oh, don't worry, dear boy, that's already been arranged thanks to Toby."

"What do you mean? Tell me who."

"That's not your concern," said Banks.

Michael bit his lip, knowing not to press the matter. He felt powerless. He downed another glass of whisky and slumped back in his chair.

"Got a bit of a drink problem, have you, boy?" Stock broke his silence. "I've heard that about you."

Michael placed the glass down and stared his fellow policeman in the eye. "Don't call me boy."

"Now, now, Brian, that's no way to welcome our newest member," Banks grinned. "Anyway, Michael, we're pleased to say your work has earned our respect, and we're going to reward you with a little treat. Keep Thursday fifteenth of December free. You're being brought into the inner sanctum."

# Fifty-one

The door crashed open at the end of the corridor, waking her with a fright. She winced as she felt the pain searing through her forehead. Her attempt at suicide had only succeeded in causing concussion and a cavernous gash. She tenderly touched the wound with her finger. It felt like it was infected.

This did not sound like a regular visit. The men were walking up and down the corridor, banging on every door and shouting. As they got to her room, the words became clear.

"Stand up, face wall. Do not fucking move."

She did as she was told, rising feebly to her feet. Her door flung open, and she was grabbed from behind. A rough pair of hands tied a blindfold around her eyes, and she was marched out of the cell door.

Instead of being taken to the shower room, she was held in the corridor. Around her, she could hear whimpers and sobs from the other girls.

"Stop your moaning," one of the men shouted. Silence immediately fell.

From the far end of the corridor, an ominous sound of footsteps started to slowly walk towards her. Every so often, they would pause for a few seconds, as if the person was inspecting one of the girls, before they started again.

As they passed her, she could see the person's shoes through the small gap under the blindfold. They were shiny brown leather, and they looked expensive. They certainly didn't belong to one of her two captors.

The footsteps reached the end of the corridor, turned, and made their way back again, still pausing at irregular intervals. The person continued to the far end of the corridor, before they exited without a word.

"In case you didn't know," a loud voice boomed out in an Eastern European accent, "it is the Christmas period. So, we are going to give you a little treat and take you to a party. You will soon be moved from here. I warn you now, if anyone tries any funny business while being moved, they will suffer grave consequences."

One of the girls started to cry.

"You will also find a little present in your room when you return. We will soon come and take you all for washing. For this party, you must be clean, and you must look nice."

Silence.

"You ungrateful bitches. Did you not hear what I just told you? Say thank you!"

The men sniggered as some mumbled replies of 'thank you' came back from the girls. She said nothing herself. She was too busy trying to hold in her tears.

She felt a hand on her shoulder that spun her around and pushed her forwards. She fell through the doorway and onto the floor. The door slammed behind her, and she ripped the blindfold off. In the corner of her cell was a black ball gown and a pair of high heels.

# Fifty-two

Rob had tracked down Bill Lowthy to Whittington Health Hospital in Islington, a small facility but one that still bore the unmistakable smell of sickness that Rob hated so much.

He didn't intend to stay in here for any longer than required, but he was determined to get answers. This case was dangerously spiralling out of control, and the sight of the Shallow Pond pub completely smashed to pieces had added another layer of mystery.

Rob took a long look at the person sprawled in bed. From a distance, he could not tell if it was Bill; it was only when he got up close that he was able to identify the stricken landlord.

Bill's entire face was coloured deep blue and harsh black. His eyes and nose were grotesquely swollen, and most of his teeth were missing. A neck brace held his head in position, and there were casts on both of his legs and one of his arms. A flicker of the bulbous swelling above Bill's left eye told Rob he was awake.

"Rough night, Bill?"

"Who's that?"

"It's DI Archer. Someone's done a right number on you, haven't they? Any idea who it was?" said Rob, pulling up a chair alongside the bed.

"I do, yeah, and I hope you're gonna nick him for me."

Rob's brow furrowed. "Go on then, who was it?"

"It was that bastard, Marius. Tried to kill me he did."

"Marius? I thought he was your mate."

"Yeah, so did I until a day before the attack. He came into the pub completely pissed, demanding money out of the till. He said he's got to disappear for a while. I told him to do one, and we had a bit of an altercation. Next day, he walks in with some cronies, all dressed in black. He battered me, cleaned out the till, and left me for dead. I had over two grand in there."

"Why didn't you tell any other officers this?"

"Because I don't trust them. The last thing I need is Marius coming back here to finish the job. I trust you though. You can be discreet and find him, can't you?"

Rob sat back in his chair and rubbed his chin. "Why do you think he needed the money?"

"He was in with some dodgy people. I think it was to do with drugs. I told him to get out of that game, but he never listened.

"Where can I find him?"

"Fuck knows. He could be anywhere."

"Rack your brains. Think of anywhere he mentioned."

Bill paused. "I know he owned a caravan down on some holiday park in Southend. He mentioned it a few times."

"Can you remember the name?"

"I can't, my mind's a bit scrambled. Maybe I would if I heard it."

Rob pulled out his phone and typed 'caravan parks, Southend' into Google.

"Tingdene, Sunnyside, Riverside…"

"Riverside, that's the one."

"Are you sure?"

"Definitely. Can you promise me you'll be careful? I don't need this coming back on me."

Rob was already in the corridor and striding towards the car park. He reckoned it would take him ninety minutes to drive to Southend from here if the traffic was kind, and he didn't have a minute to spare.

It was 11am by the time he pulled into the entrance of Riverside Caravan Park. "There's not much more depressing than a UK holiday park in the winter," he grumbled as he observed the bleak surroundings.

Rob pulled his car into a space outside a large portacabin-type building with 'RECEPTION' written above the door. He walked inside to be greeted by the unfriendliest-looking receptionist he had ever seen: a scowling, obese man covered in tattoos who looked like he hadn't washed in weeks.

"How can I help you, sir?"

"I'm DI Robert Archer, and I'm looking for information on one of your customers." Rob held his badge out in front of him.

"Certainly, Inspector. Can you provide me the name, please, and I'll get right onto it for you."

"Marius Barbaneagra."

"Hmmm, I can't see anyone of that name here. You don't have a photo, do you? Not all our guests check in with their real name."

"I do." Rob pulled up the image of Marius on his phone.

"Oh, yes, I know him. He owns a caravan down at the far end of the park." The receptionist shot Rob an uneasy look. "Not a very nice man."

"You've got that right. Have you seen him recently?"

"I haven't, but that doesn't mean he's not here. Our caravan owners can come and go as they please. Would you like me to take you down to his one?"

"That would be helpful," said Rob, regretting that he'd made the mistake of judging a book by its cover.

They walked amongst the rows of caravans through thick mud with the occasional grass patch. At the end of one row, they stopped, and the man pointed at the last caravan on the left.

"That's the one."

"Thank you," Rob said, and walked up the small metal steps to the front door. He knocked, but there was no answer. Rob put his ear to the door but could hear nothing. He knocked again. "Marius, are you in there?"

"Would you like me to open the door, Inspector? I've got the keys here."

"Yes, please," Rob replied, stepping away from the door. He wished all building managers were this helpful.

The manager took out a set of keys, and after a few seconds, located the right one. He opened the lock, pulled the door open and instantly let out a scream and stumbled backwards, down the steps and onto the mud.

Rob sprinted inside and was hit by a smell that he knew only too well.

Slumped in the corner, on the sofa, was Marius, with a huge slit across his neck, his body in a state of decomposition. Rob stepped forward and gently pulled the cuff back on the right sleeve of his jumper. There was no bracelet on him.

"Do you want me to call anyone?"

Rob turned and saw the manager, pale as a sheet, standing at the door.

"Stand back, mate. This is a crime scene now. I'll call it in." Rob pulled out his police radio, but before he made the call, something else caught his eye. There was a laptop sitting on the side table next to the TV.

\*\*\*

It was early evening when Michael received a call from David Parkinson.

"Good news, old bean. Bill done his job well. Your mate has found Marius and the laptop."

"That is good news," Michael replied calmly.

"Indeed. Our misdirection plan is nearly complete."

"It seems so, sir."

"Just one thing, though, Michael. Even though he has proved useful, The Club are getting a little concerned about DI Archer. He seems to be poking his nose around a bit too much. I thought you told me he just wanted to retire to an easy life."

"He does, don't worry. Once these pieces are tied up, he'll back off. I'll make sure of it."

"I very much hope so, Michael. I wouldn't want us to have to take matters into our own hands."

# Fifty-three

Michael stared at himself in the bathroom mirror. He'd long given up any pretence of recognising the face that stared back at him.

He knew that tonight could be the final straw. He sensed he was about to cross thresholds unchartered. The thought of the evening ahead filled him with dread. There was no chance of him backing out now though. There was no alternative route but to keep plodding grimly on.

A message came through on his phone: 'Outside. Now. DP.'

Michael trudged downstairs and past the living room. Sam, Georgia, and Becky were inside, cuddled up with a load of snacks and *Love Actually* on the TV. It was tradition that the family would watch the film together every Christmas. Michael wished he was staying in and doing it with them. He'd take a whole night with the stepdaughters over what he was about to go through.

"I'm off now. Have a nice evening," he called out. There was no reply. They didn't even take their eyes off the screen. Michael's heart sunk. He felt like he was beginning to lose Samantha forever.

He stepped outside into the cold, December night. A shiny black 4x4 with tinted windows was parked on the opposite side of the road. To Michael, it looked like a hearse.

\*\*\*

Fresh air! The first time she'd felt it in ages. It was only a fleeting taste, a sharp stab to her cheek underneath the blindfold, but it was enough. It reminded her that there was still a world outside her cell.

"Up, up," an aggressive voice ordered her from behind, and she felt a sharp shove to her lower back.

She fell forwards onto a metal floor, unable to break her fall due to her hands being tied behind her back. Someone grabbed her and propped her up against the side. She heard other girls being brought in behind her. She was forced to budge down until she was sitting in the corner. The doors slammed shut and an engine started.

\*\*\*

"What are we drinking, old boy?" asked David Parkinson, opening a plush drinks cabinet in the back of the executive vehicle.

Michael seethed inside. He hated how the home secretary was so familiar with him now. He loathed how he spoke to him, as if he was a colleague or friend. As if he was one of their own.

"I'll have a double whisky, sir. How long's this journey going to take?"

"Oh, come on, no need for sirs and formalities tonight, old boy. Tonight is about play, not work. Call me Dave. I reckon we've got a good two hours' drive ahead of us, so make sure you pace yourself on the booze. You're going to want to be fully coherent for the pleasures that await at the other end."

Michael took the glass of whisky and downed it in one.

\*\*\*

She winced as the van sped over another bump in the road, causing her back to smash against the side. It felt like they'd been in here for hours, and she was almost beginning to miss the mattress in her room. Her body was aching from the uncomfortable position she was sitting in. The flimsy dress she had been told to wear provided little protection against the cold. She heard the howling wind outside whip against the van.

The vehicle slowed, made a right turn, and stopped. She heard voices from outside, greeting the driver and engaging in a brief discussion before they started moving again, slower than before. After a few minutes, they came to another halt, and the engine turned off. The back doors flung open, and a strong gust of wind blew in.

"Out, out."

She dutifully shuffled across the floor. Upon reaching the doors, she was grabbed forcefully and pulled to her feet outside. She could feel the other girls around her, standing in a group.

After a few seconds, they were pushed forwards. She stumbled onwards, occasionally bumping into another girl. They were suddenly inside, warmth and shelter from the wind. Carpet turned to marble floor as they were herded together. Rough hands pushed her from behind.

"Sit there."

She fell limply into a chair. Comfort at last. The relief was fleeting.

"Swallow."

A pair of large fingers, stinking of cigarette smoke, pushed a small pill into her mouth. A glass of water was brought to her lips. She paused for a split second but then received the water and swallowed. There was no damage any drug could inflict that was worse than the ordeal she had already suffered.

*** 

"Heading to Norfolk, are we, David?" Michael asked as he watched the A11 speed by outside. Three drinks in, he was starting to warm up, the alcohol dampening his fear.

"Somewhere like that. We like to hold these events away from London. Helps alleviate the possibility of gate crashers, if you know what I mean."

"How do you source the premises?"

"They're all typically owned by members of The Club. We have an exceptionally well-heeled client base, as I'm sure you can imagine."

"How many of these events have you had?"

"This will be our fifth and the largest one so far. But it's nothing compared to what we've organised in January."

"Why, what's happening then?"

"Bloody hell, what's with all the questions?" Parkinson chortled into his gin and tonic. "You're going to ruin the surprise if I tell you everything before you get to experience tonight. Relax and enjoy it, would you?"

Michael turned back to the window and poured himself another whisky. Dark, ominous fields rolled by outside. Black, jagged trees swayed in the wind. Anxiety rose through him – anxiety and loneliness.

The car slowed almost to a stop and then turned off the main road into a maze of tight country lanes. There were no streetlights here. The thick and cumbersome trees that held the moon at bay ensured there was little light at all.

"This place really is in the middle of nowhere, David."

"Exactly how we like it, nice and private."

The car eventually turned right to be greeted by the sight of a closed iron fence, flanked either side by two huge security guards dressed in black. They approached the car, and David wound his window down.

"Good evening, gentlemen. David Parkinson and Michael Dack."

"Good evening, sir," one of the men nodded, and the gates started to pull open.

The car eased itself inside and crawled forwards. Far in the distance, Michael could see a huge stately home lit up eerily.

"Is this land all part of that one home?"

"It is indeed. Impressive, isn't it, Michael?"

"It's like a palace."

"We do like to have facilities fit for royalty, just in case."

Michael's eyebrows arched.

As the building edged closer into view, it became obvious how convenient this setup was. The security cameras dotted along the road, the guards, the length of the driveway. It would all come in very handy if the police suddenly arrived.

Michael let out an ironic chuckle. The police were already here, and they were powerless.

# Fifty-four

It was 8pm, and Rob had just sat down on the sofa to enjoy an old James Bond movie with Judy. He had a huge plate of cold meat and cheese balanced on his stomach and a large glass of red wine sitting on the table in front of him. This was what life was about.

They'd barely got past the opening scene when Rob's mobile began to ring. He glanced over at Judy and received a 'don't you dare' look back. He pulled the phone out with the intention of muting it, but the name calling took him by surprise: Suzanne Morgan.

"It's the commissioner, Judy, I need to answer it." He held the phone out at his wife with an apologetic look on his face. She huffed and pressed pause on the TV.

"Good evening, ma'am, to what do I owe this pleasure?"

"No time for bullshit here, Rob. We've got a real issue on our hands with that laptop you found on the dead Romanian guy."

"What sort of issue?"

"Something we've found on there is extremely incriminating to someone important. I wish you'd brought this computer to me first before handing it into evidence."

"Pardon? I did everything by the book. Why should I hand the laptop into you? You know less about computers than me!"

"Yes, I know you did everything by the book, but…"

"Go on."

"There are other forces at play here, Rob. This sort of information is something that needs to be managed before it leaks to the public."

Rob frowned. "I'm sorry, I'm completely lost. You're going to have to explain."

"It's a bit of a delicate one, not really a matter for a phone discussion. Can you get into the station?"

Rob looked at the plate of food on his stomach. "I'm sorry, tonight is not good for me. Where's Michael? Can he not handle it?

*217*

"I've tried him already a few times. His phone is off."

Course it was, Rob thought. "Can we do it tomorrow instead? I'll come in early."

"I fear tomorrow may be too late to limit this damage. You know I wouldn't be asking you if it wasn't important."

Rob let out a sigh. "I'll be there as soon as possible."

Judy leant over and pressed play on the remote without looking at him.

"What can I do, darling? It's the commissioner."

Judy stared silently at the television.

# Fifty-five

She couldn't work out if she was dreaming or not. Her blindfold had been removed, and she was standing in the middle of a grand hall that resembled something from a fairytale. She felt like she was floating around the room, a kaleidoscope of colours colliding in her brain causing a sensory overload. She had become so used to darkness and grey.

There were others in her dream too. Girls dressed the same as her, also floating. She longed to talk to them. She wished she could make friends, but the words of warning she'd been given were still ringing in her ears.

*'You do not give out your real name, you must only use the name on your ankle tag. You only speak when spoken to. You only speak to the guests, not the other girls. You do whatever the guests want you to without complaint. If anyone doesn't follow these rules, the guests have been told to inform us. We will carry out the necessary punishment.'*

Even in her delirious state, she knew those words were genuine. She recognised the voices that had spoken them. She was aware of the sort of punishment that could be dished out. She carried on floating around the room in her own little trance.

She stopped at a mirror and saw herself for the first time in ages. Squinting, she tried to make sense of the figure that stood in front of her, scrawny and beaten, void of emotion but still harbouring life inside her. She couldn't decide if the sight made her happy or sad. She lingered for a few seconds longer and then walked off, deciding to focus her attentions elsewhere. She was out of her cell and determined to make the most of it, no matter how surreal the experience was.

\*\*\*

Michael exited the vehicle and took a step back to gaze at the enormity of the building in front of him.

"Whoever owns this must have a serious bit of coin," he said out loud.

"That's the understatement of the year," David Parkinson replied, appearing at Michael's shoulder. "Follow me."

Parkinson walked through the entrance doors and handed his coat to a man dressed in a tuxedo. "This way, Michael, time for a few drinks before the party starts."

They turned right and walked down a corridor full of expensive-looking paintings on the walls. There was a heavy, oak door at the end, which two men, also dressed in tuxedos, held open for them as they approached.

The doors opened into a huge drawing room full of plush leather sofas, thick wooden tables, and a fully stocked bar. There were approximately thirty men in here, all middle- to old-aged, all dressed smartly in dinner jackets and bow ties, each involved in excited discussion with a maniacal look in their eyes.

Michael recognised a few of them straight away: Ian Stebbing, Toby Trent and Brian Stock.

"Michael Dack, you made it. Welcome to your first official Club event. I hope you brought some Viagra." Richard Banks had appeared out of nowhere.

"Viagra? No offence, sir, but no-one in here takes my fancy," Michael replied, initiating laughter from Banks and Parkinson.

"Very good, Michael. Don't worry, this is just the warmup. The main show starts in half an hour. Let's get you a drink."

The three of them walked to the bar. Banks beckoned Bernard over to him with an exuberant click of his fingers and whispered into his ear. Michael leant in to listen in on the conversation.

"Remind me, Bernie, which group of girls are we using today?" said Banks.

"Groups eleven and twelve."

"Fine. How are they looking?"

"They're all completely out of it, sir."

"Perfect. Now remember, for the January party, we're going to want at least six groups."

"Yes, sir, you have told me this three times already."

"And you'll still probably fuck it up," said Banks, shooing the huge Albanian away from him. "Go and get the grand hall ready for opening."

As Michael surveyed the room, he noticed how familiar some of the faces were. Off the top of his head, he couldn't place them, but he was sure he'd seen many of them before. No doubt they were business leaders, politicians, or high-profile individuals.

His thoughts were interrupted by the sound of a glass clinking. He turned to see Richard Banks standing in front of a large Edwardian-style door, grinning like an insane circus master.

"Gentlemen, gentlemen. We are now ready for the festivities to begin. Before they do, I would just like to thank you once more for your attendance tonight at what is our biggest ever event. We have a delectable array of treats on the other side of the door, and for those of you who don't know the rules, let me spell them out to you. There are no rules. You've paid your money. Whatever you say goes."

Michael winced as the crowd of greying, ruddy-faced men cheered.

Banks continued. "Now, before we go through, we are going to ask you to place all mobile devices with our staff. This is, of course, to protect your privacy as much as anything else. Don't worry, these will be treated with the utmost security and handed back to you when you leave. Now, let the games begin!"

The heavy-set door was heaved open, and Banks led the crowd through like the Pied Piper of Hamlin. Michael felt an arm around his shoulder.

"Follow me, Michael. Tonight is going to change your life," said David Parkinson.

I already knew that, thought Michael.

***

She was roused out of her daydream by what sounded like a football crowd approaching. The other girls had heard it too. She sensed the atmosphere in the room change.

The door at the far end of the room flew open, and a well-groomed, middle-aged man with slicked back hair walked through, closely followed by a herd of similar-looking men in expensive suits and shiny shoes.

She scanned the room for somewhere to hide. Was there an escape route anywhere? Nowhere was obvious. She recalled the words her two captors had left her with: "You do whatever the guests want you to."

A balding man with a grey goatee and a gut that hung over his trouser belt made a beeline for her. She stayed frozen to the spot, unable to move, stuck in her grim fairytale.

\*\*\*

Michael took up residence at the bar and watched open mouthed at the scene unfolding in front of him. He counted at least thirty girls, none of whom looked to be over the age of sixteen, all in skimpy dresses that displayed their flesh. They didn't seem to have their senses about them; it was like they were trapped in another world.

He watched as the leering crowd of men tore through them with no shame, groping and clutching at the young, innocent bodies with their wrinkly hands. He witnessed men grabbing a girl, or sometimes even two, and pulling them into one of the many side rooms that were manned by staff in tuxedos. He saw the doors close behind them and could only imagine the depravity that followed.

He looked on as the men emerged, sweating and ecstatic, minutes later, laughing and joking about their experiences, before moving onto the next girl. He clenched his fist and wished he could do something to stop it, but he was powerless.

To the side of him, Toby Trent emerged from one of the rooms, closely follow by a girl who looked no more than fourteen. She was in tears, black makeup running down her face, her hands cradling her stomach. Toby saw Michael and joined him at the bar.

"You must be happy I caught you, DCI Dack. You wouldn't get to experience anything like this from behind a desk at Scotland Yard."

Dack looked at Toby. "You certainly wouldn't, Toby."

"Did you see who I just had? What a cracker. The best thing is, she was delighted I took her. Look at me, I'm the youngest man in here by twenty years."

Michael looked at Toby. He was giddy with excitement, eyes bulging like a child in a sweet shop, a sick smile spread across his acne-scarred face. Michael took a deep breath, "She looked delighted for sure. So, go on then, what are each of these men paying tonight? You must be doing well out of it."

Toby squinted, unsure at the nature of the question. "Each pays their own price. There are additional benefits. This is just part of the business, Michael. There are plenty of other arms to it. Tonight is mainly about fun. Especially for me."

Michael sensed that Toby was on the crest of the wave, ready to extol his own virtues. He leant in and put his arm around him. "So, what part are you in charge of? You must be paid well, a man with your talents."

Toby pulled an oversized mobile phone out of his pocket. He clicked a few buttons on the screen and held it up to show Michael. On the screen were sixteen different live CCTV images in black and white, all beaming back live footage of what looked like a different bedroom: a dirty, grimy, basic-looking bedroom. Each room had a girl in it.

"That's group one," Toby grinned and then swiped across with his finger. "This is group two." Another range of images appeared on screen and then another one. Toby kept swiping until Michael lost count.

"I'm in charge of monitoring all our locations where stock is stored," Toby exclaimed proudly.

"How many groups are there?" said Michael.

Toby gave him a wink. "All these girls are for sale. You can see the tags around their legs. That's their online code." He then brought up another image on his screen. It looked to Michael like an online poker lobby. "These are the current bids."

Michael peered closer and saw that next to each code was an amount. One said $8,500 with 17 days remaining. Another said $24,000 with 28 days remaining.

"The technology I created is unrivalled, but that Dutch prick nearly cracked it. That's why I owe you one, Michael. That's why you're in our inner sanctum now."

Michael's stomach sank. He kept his face as straight as possible and tried to exude excitement. "So many girls. Where do you get them from?" He felt a hand come down on his shoulder from behind; it belonged to Richard Banks.

"They're groomed from a young age. We spot them when they're around ten to twelve years old, keep an eye on them for a while, and then make our move. They're all from broken homes typically. They had no life ahead of them. They may as well be used for others' needs. We keep them captive for a year or so then bring them to the parties, make the most out of them, and then sell them on. It's called the Long Game, Michael."

"Seems like a very professional operation. And who are all these men?"

"They're clients. They've all paid through the nose to be here."

"Can I ask you something, Richard? However much they've paid is probably peanuts compared to what you're worth. Why do you do it? I'm sure you could have any woman you want. Why do you take this risk?"

"Well, that's just the point, isn't it? I don't want a *woman.*"

Toby and Richard both started laughing, Michael forced himself to join in.

"Sorry, I'm just being flippant. It's not just the carnal delights that benefit me from this operation, although they're obviously a very nice perk. And I don't do this to make money, although admittedly it does turn quite a tidy profit. The main reason I do this is to exert influence."

"What do you mean?"

"You see that man there?" Banks pointed at a stocky-looking individual with a gelled-down combover that failed to hide his receding hairline. "Well, he controls the state funding for Poland. And you see that old fool there on the verge of a heart attack? He's the wealthiest man in Azerbaijan. Once they've been to one of my events, we have them onside for life."

"Where do you get the staff for an event like this? Aren't you worried about someone spilling the beans?"

"You worry too much, Michael. Everyone in here has been carefully vetted. They all have some level of attachment to The Club. And we have something on all of them. We only work with people who have too much to lose should their secrets be exposed, as you well know," Banks grinned. "Now, that takes me to my next question. When are you going to partake? You've been sat at the bar all evening."

"I'm biding my time. I need a few more drinks, first time nerves and all that."

"You drink any more and you won't be able to get it up, old boy. It's been two hours, and you haven't even spoken to a girl. It's not a window-shopping event."

"I know, I know. I'm just not really feeling it at the moment."

Banks looked him square in the eye. "Michael, we've taken a big leap of faith to let you into the inner sanctum. We did so because we thought you were someone we could trust. If you don't get involved in the activities, it would give us serious cause for concern. Do you understand?"

Michael nodded.

"Good, now go and take someone."

Michael slowly blinked and started to cast his eye around the room.

***

This wasn't so bad, she thought to herself, perching on the edge of a lurid pink sofa. At least it was more comfortable than her room. At least it was warm, and she could see the other girls. She'd only had to sleep with one person so far. She paused in grim realisation at how far her expectations had fallen.

She looked up and saw a man approaching her; there was something about him that was different. He wasn't dressed the same as the other men in here. He didn't walk with the same arrogance. He almost looked ashamed.

"Good evening. How are you?" he said.

She noticed him cringe at the idiocy of the question. She looked him back in the eyes. She couldn't see evil in there, not like the other clients.

"I'm fine, thank you. How are you?"

"Well, I'm a little drunk, but apart from that, I'm okay. So, what's your name?"

She smiled. No-one else in here had asked her what her name was. "I'm Polly, and you?"

"Polly? Is that your real name or a stage name?"

She shrugged.

"Well, in that case, my name is Rupert."

"You don't look like a Rupert."

"And you don't look like a Polly."

She watched as 'Rupert' turned and looked at the bar he had walked over from. Two men seemed to be watching, almost as if they were egging him on.

"Are they friends of yours?" she asked.

"Hmm, not really."

"They're coming over."

"Enough chit chat, Michael. They're not here for talking to. Get her into a room. Now!"

Banks forcibly lifted Polly from the edge of the sofa and pushed her towards Michael in the same manner a schoolboy would in the playground.

"All right, all right," Michael replied, taking her by the hand and leading her towards one of the side rooms. Behind him, Richard and Toby started to cheer.

Michael walked her into the room and closed the door behind them. His heart was racing, and he was starting to sweat. The room was sparse, just a bed and a side table. Michael scanned around to see if there were any cameras.

"So, Michael, is it?" Polly slurred from behind.

Michael spun to look at her. "What have they given you?"

"What do you mean? I've just had a couple of drinks."

"Don't bullshit me. I can see you're on something else."

"And don't you bullshit me, Michael. Why do you care what I've been given? I can tell you're not one of them. I can see it in your eyes."

Michael grabbed her around the cheeks and leant in, whispering in her ear.

"Tell me your real name."

"Ow, you're hurting me."

"Listen to me. I haven't got time for games. You're going to tell me your real name, and then you're going to do exactly as I say."

\*\*\*

DCS Brian Stock was nursing a ginger ale and counting down the hours until he could leave. He didn't think that much could shock him anymore, but the depravity in this room was proving otherwise. These events were getting out of control.

A door to one of the side rooms flung open, and a small girl burst out, clearly in tears. She was one of many that night that he'd seen in such a state. He shook his head and waited to see who had caused the anguish. His eyes widened as DCI Michael Dack walked out of the room and trudged towards the exit at the far end of the hall. Stock got off his stool and strode after him.

\*\*\*

She just wanted to get away. She saw a spare stool at the bar and made her way over there. Maybe a drink would help. Suddenly, she felt someone grab her around the wrist.

"Did you give him a good time?" Richard Banks snarled in her face.

"What do you mean?" she stuttered.

"What do you think I mean?"

"I… I… I don't know." Tears began to pour from her eyes again.

"Did he shag you, you silly cow?"

"Yes! Yes, he shagged me. You happy now?" she shouted back, broke out of his grip, and dashed towards the toilets.

A huge grin appeared on Banks's face.

\*\*\*

Michael found a quiet space outside and bent over a wall, head in hands. He needed fresh air. He had a feeling in his stomach that he couldn't shake. He leaned over the wall and started to vomit.

"DCI Dack, what a disgrace you are to your profession!"

Michael looked up, wiped his mouth, and saw Brian Stock approaching him.

"What did you do to that girl in there, you dirty bastard?" Stock hovered over him.

"What do you care? You've been doing this for a lot longer than me." Michael squared up to him.

"I don't touch the girls, that's not what I'm about." Stock pushed his forehead into Michael's.

"What, you think that gives you some sort of moral superiority, do you? You're just as bad, Stock. You're an enabler. You're just like them." Michael grabbed him around the throat and pushed him away.

"I'm nothing like them, and I'm nothing like you, you fucking pervert." Stock lunged forwards and threw a right hook to Michael's temple that sent him crashing over the wall.

"You're a fucking copper, Dack, we don't touch the girls." Stock turned and walked back inside, leaving Michael lying in the mud, covered in his own sick.

# Fifty-six

Nisha groaned in agony. She had been in hospital for two weeks now, and her recovery had been slow. She'd set herself the target of being out of this wretched place by Christmas Eve. Her confidence in hitting this deadline was starting to wane.

She looked over to her bedside table and saw that the nurse had already visited this morning. A neatly packed but tasteless-looking breakfast lay uninvitingly in its plastic container. A copy of the Guardian rested on top. Nisha smiled. She'd grown close to nurse Katerina over the last few weeks. Small touches like this were what made the NHS great.

She leant over and picked up the paper. The headline on the front page grabbed her attention.

"Commons Child Abuse Disgrace. Home Secretary implicated."

"What!" Her eyes widened as she scanned the pages.

'The former home secretary, Lord Pcter Marshall, todays stands accused of involvement in a sex trafficking ring. Documents and images, seen by this newspaper and recovered from a laptop belonging to an alleged associate...'

The paper fell from her hand and onto the floor. She grabbed her phone and dialled Matt, but it went straight to answerphone.

"Matt, call me back. We need to talk. How can this information have made the papers already? We only found out yesterday."

***

Matt felt his phone began to vibrate in his pocket but decided now was probably not the best time to answer it. He and Rob were in the middle of a tongue lashing from Suzanne Morgan.

"There were only five of us who knew about the information on this laptop. Three of whom are in this room, one is in hospital, and the other one I was with all night going through the files." Suzanne glared again at the Guardian front page, her face turning redder by the second.

"You're not seriously intimating that either of us would leak a story like this, are you, ma'am?" said Robert.

Suzanne ignored the question. "Where is Michael? His phone's been off all night. You're telling me that neither of you have spoken to him about this?"

Both men shook their heads.

"I haven't even seen the files yet, ma'am. All I know is what Rob told me last night. Just how bad are they?"

Suzanne raised her eyebrows.

"What are we doing about Lord Marshall? Have you spoken to him? Are we arresting him today?" said Rob.

"I've been trying to call him for the last hour. There's no answer. I don't even know if he's in the country. We've got unmarked cars monitoring his road. I'm going down to his house before the press get there, and you're coming with me, Rob."

Rob nodded. "Okay. Matt, you stay here. Keep trying to contact Michael, and give Nisha an update, would you?"

"No problem, sir."

When Matt had left the room, Suzanne turned to Rob. "Let's take my car, Rob. We need to have a chat on the way there."

Ninety minutes later, they turned into Lord Peter Marshall's Road in Surrey. Suzanne breathed a sigh of relief to see there were no press outside.

They pulled up to the gates and pressed the buzzer on the intercom. No-one answered.

"What do you reckon, ma'am? Has he done a runner?"

"Hmm, that doesn't seem likely to me. He's a bit old to be pulling a Ronnie Biggs. Plus, his car's still in the drive. Something doesn't feel right."

Suzanne got out of the car and peered through the gates, "I can see one of his Labradors running around in there. He'd never have left without them. We need to get in there."

Rob sighed, looked both ways down the street, and walked up to the gates. He leant his considerable body weight against them and then rocked backwards and forwards with as much force as possible.

"You sure you know what you're doing, Rob?"

"Let me know if you have any other suggestions," Rob panted. A few seconds later, they heard the lock break. Rob carried on pushing, and the right-hand gate slowly gave way under the pressure, bending back to create a gap large enough for them both to fit through.

"Apologies, I underestimated you," said Suzanne. "I underestimated how much you weighed!"

"Very funny, ma'am. Some people would report their boss for fat shaming, you know."

They knocked at the front door and heard the dogs start to bark. There was still no sign of Peter.

"Stand back, ma'am." Rob pushed his elbow through the pane above the door handle, sending glass shattering onto the floor. He reached through the hole and unlocked it from inside.

As they entered the house, both Labradors rushed up to them, barking excitedly, and then sprinted off again towards the back of the house.

"Peter," Suzanne shouted out, "are you here?"

"Where's that music coming from?" asked Rob. There was the sound of classical jazz playing somewhere. They walked towards the direction it seemed to be coming from – the back of the house.

Rob opened a door into a large drawing room that led out into the garden. The patio doors were ajar, and the dogs were in the garden, still barking. There was an old-fashioned record player in the corner of the room spinning a vinyl record of what sounded like Miles Davis. Suzanne walked up to it and lifted the arm off.

"Ma'am," Rob's voice sounded serious. She turned and saw him pointing to the garden.

She squinted through the morning fog to a large tree the dogs were barking at. Out of the grey gloom, the sight hit her like a runaway train.

Hanging from a noose, tied around the tree's thick branch, was the limp and lifeless body of Lord Peter Marshall.

# Fifty-seven

Michael awoke with a headache more intense than any he'd had before. He tried to open his eyes, but only the right one would obey. He reached up to his left and winced as the touch sent pain soaring through him. It was then that he remembered his confrontation with Brian Stock.

He sat up and tried to get his bearings. He was home at least, in his own bed, but Samantha was nowhere to be seen. He squinted at his watch: 1.30pm! He jumped out of bed and rifled through his discarded clothes on the floor. Where was his phone? Why hadn't his alarm gone off?

He found the device in his trouser pocket; it was switched off. A blurry memory appeared of his phone being returned at the end of the night. Did he ever switch it back on? He started to recall other events of the evening. He froze, staring at the floor as it all came rushing back to him. Knots formed in his stomach. He felt like throwing up again.

He heard Samantha on the landing outside the bedroom.

"Sam, Sam," he shouted. She opened the door, anger etched on her face.

"Why didn't you wake me up?" Michael shouted. He instantly regretted his tone.

"Are you kidding me? How dare you! How dare you! I've hardly seen you in weeks. You crash back in here at five AM stinking of booze and perfume, completely out of your head. Look at the state of you. Hungover again, black eye. You're an embarrassment."

She slammed the door and stormed downstairs, leaving Michael with his head in his hands.

He turned on his phone. Multiple alerts started springing through; text, voicemail, missed calls. He closed his eyes as anxiety encompassed him.

35 missed calls, 12 voicemails, 16 texts.

He couldn't face reading them; he knew something big must have happened. He'd missed it again. He rubbed his forehead and dialled Suzanne's number.

"I'm sorry, ma'am, I've just woken up. my phone was turned off." He paused and waited for the inevitable backlash, but none came. Instead, he could only hear sobbing.

"Sue, what's going on? Are you okay?"

"You haven't seen, have you? For god's sake, Michael, turn on the news, get your head straight, and call me back."

\*\*\*

Suzanne pulled the blinds down in her office and locked the door. She needed to be alone; she didn't want anyone to see her tears. Ten minutes later, there was a knock on the door. "Go away, I'm busy," she shouted.

"You're not too busy for this. Open up, Morgan."

Suzanne recognised the voice straight away: David Parkinson.

"Commiserations on your loss. I know this must be very hard for you, and I know how much you respected the man. To have the wool pulled over your eyes like this must be upsetting, and also slightly concerning, seeing as you're supposed to be the top police person in the country," rasped Parkinson.

Suzanne gritted her teeth as she sat back at her desk.

"Wipe the tears away, dear girl. That pervert doesn't deserve your sympathy. We need to talk about next steps."

It took all of Suzanne's strength to hold back from punching him. "The next steps, sir, are that we investigate this crime fully. We shouldn't jump to any conclusions on Lord Marshall. One laptop of evidence doesn't prove the whole case. We need to fully investigate his links to Marius and Strevens. This could have been a set up," she said.

"Oh, open your eyes, Morgan, Jesus Christ. We have clear evidence of him sending emails with instructions on kidnapping and people smuggling. We found hundreds of vulgar images of children. Heaven knows what we'll find when we go through his personal computer. And not only that, but he's then gone and topped himself to avoid prosecution."

"We don't know that he topped himself. Here in the Met, sir, we still work on the basis that people are innocent until proven guilty."

Parkinson sat forwards in his chair and fixed Suanne with a steely glare. "Yes, but then the problem comes when you in the Met fail to prove anyone guilty, doesn't it? Now, this is what's going to happen next. You need to get onside with it, or you will find your impartiality in this matter being questioned publicly, and shortly after that, you will find yourself out of a job."

Morgan took a deep breath.

Parkinson continued. "I will be holding a press conference in which I will offer a heartfelt apology on behalf of the UK government, and the Metropolitan Police, regarding my predecessor's crimes. I will announce a full investigation into how he operated with impunity for so long. I will also announce that, with the deaths of Marshall, Strevens, and Barbaneagra, we now consider the investigation closed. By giving the press this information and at least a semblance of success for the taskforce, I hope to alleviate some of the criticism aimed at you."

"What on earth do you mean? You can't announce the investigation as closed. We still have multiple missing girls out there."

Parkinson paused. "Yes, well, I'll announce that we will keep looking for the girls but that we consider our search for the perpetrators complete. Marshall was the ringleader, Barbaneagra the muscle, and Strevens the demented I.T. pervert. That should take some heat off."

"You really are clueless, aren't you?" Suzanne shook her head. "This isn't some sort of PR exercise. There are real lives at stake here. We are not shutting the taskforce down. I won't allow it."

Parkinson let out a patronising laugh. "Oh, dear girl, you really do get ideas above your station. You don't have the power to make those sorts of decisions. I do. And if you ever talk like that to me again, it will be the last thing you do as commissioner of the Metropolitan Police."

# Fifty-eight

Michael woke alone in bed for the eighth day in a row. He reached for the bottle of whisky that he remembered bringing home from the pub the previous night. It was empty.

It slowly dawned on him that it was Christmas Day. He heard excited chatter from downstairs as Sam and the girls' exchanged gifts. Christmas songs rang out from the radio. Everyone was having fun except him.

He hadn't bought any presents this year; the family wouldn't have accepted them if he had. Sam hadn't spoken to him since their last argument. He felt like a pariah in this house. He wondered how he could go downstairs and bring a bottle of booze up to the bedroom without having to talk to anyone.

Michael fumbled for his phone. He needed to call Jacqui and wish her a happy Christmas. She'd be happy to hear from him, he hoped.

He went to dial her number but saw something out of the corner of his eye that diverted his attention – a present wrapped up from Sam for her aunt, who she was due to visit on Boxing Day. It was a bottle; he didn't know what of, but he didn't care. Without a second's thought, he ripped the wrapping off. Sherry. He screwed the top off and gratefully took a lug.

As the liquid settled into his body, his mind drifted back over the events of the last ten days.

He still hadn't got over the night of The Club's party. It was the first time he'd comprehended the full scale of their activities. The faces of the girls forced to work that night were etched in his mind.

He recalled his conversation with Toby and the sickening images he'd been shown of the other girls in captivity; cold, scared, and alone. He was a policeman; he was supposed to be protecting them. He should have been trying to free them.

And then there was Lord Peter Marshall. His funeral had taken place two days prior, though only close family were aware of it. He was buried in private with lurid allegations hanging over him.

Another victim of The Club and it's unscrupulous manner. A reminder of what would happen to Michael if he dared cross them.

Hatred grew within him. He pictured their faces: Banks, Parkinson, Trent, Stebbing, Stock, Bernard, and Murat. He wanted to destroy them, but he was part of them now, and he didn't know how to fight his way out. He took another lug of Sherry and tried to numb the pain.

After half the bottle had been consumed, he'd calmed down. He felt confident enough to make his way downstairs. Maybe they could all be civil. It was Christmas, after all.

As he got to the bottom of the stairs, he stumbled, causing an almighty noise, which startled Sam, Georgia, and Rebecca. He walked through to the kitchen with an apologetic look on his face.

"Merry Christmas, girls."

All he received back were scowls.

"Oh, come on, we can call a truce for Christmas Day, can't we?" he slurred.

Samantha walked towards him, a stern look on her face. "Come here, now," she said, pulling him into the living room and closing the door behind her. "I can't do this anymore, Michael. I'm not having you ruin today. I'm not having you ruin any more days for us."

Michael held his arms out by his side. "Come on, Sam, you can't do this on Christmas Day."

"I can. I don't love you anymore. In fact, I hate you. We're finished. I need you to get out. And I'd like it to be today."

"Sam, you can't kick me out on Christmas Day. Where will I go?"

"That's not my problem anymore. I just need you out of our lives. I'm sorry."

Michael tried to protest but stopped. He looked in her eyes and saw a determination in them he'd never seen before. He saw a sadness too, a feeling that he had failed her. His heart sank; it was over. "I'm sorry, Sam. I'm sorry I couldn't be the man you needed. I'll give you a call in a day or two and arrange to collect my things when I've sorted somewhere out."

He gave her a hug, turned, and walked out of the front door. As it closed behind him, Sam buried her head in her hands and started to cry.

Where to now? Michael thought as he walked along the cold streets of Islington. Jacqui hadn't answered his call; he hadn't spoken to Rob since Peter Marshall's death. Nisha was still in hospital. Matt was ignoring him.

The streets were grey and deserted. Normal people were tucked up inside, enjoying Christmas with family and friends. Michael was walking through desolation, aimless and bereft of hope. He kept moving, stopping only to pick up a bottle of whisky from a Turkish minimarket.

He walked for about two hours, thoughts echoing through his head. He looked up to gather his bearings and realised where he was. He knew what was nearby. Was it coincidence, or had his conscience led him this way? He turned the corner, and there it was in front of him: the Shallow Pond, and it was back open.

Through the dimly lit windows, he could see a few of the regular faces in there. He craned his neck and saw Bill sitting at a table, still battered and bruised, with crutches resting next to him, but he was smiling and drinking.

As Michael walked forwards, his phone started to ring in his pocket. It was Jacqui. He paused for a second, pressed decline, and pushed the door to the pub open.

# Fifty-nine

Rob could think of a thousand things he'd rather be doing tonight. He'd spent the last two days – Christmas Day, and Boxing Day – at home with his family, having the most relaxing time. He'd enjoyed it so much, he almost considered calling in sick today, but loyalty to an old friend had persuaded him otherwise. Suzanne's last words were ringing in his ears: "You need to keep an eye on Michael. He's going off the rails, and I'm worried for him."

Rob now found himself parked up in his car, with the heaters on full blast, outside the Shallow Pond pub.

He'd managed to track Michael down after receiving a phone call from Paula, worried that he hadn't called Jacqui back on Christmas Day. A call with Sam revealed that she'd kicked him out and hadn't heard anything since. By process of elimination, he was either dead or holed up in a pub. The Pond was the fifth one Rob had visited.

He'd briefly considered going in and joining his friend for a drink but decided against it. He hadn't spoken to Michael for nearly two weeks, and while he cared enough to be concerned about his health, he wasn't ready to sit down and socialise with him yet. Things were too raw.

The door to the pub swung open, and Michael stumbled out, speaking on the phone. Something looked awry; he was in animated discussion with whoever was on the other end. He appeared agitated. Rob turned the radio off and wound his window down. He could just about discern the sound of Michael's voice, but he couldn't decipher the words.

Michael hung up the phone and shook his head before checking his watch. To Rob's horror, instead of going back inside, Michael turned and stormed up the road in Rob's direction.

Rob ducked down in the front seat and prayed that the running engine wouldn't attract Michael's attention. He saw Michael pass by his passenger window and realised that there was no need to worry; Michael looked far too out of it to be able to notice anything.

He watched in his rear-view mirror as Michael reached the end of the road and hailed a taxi. He waited until Michael had closed the door behind him before he spun the car around and started to follow.

\*\*\*

Michael had not stopped cursing since he'd gotten into the taxi. "Richard fucking Banks! Who does he think he is, ordering me around like this?"

"Everything okay, mate?" the cab driver asked, concerned at the state of his inebriated passenger.

"I'm fine, just drive, would you?"

"You haven't told me where to!"

"Oh, just carry on straight. It's in, erm, Camden. Here's the address." Michael leant over and showed the driver his phone.

"Are you sure, mate? That pub's been closed for months."

"I'm sure." Michael nodded and collapsed back into his seat.

\*\*\*

Rob tailed behind as the cab weaved its way through the sea of people at Camden market before turning left into a side road. He followed, and saw the taxi take another road on the right. Rob crawled along, careful not to get there too quickly in case he was spotted.

He drove around the corner just in time to see Michael stumble out from the cab and walk to the front door of a pub called the Cowper's Arms. It looked like it was closed. Rob pulled up on the pavement and switched the lights off.

Michael knocked on the door and waited a few seconds before hammering on it again. Rob went to open his window and call out to him, but the door of the pub swung open, and a huge, evil-looking man stepped out, stared at Michael, and let him in.

Rob weighed up his next move. He decided to sit tight for the time being; it didn't look like the sort of establishment where strangers would be welcome.

Fifteen minutes passed, and there was no sign of Michael. It was probably just some private card game going on, Rob told himself. Nothing to be concerned about. Headlights appeared in his rear-view mirror. Another car had turned into the road and was heading towards the pub. Rob lay back in his seat again and promised himself this would be the last time he ever carried out surveillance work.

The car drove past – a black 4x4 that looked completely out of place in this part of town. Rob watched it pull directly outside of the pub and a tall, well-groomed man jumped out and knocked on the door. Rob craned forwards to try to get a better look at him. There was decent light from the nearby streetlamp, but Rob could only see the back of his head.

The door opened again. A different brute this time, equally as large and intimidating as the last. The visitor walked inside, but just before he disappeared out of sight, he turned to look behind him and Rob caught sight of his face. "Holy shit, that's the bloody home secretary."

\*\*\*

David Parkinson walked into the pub with a pained expression on his face. "These meeting places get dirtier each time." He theatrically wiped his seat with his pocket chief and sat down at the table, around which Michael, Richard Banks, Brian Stock, Toby Trent, and Ian Stebbing were already sitting.

"Oh, stop being such a snob, would you, David?" laughed Banks. "It does you good to get out of your ivory tower every once in a while."

Michael hadn't said a word since he got there; he'd spent most of the time eyeballing Brian Stock. It was the first time he'd seen him since the altercation at The Club event.

Banks noticed the tension. "I hope we're not going to have a problem here. I really thought you two were going to be close when Michael came on board." The rest of the table sniggered as Michael and Stock shook their heads but maintained eye contact.

"Good," Banks continued. "I'm sorry for the late notice in calling some of you here, but I have some huge news. We have had confirmation from HRH that he will be attending the event on January seventeenth."

This caught Michael's attention. His glare immediately diverted from Stock to Banks. He'd heard whispers that a member of the

Royal Family was interested in attending Club events. Now, Banks was confirming it.

"This is going to be our biggest ever event. The venue is secured. We're doing it at Swelton Hall in Wiltshire. We'll have more girls working and more guests than ever before," said Banks.

"Michael, Brian, I've called you here today because we're going to need to make sure the venue is completely secure. HRH attending obviously takes things to a new level. Someone of his profile carries the permanent possibility of being followed by the press, and to be honest, he's not the sharpest tool in the box. I need to lean on your experience. I want you to go up to the venue prior to the event and carry out a security scan on it."

"What, just me and him?" said Stock.

"Yes. Is that going to be a problem, Brian?" said Banks.

Stock turned away; his anger was clear to see, but he knew not to protest any further.

"Is that okay with you, Michael?"

"Fine with me, Richard."

"Good, now let's quickly go through some of the logistics."

In an alleyway outside the pub, Rob had found a small window which opened into the kitchen. He stood on an empty beer barrel and pulled the window open, listening intently to the conversation taking place in the room next door. He couldn't believe what he was hearing.

Not only was Michael inside, discussing the arrangement of an event involving underage sex trafficking victims, but it also sounded to Rob like the man running the meeting had just confirmed the attendance of a member of the Royal Family. His eye's widened as the discussions went on. He pulled his phone out of his pocket. He needed to call Suzanne.

Inside, Banks finished his summarising of the event. "So, does anyone have any questions?"

"I do, Richard," Michael said.

"Go on then."

"To assist with my security planning, it would be helpful to know who HRH actually is."

"Ah ha, I thought you might..." Banks was interrupted by the sound of a commotion at the entrance. The group stood up as the door burst open and Bernard and Murat walked in, dragging someone with them.

Michael saw who they had and felt like his world had fallen apart.

"We just caught this fat pig listening in through a window," said Bernard as he pulled Rob up from the floor. He sat him on an empty chair and stuffed a bit of rag into his mouth. He then cracked him around the face with a right hook that sent Rob flying to the floor again, "He's a fucking copper."

"For fuck's sake," said Parkinson. "I told you Camden was a terrible place to meet. It's far too busy."

Michael stared at Rob as he was pulled onto the seat by Murat, blood weeping from a wound on his cheek. His eyes were saturated with terror; he stared back at Michael, silently imploring him to help.

"Well, this is a bloody mess. Do we know if he's called anything in?" said Banks.

"I'll get on my radio and check," said Brian Stock, walking through to the kitchen.

"He was just about to ring someone when we caught him. The call hadn't gone through. We checked, and there were no other calls on his log," said Bernard.

Banks walked forwards, grabbed Rob around the cheeks and pulled out the gag from his mouth, "What did you hear?"

"I promise you, I haven't heard anything, and I haven't called anything in. I don't know what's going on in here, but I've got no knowledge of it."

"Bullshit! He's part of the fucking taskforce. It's Robert Archer. He's Michael's mate," David Parkinson shouted out.

All eyes turned to look at Michael. "Is this true? Have you set us up, Michael?"

"Of course I haven't set you up. Why would I do that? What are you doing here, Rob?"

"I followed you. I've been concerned about you, that's all. I saw you come out of the Shallow Pond and wanted to check you were okay. That's all I was doing. There's no need for this to get nasty, fellas. I've got a family."

Michael's heart sank as he thought of Judy, Latisha, Michael, and Patti and the unborn grandchild. He knew the two Albanians could inflict severe damage without a second's thought. His mind raced as he tried to think of a way out of this mess.

"I can vouch for him. I promise, he won't tell anyone. Honestly, he'll walk away from this and won't mention a word. I'll make sure of it."

Stock burst back in from the kitchen. "Nothing's been called in. We're okay for the moment."

"See, he's fine. We can trust him," Michael pleaded. "Just let him go. I'll stay with him. I swear to God, he won't talk."

Toby Trent broke the silence. "No way. We can't have this, Richard. He's got to go."

Rob let out a wail that earned him another punch from Bernard.

"Shut up, you silly prick. Killing a policeman would be the worst thing for The Club to do. Tell them, Brian." Michael looked at Stock and prayed for some police solidarity. All he received was a shake of the head.

"He's heard everything, Michael. He's seen our faces. He knows you're a part of it. We can't have that. It's too risky," said Stebbing.

"Fuck you. He's got a family. He's got a grandchild on the way. The last thing he'll do is talk."

"Oh, come on. He's a copper, of course he's going to bloody talk," said Parkinson.

"Richard, don't do this. It's suicide. Think about it. They'll track his phone down here when he turns up dead. They'll check CCTV."

Banks looked back at him. "Good point, Michael. After we kill him, I want someone to drive his phone to the other side of London and dump it there."

"No!" screamed Michael. "The CCTV, they'll track it here."

"Do you think we're stupid, DCI Dack? That's the reason we choose these venues. They're on streets with no CCTV," smirked Stock.

"Fuck you. Fuck you Stock! If you kill him, I'm out. You can't do this."

Banks laughed. "Dear boy, you can't be out. We have way too much stuff on you. You'll do life for the murder of Simina Albescu alone." Banks looked at Rob, "Oh, silly me, he doesn't know, does he?" Banks stared Rob straight in the eyes. "Your partner here, your best friend, he raped and killed Simina Albescu. We found out. That's how we've got him working for us. I'm glad you found out before you go to your grave. Bernard, please do your thing."

"Noooo!" Michael jumped out of his chair to get to Rob but was instantly grabbed by Stock and Murat. They forced him to the floor, smashing his face into the ground as they did.

Michael looked up at his old friend. He tried to scream, but no noise came out. Rob's eyes were bulging out of their sockets, sweat pouring down his forehead. They stared at each other, powerless, terrified, broken.

Bernard grabbed Rob's head and yanked it back to expose his neck. He pulled his knife from his jeans, and with a demented smile spread across his face, he slit Rob's throat from ear to ear.

# Sixty

Darkness. Whether his eyes were open or closed, Michael could see only darkness. The void that had been slowly consuming him for over a decade had now completely overcome him.

The last week was a blur. New Year had come and gone without even a hint of recognition. Each day felt the same when you spent them at the bottom of a bottle.

He stood at the edge of Waterloo bridge and looked down into the river below. There was only darkness. He gently leant forwards and felt his weight lift, almost as if he was floating. He took one last look up and cast his eye across the scene. In usual circumstances, the view would have been spectacular; the River Thames came to life at night over the festive period.

Beneath him, on the Southbank, the pop-up Christmas market was still open and bustling as families and tourists enjoyed the last remnants of seasonal cheer. Lights twinkled and danced along both sides of the river for as far as he could see. He almost felt a dash of inspiration, and a tiny glimmer of positivity flickered, but it was immediately crushed by the force of his memory, and the weight of his guilt.

There was no coming back from what he had done. He'd caused the death of his best friend. Once again, he had lost someone he loved. Once again, it was his fault.

He closed his eyes. Involuntarily, his mind flashed back to that day eleven years ago, when the darkness first arrived.

\*\*\*

"Right, Josie, stay here, I'll just be a minute. I want this sandcastle fully built by the time I'm back."

"Where are you going, Daddy? Don't leave me."

"I'll be just over there. I promise I won't take my eyes off you." Michael pointed towards a small, ramshackle-looking bar he'd been eyeing up ever since they'd arrived at the beach. It looked like the Spanish barman was finally ready to start serving drinks.

"Can't I come with you, Daddy?"

"I need you to stay here and look after our stuff. We've got a lovely spot. You don't want to lose it to the Germans, do you?"

"Who are the germs, Daddy?'

"Someone who will come and knock your sandcastle down. You don't want that, do you?"

Josie frowned back at him and shook her head.

"Good girl. I'll only be a few minutes. I'll bring you back an ice cream. What flavour do you want?"

"Strawberry, please."

Michael got up from his knees and started to walk backwards to the bar. He knew Josie would check if he was still watching her, and every time she looked up, he smiled and gave her a little wave. Each wave she gave back sent warmth running through him. He'd never felt a love like this before. Several years earlier, at 38 years old, he'd felt like he'd missed his shot at fatherhood. He thanked God every day for meeting Paula and for her determination to start a family. He couldn't imagine life without Josie now.

Michael reached the bar and positioned himself, so he had a clear view of Josie playing in the sand.

"Ola. Dos cerveza and un strawberry cornetto, por favor," said Michael.

The young barman smiled and started to pour the beer.

"Let me guess, you are from… Madrid," a voice behind Michael took him by surprise. He turned to see a woman laughing at his attempt at Spanish. He was momentarily caught off guard by her beauty: long, brown, wavy hair and tanned skin, decorated perfectly by bright white teeth and sparkling blue eyes.

"Barcelona, actually, but not a bad guess."

She let out a laugh and gave him a playful slap on the arm.

"And whereabouts are you from, may I ask?" Michael turned around to face her.

"Well, that's not the rules. You must guess."

"Okay, well, your English is very good, but there's a definite accent there. It would be easy for me to say some part of Spain, but something tells me it's slightly further afield. I'm going for... Egypt."

"Ohhh, so close! Morocco, actually. Casablanca."

"Of all the bars in all the—"

"—Please, don't."

"Heard that one before, have you?"

"Only a thousand times!'

"Ha, I'm sorry. Your English is so good. How come?"

The barman appeared and put the two pints of lager and ice cream between them. "Twelve euros, please."

"Oh, you are with someone else?" the woman asked, motioning at the two glasses.

Michael blushed. "Erm, they're actually both for me. You know, holiday time and all that."

"Oh, I see, you English, hey! Two beers and an ice cream for breakfast."

"Well, the ice cream is actually for my daughter. She's just over..."

Michael's heart fell into the pit of his stomach. He sprinted from the bar to where he'd left Josie, praying she was hiding under a towel or behind a wind breaker. She was nowhere to be seen.

He pulled his towels up, spraying sand everywhere, and then did the same to others' towels who were sitting nearby, earning rebukes from them in German and Spanish. "I'm sorry, have you seen a small girl? She was here. About this height?"

He asked everyone but only received confused looks, shrugs, and shakes of the head. Michael ran towards the sea. Maybe she'd gone down for a swim. There was still no sign of her. He cast his eyes across the beach, but it was vast and busy. He felt the urge to throw up.

Michael rushed back to the bar. The beers and ice cream were still there, the woman had disappeared. He leant over and grabbed the barman, who was now serving someone else. "Please, por favor. Sir, can you call police? Polizia? Guardia Civil?"

His recollection of the remainder of that trip was vague, locked in a place he dared not revisit. There were some vivid points that stood out. He remembered his phone call to Paula, almost word for word. He remembered the tears that poured from the handset.

He remembered being locked up in a cell a few days later, treated as a criminal, questioned as a suspect as he shouted and swore at incompetent Spanish policemen.

He remembered flying home alone, empty, broken, finished.

He often thought about that woman. He never saw her again. She disappeared without a trace. He regularly wondered if she was part of the ploy or just an innocent stranger in the wrong place at the wrong time.

The next years of life passed in turmoil. Michael became a ghost of a husband. He became a spectre of a father to Jacqui. Paula forgave him for that day. He never forgave himself.

∗∗∗

A horn beeped from a vehicle behind him, snapping Michael out of his trance. He stumbled forwards, nearly losing his footing, but his hand instinctively clasped onto the post. He held on.

He'd been holding on for the last eleven years.

He stepped back from the ledge.

"Hold on."

# Sixty-one

"Matt, are you still alive?"

"Go away, Liam. I'm sleeping."

"You've been in bed for five days straight, mate. It's not good for you. There's someone here to see you."

Matt huffed. "Tell them I'm not in. I don't want to see anyone."

"Erm, it's a bit late for that. She's in the kitchen. She didn't give me much choice."

"Who is it?"

"She said she's a colleague of yours. She also said that if you weren't downstairs in fifteen minutes, she'd come and drag you out of your pit."

Matt rolled his eyes.

"Jesus Christ, mate, when was the last time you had a wash?" said Liam, rocking back as he saw the state of his flatmate exiting the room.

"Yeah, well, now you know what it feels like to live with you," Matt replied, pushing past him and trudging downstairs.

"Did you not get the hint after your tenth unanswered call?" Matt said as he got to the kitchen and saw Nisha sitting with a cup of tea.

"Bloody hell, I would give you a hug, but I'm worried I'll catch something," said Nisha.

"Good one. How's the recovery going? You got long left on those crutches?"

"Hard to tell. At least a few more weeks. But I'm feeling okay, to be fair. Now, how have you been? What's with the radio silence? I've been concerned about you."

Matt forced a smile and sat down opposite her. "I've… I'm, err, not doing too well, to be honest. I can't get over Rob's death. I keep thinking about his family and how much he was looking forward to settling down with them. He was so close to retirement."

"I know, mate, it's heart-breaking. I'm devastated as well. He was a good man. But you need to pick yourself up. We haven't heard from you in a week. We've still got work to do."

"I don't even know what the situation is with work, Nisha. Last I heard, the taskforce was basically suspended. We've got no-one in charge. It's a mess."

"I agree, it's a complete shambles, but you've got two choices. You either let it drag you down, or you fight back. You look like you're wallowing in pity, and I didn't expect that from you."

"Well, what do you suggest we do instead?"

"Suzanne Morgan is at the funeral tomorrow. She sent me a message and said she'd speak to us after that."

"I don't think I can face the funeral."

"Enough of that talk. It's Rob's funeral, and you're coming. End of. We need to get justice for Rob, and we need to find out once and for all what the deal is with Michael Dack."

Matt looked up. "You think Rob's murder was linked to the investigation, don't you?"

"Oh, come on. You're not buying that 'street mugging gone wrong' line, are you?"

Matt shook his head. "You don't think Michael had anything to do with it, do you?"

"I don't know. But I'm going to do everything possible to find out, and I need you by my side."

Matt nodded. A look of resolve appeared on his face. "I'm in. Where do we start?"

"We start with you having a shower, a shave, and putting on some clean clothes. And then, you're going to drive me down to Bow."

"What's down there?"

"I've managed to track down Harriet Kennedy. I'm going to find out exactly what happened in the meeting room that day she came in for an interview. Then, we're going round to his partner, Samantha's, house and we're going to question the girls about him."

"Won't Michael be there though?"

"Nope, she kicked him out a few weeks ago. I'd love to know what for. Never a better time to get the dirt on someone than from an angry partner."

"Bloody hell. Where's he living now?"

"Who knows? Who cares? Now, go and get changed."

***

Fifty minutes later, they pulled up alongside a council playground in Bow.

"She's meant to be working from here," said Nisha.

"Working? Drugs or…?"

"Well, let's find out," said Nisha, squinting over at a group of youths huddled around the roundabout. "I'm sure that's her there, in the pink top."

Matt jumped out of the car and sprinted over. Nisha followed behind, hopping as fast as she could on her crutches. The group only noticed Matt when he was twenty metres away. They scattered in different directions, but Harriet was the slowest of the lot. Matt caught her easily.

"Get off me, I ain't done nothing." Harriet thrashed around, cursing at Matt.

"Calm down, you're not in any trouble. We just need to talk to you."

"Who's we?" replied Harriet before she noticed Nisha approaching. "Oh, not this stuck-up cow again."

"Nice to see you too, Harriet. Now, stop struggling, I just need to ask you some questions."

"Yeah, well, I've got nothing to say to you lot."

"There's two ways we do this," said Matt. "You either answer our questions honestly and we'll leave you alone, or we turn out your pockets and find what you're selling."

Harriet stopped struggling, "All right, go on."

"That day you came in for an interview and met me and my colleague. Do you remember it?"

"Shush." Harriet's eyes darted around the vicinity. "Do you know what they do to grasses around here? Yes, I remember it. Why?"

"When I walked off to the kitchen, I left you alone with him. When I returned, you were crying. What happened in that room?"

Harriet's face dropped. She stared down at the floor.

"Harriet, you're not in any trouble. I just need to know what he did."

"He told me to never breathe a word of it. He said that no-one would believe me anyway."

Nisha and Matt exchanged a glance. "Harriet, that man cannot hurt you, I promise that. But it's really important you tell us exactly what happened. What did he do to you?" said Nisha.

Harriet looked up, confused. "Do to me?"

"Yes. What did he do? Was he inappropriate?"

Harriet screwed up her face. "Ugh, no way. I wouldn't let an old man like that touch me."

Nisha frowned. "Well, then what? Why did you run out crying?"

"Cos he scared me, didn't he?"

"How?"

"He told me all about the men who killed Natasha. He said they were linked to some horrible people. He told me they'd come for me, too, and that only he could help me, but I had to help him. I had to tell him everything, or he wouldn't protect me. He'd let me get killed." Harriet started to sob.

"What did you tell him?" asked Matt.

"I told him about the Shallow Pond. I told him I was the one who took Tash down there. That I'd introduced her to a couple of men. They used to look after us in there if I brought a friend in. Gave us free drinks, sometimes drugs."

"Did you ever have to give them anything back for it?" said Matt.

Harriet shrugged.

"And that was it?" said Nisha. "That was all my colleague did? You can tell us the truth. You don't have to be worried because he's a policeman."

"Yes, I swear that was it. He said he'd help keep me out of the investigation after I told him about the pub. He said he'd protect me, but then I never heard from him again. I've been petrified ever since. Living out on the streets or bunking down at mates. It's ruined my life."

Matt let go of her wrist and looked at Nisha. "Okay, thanks Harriet. You can go."

"Is that it? That's all you can say? You're not going to protect me or anything?"

"You're fine, no-one's after you. Go home and stop selling drugs. Pull your life together," said Nisha.

They both turned and walked back to the car, leaving Harriet crying in the playground.

"What do you make of that?" said Matt.

"Not exactly what I was hoping for. Let's get over to Islington and speak to Samantha."

***

"Mum, there are some police here," Georgia's voice rang through the house, startling Samantha. She made her way to the front door and saw Nisha and Matt standing there.

"What's happened? He's not dead, is he?"

"Not yet. Can we come in?" said Nisha.

"That's a shame," said Georgia, turning away and walking upstairs.

"Yes, of course. Would you like a cup of tea?" Sam walked them through to the living room.

"No, that's fine, we won't be here long. We just have a couple of questions to ask about Michael," said Nisha.

Samantha's brow furrowed. "Questions about him? What's happened?"

"It's a bit delicate. Sorry if this comes out of the blue. We'd like to know if you ever saw Michael act inappropriately around your daughters."

"Inappropriately?' Sam rocked back. "What do you mean? In a sexual sort of way?"

Matt nodded.

"Never, no. Not at all. Why on earth are you asking this?"

"Are you sure? There's no need to defend him."

"Oh believe me, he's the last person I'd want to defend. There are lots of accusations I could throw at him but that is not one of them."

"It's just that I was once on the phone with him, and I heard one of the girls shouting in the background. They said he was naked in front of them," said Matt.

"Oh, that was just, you know… He was a complete mess when he had a drink. You do know he's an alcoholic, don't you? He never knew what he was doing when he got into those states. And I'm pretty sure he was wearing pants."

"So, the girls never mentioned anything at all? Never acted uncomfortably around him?"

Samantha rubbed her chin. "Well, thinking about it, I guess they did call him a few names."

"Like what?"

"Dirty old man. But that's just the sort of thing that teenage girls say."

"Are you sure?"

"I'm quite certain. Why do you ask? Has he been caught doing something?"

"Would you mind if we asked the girls themselves? In front of you, of course. Are they both in?"

"No problem at all." Sam got up and walked to the bottom of the stairs. "Girls, could you come down here a minute, please?"

"I'm watching TV," Rebecca shouted back.

"Well, put it on pause and come down. It's important."

"Ugh." Rebecca let out a dramatic huff and stomped down the stairs with Georgia following behind her. They walked into the living room and slumped down on the sofa.

"Now, girls, the police are going to ask you a couple of questions about Michael. It's important that you're completely honest with them, okay?"

They both nodded.

"Thank you for your help, girls. We were just speaking with your mum about Michael. She told us that sometimes you'd call him names. Things like 'dirty old man.' Is this right?" said Nisha.

Rebecca and Georgia both started giggling.

"Was there a reason you did this?"

"Yeah, course, he was a right dirty old perv," Rebecca snapped back.

"Rebecca," Sam gave her a stern look.

"If there's a valid reason that you're saying that, then it's vital we know. Don't feel embarrassed. Please, tell us. Did Michael ever say or do anything inappropriate with either of you?"

The girls looked at each other and shook their heads.

"Are you sure? Nothing at all?"

"Nothing," said Rebecca.

"No." replied Georgia.

"What about when you said he was walking around naked in front of you?" said Matt, looking at Rebecca.

Rebecca huffed. "I was just winding him up. He came in drunk, and when he went to the toilet, he woke me up. I walked out of the room to have a go at him, and I found him struggling to pull his trousers up. Silly old drunk."

"So, why did you call him a dirty old man?" said Nisha.

"I dunno, just something to say, isn't it? We don't like him, but he was never inappropriate. He tried to make an effort to get on, but we didn't let him. He's just not our dad, is he?"

Matt looked at Nisha and shrugged.

# Sixty-two

Michael pulled his car into Golders Green crematorium and parked in the last remaining space. He was relieved to see that the attendees of Robert's cremation were already funnelling inside for the service. He had purposefully turned up late to try to avoid awkward conversation. There were plenty of people here who wished it was him rather than Robert lying in that coffin. Michael was one of them.

This was the first time in over two weeks that he hadn't poured himself a drink as soon as he woke. The importance of today had trumped even his insatiable appetite for alcohol. He stared down at his shaking hands and regretted not bringing a bottle with him.

Michael waited until the last guest had disappeared inside before he stepped out of his car into the cold. Crematoriums were grim enough places at the best of times, but a rainy January morning only added to the sense of gloom.

He slipped into the service just before the door closed and managed to find an empty seat in the back row, next to a lady he didn't recognise. At least he could sit here in anonymity for the next thirty minutes.

Michael surveyed the room. He recognised numerous friends and colleagues of Rob's from years gone by. It was an excellent turnout – a testament to Rob's popularity. He saw Rob's family on the front row, and a lump formed in his throat. How would he be able to face them later?

He had yet to speak to Judy since Rob's death. He'd tried to call her once, but she'd ignored him. Deep down, he was pleased she did. He didn't have the right words to say to her then. He still didn't now.

Michael saw Paula and smiled. She was sitting with Jacqui. At least he had a couple of semi-friendly faces in attendance. They didn't hate him like others did. He hoped.

Directly behind them were Nisha and Matt. He felt ashamed that he hadn't spoken to them in weeks now. He'd avoided them for their own good, but he knew they wouldn't see it that way. He was supposed to be their boss, the one they came to with their problems. He'd become their problem.

Michael's blood boiled as he realised who was sitting behind them. He blinked and looked again to make sure he wasn't imagining it. David Parkinson, Ian Stebbing, and Brian Stock were there, sitting next to Suzanne Morgan. How dare they turn up; they were the ones who'd condemned Robert to death.

Slow, haunting music began to play. The congregation stood as the vicar walked in from the back and took his place. Michael heard nothing of his speech. He stared at the coffin and zoned into memories of Rob. Tears started to pour from his eyes. He thought back to happier times spent with his best friend. He cursed the day he'd agreed to become part of this investigation.

"And now to the stage, we welcome the home secretary, the Right Honourable David Parkinson."

Michael looked up. He must have heard the vicar incorrectly. He watched in horror as Parkinson rose from his seat and took his place at the microphone. Michael clenched his fists. He wanted to shout out and tell everyone that this man was one of the people who gave the order to end Rob's life.

"It is with the greatest sadness today that we lament the loss of a fine police officer and a much-loved family man," Parkinson read out.

Michael couldn't take it anymore. He jumped up out of his seat and stared at Parkinson, silently daring him to continue. Parkinson noticed him and paused, causing several heads to turn around. Michael saw Judy, Paula, and Nisha looking at him. His face dropped, and he turned and ran out of the crematorium.

"What do you reckon that's all about?" Nisha whispered to Matt.

The coffin rolled back into the flames, and the curtains closed behind it. The congregation filtered out of the room and onto a terrace which overlooked the gardens. The flowers for Rob were laid against the wall, displayed so guests could read the final messages written for him.

Rob's family took time to read every single one. As they got to the end of the row, Judy looked up and saw that Michael was standing in the car park, smoking a cigarette and looking over at the group. They held each other's stare for what seemed like an eternity before Judy walked over to him.

As she got closer, she noticed the expression on his face begin to change. It was slight at first, a quiver which grew into a jowly wobble. Judy came closer; they were nearly face to face, and Michael broke. Tears began pouring uncontrollably down his cheeks, like a schoolboy who'd been told off for the first time.

"I'm sorry, Judy, I'm so, so sorry. I don't know what to say."

One half of Judy wanted to scream at him in front of the watching crowd, admonish him for failing her husband, and perhaps give him a slap across the face for good measure, but she was too classy for that. She knew Rob wouldn't have wanted it.

She took Michael's face in her hands and spoke to him softly but firmly, "You were his weakness, Michael, you know that don't you? He could never say no to you. We were always grateful for how you looked after him when he joined the force, but you could never let him go, could you?"

Michael shook his head and tried to wipe away his tears.

Judy continued, "As much as I want to, I cannot hate you. I wish he hadn't followed you this time, but Robert was a grown man, and he was free to make his own decisions. So, I'll forgive you, Michael. But what I won't forgive you for is if you give up now. I can see you're close to breaking point, but Rob's killers are out there, and I will hate you forever if you cannot bring them to justice. So, pull yourself together, and find them."

Michael collapsed into Judy's arms and hugged her. His eyes caught the sight of Brian Stock and David Parkinson watching from the terrace, both with smirks on their faces. Michael whispered into her ear, "I will bring them down. I promise you that, Judy."

# Sixty-three

"Do we know what this is about at all, Nisha?" said Matt.

"I haven't got the foggiest. Suzanne approached me at the wake yesterday and said we both need to report to her office at ten AM. That was all the info I got," said Nisha.

"Weird."

"Very. I'm guessing it's going to be some sort of formal ending of the taskforce or something like that."

As they waited outside Suzanne's office, Lizzie Alexander appeared from the side of them.

"I'm very sorry, Suzanne is running slightly late. She's just been called into a meeting with the home secretary upstairs. Can I get you both a drink while you wait?"

"We're fine, thanks," Nisha answered for both.

"Okay, great, she shouldn't be too long."

Two floors above them, Suzanne Morgan walked into a briefing room expecting to meet with David Parkinson. She hadn't accounted for Brian Stock being there as well. Something felt off.

"Please, take a seat, Sue. You know DS Brian Stock, don't you?"

"I do, although I'm not sure what he's doing here."

"We thought it may be beneficial to have at least one competent police officer in the room for this meeting," Stock sneered.

"Is that how you address a superior officer, Brian?"

"There's no superior officer in here."

"Now, now, Suzanne," Parkinson intervened. "I've asked DS Stock to be in here as I've been taking advice from him on what to do with you."

"In what way, sir?" said Suzanne.

"It's come to our attention that you are still communicating with the taskforce as if they are operational."

"They haven't been officially disbanded, sir."

"Come on, woman. One of the taskforce is dead, one is an absent alcoholic and one of them has just got out of the hospital. Don't you think it's time to call it off?"

"And why on earth would I do that when there are still missing girls out there?"

"Because you need to know when it's time to cut your losses. We have our suspects, albeit they're in the ground. I think it's safe to assume that the girls have suffered the same fate. You don't seriously expect them to turn up alive, do you?"

"I've always been of the opinion we carry on working until indisputable proof is found. I've seen no evidence to suggest the girls are dead. I'm also of the opinion that other people out there are involved in these crimes."

"So, you're saying the taskforce has been a failure, then?" said Stock, leaning forwards to eyeball her.

"Not at all."

"But if you still have missing girls, and if you're saying that there are other suspects, how can you conclude anything else?" said Parkinson.

Suzanne said nothing.

"You see, dear girl, the best thing for your reputation now would be to close the taskforce down on the basis that it managed to establish who was responsible for these crimes and that it's confident there is no-one else involved," said Parkinson.

Suzanne paused, "Well then, sir, it's bloody lucky that the last thing I care about is my reputation. All I'm interested in is finding the girls and bringing everyone involved to justice."

Parkinson stared back at her. "I will be ordering that the taskforce is disbanded. You either get behind that decision publicly, or you will find yourself at the end of a shitstorm of negative PR, which will result in your removal as commissioner of the Metropolitan Police."

"And then we can get someone in who actually knows how to do the job," said Stock.

"And I guess you think that's you, do you?" Suzanne shot back.

"I bloody well do, woman. I think you've been an absolute disgrace in this position. You were brought in to tick a load of boxes, but the one box you couldn't tick was professional competence."

Suzanne stood up and looked both men up and down with contempt. "I won't be backing your decision up in public, David."

"You should address me as—"

"—I'll address you however I bloody well want to. I'm the commissioner of the Metropolitan Police, and I'm sick of bowing down to weak-minded men who bully their way into positions of power. Now, you may be happy with leaving jobs half done and crimes unsolved, but I'm not. You do whatever you feel needs to be done, and we'll see who's standing at the end of it."

Suzanne stormed out of the room, leaving two red-faced men behind her.

A minute later, Nisha and Matt saw Suzanne walking purposefully towards them.

"Right, you two, get in here," she said, holding open her office door for them.

They walked in, wondering if they were in trouble.

"Thanks for coming in today. I'd like to place on record my thanks for your work on this taskforce. I know it's been an extremely hard investigation to be a part of," said Suzanne.

"You don't know the half of it, ma'am," said Nisha.

"I know more than you realise, DS Sharma. You're probably both thinking that this is the end of the taskforce. Well, it's not. In the absence of Michael and Rob, I'll be assuming direct command. We have one more play to make, and it's a big one."

# Sixty-four

Another van appeared at the entrance gates, the sixth one that Michael had counted today. He watched from Swelton Hall car park as the van passed the security checks and then weaved up the mile-long driveway towards him.

Michael had been staying at Swelton Hall for the past two nights in preparation for the evening's event. This grand thirteenth century building was one of the best-kept secrets in Wiltshire. Surrounded by hills on either side, the place was secluded and private.

Michael had tried to research the building but came upon very little information. No-one really knew who lived here, who owned it, or what it was used for. Various rumours swirled amongst residents of nearby villages. Some said it was the masonic headquarters in the UK; others spoke of satanic rituals and devil worship. Dark and foreboding, with a sprinkling of Gothic architecture, it certainly looked the part.

The van pulled into the car park and was directed to the back of the building by Bernard. The passengers holed up inside the van weren't to be allowed anywhere near the guests' entrance; they could only be taken in via the service entrance.

Michael pulled heavily on a cigarette as he did the maths in his head. Six vans, approximately twenty girls in each. All of them sedated, dressed up, and put on show to be used as entertainment for the eighty guests in attendance. He looked to the heavens and closed his eyes as a smattering of raindrops started to fall from the sky.

The longing appeared within him again. He needed a drink. He fantasised about taking that first sip of whisky. He could almost taste it. But not today. He had promised himself that no matter what happened, no alcohol would pass his lips today. He needed his wits about him.

Another car appeared at the entrance. Michael recognised the vehicle as David Parkinson's. He must have arrived early to inspect the preparations.

Michael walked inside; he had no time for the home secretary right now. He made his way upstairs to his bedroom and started to prepare for tonight. The first of the guests were due to arrive at 5.30pm, just a couple of hours' time.

On the stairs, he passed Brian Stock, no doubt going down to greet Parkinson. The pair exchanged glances but nothing more. Despite them both staying at Swelton Hall for the last two nights, they had barely said a word to each other.

An hour later, Michael was showered and ready. He observed himself in the mirror, dressed in black tie - the formal dress code for tonight's event. Not too shabby, he tried to joke to himself, but a smile didn't appear. It hadn't for weeks.

Parkinson was holding a pre-event briefing in one of the sitting rooms downstairs. Michael made it there just in time. In attendance were Brian Stock, Ian Stebbing, Toby Trent, Bernard, and Murat. Michael slunk into the back of the room and stood quietly while Parkinson addressed the group.

"Gentleman, I hope you are as excited as I am about tonight's event. This will be, without a doubt, the biggest and best in The Club's history."

'Here, here," Ian Stebbing shouted, raising his glass.

"As you know," Parkinson continued, "we will be welcoming an extremely important guest to tonight's function, and it is vital that the evening goes without a hitch. As such, there will be a few of you on working duty tonight. Obviously, we do want you to try to enjoy the event, but please be aware that your main priority is to ensure its smooth running."

Michael nodded. He'd already been informed that he was to assist with security and surveillance.

Toby leant over and whispered, "Come with me after this. I'll show you where we'll be enjoying tonight from."

After Parkinson's speech concluded, Toby led Michael upstairs. He opened a door and proudly showed Michael what lay behind it – a surveillance setup that wouldn't have looked out of place in MI5. There was a plethora of screens, all beaming back live images of the many various rooms in Swelton Hall that would be used tonight.

"When on earth did you set all this up?"

"I've been here for five days doing it."

"Really? I've been here for two. I haven't seen you."

"Don't worry, I've seen you," Toby grinned.

"So, we'll be working from here tonight, then? Thought you would have preferred to be down experiencing the action," Michael asked, trying to keep a steady face whilst scanning the screens to see if his bedroom was on one of them.

"I'm sure I'll be able to have a bit of fun later, but there are more important things, Michael. The people we have coming tonight are amongst some of the most influential in the world. Richard has asked me to make sure we have damning leverage material on them."

"Even the royal?"

Toby smiled.

Twenty-five minutes later, the first guest arrived – a rotund man whose cummerbund struggled to contain his bulbous stomach. Even through the CCTV images, Michael could see the beads of sweat pouring from his forehead. He was greeted as an old friend by Ian Stebbing and shown through to the drawing room for pre-drinks.

Michael walked down to the ground floor and watched on over the next half an hour as the guests trickled in, each of them with a look of arrogance and entitlement that made him feel sick to the core. He witnessed the dismissive way they threw their coat at the staff or demanded their favourite drink was made. A room full of egotistical perverts, firm in the belief that their money or status meant they were above the law.

Michael imagined how they'd be when they were let loose on an innocent young girl. He wanted to make them pay. The thought of a large glass of whisky crossed his mind again, the umpteenth time today. He closed his eyes and fought it back. He walked up to join Toby in the surveillance room, away from the temptation of the bar.

Michael watched on the screen as Richard Banks stood to address the room. He glanced at Toby's smirking face and an urge came to attack him. He took a deep breath.

On the largest screen, the main room started to fill up with girls ushered in from a door by Bernard and Murat. Undoubtedly already under the influence, the girls ambled around, most unaware of the horrors that were about to unfold. They dared not to speak to each other; they followed orders and took up solitary positions around the huge hall, some of them barely managing to stand.

Banks's speech ended with a raise of glasses before the men piled out from the drawing room through a small side door. A few seconds later, they exploded into the main room, a sea of sweating, ageing predators. They wasted no time in accosting the nearest female like a pack of hyena's tearing into a group of baby antelopes. Michael turned away from the screens.

It felt like he had only stopped watching for a few minutes, but when he turned back, most of the screens were depicting depravity. Michael watched in horror as girls were taken into bedrooms and subjected to all kinds of brutality. He could only look on as the guests used this opportunity to unleash their most debauched fantasies on their defenceless victims before casting them aside and moving onto the next one.

"Any news on when the special guest is arriving?" Michael asked.

"Not yet. You'll know when he is. And remember, he's referred to as 'VIP One' tonight. Nothing else," Toby replied without taking his eyes from the screens.

"Okay, well, I'm going out for a cigarette, then."

"Take one of those with you in case I need you. Use line three," Toby said, pointing over at a batch of walkie talkies.

Michael grabbed one and marched downstairs into the car park. Never in his life had he needed a drink more. He lit up a cigarette, leant back against the wall, and stared into the horizon. It was dark, but against the backdrop of the moon, Michael could just about make out the vast expanse of hills in the distance.

# Sixty-five

Swelton Hall was surrounded by rolling hills and sprawling fields. It was isolation in the extreme. The nearest building was a farmhouse over eight miles away, and the closest main road was six miles away.

There was just one route into Swelton Hall – a winding country lane that was sometimes impossible to drive down during the winter months. The Club had already positioned a spotter at its junction with the main road to ensure an extra level of security.

Commissioner Suzanne Morgan was well aware of the complexities of conducting a raid on Swelton Hall. She knew that vehicles approaching from the road would give The Club notice to either evacuate or cover up – something she couldn't allow to happen.

At 5.30pm, under cover of darkness, she was dropped off along with DS Matt Gardiner and twelve other policeman at the edge of a farmer's field approximately four miles away. From there, they walked cross country to get to their designated position – a small patch of trees on a hill overlooking Swelton Hall, approximately five hundred metres away.

They crouched under the cover of the trees and used night vision binoculars to take a look at their target for the first time.

Matt shuffled up to Morgan's side and whispered in her ear, "Who are these coppers again, ma'am? I don't recognise any of them."

"I've had to call in a favour from my force back home in the Northeast. I couldn't risk bringing anyone from the Met. This is too important an operation, and the chance of a leak would be too high. I've kept it nice and small. I trust all these men, and so can you."

"That's good to know. I'd be even more reassured if you'd have let us come armed."

"Armed operations require a level of clearance from the powers that be. I couldn't have anyone alerted. Trust me, all these men know how to handle themselves."

Matt nodded. They were all big, burly men, and he was comforted to have them by his side. He pulled out his binoculars and surveyed Swelton Hall. The car park was full of vehicles, and the lights were on inside the building; there was definitely an event taking place.

A movement caught Matt's eye; someone had walked out of the front door. Matt followed the figure. It looked like he was pulling something out of his pocket – a cigarette. Matt focused in on the man's face as he brought the lighter to his mouth. He looked familiar. He looked like…

"What the fuck?"

*** 

Michael had just lit up his fifth cigarette of the evening when his walkie talkie crackled into life. Toby's voice come over the radio.

"Attention, we have had confirmation that VIP One has left London, please commence preparations."

Michael grabbed his device. "He's just left London? He won't be here for another couple of hours. The party will be nearly finished."

"He's not arriving by car, you idiot," came Toby's reply.

"Copy that, starting preparations," said Brian Stock over the line.

Michael felt a hint of panic. What did they mean, he wasn't coming by car? He threw his cigarette on the floor and walked inside to speak to Toby.

*** 

"Ma'am, we've got a big problem," said Matt. "I've just spotted DCI Dack in the car park."

"Good to know he's in position."

"What? You knew he'd be here?"

"Who do you think we're getting our information from?"

"But, he's been compromised. He's not a valid source of information."

Suzanne shook her head. "I think it's time for me to tell you the truth about DCI Dack."

\*\*\*

Michael walked back to the surveillance room, but Toby was nowhere to be seen. He scoured the screens, but there was still no sign of him. He decided to check out the main hall; he regretted it as soon as he got there.

The insatiable appetites of the guests had not dwindled. Girls were being passed around and manhandled like pieces of meat. "Not long now, keep your cool, don't do anything stupid," Michael told himself.

He felt a tap on the shoulder and spun around to see a girl standing in front of him. It took a moment for him to realise it was the girl he'd met at the last party, the one who Banks had forced him into a room with.

"Do you remember me?" she asked.

"I do."

"Please, you must help me. These men are animals," she grabbed Michael's hand.

Michael looked behind her and noticed Stock staring. He pulled his hand away.

"Why would I help you?"

"Because I know you're not one of them. Please, help. Hide me somewhere, I beg you. Look what they've done to me." She turned around and pulled up her dress. The back of her legs were covered in welts and bruises.

Michael grimaced, but Stock was still looking over. "I can't help you, I'm sorry."

"Why didn't you touch me at that other party? Why did you ask me to pretend? I know you want to help."

"I just… I'm sorry, I can't. You need to leave me alone, for your own good." Michael pushed her away and walked out of the hall and back to the surveillance room. Toby was in there.

"Where have you been?" Michael asked.

Toby grinned.

"Actually, I don't want to know. What's the ETA on VIP One?"

"Should be landing in around ten minutes," Toby said. "Oh, look at this, there's a turn up for the books. Brian Stock is having a go on one of the girls."

Michael froze as his eyes fell on the screen for room number eight. Brian Stock had his hand around a girl's neck and was screaming in her face. It was the girl Michael had just been talking to. He watched as Stock delivered a slap to the side of her head that sent her reeling onto the bed.

Michael closed his eyes and tried to phase out the scene. Be patient, his time will come. When he opened them back up, the violence had escalated. Stock was now on top of her on the bed, left hand holding her down, right hand delivering blow after blow to her helpless body.

Michael closed his eyes again, but instead of darkness, he saw red. Images from his past flashed through his head. He saw the dead body of Natasha Shaw; he saw Rob's throat being slit; he pictured Nisha sitting in hospital; he saw Josie, sitting on the beach. Michael snapped.

He grabbed Toby from behind and enveloped him in a choke hold. Toby's limbs flailed, and he tried to scream, but no words came out. He was weak, exactly like Michael knew he would be.

Michael squeezed harder, rage burning through his veins. He felt like he could rip Toby's head clean off his shoulders if he wanted to, but Toby's body fell limp, and Michael loosened his chokehold just in time. He dragged Toby from his chair, pulled out a plastic zip tie from his pocket, and secured Toby's hand to the table leg.

On screen, Stock was still administering his punishment. Michael stormed downstairs, past the main hall and down the long corridor of bedrooms. He reached room number eight and burst through the door just as Brian Stock had his arm cocked back to deliver another blow. Michael never gave him the opportunity.

As Stock turned to see who had dared interrupt him, he was met with a powerful right fist to the temple. As he tried to regain his senses, Michael sent a left fist buzzing to his nose. Blood sprayed out of it as Michael felt the bones crunch beneath his fist. He wasn't finished. Michael leapt on Stock and landed punch after punch until he was unconscious, his face a bloody pulp. He pulled out another zip tie and secured Stock's hand to the bedpost.

She was cowering in the corner of the room, blood smeared across her face and dress, tears pouring out of her eyes. She flinched as Michael approached her.

"You don't need to be scared anymore," Michael reached out his hand to her, but she didn't move, "I'm an undercover policeman. My name is DCI Michael Dack. That's why I didn't touch you at the other party, and that's why I asked you to pretend for me."

"He was asking me about you. That's why he was beating me. He was asking what we were talking about," she blurted back, pointing at the prostrate figure of Stock.

"It's okay, he can't hurt you now. He was asking about me because he knows I'm not one of them. I'm here to help you, but we need to move quickly. Now, what's your name?"

"It's Polly."

"Tell me your real name."

"It's Lisa. Lisa Cattermole."

Michael's heart jumped, the first bit of positivity he'd felt in weeks. "I knew it. I knew it was you. We've been looking for you, Lisa. I've been speaking to your family. We're going to get you home, but you must come with me now."

Lisa jumped up from the corner and threw her arms around Michael. Her strength returned to her, and the fogginess in her brain eased. This was her chance of escape from hell. "Tell me what we need to do, Michael."

Michael grabbed Lisa's hand and ran out of the door, pulling her behind him. They ran upstairs and along a winding corridor at the end of which was a huge bedroom. As they burst in, two figures jumped in unison in the bed.

A young brunette, barely into her teens, was lying helpless underneath a naked, scrawny-looking man in his fifties.

"What is the meaning of this?" the man shouted, trying to scramble to his feet, but Michael had no time for words. He delivered a left hook to the man's jaw that sent him crashing into the corner of the room. He ran to the window while Lisa tried to console the distraught girl in the bed.

Michael picked up a heavy-set wooden chair from under a desk, and with all his might, he launched it through the window.

\*\*\*

From the hillside, Suzanne had been keeping her eye on the window on the first floor at the far right of the house. From nowhere, a large object suddenly came hurtling through it, crashing onto the car park below.

"That's the sign," she bellowed to her team. "Get in there now. Arrest any adult you find. Use any force necessary"

# Sixty-six

Nisha checked her watch. She'd been sat in her car for over five hours now and was eager for an update. She cursed her crutches again for preventing her from taking part in the operation.

Despite being ten miles away from the action, she consoled herself with the fact that she still had an important part to play. As soon as Commissioner Morgan gave her the nod, she would get on the radio and call in back up. She looked across the dark, desolate fields and tried to imagine the current scene at Swelton Hall.

"DS Sharma, DS Sharma, do you read me?" The voice sounded faint through the radio.

"Ma'am, this is DS Sharma, can you hear me? What is that noise?"

"We need backup here now, DS Sharma. I also need you to speak to air traffic control. We have a helicopter that has just arrived, and I think it contains the Royal. Call air traffic control, try to get an identification on it."

A helicopter roared over Suzanne's head, barely twenty metres from the floor and flew down towards Swelton Hall. Her team had just reached the edge of the car park.

The helicopter started its descent towards the open field directly next to the car park. She could see what was coming, but there was nothing she could do. The helicopter stopped about five metres from the floor. Her team had been spotted.

The helicopter paused and then veered dramatically away to the right, pulling upwards and flying off in the same direction, back over Suzanne's head. "Fuck it!" she screamed at the top of her lungs.

# Sixty-seven

Michael delivered a boot to the face of the spindly man, sending his head smashing back into the wall.

"Come on, we need to move," he shouted at Lisa.

"We're taking her with us," Lisa screamed back, cradling the young brunette in her arms.

"Fine, but we need to go now!" said Michael. "They could have heard that window smashing."

Lisa tried to pull the girl up, but she was in a state of shock. She curled into a ball on the bed and wouldn't move. "Please, come on. We'll look after you," Lisa implored, but the girl would not budge.

"Lisa! We need to go, NOW!"

Lisa nodded and threw a duvet over the girl to try to hide her. "Stay here and don't move. We'll come back for you," Lisa ran out of the room, following Michael. They sprinted back along the corridor, passing the surveillance room as they did. Michael looked inside and noticed that Toby was no longer tied to the desk.

"Hey!" a shout from behind caused them both to stop. Lisa recognised that voice. It was engraved in her nightmares. At the far end of the corridor, about forty metres away, were Bernard and Murat. The two Albanians sprinted towards them, veins pulsating on their foreheads.

"Come on." Michael pulled Lisa by the hand. They ran to the other end of the corridor towards a fire exit, they burst through it and onto a large metal staircase. Out of breath and panting with fear, they ran down the stairs, not knowing where they would lead to. After a few seconds, they heard the fire exit door smash open again. Lisa screamed. Bernard and Murat were closing on them.

Lisa reached the bottom of the staircase first. There was just one door in front of her and nowhere else to go. She grabbed the handle and tried to open it, but it would not budge. Her heart sank.

"Out of the way," Michael screamed at Lisa. He charged down the final few steps and flung himself at the door, sending it flying open. They were in another corridor. Lisa helped Michael up, and they carried on running.

They passed various doors, but each one they tried was locked. They turned the corner, and ahead of them was a pair of white double doors. They sprinted towards them, praying they would open. Behind them, they could hear the shouts of Bernard and Murat getting closer.

Lisa pushed the doors; they opened, but their joy was short lived. On the other side was an old, abandoned kitchen full of pots, pans, and fridges. To their horror, there was no other way out. They were trapped.

The doors flew open as the two Albanians hurtled through them. Bernard saw Michael and Lisa backing away to the corner of the room and started to laugh. He pulled a huge knife out from the back of his trousers.

"I'm going to enjoy gutting you both," he said as he walked towards them. Murat pulled out a similar knife and followed behind him, a sick grin on his face.

"I knew we shouldn't have trusted you, pig," said Murat.

"You fucking cowards!" shouted Michael, pushing himself in front of Lisa. "An old man and a young girl, and you both need a knife."

As they got to within five metres of them, Michael held his fists out in front of him; he wasn't going down without a fight. There was a time in the past he may have fancied himself against one of them, but those days had long gone.

"You silly old bastard, I'll tear you apart with my bare hands," said Bernard, handing his knife to Murat.

The two men squared up, Bernard towering over Michael. An eerie silence fell upon the room. Michael knew there was little hope, but trying to take the initiative, he threw a punch that Bernard easily sidestepped and countered with a heavy right hand that sent Michael flying backwards into some shelves.

Michael tried to regain his senses but was immediately met with a flurry of blows from Bernard that left him sprawling on the floor. In the back of Michael's mind, he heard Lisa scream. He semi staggered to his knees but received a brutal kick to the head from Bernard's huge steel toecap boot.

Michael lay prostrate on his back as the ceiling above swirled and spun. He managed to raise his head from the floor and saw Bernard take the knife from Murat. Michael closed his eyes, said a prayer to himself, and prepared to finally be put out of his misery. He awaited the welcoming thrust of the blade, and a small grin appeared on his cracked and bloodied face. But the fatal strike did not come.

Something had attracted the attention of the two Albanians; they were staring at the open double doors. Michael heard a sound coming from that direction – a slow, monotonous thud. It seemed to be getting closer; the sound got louder. It was the sound of footsteps.

Michael squinted as a figure appeared in the doorway and stopped, looking around to survey the scene.

"You all right, Michael? Are these the two bastards who killed Rob?" Matt had arrived.

Murat charged forwards and slashed at Matt with the knife, but Matt evaded the attack expertly and threw a sharp left hand with precision-like timing that detonated on the Albanian's temple, sending him flying to the deck.

Michael watched on, at first sure he must be daydreaming until he remembered Suzanne Morgan's description of Matt after that first press conference.

"He won't be intimidated easily. He's six-foot three and full of muscle. He does cage fighting or some bollocks like that. Either way, I think you need a physical presence."

Michael hadn't seen his colleague like this before; he hadn't witnessed him in any sort of physical action, but now, a new light shone on him. As Murat stood up on shaky legs and a confused look on his face, Michael hauled himself from the floor, adrenaline coursing through him. The odds had been evened.

Bernard walked towards Matt, cautious of the damage his friend had just received. They eyed each other up and down. Matt started throwing the occasional jab out, keeping Bernard and his knife at arm's length; he knew that one slip against a man of that size could be fatal.

With Murat still recovering his senses, Michael saw his opportunity. He rushed forwards and punched him flush in the nose, following up with a left to the jaw. Murat was temporarily stunned, and Michael delivered a headbutt, which landed on the bridge of his nose, causing it to bust open. Murat let out a scream and tackled Michael around the waist. The pair crashed to the floor, and the knife fell out of Murat's hands.

Bernard overstretched with a lunge of the knife, and Matt immediately recognised it. With over fifty mixed martial arts fights under his belt, Matt knew the best way to overcome a larger opponent was to use timing and speed. As soon as he saw Bernard's balance waver, he sent a low kick to the Albanian's knee that toppled him over. Matt followed up with a kick to his head.

Bernard managed to get to his feet but was greeted with a spinning elbow that sliced open his right eye. As blood poured down his face, he started to panic. He had never fought anyone like this before. He held his arms over his head and tried to guard from the punches that Matt was now firing at him.

Michael was similarly trying to guard his face from the flurry of wild haymakers Murat was throwing at him on the floor. Not many were connecting, but the ones that did were painful. Michael scrabbled underneath Murat's legs, trying to get out from danger, but the weight of him was too much; he was stuck.

Lisa watched as Michael flailed on the floor, trapped underneath the monster – one of the monsters who had taken her against her will, who had abused her, and assaulted her. A monster who had separated her from her family and treated her like a piece of meat. She saw the knife on the floor at her feet; she saw that the monster hadn't noticed her. She saw her chance at revenge.

Matt was in complete control of his confrontation. Bernard was now backing away, arms over his head, not throwing anything back. Matt paused his attack and waited, sizing up the chance for one perfect punch to end the fight. Bernard looked up to see why the attack had stopped, and his arm dropped slightly, leaving the underside of his jaw open. Matt reacted in a split second with a vicious uppercut that landed right on the mark. Bernard dropped to the floor, his head crashing into the concrete.

"Agggh." Michael heard a scream and felt the punches stop. He opened his eyes; Murat was still on top of him but with a stunned look upon his face. He was reaching behind with both arms, trying to grab something on his back.

Lisa was standing behind Murat, her face a jigsaw of emotions. She had stabbed him from behind, the knife embedding itself deep into his spine, just below the neck area.

Michael sat up and pushed Murat off him. He took Lisa in his arms and cuddled her as the Albanian thrashed around on the floor, still trying to pull the knife out. Michael looked across the kitchen and saw Matt kneeling on Bernard's back, handcuffing him.

"Have I killed him?" Lisa's face turned pale. Michael held her close and tried to shield her from the scene, but she started to panic. "Will I get in trouble? I don't want to go to prison. Please, don't let me go to prison."

Michael reacted impulsively. He let go of Lisa, walked up to Murat, and pulled the knife out of his back. He sat on Murat's back, pulled his hair backwards, and whistled at Bernard to make sure he was watching. Michael looked deep into Bernard's eyes, smiled, pulled the knife around in front of Murat's neck, and slowly slit his throat.

"Noooo!" Bernard screamed. He watched on helplessly as his childhood friend's life drained from his eyes and blood cascaded from the open neck wound.

"That's for Rob," Michael said to Bernard, letting Murat's head crash onto the floor before he stood up to embrace Lisa.

"You didn't kill him, I did, and I'll suffer the consequences."

# Sixty-eight

Suzanne Morgan strode through Swelton Hall like a victorious army general on the battlefield. Her officers had done her proud.

Strewn across the floor were at least sixty men, handcuffed and all in various states of undress. Most of them were indignant with rage, shouting out verbal threats as she walked past.

"You can't treat me like this."

"You'll be hearing from my lawyers."

'Ah, the delusional rantings of privileged males," smiled Morgan.

She walked through to an adjoining room which was full of young girls. They were crying and hugging each other, looks of disbelief and relief on their faces. Morgan took time to comfort each one individually. "It's okay, you're safe now. They can't hurt you anymore."

She watched as more girls were brought down from different bedrooms. She made a count, stunned at the numbers. There were over a hundred victims.

Morgan heard a commotion in the main hall and walked through just in time to see David Parkinson and Richard Banks being escorted in handcuffs by two officers. A huge grin spread across her face. "Fancy seeing you here, David."

Parkinson looked up with wild eyes and a reddened face. "Morgan. You'll pay for this!"

Suzanne shook her head. "So, now we know why you wanted the case closed, you disgusting bastard. I'm going to make sure you spend your whole life in prison."

Parkinson's mouth opened, but no words came out, just an angry spluttering noise. He looked at Banks for support, but none came. The billionaire was silent and pale, staring at the floor, looking like he might be sick at any minute.

Morgan smiled at Parkinson and gave him a wink. "God, this feels good."

At the far end of the hall, Michael appeared, covered in blood and walking with a limp. Beside him was Lisa and behind them walked Matt, escorting Bernard in handcuffs.

"What the hell's happened to you, DCI Dack?" said Morgan.

"There's a body downstairs, ma'am. I killed him in self-defence."

"That was not self-defence, that was murder!" shouted Bernard.

"Shut up," shouted Matt, throwing Bernard onto the floor. "It was self-defence, and there are two witnesses to prove it."

Michael scanned the room. "Where's Toby Trent?"

"We haven't found him yet. Don't worry, we're still looking. We have an ambulance outside. Michael, I think you should go get yourself looked at," said Suzanne.

"I'm fine, don't worry about me, ma'am," Michael caught Parkinson's glare.

"Dack, you fucking traitor. Do you know what you've done? Have you forgotten what we've got on you, you silly little man? You've just ruined your life," shouted Parkinson.

Michael approached him, his face barely an inch from Parkinson's, and stared straight into his eyes "You may be right, you may be wrong, but one thing's for sure. I know I've ruined your life, you depraved arsehole."

# Sixty-nine

Jacqui was beaming with pride as Paula read out the morning news over breakfast.

"The investigation led to some of the most high-profile arrests in British history, smashing a sophisticated sex-trafficking ring that had seemingly been in operation for years. The prime minister has called an emergency cabinet meeting to discuss the detainment of the home secretary, David Parkinson, billionaire Richard Banks, and many other high-profile individuals.

"The dramatic sting, which took place in a sleepy Wiltshire village two nights ago, has led to the release of nearly a hundred girls from captivity. Among them were Claudia Tyler, Lisa Cattermole, Joanne Buckley, Lena Nowak, Lucinda Wallace, and Christina Petrescu, all of whom have been reported missing in the UK over the last few years.

"The names of the other victims are still to be released, but they are believed to be a mix of girls who were homeless and taken from the streets, or immigrants who arrived in this country without families and were forced into modern slavery."

"And this was Daddy's work? He saved all these girls?" said Jacqui.

"Yes, he led the case. He's a hero, Jacqui!"

# Seventy

"You're on mute, Michael!" Suzanne, Nisha, and Matt shouted at the screen in unison.

"Oh, for god's sake, sorry, give me a sec. There you go. Can you hear me?"

"We can now, you caveman. How have you lasted so long in the police force without learning how to use a computer?" said Morgan.

"Oh, shut up," Michael laughed. "I thought I'd never have to do another Zoom call again after lockdown."

"Yes, well, needs must, Michael. We can't afford to have the star witness walking freely around town."

"Have you got enough protection, guv?" said Matt.

"I've got no-one here. We decided against it."

"Why?"

"Until we arrest DCS Stock, we can't risk it. Who knows how many bent coppers he still has on his side. I'm safer being here on my own."

"Why haven't we arrested Stock yet?" said Nisha. "I still can't believe he managed to get away from Swelton Hall without being nicked."

"All will be revealed on this call, DS Sharma. We have a lot to fill you in on," said Morgan. "First thing's first, have we had any update on that helicopter?"

"I'm sorry, ma'am, air traffic control has no record of a helicopter in the area at that time. It's like it was never there."

"Or the evidence has been wiped," said Morgan, shaking her head. "That's very frustrating. Still, we can press Banks or Parkinson for information, they might cave and give us the name."

"I'm sorry too, ma'am," said Michael. "I had to pull the trigger to alert you. I'm gutted it was a minute too soon."

"Don't be stupid, Michael, you've done fantastically. This just would have been the icing on the cake. I'm sorry I had to ask you to go so deep on this investigation, I know the sacrifices you've made."

"I apologise too, guv. I suspected you of being involved in all this, and I know I made your life hell. Commissioner Morgan has put me straight on a few things," said Nisha.

"There's no need for your apology, DS Sharma. You wouldn't have been doing your job properly if you didn't suspect me. I'm sorry that I had to keep a lot from you and DS Gardiner on this job, and there's still more that you don't know. I didn't want to do it this way, but hopefully you'll see that there wasn't much choice. Also, my drinking got well out of control during this case. That wasn't an act. I can blame the pressure of the case and all that, but I need to hold my hands up. That was unprofessional."

"All right, all right, stop the soppiness, it's making me nauseous. Let's get on with this debrief," said Morgan.

"Compassionate as always, ma'am," said Michael.

"So, as you know, we have now arrested Bill Lowthy. Michael, from all the arrests at Swelton Hall, are you confident that the only two people we're missing from The Club are Brian Stock and Toby Trent?" said Morgan.

"Correct. How on earth did Trent and Stock get away from that place? It was in the middle of nowhere," said Michael.

"We're currently looking into that, and we'll question Stock about Trent when we arrest him. There's a chance they may have escaped together."

"I take it Stock is still in work, ma'am?"

"He's bowling around as if nothing happened. The balls on that man! But don't worry, we've got surveillance on him twenty-four seven."

"I cannot wait till that arrogant prick gets arrested," said Nisha.

"Well, you don't have to wait too long. The plea hearing is on Monday. We're going to do it there."

"And why are we waiting until then?"

"All will become clear on Monday. There's one more part of the jigsaw remaining," said Michael.

# Seventy-one

'Would all participants in the case, the Crown versus Banks and Parkinson, please take their place in Court Number One.'

A ripple of excitement ran through the building. There hadn't been a trial this big in years, maybe ever.

Michael walked into the courtroom, followed by the Prosecution Barrister QC Henry McIntyre and Suzanne Morgan. Nisha and Matt took up seats in the row behind them. David Parkinson and Richard Banks were already in the dock, seated next to their respective barristers.

McIntyre turned to Suzanne, "Look at those smug grins on their faces. Why are they so confident? Do they honestly think they're going to get away with this?"

"Don't you worry, Henry, these bastards aren't getting away with anything," said Suzanne.

The judge was prompt and officious, clearly revelling in her position as head of proceedings for such a high-profile trial. As she was about to start reading the charges, she was interrupted by a court official who burst through the door and ran down the aisle to hand her a note. She read through the note, and a discernible look of shock appeared on her cragged features.

Simultaneously, a noise began to reverberate around the courtroom from those in attendance. Michael turned to see many of them reading their phones, open mouthed, before glaring over at him. Suzanne passed him her phone, and he looked down at the breaking news headline. His stomach flipped.

'Hero cop implicated in murder of missing girl Simina Albescu.'

*The Daily Mail has received a disturbing video which shows DCI Michael Dack and what is purported to be missing Romanian schoolgirl...*

Michael looked around the court. He felt like all eyes were bearing in on him. He carried on reading, his face drained of colour, as he pictured his friends and family soon reading the same article.

*The sender of the video was also witness to DCI Dack's involvement in other offences - the sexual assault of an underage girl at a party and the perversion of justice in providing information on witness locations to the criminal enterprise.*

The sender of the video? Michael sat back in his chair and closed his eyes. Toby. He'd timed it perfectly to coincide with the start of the trial.

The door opened again, and in walked DCS Brian Stock, followed by four uniformed officers. He strode towards the front of the courtroom, a scowl etched across his face. "Your Honour, I apologise for this interruption, but as you have seen, new and damning evidence has just come to light regarding DCI Michael Dack. Due to the serious nature of these crimes, I have no other option but to take him into custody immediately. Officers, arrest DCI Dack."

The defence barrister stood up on cue and read out what seemed like a conveniently pre-prepared speech. "Your Honour, we move to get DCI Michael struck off as a prosecution witness. In light of this new evidence, he is clearly not suitable to take the stand. He is a disingenuous, violent sociopath who has used his position in society to cover up the fact that he is, in fact, the real criminal. We believe he is the actual ringleader of a sex-trafficking group and has concocted an elaborate plan to frame my clients. He needs to be immediately arrested for the rape and murder of Simina Albescu, and this case should be adjourned whilst we investigate the situation surrounding his crimes and whether, indeed, this case is fit to go to trial at all."

Banks turned to Parkinson and winked before both looked over at Michael and smirked.

The courtroom gasped as one as the uniformed officers moved towards Michael. They found their path blocked by the imposing frame of Suzanne Morgan, who stood between them. "As commissioner of the Metropolitan Police, I order you all to stand down. DCI Michael Dack is no criminal. He is a law-abiding policeman, something that cannot be said about you, Brian Stock." She pointed at Stock, a steely glare in her eye. The uniformed officers paused, unsure what to do.

Henry McIntyre stood and faced the judge. "Your Honour, there is no doubt that this case is one of the most unique in British history.

The undercover operation that DCI Dack carried out was probably one of the deepest that has ever taken place. Due to the nature of this case and the powerful status of those indicted, it has been necessary to keep some of the information as secret as possible until now.

"Due to the lack of trust in the police force and Westminster, commissioner Suzanne Morgan has gone to extreme lengths, and today, you will hear details of those. Whilst some may not agree with her methods, we are confident that this was the only possible way a network of criminals as influential as this could be infiltrated.

"As such, and to ensure that DCI Michael Dack can be trusted as a man of good faith and moral standing, we would like to call someone forward."

The defence barrister stood up. "This is a plea hearing, there are no witnesses to be called."

"I think you're going to want to hear from this person, Your Honour," said Henry. "We would like to call Simina Albescu."

# Seventy-two

**2nd March, 2020**

DI Michael Dack was sitting in the beer garden of his favourite Islington pub, soaking up the last few rays of afternoon sun. He finished his pint of lager and was contemplating ordering another when his phone rang. He smiled as he saw the name on the screen: an old friend he hadn't spoken to in a while.

"Well, if it isn't Commissioner Suzanne Morgan. I didn't think you had time for us lowly inspectors anymore."

"Stop it, you silly sod. How have you been?"

"Not too bad, thanks, ma'am. Do I really have to call you ma'am now? How awful. Anyway, how are you enjoying the new role?"

"It's horrendous. I'm dealing with snakes, rats, and slimeballs every day. It's lucky I had the experience of working with you to draw back on. What are you up to right now, Mike? Let me guess, you're in a pub?"

"Correct, ma'am."

"Which one?"

"The Canonbury."

"Stay there, I'll be with you in thirty minutes. Get me a large G and T, will you?"

"How do you know I've got no other plans?"

Suzanne let out an exaggerated laugh. "Good one, Michael. See you soon."

Twenty-eight minutes later, Suzanne walked into the beer garden. The sun had disappeared, and a chill had swept in. Michael was alone at a table, the only customer still outside. The pair enveloped in a warm embrace before Michael jokingly pushed her away.

"Hold up, are you sure we should be hugging? There's a killer virus going around."

"I'm sure you've had worse. I remember your late-night antics up North. Now, give me that drink, and sit down."

"Shall we not go inside? It's getting a bit nippy."

"Out here is perfect. We need complete privacy for what I'm about to ask."

Michael frowned. The tone in Suzanne's voice was serious.

They sat down, and Suzanne cast her eyes around the garden before she spoke. "How are you feeling, Mike? Healthwise."

"I'm good, thanks, keeping the pounds off, eating reasonably healthy."

"I'm talking mental health."

"Never been better. Why?"

"I've got a job coming up, and I need someone I can trust."

Michael paused. "You know you can trust me. Why the cloak and dagger approach? I'm always available to work with you."

Suzanne paused. "This job, Mike, it's like no other. What I'll need you to do has probably never been done in the history of British policing. I need someone to go so far undercover, they could well lose touch with reality. I don't want to sugarcoat this. It's a case that could easily break someone."

"You're really selling this to me."

"I wouldn't be asking you to do this if you didn't tick every box required. I've racked my brains, but I can't think of anyone else better suited to the role and anyone else I trust more. It's got the potential to be the biggest case this country has ever seen. If you crack it, you'll be a national hero. If you don't, your reputation could be damaged beyond repair."

Michael smiled, "You've got my attention. Tell me everything."

"We've been approached by a young girl from Romania, called Simina Albescu. Her sister was abducted, raped, and murdered in Bucharest. She was only fourteen."

"What's that got to do with us? Is it not a case for the Romanian police?"

"They've washed their hands of it. It seems like there was the involvement of a high-profile Englishman who invests a huge amount of money into the country. Politicians got involved, and suddenly, the case went away. You know what that Eastern Bloc is like."

"What Englishman? And how did you find out about that?"

"I've done a bit of digging around. I spoke to a guy I used to go to Durham University with. He's called Florin, a Bucharest native. He ended up working in the police force over there. He told me some disturbing shit."

"Go on."

"He's convinced that a major sex-trafficking operation has recently started up. It involves high-profile individuals from European locations, London, Berlin, Amsterdam. He's heard stories of girls being taken from homeless shelters, halfway houses and off the streets. Apparently, they're trafficked across Europe. The Romanian police don't have the resources or power to investigate. It's all conducted on the dark web. Girls are being taken from places like Poland and Albania as well. Politicians and policeman are being paid off to look the other way. It sounds huge."

"Fucking hell, Sue."

"Exactly. So, Florin told me he had proof of involvement from a UK politician and a high-profile businessman."

"Okay, so where's the proof?"

"The day after I spoke to him, his body was found in the Dambovita River with his throat slit. A mugging gone wrong, apparently."

Michael's eyes widened.

"I spoke to Lord Peter Marshall about it. He's someone I can trust. He believes it, says he heard a few whispers himself in Westminster circles. He told me about something he'd found on the computer of a politician just before he retired."

"What was it? And who?"

"I'm not telling you that. If you take on the case, I want you to draw your own conclusions and see if they align with what we know."

"Okay."

"This could be huge. So big that I don't think we're going to get anywhere near cracking it without taking extreme measures. Do you want me to go on?"

Michael nodded, his heart rate quickening.

288

"Officially, on police records, we've sent Simina away and said there's nothing we can do to help. Unofficially, she's going to work with us."

"Work with us how?"

"I have a plan, a long-term plan, that needs to be played to perfection. You'll think I've gone mad, but I'm sure it will work. I'm sure it's the *only* way that can work. I want to stage a crime."

"Yep, you've gone mad."

"Hear me out. I want Simina to be snatched off the streets in a viable location with active CCTV. I want the person who snatches her to enact a realistic home video of her being tied up and abused. Make it look as genuine as possible. She'll then disappear back to her homeland, in witness protection, with a new identity."

Michael shook his head. "Have you been at the G and Ts all day, Sue?"

"I wish I had. Listen to me, this group have got people everywhere, and they have someone who is technologically special, a hacker. We need to go this deep to infiltrate them."

"There's deep and then there's up-to-your-neck in shit."

"The video would lie dormant, maybe for years, until the time is right. I'd then hire that person into a high-profile role in the Met, maybe even to investigate crimes by the trafficking ring if they've started to come to light by then, that would grab their attention."

"And you want that person to be me?"

"An old white male in a position of power. Could be useful to the group if corrupted. If they get evidence of you doing this, they'll think you can be manipulated."

"And you'd want me to let them?"

"Exactly."

"And what about the girl? Do you think she's capable of seeing this through?"

"She's a strong young lady, desperate to ensnare the people who ruined her family. I think she'd go to much further lengths than this."

Michael took a huge gulp of his drink and stared at the floor, trying to get his head around what he had just been asked. "This sounds crazy, Sue, even for you."

"You know I wouldn't ask you if I thought there was another way. By doing it like this, there's no chance of them suspecting you. The crime would have been committed years before."

"You're asking me to pretend to be a nonce. Your insensitivity is astounding. You know what happened to my daughter."

Suzanne nodded. "And I know how much you'd love to put monsters like this behind bars."

## 19th November, 2021

Suzanne hit the stop button on her phone's alarm and let out a yawn. Squinting through the early morning light, she noticed a message alert flash up on the screen.

'Call Me – Michael.'

She immediately rang it back.

"It's done," Michael answered.

"How did it go?"

"It was horrible."

"I know that, Michael. But will it pass? Does it look genuine?"

"Too genuine."

Suzanne nodded. "Are you okay?"

"Don't worry about me, take care of the girl. She's at the safehouse now."

"I'm on it," Suzanne replied, jumping out of bed.

## 1st August, 2024

Michael walked through the front door of Barnet Police Station with a spring in his step. He felt well again for the first time in months. He had his drinking under control. His recent holiday to Malaga with Sam and the kids had been a success and had left him with a healthy glow on his skin. He was performing well at work, life was good.

"DI Dack, in here, please," a voice rang out from across the office. It sounded serious.

"Congratulations, DI Dack, you've been given a promotion. We're going to miss you here." The superintendent showed Michael into his office and walked off in the direction of the canteen.

Michael's confusion only lasted a few seconds. Sitting in the office was Suzanne Morgan. His life was about to be tipped upside down.

"Michael, it's time to make our move. There's been another murder. Are you ready?"

"Can anyone ever be ready for something like this?"

"You're going to be DCI, heading up a taskforce into these crimes. If you can manage to solve them without having to resort to the infiltration, then congratulations, I really hope you can. If not, though, we'll need to decide in a few months how that video can find its way into their hands."

Michael nodded.

"This must be played perfectly, Michael, no slip ups. If they catch wind of it, then we're both finished. We'll be announcing your hiring and the formation of a taskforce in three days. After that, any communication about this side of the investigation will have to be done in person and stays purely between you and me. There can be nothing over phone, email, or anything digital. They've got an IT genius in their organisation, and you can guarantee they'll be monitoring us. I don't know who in the force I can trust yet, so we have to rely on each other. Understood?"

Michael nodded again.

"When you do infiltrate them, I need you to ignore any crime you see that would compromise you if you're apprehended. If you need to commit a crime to establish your credentials, then do so. The priority here is getting right to the bottom of this murky swamp and draining it."

## 20th November, 2024

Suzanne heard a knock at her office door and looked up to see Michael staring through the pane. She beckoned him in, immediately noticing his haunted look.

"Why the long face, DCI Dack?"

"It's happened, they've got me, ma'am. They've found the video. They kidnapped me and then showed it to me last night. I'm all theirs now."

"And you definitely think they bought it?"

"One hundred per cent."

"Fantastic." Suzanne punched the air.

"I'm glad you're happy, ma'am. I'm about to go through hell."

"Yes, but just imagine the result at the end. You could be about to crack the biggest case of all time." As she finished her sentence, her phone started to ring. She looked down at the screen and shrugged before answering.

"DI Archer, to what do I owe this rare pleasure?"

"Hi, ma'am, sorry for ringing your mobile, but I thought it shouldn't wait."

"Oh dear, that sounds ominous. Go on."

"I'm afraid to say that we've got a bit of a problem with Michael."

"Right, and what seems to be the problem?"

"I don't know where he is. He's been missing for a few days now. I can't get through to him on his mobile. I'm starting to get worried."

"That is a huge surprise that you can't find him."

"I know, I've been looking everywhere I can think of."

"Well, you can't have been looking hard enough. Are you sure you're still up to being a detective?"

"Pardon?"

"I'm sitting with Michael now. He's right opposite me. I'll put it on speaker phone for you."

"What?"

"Hello, Rob, no need to panic, mate, I'm here at the station," said Michael.

"We've been worried sick about you. Where have you been?"

"You couldn't have been that worried, mate. You didn't tell Suzanne or any other Old Bill to come looking for me. Anyway, I'm fine. Get yourself home and be ready for a briefing at nine AM tomorrow. We've got a case to crack."

The phone went dead, and Michael hung his head. "He doesn't trust me anymore. I've lost the trust of my whole team and my best friend."

"It's for the greater good, Michael," Suzanne replied.

Michael prayed that Suzanne was right.

## 3rd December 2024

Suzanne watched through the windscreen of her car as a pathetic figure came towards her. A pang of guilt flashed over her as she noticed his hunched shoulders and saw how he was struggling to walk in a straight line. He'd started to hit the bottle hard again; the pressure of the case was weighing on him.

"I think I've fucked up, ma'am. I've gone too far."

"What's happened?"

"I gave them the location of Joost. I'm the reason he's dead. I'm the reason DS Sharma was nearly paralysed!'

Suzanne stayed silent.

"He told Matt he'd cracked the code. If Matt had got that info, The Club would have been compromised without us finding out who the royal was. I panicked and told them where Joost was housed. I only wanted them to destroy the evidence though, not to kill him!"

After a minute or so, Suzanne broke the silence. "Fuck him, he was a crook anyway. Sharma is going to recover. We carry on with the plan and never mention again the reason Joost was compromised. You followed my instructions so don't blame yourself. We need to drain the whole swamp. If there's a royal involved, then we need to know who it is. Now, get yourself home and have a shower."

As Michael staggered out of the car, he wondered how far they were both willing to go for justice.

## 16th December 2024

Michael knocked on the front door of Suzanne's flat and was taken aback when she opened it in tears. It was rare that he saw her emotional; he'd often joked about her having a heart of stone.

They walked into her living room before she turned and grabbed him around the shoulders. "They've killed him, Michael. They've killed Lord Peter. They've soiled his name, and it's all my fault. We need to bring these bastards to justice. I want them behind bars for the rest of their lives."

"Well, sit down then, and I'll tell you about the party I was at last night."

Suzanne listened open mouthed as Michael poured his information out. As he finished, she sat back in her chair, shaking her head.

"I had no idea there were so many victims. How have we not been aware of this?"

"I don't think they've all been taken from the UK. They could have been trafficked here from anywhere. Listen to me, Sue. I think it's time to act now. We can arrest them all and have them on people trafficking charges. We can stop these girls from more suffering. It's time to end this."

Suzanne sat bolt upright. "No chance. You know the rules here. We keep going until we get right to the bottom of the swamp."

"Look at what this is doing to us," Michael pleaded. "We're ignoring serious stuff here. I'm a full-blown alcoholic again. The stress is killing me. I'm losing my family. My team don't trust me. We need to stop this now before anyone else gets hurt. Let's bring them in. It's the biggest bust ever, even without the royal."

"Michael, we can't give up now. From what you've said, the royal will be attending the next party. It's the end game now. We're so nearly there."

## 10th January 2025

Suzanne beckoned Michael over to her car. As the rest of Rob's mourners milled around, checking out the flowers and condolence notes, Suzanne pulled onto the road and drove towards the pub where the wake would be taking place.

It was Michael who eventually broke the silence after wiping away his tears. "The party's going ahead on the seventeenth of January. I'll fill you in with details as I get them. I've had confirmation the royal will be there. Make sure you get a team in place that you can trust. Stay out of sight, and I'll make it known when you should raid. Let's bring these bastards down."

# Seventy-three

A gasp echoed around the court room as Simina Albescu walked in and made her way to the witness box. Banks, Parkinson, and their legal teams looked on open mouthed. The girl from the video with Michael, the girl who disappeared years ago, now stood there. There was a different hairstyle, and she was wearing glasses, but it was definitely her.

Brian Stock's face turned white. He looked nervously around the courtroom and then started to edge his way towards the exit. He was stopped in his tracks by the booming voice of Commissioner Suzanne Morgan.

"Arrest that man, now!"

All heads in the courtroom pivoted to look in his direction. As Stock turned back towards the exit, his way was blocked by Nisha and Matt.

"DCS Stock, you are under arrest for accessory to the murder of Joost Leenthijouts, human trafficking, assault, and gross misconduct as a police officer. I'm sure there'll be other charges along the way. And may I just say, this is definitely my favourite arrest I have ever made," Nisha grinned as she read out the rights whilst Matt handcuffed him.

As they led him out of the gallery, Stock turned to shout something but could find no words. The last thing he saw before being bundled out of the door was Suzanne Morgan smiling at him.

"Order, order!" shouted the judge as an excited chatter vibrated around the courtroom. Calm was eventually restored, and the judge addressed the courtroom, "Whilst these are most unusual circumstances, I believe it to be in the court's and the public's interest for us to hear from Simina Albescu, so the facts can be clearly established. I take it there will be no more revelations after this?"

"I can assure you that this is the last one, your Honour," said McIntyre.

Simina took to the witness stand, and as she gave her testimony, Michael's gaze did not divert once from Banks and Parkinson. He revelled in every excruciating minute as they listened to the story unfolding in front of them. Their faces displayed anger, then shock, then hopeless acceptance as Simina set out in clear detail how her kidnapping had been pre-arranged by Michael and Suzanne Morgan and how the video of her being captured by Michael had been a set up. She finished her testimony with a defiant outburst at Banks and Parkinson.

"You killed my sister, you weak, spineless men of supposed power. But now I have turned it on you. I hope you rot in hell for what you have done."

As she walked off, happy for the first time in years, QC Henry McIntyre stood.

"Your Honour, I appreciate the revelations of the last half an hour have probably come as quite a shock to most. I feel it appropriate to call Commissioner Suzanne Morgan to the stand to explain more."

"First of all, your Honour, I would like to apologise for the dramatic events today. We would not typically like to carry out a live arrest of a senior officer in your courtroom. However, we have solid information that DCI Brian Stock was an integral member of the trafficking gang we are prosecuting. We therefore felt that if any prior indication was given of Simina Albescu being alive, it could have jeopardised the case. We believe that Brian Stock has used his police powers for criminal gain multiple times before and relayed many valuable police secrets back to this gang."

"It's certainly been an eventful start to the day, I'll give you that," replied the judge. "But if the ends justify the means."

"Thank you, your Honour, I couldn't have put it better myself. Today is the culmination of the most unique undercover operation I have ever been involved in. Never before have the Met framed its own officer with such a crime to provide him with an infiltration route into a criminal organisation. I know we will have our critics for the route we took, but to those critics, I tell you now, there was no other way."

The courtroom was deathly silent, each person hanging on Morgan's every word.

"This gang, led by the two men you see here today, had its tentacles so far into the highest levels of government and law in this country that we had to use this approach to bring them to justice. Only four people knew of the true extent of our plot, and one of them, Lord Peter Marshall, now lies dead." Morgan turned to look at Banks and Parkinson, "And that's another death I lay firmly at the feet of these two beasts. Simina Albescu has shown extreme bravery to work with us in bringing these criminals down, and I cannot thank her enough for this."

Morgan paused, and her eyes appeared to moisten. "And then to my colleague and good friend, DCI Michael Dack. This man has sacrificed everything to bring this criminal gang to justice. He risked losing his reputation, his health, his life. He lost his best friend, he lost his family, but he succeeded, and he stands here today as a hero."

The courtroom erupted into a raucous chaos that the judge struggled to get under control. Above the cacophony, Banks shouted at Michael, trying to get his attention. "Oi! Dack! Dack!" Eventually, he was heard. "You've really been planning this for over three years? You've been pretending for all this time? You're as messed up as us!"

Michael smiled back at him, "It's called the Long Game."

---

**Michael Terence Publishing**

www.mtp.agency

mtp.agency

@mtp_agency

www.ingramcontent.com/pod-product-compliance
Ingram Content Group UK Ltd.
Pitfield, Milton Keynes, MK11 3LW, UK
UKHW041012100425
5389UKWH00003B/180

9 781800 949904